Ave Antonina

"Now I will tell you a little story of my own, and then we sleep," she said. "In the last winter of fighting, the Nazis caught me when I was trying to deliver a message in a town beside the Oder River. I was a little careless, and I was caught. They took me to a jail and they called the SS. The SS came and they beat me, I do not talk, they beat me some more, I still do not talk, and the SS went away and I am alone in my cell. The jailkeepers were Sudeten Germans. Regular German Army, not SS. They were not bad guys. Then one day they brought in a little Jewish girl and put her in the cell next to mine, all by herself. Her name was Joanna. I think these Sudeten men thought they could keep her safe there and no one would notice. She cried and cried, and I began to talk to her. I would hold her hand through the bars. After a while the jailers sometimes let her come from her cell into mine, and I would take her on my lap and sing to her and tell her stories. My father had a wonderful voice. When I was a child, I loved to hear him sing. My voice was not so good, but I would sing her the songs my father sang to me. Sometimes she would go to sleep on my lap. And then one day the SS came again, but this time they did nothing to me. They took Joanna from her cell, and they took her outside my window into a little courtyard, and they shot her. And a few days after that I was put on a train to Ravensbruck. So no, little chisel, I do not think about your friend, the child I was able to save. But I think every day of Joanna, the child for whom I could do nothing but sing badly."

Table of Contents

Ave Antonina 1
Table of Contents 3
What They Are Saying About Ave Antonina 5
Ave Antonina Title Page 7
Dedication 9
Glossary 11
Ave atque vale 13
—Catullus 13
   PART I 1
      One 3
      Two 8
      Three 17
      Four 26
      Five 30
      Six 41
      Seven 56
      Eight 66
      Nine 80
      Ten 84
      Eleven 91
      Twelve 103
      Thirteen 113
      Fourteen 123
      Fifteen 126
      Sixteen 145
      Seventeen 149
      Eighteen 158
      Nineteen 169
      Twenty 190
      Twenty-one 199
      Twenty-two 226
      Twenty-three 247
      Twenty-four 251
      Twenty-five 256
      Twenty-six 268
      Twenty-seven 286
      Twenty-eight 299

PART II..313
    Twenty-nine 315
    Thirty..322
    Thirty-one...340
    Thirty-two...355
    Thirty-three..384
    Thirty-four..390
    Thirty-five 406
    Thirty-six..415
    Thirty-seven 432
    Thirty-eight...458
    Thirty-nine..475
Acknowledgments 481
Meet Michael Jennings..483

What They Are Saying About Ave Antonina

"Raising disturbing questions about America's involvement in Vietnam and what the American government was willing to overlook in order to compete with the Soviets in the exploration of space, *Ave Antonina* effectively brings back the days when the Vietnam War and the race to be the first nation to set foot on the moon competed for the headlines."

—Chris Helvey, Editor in Chief, *Trajectory Journal* and author of *Snapshot*

"*Ave Antonina* is thought-provoking, insightful, and entertaining, an original novel that is sure to satisfy readers on many levels."

—Michael Embry, author of *New Horizons*, the third book in the John Ross Boomer Lit series.

Ave Antonina

Michael Jennings

A Wings ePress, Inc.
Literary Fiction

Wings ePress, Inc.

Edited by: Jeanne Smith
Copy Edited by: Christie Kraemer
Executive Editor: Jeanne Smith
Cover Artist: Benjamin Stewart Anderson

Wings ePress Books
www.wingsepress.com

Copyright © 2020 by: Michael Jennings
ISBN 978-1-61309-590-4

Published In the United States Of America

Wings ePress Inc.
3000 N. Rock Road
Newton, KS 67114

Dedication

This book is dedicated to Miroslawa Perham, Polish partisan. In the darkness of a Nazi prison, she sang to a doomed Jewish child named Joanna.

Glossary

The following terms were commonly understood among American military members during the Vietnam War:

Arvin - Army of the Republic of Vietnam (ARVN).

Cadre - A Viet Cong squad leader. Americans often applied the term to any Viet Cong combatant.

di di mau - Scram; beat it.

JAG - Judge Advocate General. The JAG Corps is the branch of the military concerned with justice and law.

LCI - Seagoing amphibious assault ship used to land infantry directly onto beaches.

LST - Ocean-going ship capable of shore-to-shore delivery of heavy military equipment.

NVA - North Vietnamese Army.

ROK - Used by Americans to refer to their South Korean allies during the Vietnam War. The Republic of Korea (ROK) sent more than 300,000 troops to South Vietnam between 1964 and 1973.

Veenaf - Republic of Vietnam Air Force, also known as the Vietnam Air Force (VNAF).

Ave atque vale
—*Catullus*

PART I

FQB

One

It would always be late afternoon, the shadow of the long main classroom building would already have engulfed the bare, rusted frame of Major Duong's Citroen, when the new recruits came slithering down the street from the academy's main gate and Lieutenant Pham ran out of his office to kick them. The Vietnamese drill sergeants made the recruits crawl on their stomachs the half-mile from the gate to the recruit barracks. The sergeants would kick only the laggards, but if Pham was in his office when they crawled past, he would kick the first recruit he came upon outside his office door. His pale, delicate face impassive, wearing a crush cap and wraparound sunglasses and sometimes, in cooler weather, a blue silk scarf carefully puffed to fill the opening at his collar, he would stroll along the crawling line, picking out other recruits to kick in the ribs or stomach. If they were crawling too high on their knees and elbows, he would kick them in the groin. The recruits still wore their civilian clothes. By the time they had crawled as far as the language school, most of them appeared to be in shock. Rarely did they cry out or alter the pace of their crawling when they were kicked. The drill sergeants kicked the recruits with a purely perfunctory though pyrotechnic show of rage. Pham packed far greater force into his choppy and wordlessly delivered kicks. Often he would spin an undersized body halfway around in the street. Peter Dandridge would watch this from the doorway of his classroom if, as often happened, the recruits crawled by during the final break of the school day. Peter could never, except for the ones who were kicked in the groin, tell why Pham chose to kick one recruit rather than another.

Like the other Army and Air Force enlisted men who taught at the language school, Peter had learned to choke down his anger at Pham's attacks on recruits. Once, it had flashed across Peter's mind that all of them, himself included, had made the kind of collective agreement that German civilians must once have made to neither see the hands that reached from cracked doors of rumbling boxcars nor smell the wind-borne fumes of burning flesh. But then he told himself, *No, that's ridiculous. What Pham dishes out is just a notch up from the split lip I got in basic training. Well, maybe two notches up. But it's not Dachau.*

Then Rabinowitz showed up. Rabinowitz told Peter he'd volunteered for duty in Vietnam after enlisting in an Army Reserve unit in New York. He'd been offered options, and he picked the language school at Nha Cat, part of the air academy there. Vietnamese airmen in ranks up to field-grade officers were supposed to absorb enough English at the language school to fit them for training in the States, whether as ground crewmen or pilots or squadron commanders. Rabinowitz didn't bother to explain why an Army reservist should be able to pluck at will such a plum assignment. He didn't explain, either, why he felt unbound by rules that applied to other enlisted men, such as wearing a helmet and loading his weapon when he pulled guard duty, or saluting junior officers even if their personal worth wasn't, to his eye, readily apparent.

It took Rabinowitz less than two weeks after setting foot in the school to fall into a show of rage at Pham each time a fresh batch of recruits came crawling down the street from the gate. That made it impossible for Peter to keep his own anger switched off.

"You precious bastard!" Rabinowitz would scream, his cap off, slamming his eraser against the side of the classroom building three doors

4

up from Peter. There was no mistaking his genuine anger—a muscle in his jaw would twitch furiously—but it struck Peter that there was something controlled, even staged about it.

Sometimes Pham would glance back at Rabinowitz. Still there would be no expression on Pham's pale, childishly smooth face. "Yes it's you I'm talking to, you son of a bitch!" Rabinowitz would yell, charging out onto the curried dirt in front of the building and shaking his fist. "Come on. Come on up here. I'll yank that sweet scarfy-poo through your ears, you hear me, you half-pint of rancid ant piss!"

Pham would not answer. His blank expression would grow more poised in a way that was not quite a smile. Finally he would lift his delicate chin and lower it, once, sharply, in what seemed a kind of salute. Then he would go back to kicking the recruits. When the bell for the last period sounded, Rabinowitz would go back inside with his students, but he would go on cursing Pham through the open doorway.

The more time Peter spent around Rabinowitz, the more certain he felt that Rabby had sought a posting to the war—if duty at the language school even deserved to be called that—precisely so he could engage in the kind of role-play for which Pham seemed the perfect foil. Apart from that afternoon hour when new recruits crawled down the blistering-hot asphalt street from the gate and the few other times when he found an excuse to mimic a Jersey-born street tough, Rabby acted and sounded like what Peter had concluded he was: a son of privilege—privilege no doubt hard-won, but not won by him—who was primed for entry to his father's Manhattan law firm. In Rabby's telling, having received his Princeton degree, he swiftly saw his draft eligibility reduced to a minor inconvenience, thanks to the presence among the Harlowe & Rabinowitz lawyers of an Army Reserve colonel who had no difficulty finding a place in his unit for the managing partner's son. By cutting a delayed enlistment deal, Rabby was able to get in a full year of law school before he was sworn in.

"Princeton for that too, huh?" Peter said. Rabinowitz merely pursed his lips—an attempt, Peter assumed, to stifle a smile.

As he enumerated for Peter the charmed steppingstones that had been placed before him one after another at his request, Rabby actually used the word "wangled," as if orders for Vietnam were a prize to be sought. Rabby described all of this to Peter with a smiling offhandedness that communicated this was simply the way things worked in his sector of the world. Peter only half-listened to the details, but he heard with painful clarity that Rabinowitz didn't have to be in Vietnam, and that he was unlikely to find his subsequent career blemished by his having been there. Rabby could afford to treat his time at the war—assuming he stayed out of the actual line of fire—as a lark. The more Peter reflected on how much his own case, with its tortuous turns of bad choices and blind luck, differed from what seemed the smooth trajectory Rabinowitz was destined to follow through and beyond this war, the more resentment he felt. Which posed a problem, because along with resenting Rabinowitz, Peter had never felt so powerfully drawn to anyone apart from his parents and Stephanie Ames, the woman he had loved since the day she drew blood from his throbbing knee. In Rabby's case, what he felt was not liking, exactly, or not only that. Rather, it was an instinct that the better he understood Rabby's story, the better he might understand his own.

~ * ~

Major Duong complained several times to Colonel Jesperson about Rabby's screaming at Pham. The first time, when Peter saw Rabinowitz coming back from Jesperson's office, he grabbed his rifle and skipped out of the classroom. The sweat and chalk dust dappling Rabinowitz's uniform and the way he plodded with his head slung forward and his shoulders rolling called to Peter's mind the incongruous image of an aging leopard.

"What'd he say, Rabby?"

Rabinowitz toiled on. He was still new in-country then, and walking in the heat seemed to cost him enormous effort. "Healthy American response my ass," he panted. "What he tells every calf-faced PFC who catches clap." That was all Peter could get out of him.

The following week a new batch of recruits came in and, even though it wasn't break period, Rabinowitz ran out of his classroom to yell at Pham. When Rabby got back from Jesperson's office that time, he told Peter that all the colonel had asked of him was a promise he wouldn't interrupt class again.

Peter fully expected to hear next of something beyond a complaint, such as Rabby's sudden dismissal from the staff, an Article 15 slapped on his record and his sudden departure for the States. Peter had expected something on that scale after Pham brought barbed wire into play. When Pham did that, as Peter came to realize, he touched depths of anguish and hostility in Rabinowitz that neither Pham nor anyone else could have suspected were there. That wasn't clear at the time, though. What was immediately clear was that Rabinowitz had deepened the cause for hostility on Pham's side. He had done that by humiliating Pham in front of recruits, students, Vietnamese NCOs and American instructors alike. He had done it almost offhandedly, with a show of calm wholly unlike his previous fits of rage.

Nothing, as Peter understood in time, could have more deeply wounded a puffed-up martinet like Pham or made him want to inflict a still deeper wound on his adversary. But by the time Peter understood all that, it was too late to cut short the risk it would lead to something deadly.

As far as Peter could ever tell, Rabby either didn't know or didn't care about Duong's complaints to Jesperson. Colonel Jesperson was a lank Arizonan whose eyes were the color of bleached jean cloth, and whose voice sounded like something worn down to bare gray boards in a dust storm. He liked to sit in front of his villa in the evenings under a mosquito net supported by an igloo tent frame, and there to write on ruled yellow paper with a collection of pencil stubs he kept sandwiched in a legal pad binder, letters to his wife.

Two

The first time Pham appeared in the doorway of Peter's classroom and called out the names of three students, Peter had not asked his authority or his reason. One of the students whose names Pham called had come to class that morning shivering with malaria. Peter assumed this porcelain-faced lieutenant with wraparound sunglasses was taking them to sick call.

After the three boys left with Pham, the other students clicked their tongues and muttered in Vietnamese. One of them, a young warrant officer who had instigated and won an arm-wrestling contest during the break between the first two class periods, jabbered something angrily and chopped the air with his hand, as if he were delivering karate blows.

The older man who sat next to the one who had lost his temper smiled at Peter. "Sir, that man who takes them, he is a very bad officer."

"Why bad?" Peter said.

"He takes them for punish."

"What? Why? What is it they've done?"

"You no know Lieutenant Pham?"

The young warrant officer told Peter the student with chills had been written up because he arrived late at morning muster. Once the older man had briefed him on Pham's official and functional roles—administrative factotum and petty sadist—Peter left the classroom. His rifle stock pummeling his hip, two clips of ammunition clattering in a pocket of his fatigue blouse, he ran down the row of classroom buildings and past the student barracks to the ditch.

There were about a dozen students arched over a shallow ditch beside the embankment of a narrow-gauge flight line service railway. The students' feet were braced halfway up the sand embankment. Their rear ends stuck high in the air and their weight was thrown forward onto their hands. The shadow of the embankment reached as far as their waists. The sun beat down on their backs and bare heads. Their caps were lined up on the ground in front of them. Peter saw that the idea of the ditch was to allow them no inconspicuous way to rest. The only alternative to remaining arched over the ditch was to fall into it.

Lieutenant Pham was standing in the shade of the last building in the row of student barracks. He held his clipboard at an upward slant from his chest, and he lifted a page and read the page under it. When one student lowered himself onto his elbows, Pham looked up and, shouting, took several steps forward into the sun. For an instant, the student turned his flushed, frightened face toward Pham. Then he raised himself, tremblingly, onto his hands. Peter saw that it was the boy who had come to class that morning shaking with a malaria chill.

"Duc, get up from there," Peter said. When Duc did not answer or move, Peter's rising and unfocused anger fastened on the boy. "For Christ's sake," Peter said. Stooping, he placed one hand under the boy's stomach and the other hand under his chest, and hoisted him forward over the ditch. The boy spun his legs helplessly until his big chukka boots found purchase in the sand across the ditch. As he was lifting the boy, Peter's rifle slipped from his shoulder and dangled by its strap from his elbow. Peter cursed the weapon and hurled it free onto the sand. The boy babbled something high and despairing in Vietnamese as Peter forced him to stand. "Yeah, that's right," Peter muttered through his clenched teeth. "My grandma could spit over the corn crib too."

Then he saw Pham running forward from the barracks. Pham ran in a mincing way that did not jostle his crush cap or his sunglasses. "Ho! You!" Pham called, pointing with the clipboard. "You do not have here this your business. I am officer here."

"Who in hell do you think you are?" Peter bawled. "You don't pull a sick kid out of my class! Not to take him to your goddamned ditch, not for anything!"

Pham smiled a small, thin-lipped smile. "I am officer here," he said, tapping the edge of his clipboard lightly against his chest. "You no want my coming in your class? Very good. I come for finding your students in the morning when they do not yet leave their barracks. Then they do not have still two hours of learn English before they report for be punished. Then maybe they do not pass their test. Then they must go for infantry. Oh, tsk tsk," Pham said, shaking his head and smiling. "That is too bad."

"Cut it any way you want," Peter said. His mouth was filled with the stale, brassy taste of spent rage. "Just stay the hell out of my classroom. And don't you take any kid that's as sick as Duc to your damned ditch, not from my class. Comprends?"

Peter picked up his rifle. Sand had gotten into the ventilator holes along the top of the casing and he shook it out. Peter grabbed the boy's wrist, and the bare flesh felt hotter than the rifle's metal casing. "Let's go, Duc," he said.

It seemed to Peter later that—even before Pham said something incredibly fast and Duc yanked his arm free and stretched himself again over the ditch—he, Peter, had already known that was what was going to happen, and had already ceased to care.

~ * ~

So Peter had left it alone. He had slipped into the going rationale for leaving things alone: Let them do it their way; don't interfere with the Vietnamese way of doing things. As though theft and petty brutality were as much mere matters of custom as the oddly touching, musical giggle they used to show polite attention, or the way combat veterans would stroll along the beach toward town on Sundays, holding hands like schoolgirls.

After all, what were his students to him, that he should risk on their account the short-time discharge that awaited him if he went home with his record clean? If Major Duong, on his way to the black market downtown, drove past the advisory team villas on Saturday mornings with cartons of contraband cigarettes and liquor stacked to the top of his decrepit Citroen's rusted frame, what was that to Peter? What should any of it mean to him when, in a few more months, at a nearly diametrical point of the globe, he would walk into a room where a woman who held a yellow marker like a dart above a medical textbook would lift her eyes, and a slight smile would dent her New Hampshire stolidity. She would say to him something in keeping with that smile, and it would sweep away the memory of his student arched on trembling limbs over a ditch like a fan sweeping away the vapors of a chemistry experiment gone wrong.

He was too far gone at narcotizing himself with these thoughts to do more than mock and feebly admonish when Rabinowitz turned up at the language school and jumped on Pham's case and stayed there. Peter could have refrained from the mockery if Rabinowitz had been a patent Jewish wild man, but Rabinowitz was no such thing. Rabby had that street-slangy brand of urban elitism that Peter knew just well enough to see past the swagger to the pride of caste. It had little to do with strident Jewish intellectualism, or with wealth, Peter felt. It was more like a cavalier's pride in his family's service to the crown, and his serene confidence that he would further that tradition.

And, with all of this, for Rabinowitz to transmogrify into a screaming Jewish goblin whenever a fresh batch of recruits came in and Pham ran out to kick them—that was what baffled Peter and unnerved him. For Rabinowitz, of all men—an Ivy League law degree within reach and a job in his father's Manhattan law firm awaiting him—to risk all that he would go back to, all that mattered to him so rightly and so much, for the privilege of cursing a Vietnamese lieutenant, angered Peter as much as it troubled him. Where did Rabinowitz get the right to have it both ways?

Only once did Rabby seem to tip over some brink, and it was his abrupt, complete silence that signaled his plunge. It was on one of those evenings when recruits crawled in an ant line past Peter's classroom. The drill sergeants were screaming at them as usual. Through his open window Peter heard the thumping of boot leather against clothed flesh, which meant the sergeants were kicking the laggards. Then he heard the sound of an approaching motor scooter. Turning, he saw through his window the trim little figure with the wraparound sunglasses park his scooter, then jog toward the street. Peter knew by then that Pham often left the academy for several hours during the day, but that if new recruits were due to arrive, Pham would hurry back in time to abuse them.

This time Pham carried a canvas bag by its sewn-on handles. Small metal stems stuck out of the top of the bag. Pham barked an order, and all motion in the street ceased. All Peter could hear was the recruits' panting and Pham's footsteps on the pavement. Then Pham ordered one of the recruits, who lay prone in front of Peter's classroom window, to stand up. The kid, wearing a checked shirt that had come completely unbuttoned during his crawl from the gate, staggered to his feet. Pham extracted one of the strands of metal from the bag. It was a piece of barbed wire, about two feet long. Pham ordered the recruit to hold out his hands, and he wrapped the wire around the boy's wrists. Then Pham took a quick step backward and, with the heel of his other foot, swept the recruit's feet out from under him. The boy cried out as he fell on his elbows onto the pavement. Blood oozed from his wrists where the barbs cut into them.

Several of Peter's students, including the young warrant officer who had earlier vented his anger at Pham, had left their desks and clustered behind him to look through the window. When Pham tripped the boy in the street, the warrant officer shouted what sounded to Peter like a threat, but Pham gave no sign of having heard it. Pham strolled toward the end of the line of prone recruits, looking them over with the casual air of a shopper eyeing a rack of produce, until he reached the one at the very end.

He beckoned to one of the drill sergeants and handed the sergeant another two-foot length of barbed wire. Like many of the recruits, this one wore sandals. The sergeant stooped and wound the wire tightly around the recruit's bare ankles.

"Good Christ!" Peter said through clenched teeth, and the students nearest him muttered "*trời ơi!*"—with, as he knew, the same meaning. "He's just experimenting," Peter said. "He's testing out a new way to torment them."

Then Peter saw Rabinowitz step from the door of his classroom. Unlike all the times he had raged at Pham's abuse of recruits, Rabby said nothing. His lips drooped as if he were so completely immersed in thought that he had lost control of his facial muscles. He started toward Pham, plodding with his head slung forward and his big shoulders rolling and that faraway look on his face. He squinted a little as he crossed the sunlit gap between the shadows of two classroom buildings. Rabby carried nothing, not even his M-16, and Peter made a mental note to berate him for leaving his weapon in his classroom.

Lieutenant Pham had set the canvas bag on the ground behind him to watch the sergeant bind the recruit's ankles with the barbed wire. When the sergeant had finished, he noticed Rabinowitz approaching. Pham turned around in time to see Rabinowitz pick up the bag of barbed wire by its handles. As far as Peter could tell, Rabby said nothing to Pham or the sergeant. He headed back toward his classroom at that steady pace, slump-shouldered and still appearing to have his thoughts fixed elsewhere. Pham shouted something short, sharp and a little shrill, like a puppy's bark, but Rabby plodded on. Pham strode after him, fast enough to catch up quickly. Rabby stopped and looked down at the recruit whose wrists were bound with barbed wire. Then he glanced at Peter and the students in Peter's classroom window. Then he began fumbling at the canvas bag.

"Excuse me, Private, I think you are making very big mistake," Pham said.

"Nope," Rabby said, shaking one length of wire to disentangle it from others in the bag.

"You have your business here teaching English," Pham said, "You too much interfere of things not your business, I think."

"Think again," Rabby said, pulling the piece of barbed wire clear of the bag. He looked at it with a lip-curl of disgust, as if he'd picked up a snake.

"Okay, I think again," Pham said in a rising voice. "And now I think very clear you interfere of things not your business!"

Pham reached for the bag. Rabby jerked it out of reach, held it behind him with one hand and took a step backward toward Peter's classroom. With his other hand he waved the length of barbed wire like an absurdly wobbly fencing foil.

"Have—a—care," Rabby said in a low voice.

With an impulse to laugh, Peter recognized in Rabby's words a warning unlikely to be understood so far from an Ivy League fencing club. Keeping his eyes on Lieutenant Pham, Rabby reached the bag of barbed wire strands behind him until the bag bumped the wall below the window.

"Take them," Rabby said, shaking the bag. "Share and share alike."

The young warrant officer seized the bag, pulled it inside the window and held it open for the other students. There were about a dozen pieces of barbed wire still in the bag. Peter's class included two air force captains and an army major, as well as the warrant officer and several enlisted men. The warrant officer waved two pieces of barbed wire through the open window and shouted furiously at Pham. After exchanging hesitant glances, several of the enlisted men took pieces of wire from the bag too. They giggled nervously as they waggled the lengths of wire from the window like children fishing with cane poles.

Pham pointed a finger at Rabinowitz and said something that Peter was unable to hear over the hotheaded warrant officer's shouting. The major and the two captains spoke quietly among themselves inside the classroom door. Then the major, whose name was Hung, stepped outside and gave what sounded to Peter like a direct order. The sharp tone surprised Peter, because Major Hung had always been soft-spoken and deferential in class. Peter looked closely at the small, rigid figure facing Pham to make sure, from the single silver blossom on each epaulette and the hair graying at the temples, that it was in fact Hung.

From the tone, Peter understood the gist of what Major Hung and Lieutenant Pham said to each other. The young warrant officer filled in the gaps for him later. Hung said tying recruits' hands and feet with barbed wire was a disgrace. Pham said he had his own separate chain of command, and no language student of any rank could intrude on it. Hung said chain of command be damned, the barbed wire had better come off those two recruits pronto.

A faint flush showed through the pale skin of Pham's face. Then, saying nothing, he turned and walked quickly toward his office across the street. Major Hung ordered the Vietnamese sergeants to remove the barbed wire from the wrists and ankles of the two recruits, and he watched as they did it. Then Hung turned toward Rabinowitz and made a shallow bow. It was a soldier's bow, with shoulders squared and head high. Rabby, though, didn't even seem to see it. Once again, he appeared lost in thought.

"Damn, Rabby, can't you thank the man?" Peter said. "He just might have saved your butt."

"What?" Rabby said. He glanced at Peter, and it seemed to take a moment for his eyes to focus. "Oh, yes," he said. He threw Major Hung a sloppy salute, and Hung, with a polite laugh, returned it.

"And listen up, Cyrano," Peter said. "Never leave your weapon unattended, okay? You know, the rusted-up one you left back in your classroom?"

Rabinowitz, slouching toward his classroom door, waved one hand in acknowledgement. Then he stopped. "Pete, can you get rid of the barbed wire?" he said over his shoulder. "I mean, really get rid of it?"

"Rid of it?" Peter said. "Well, there's a big trash bin by the orderly room, and I could throw these pieces in—"

"Not good enough," Rabby said, still speaking over his shoulder with that faraway look. "Could you maybe bury it?"

"Huh? Well, yeah, but—"

"At least bury the pieces with blood on them, the ones he tied on those two kids." Rabby said. "Be sure you bury those, okay? Bury those two pieces good and deep."

"Yeah, I guess I could do that, Rabby. But, look, it's just barbed wire. It's not like there isn't God's plenty of that around."

Rabby had still only half-turned, but for the first time since Rabby had set out to confiscate the bag of barbed wire, Peter could see the twitching in Rabby's jaw that marked his fits of rage.

"It's the intent, goddamn it!" Rabby said. "It's the blood, and the intent! Just bury it, will you? It's not like I'm asking you to do anything high-risk. God forbid I should ever ask that of *you*."

Without waiting for an answer, Rabby headed on toward his classroom. It wasn't until Rabby had disappeared through the door that it struck Peter that his own role in the spectacle he had just witnessed had been that of a timid scold.

"All right, I'll bury it," Peter muttered.

Peter borrowed an entrenching tool from the orderly room. After the 11 p.m. signoff on Armed Forces Radio, he left his villa with the strands of wire Rabby wanted buried. He picked a spot behind some scrub bushes, well away from the street, hoping no one would see him digging. "Good and deep," he muttered as he drove the little spade into the sand. "This is just nuts."

When he returned the spade next morning, he checked the guard duty roster and got the orderly room sergeant to switch him to the same shift Rabinowitz would pull the following week. Maybe I'll learn something, Peter thought. Maybe it will do one or both of us some good.

Three

Only long afterward, after layers of self-deception had flaked away like cheap paint beneath the tropical sun, could Peter Dandridge see what that day's comic-opera dance in the guard post had been about. Only then could he see what had drawn Rabby to a war he could have sidestepped with ease. Sketched out there, too, at least in dim outline, had been the truth about the two Antoninas. But so much had to happen before Peter could see that there were two Antoninas, and that Rabby's need for both was absolute. Rabby had needed the tall, noble Antonina, gray-eyed like Athena, to lead the life he'd created for himself. He'd needed her because he had so little else to work with except loss and pain. And he'd needed the runtish, cunning, ferret-eyed Antonina—the one who could rescue or kill with the same cold indifference—so that he could live at all.

But at the time, there'd been no hint of any such revelation. It was a mid-day guard duty shift in a post with a corrugated steel roof, and Peter knew it would be like four hours in a Dutch oven. When he ducked through the entry of the guard post and looked up, he saw a foot-long gecko dangling from Rabby's hand. Peter took an involuntary step backward, and his helmet clanged against a steel beam at the roof's edge. Rabby's hand was clamped on the gecko's back. The lizard, its splayed feet scrambling in air, yapped like an irate puppy.

"You just cannot, will not, leave well enough alone," Peter muttered through clenched teeth.

Rabinowitz lifted the gecko higher. He held it at arm's length between the tin roof and the sandbag parapet. That exposed the lizard to what such a nocturnal creature would want least: sunlight that beat down brutally on its exposed flesh.

Head cocked, Rabby contemplated the apricot-colored speckles on the gecko's back. Then he slowly turned the animal until he was looking directly into its mouth. While both men stared wordlessly at the gecko, its frantic yaps were gradually drowned out by the cymbals and bizarre trumpet runs from a funeral procession that was coming, unseen beyond a classroom building, down the street from Nha Cat.

Finally Peter said, "For God's sake, Rabby, throw it out. When those big geckos bite, they mean business."

Rabinowitz gave no sign of having heard. His eyes softened and his lips curled in a smile both mocking and tender. He brought the gecko closer to his face, until its jaws, lined with tiny, needle-like teeth, gaped in front of his nose.

"Rescue," he whispered. "Rescue is at hand."

The gecko stopped thrashing. Its tongue looped slowly out and brushed the front of Rabby's chalk-stained fatigue blouse. Rabby's free hand moved toward the lizard's tail, and Peter realized he meant to grasp it and swing the creature out toward the swirled razor wire staked to a row of metal poles between the guard post and the street.

"Don't do that!" Peter said. "Just hold him where he is."

Peter unslung his rifle from his shoulder and stuck the muzzle against a sandbag. He cocked the weapon, checked the breech to make sure it was clear and clicked the trigger. The racket of the trumpet and cymbals grew louder, and a stocky little sorrel horse drew a rattling wooden cart past a jagged-looking corner of the nearest classroom building. It had been a little over a year since minigun fire had chewed chunks from that building's concrete wall. Peter felt a familiar twinge of dismay that he hadn't been there when the Viet Cong forced their way into it and held it until the gunships and Korean infantry drove them out.

As the cart drew closer, Peter saw flaking gilt atop a casket in the cart's bed. Four women wearing white áo dàis and white shawls walked behind the cart. Behind the women walked a half-dozen male mourners wearing white headbands, then a shuffling gaggle of other mourners, then the two men with the trumpet and cymbals. The procession was headed, Peter knew, toward the cemetery near the old French beachside villas where he and Rabinowitz and the other American instructors at the air academy were billeted.

Seems there've been a lot of funerals lately, Peter thought. Well, there's a war on.

"Now hold him out over the sandbags, and let go when I say," Peter said. He held the rifle by the muzzle and pressed its stock against the lizard's back, beneath Rabby's hand.

"What are you doing, Pete?" Rabby said. His voice quivered with annoyance.

"Simple act of propulsion, that's all," Peter said.

"You'll get him over the wire, right? You'd better get him over the wire. With plenty of clearance. Understand?"

"Guaranteed, if you'll just fucking do what I tell you," Peter told him. "All right. Now!"

Rabby let go of the lizard's tail and Peter swung the rifle. The slow arc of the gecko's body in air seemed almost languorous despite the frantic scrambling of its feet. It landed on the earth beyond the concertina wire, danced a frenzied tarantella through its own dust and made off toward the classroom building.

The man with the cymbals lifted them above his head and hit them together half a dozen times. A smile of pleasure and relief spread across Rabby's face.

"Exit lizard, stage left," he said. "Lacking only—only that."

Peter punched a sandbag in exasperation. "Lacking only you getting bitten for tormenting the damn thing," he said.

"Why wouldn't you let me give him the tail toss? I wouldn't have thrown him into the wire, if you were worried about that." Rabby paused, then laughed loudly, for what seemed to Peter an unnecessarily long time.

"No, Rabby, you wouldn't have tossed him into the wire," Peter said. "In fact, you wouldn't have gotten him over the sandbags. You don't know what lizards do when you pick them up by their tails, do you?"

Rabby eyed him archly. "Sure, he said. "They wag those appendages with great ferocity."

"No, Rabby. The tail just pops off. It might squirm in your hand a few seconds, but the rest of the lizard would be scuttling around our feet, scared and mad as hell."

"Oh, I see," Rabby said. "Cityboy fuckup, then. I haven't had much history with lizards. Little ones with blue tails—I'd catch a glimpse of those at summer camp in the Berkshires."

"So, first opportunity, you just naturally pick up a foot-long gecko and hold it close enough to spit in your eye?" Peter said. "And what was that crap about rescue at hand?"

"That?" Rabby gave a single sharp bark of dismissive laughter. "I was just helping him steer clear of slothful habits. We're teachers, right?"

Peter snorted. "Horseshit," he said. "When you came in here five minutes ago, that gecko was hanging upside-down over in that corner, asleep, right? Just like he was every other time I've pulled guard duty in this post. That's what geckos are supposed to do all day. All he needed from you was to be left alone."

Rabinowitz took a clear plastic cigarette case and a book of paper matches from the broad cuff of a rolled-up sleeve. The way Rabby's eyes moved in squinting takes between the task of lighting up and the funeral procession seemed to Peter curiously at odds with Rabby's big-boned, homely face. Rabby's rifle was still slung from his shoulder. Algae-colored rust coated the barrel.

"Hey, there's another one in there," Rabby said. "Looks like it's just a box, though."

As the cart rattled up the street, Peter could see a second casket through the crowd of mourners. It was painted bright red, but unlike the gilt-edged one, this one appeared to be made of plain boards, and it was oddly short and narrow for a coffin. As Peter was wondering what to make of this, a young male mourner near the rear of the procession caught sight of him and nudged another young man beside him. The two of them glowered at Peter and spoke briefly to each other. Then, weirdly, they both smiled at him, and they each raised two fingers in the peace sign. Peter saw that the one who had spotted him first had a thick white scar running diagonally from below his chin to his collarbone.

"Unless I miss my guess, that's an ordnance crate," Peter said. "I've seen them stacked outside the weapons depot on base. That'd be an awfully tight fit, unless it's for a kid."

"Maybe it's just for ropes, right?" Rabby said. "I mean, to let the casket down?"

"Then why not just throw the ropes in the cart?" Peter said.

"Appearance's sake," Rabby said. "Presentation, presentation, you know?"

"Maybe those two dudes that cased us out could give us some answers," Peter said. "Did you see the scar on that guy's throat? How would you even get a scar like that?"

"From my limited knowledge of matters surgical," Rabby said, "I'd rule out tracheotomy. Which I guess leaves either accident or hostile action."

They watched the cart and the mourners until they passed out of sight around a bend in the street, leaving a faint caterwauling on the air. A wavelet of unease washed over Peter, then dissolved in distant ripples.

"Well, it's not our business, is it?" he said lightly. "You know, Rabby, there are two kinds of short list you need to keep over here. One for the number of days till you rotate stateside, and one for the things you need to worry about till that day comes. As you tick off the days, you also cross items off that give-a-fuck list. Figuring out what's inside that box in the cart—the body of a three-year old, or ropes, or tools, or bones, or whatever? That's definitely off the list. A gecko taking his noontime nap? Off the list. And, listen: Lieutenant Pham? Nowhere on the list. Do you have any idea how much you owe that little gray-headed major for lacing into Pham, after you freaked out the way you did the other day? Pham just does things the Vietnamese way. Nothing you do is going to change that."

Rabinowitz took a long, contemplative drag at his cigarette. He wore no helmet, and his fatigue cap perched high on his dark, knotted curls. Splotches of sweat and chalk dust dappled his fatigue blouse.

"Kicking recruits and making our kids spreadeagle over a ditch till they fall in it is the Auschwitz way," he said. "And then trussing them up with barbed wire, and him in his spit-shined combat boots and wraparound shades and puffed-out little cravat. It's almost like he wanted to underscore the SS likeness, you know? You bet I'll go after him if he tries that again. Only next time I won't just waggle a strip of wire in his face."

"Spoken by the man who played tailback for the ghetto varsity on Kristallnacht," Peter said. "A humanitarian icon. Come off it, Rabby. Think of it this way: Pham's just something funny that happened to you once on the way from the Princeton locker room to the land of torts and swizzle sticks."

Rabinowitz snorted cigarette smoke. He squinted at Peter. When he chose to take offense, Rabinowitz had a way of spreading out his mouth in a flat, sardonic line and then saying something very short and arrogant.

"Kristallnacht and ghetto varsity, huh?" he said. "Peter, if I were a man of your cultural background talking to a man of mine, I wouldn't assume that works as a gag line." He slid his thumb under the strap of his M-16 and threw the rifle against the sandbag wall. The butt struck the ground sharply, and a puff of chalk dust bloomed from the muzzle.

"Jesus F. Christ, Rabby!" Peter said. "Do you know how likely these tin cannons are to go off when you sling them around like that?"

Rabby peered at the street. "There's our pard," he said. The gecko waddled sluggishly past a pile of steaming garbage beyond the wire. It was searching, Peter knew, for some other dark corner where it could wait out the fierce daylight. Sort of like me, Peter thought. Sort of the way I've chosen to hang upside-down in a shadowed corner of this war.

"It can't go off if I never load it," Rabby said. "If I can get through this war without loading that thing more than once, I may ask for a tickertape parade through downtown Hackensack."

Peter took the two full ammunition clips from a lower pocket of his fatigue blouse and laid them on the parapet. He fitted one clip into the breech of his rifle and slapped it home.

"Hey, Pete, you know about the soccer game we've got lined next Friday, right?" Rabby said. "You want to play? We've got two large jerseys still."

"Can't do it, Rabby," he said. "My knee."

"Why didn't you get your fiancée to fix that for you?"

"Stephie's not my fiancée. And she tried to make the only fix she could. She could've used her med school connections to make me draft-exempt. Silly me, I declined."

"She waiting patiently for you back there? Bowl of buttered grits in one hand, gleaming scalpel in the other?"

"They don't do grits in New Hampshire. She's from there and intends to head back. Got a residency at Dartmouth's hospital. And waiting patiently? That's something else she doesn't do."

The guard post's metal roof radiated heat, and Peter's eyes started drifting shut. To fight off sleep, he spoke the first words that came into his head.

"So what's it with you and barbed wire?" he said.

For a while Rabinowitz didn't answer. Then he said: "Nothing. Empty theatrics. Forget it."

"Well, I just thought, since you said you wouldn't even toss a lizard into barbed wire, you must have some reason. Sounds like you must have had some bad experience with the stuff. Of course, you never had to track down a runaway cow and drive her back into fenced pasture, the way I did time and again."

Rabby heaved a bored-sounding sigh. "Well, I could probably come up with some plausible story of early-life trauma, and you'd probably believe it," he said. He chuckled briefly. "I'm gifted that way, you see. I mean, at stitching together narratives so airtight even I buy into them, while at the same time I recognize the artifice. Good advocacy requires that, you know? You have to put the best, most useful construction on facts, and deliver that version with conviction. Quite a different thing from lying. And I always had that talent. Not a boast. Simply a fact."

"Damn it, Rabby!" Peter said. "All I asked was why barbed wire freaks you out, and you lecture me on your fitness to con juries."

Rabinowitz slowly turned his head with what Peter took to be a lip-curl of disgust. "I will tell you bluntly, then, that I hate the stuff," Rabby said. "Barbed wire, I mean. Always have, though Pham's use of it on those recruits has, let's say, heightened my visceral distaste for it. And for him."

Rabby had not put a clip in his rifle. Smoking, resting his freckled forearms on the parapet, he clearly did not intend to, though standing orders for guard duty specified a loaded weapon and a helmet.

Peter looked down at the rust-flecked barrel of Rabby's rifle. "Got a visceral distaste for cleaning your weapon too, looks like," he said.

"I'll clean and load it at the proper time." Rabby's voice sounded oddly strained.

"Charlie's lousy at giving notice," Peter said. "I think that's why we went to war here. To teach him proper etiquette."

"I'll know when it's time," Rabby said. "Which it will be, I expect. Once."

"You've got a sixth sense, huh?"

"I suppose you could call her a sixth sense."

"Her? What's that supposed to mean? You got a hotline to Hanoi Hannah? She updating you on VC battle plans?"

"I don't relish the derogatory tone, Pete," Rabby said evenly.

"Well, call us even then. Because, funny, I was just thinking how little I enjoyed digging a cat hole by the beach at midnight, just to give tainted barbed wire a fit resting place."

Rabby sighed heavily, in what seemed to Peter a strenuous effort to sound offhand.

"Well, the name won't mean a thing to you without the backstory," Rabby said. "Lay off the slurs about the SS and Kristallnacht and I might fill you in sometime. Her name's Antonina. Crucial figure in my family's history. Perfect model of behavior in times of peril. Long dead herself, understand."

Four

Peter liked to walk to the villa after the last class period. Sometimes he would stop at the Vietnamese soup kitchen inside the main gate of the training base. He would eat a bowl of soup at a corner table where he could see, through the screened window, the Vietnamese officers practicing karate outside the main gate. Atop the gate's yellow columns perched two concrete entities that were supposed to represent eagles. Peter thought of them instead as obese stingrays.

A lieutenant who worked in the student dispensary came regularly into the café in the evenings. He had a warm, harried look about the eyes that Peter liked. His name was Lieutenant Thanh. Thanh would order soup and tea and a liqueur glass of rice wine for his dinner. Once he had been a medical student in Hue. Now he worked nights at a hospital in Nha Cat, where he often delivered babies. Sometimes Peter would sit for an hour with Lieutenant Thanh, drinking rice wine and watching the sunset turn the stingrays a bright, newborn pink and then a pale, asphyxial blue.

When the final bell marked the end of their shift in the guard post, Rabinowitz picked up his rifle and started in his slung-headed prowl toward the villa shuttle trucks parked inside the gate. Peter cleared his rifle, walked into the café and asked for a bowl of pho at the counter. He was gingerly lifting a mass of noodles and bean sprouts out of it with his chopsticks when Thanh came in.

"Ho, Dan'ridge!" Thanh called from the door.

Thanh brought his soup and his tea to the table, and then Peter learned that there was no getting away from Rabinowitz anymore.

"Your friend is for long time now making Major Duong very angry," Thanh said.

"For sticking it to Pham? Well, that's not exactly news."

The small, steady, glistening eyes stayed fixed on Peter through the steam rising from Thanh's soup.

"Your friend is a good man," Thanh said. "I think so. Many of Vietnamese officer think so."

Peter said nothing. He did not want to answer to anything that had to do with Rabinowitz. Beyond the stingrays, about a dozen young Vietnamese officers were warming up in white robes beside a big Quonset that had once been a hangar.

"Pham *n'est pas populaire avec les autres officiers*," Thanh said. "He is—what you call?—have without ruth."

"Ruth, huh?" Peter tried to rein in his annoyance. "My friend has a fair ration of her, all right. Trouble is he doesn't know it. He thought he was just your average Princeton intramural football captain waiting to sandwich his brain between the covers of books with colorful titles like *Civil Procedure*."

Peter still looked out the screen window. As the sun dipped behind the palms toward the bay, the violently flexing white robes appeared more and more untenanted. When finally Peter looked again at Thanh, he was surprised by the intensity in the small, luminous eyes. But apart from the eyes, Thanh's harried look and with the schoolmarmish downward set to the corners of his mouth seemed the same as always.

"Your friend is a good man for me, many officers, all students," Thanh said. "He is one American man is thinking here, this place, his students, Vietnam. Is not all of time thinking someplace else, wife, offspring, be happy, go to work, automobile."

"That's right," Peter said. "Rabby is the only American this side of Montgomery Ward headquarters the inside of whose head is not a well-thumbed catalogue. He's got some Ruth, all right. But he's got a fair amount of Judith mixed in there too."

Peter realized how small-minded it was of him to unload this toxic rant on this gentle man. Thanh sipped his tea, and his eyes stayed fixed on Peter's.

"Oh, I come here too late, I think," Thanh said. "Already time for me now to go to the hospital."

"But your soup?" Peter said.

"Yes, but I must go. My hospital is close to the river, you know? Takes more time to go there now, because this time of day is lot of—how you say it?"

"Traffic," Peter said.

"Yes, yes, a lot of traffic."

Again Thanh's dark eyes came to rest on Peter's face. He's measuring something, Peter thought. But what? How much he should trust me? How much I already trust him?

"One thing I think maybe you don't know, Dan'ridge," Thanh said. "I think maybe too your friend not know this. Pham is from the North. You know this already? No? All Vietnamese officers know this. You see Duong treating Pham in special way? You maybe see Jes-pah-sung is treating Pham in special way? You see Pham leave from academy sometime for three, four hours, and Duong and Jes-pah-sung say okay? You think they treating him special way because he is very good officer? You think they have other reason? I think so. Other Vietnamese officers think so. Maybe it will help your friend if he know we think this. Maybe you will tell him. Pham come here from Haiphong. Only two years in the South, and already very special officer."

"Special in an unholy abundance of ways," Peter said.

Thanh glanced at his wristwatch and his head jerked slightly. "Oh, I think now I will be late!" he said. He downed the last of his tea and stood abruptly.

Peter looked away toward the concrete stingrays. They had started to take on that blue cast he associated with stillbirth. He had gotten that notion from a story Thanh told him about delivering a stillborn baby at the hospital. The mother had wanted to bathe her dead baby, and Thanh had brought her a basin of warm water and a washcloth. Then Thanh had stood quietly aside, not watching her, while she bathed her baby and wept. Finally she had handed the basin back to him with the tiny corpse still in it.

Thanh turned in the open doorway of the soup kitchen.

"I think you will tell your friend this, yes, Dan'ridge?" he said. "Pham is from the North."

"Well, we've all got to be from somewhere," Peter said.

Five

When he thought of the gulf between his own world and the one that could produce a Rabinowitz, Peter could only shake his head and wonder how the two of them could even speak a common tongue. Given their difference, he wondered why he bothered to bicker with Rabby over the importance of steering a disaster-free course back to the lives they had put on hold. Peter had grown up in a tin-roofed farmhouse across a gravel road from a barn built of hand-hewn logs so immense that his mother would point to them with mock indignation when her small son questioned her tales of a vanished race of giants. As a child, Peter would often climb the stacked hay bales in the barn to read the inscription his maternal great-great-grandfather had carved on a rafter: W.H. Leinbach, May 1873.

Peter had grown up listening to his father and other men swap tales—most of them amusing and none involving bloodshed—about their experiences in World War II. He loved the story, told by the father of the twins who were his best childhood friends, of the weekly surveillance runs flown by a German pilot over an American weather station in Iceland. The German would wag his wings in warning to the weather station's crewmen, who would dart under cover sufficient to protect them from the only ordnance the Nazi plane would ever deliver: a single brickbat. He loved his father's story of swiping fresh-baked bread from a field kitchen, hiding it in his helmet and bringing it to a Polish refugee woman who was living with her children in a bombed-out building. His father said the woman would slice the bread wafer-thin and serve it as if it were cake. He even loved the way his father disclaimed credit for the Bronze Star that Peter, at age 10, had discovered inside his father's big walnut desk in one of the cubicles behind the door that swung down on hinges and doubled as a writing surface. Whenever Peter asked him about the medal, his father had said it was simply a mistake, but that he valued it as a sign of his luck in coming through the war with nothing to deeply regret. Peter had assumed, without ever thinking much about it, that if there were ever a war for him to go to, he would go, and in it he would have the same sort of zany, goodhearted adventures as those his father and his friends' father had described, and he would bring home the same sort of incommunicable gratitude his father felt for whatever he had done to earn the Bronze Star.

In Peter's senior year of high school, his knee crumpled in a football tackling drill. The surgeon removed most cartilage from his knee and put a big metal screw in the bone above it to hold the ligament taut. The surgeon called it a pin, but to Peter the X-ray image looked like an outsize wood screw. He got the surgeon to give him a copy of the X-ray. Having had little success with girls by other means, he had fallen into the habit of doing or saying something mildly shocking to girls whose attention he craved. He showed the X-ray to a girl who sat beside him in study hall, hoping the darkened image of the screw piercing the stark white bone would somehow excite her. She looked at the X-ray and then at him. Her nose and lips wrinkled with disgust and she said, "Ee-yew!"

He enrolled at a land-grant university where male students who passed a physical were required to take two years of ROTC. The doctor who examined his knee at the ROTC armory on campus told him he was exempt. Peter told him he didn't want to be exempt. The doctor told him with an impatient wave of the hand that it made no difference what he wanted.

For the rest of his college years, Peter lowered his head whenever he walked past the field where students in their crisp khaki or dress green uniforms were mastering the intricacies of close-order drill. He told himself it wasn't his fault that he wasn't out there with them. Still, he kept his head down and bit his lip.

He felt a little ashamed, too, about his love of drawing and design, though he told himself he deserved credit for wanting to design only useful things. He had never had much interest in sketching people or landscapes, but since he had been about ten he had drawn buildings, starting with sketch after sketch of the barn. As he thought through the challenge of lifting the immense logs into place, he decided his ancestors must have used a horse-powered pulley system. He drew all the farm's other outbuildings too—the granary and chicken house and corncrib, the brick smokehouse, the tobacco barn and the shed that housed the threshing machine and baler—as well as the old farmhouse itself. Later, in architecture courses in college, he designed or copied more elaborate buildings, but he never lost the unspoken feeling that the simple structures on his home place mattered more.

Peter's father taught eighth grade and farmed the land his wife's family had farmed for three generations. He told Peter his one condition for paying his college tuition was that Peter would get a teaching certificate. As long as he was certified to teach, his father said, he would never have to work at a sawmill. Peter's father was good-humored in setting this condition. Not having to work at a sawmill was a recurring theme with his father, who had an uncle who was killed at a sawmill when his sleeve snagged on a log in a moving conveyor.

Peter's mother, who taught tenth grade English, listened to this conversation between Peter and his father. She took no issue with it, but a few days later when Peter walked into the kitchen, she asked him how long it had been since he had learned to read. She tossed the question at him over her shoulder while turning her attention between onions she was sautéing on the stove and a paperback book held open with an uncut red onion on the kitchen table. She would read from the book for a while, frown for a moment, then turn and stir the onions. Peter had watched her cook and read this way since he was a child, and he knew she was not reading a cookbook.

"When did I learn to read?" he said. "You ought to know. You taught me."

"That's right." She turned toward him and waved her wooden spoon in his face. A fleck of hot onion hit his cheek. "And don't ever let anybody un-teach you to read, either," she said. "Even at college, some of them will try. Don't confuse plowing through a textbook your professor wrote with reading."

At the university, Peter found he occupied a lower order of being than the sons of doctors and lawyers who lounged in and out of frat houses that reeked of the beer spilled there during weekend bacchanals. Over his four college years, this sense that he was irredeemably déclassé got mixed in with the disappointments his injury cost him and his frustration that his intellectual efforts gained him nothing socially, especially with women. The result was a toxic brew that spilled from his mouth at unanticipated moments, and that contrasted weirdly with his native mode of country-bred courtesy.

Peter earned a degree in history and a certificate to teach it. He liked his history courses and did well in them, but he decided while practice teaching at a rural high school that—though teaching was preferable to getting bisected by a sawmill blade—he'd rather do something else.

Peter also took enough design and architecture courses that he would be able to earn a master of architecture degree in two and a half more years if he could come up with the tuition money. Toward that end, in his final year he signed on to work over the mid-year break as a masons' helper on a crew building a kiln that would supply bottles to a brewery.

The work promised to pay well, but it was anything but light. He had been on the job less than two weeks when he stumbled while steering a wheelbarrow loaded with mortar along a catwalk. He did a quick sideways shuffle that prevented the wheelbarrow from tipping over, but it wrenched his knee so badly that the swelling forced him to drive to the hospital before his workday was done. By the time he got there, he could barely lift his left foot to the clutch pedal. His knee was still swelling in the X-ray lab. By the time he was taken to an examination room, his knee was the size of a cantaloupe and he needed a wheelchair.

A little nurse who looked barely out of her teens had him hoist himself onto an examination table where his feet dangled clear of the floor. She took his temperature and blood pressure, told him the doctor would be with him soon and started to leave the room, pushing the wheelchair ahead of her.

"Hey!" he shouted. "I need that!"

She gave him a prim smile, looking a little frightened. "We always take the chairs out front," she said, "for other patients who might need them.

"Well I need it right now," he said. "So bring it over here. Please."

He started to ease himself down onto his good leg, tearing the table's white paper covering as he did so, but when he glanced toward the nurse he saw she had pushed the chair outside.

"Just lie down on the table," she said. "That's what you're supposed to do."

"Jesus Christ!" he muttered as the door snapped shut. He struggled back onto the table, completing the tear he'd made across the sheet of paper. He wadded up the torn-off piece and threw it at a wastebasket.

After a few minutes, another, taller young woman in a white lab coat came through the door. She stood with her shoulder toward him and her eyes fixed on the clipboard in her hands. She flipped several times between an X-ray and a couple of pages beneath it. Peter felt his pain and annoyance veering into anger, but he didn't want to interrupt the spell cast by this strangely silent nurse. Something pixie-like in her profile—a slight parting of her lips, a faint golden aura above her cheekbone—summoned in him the unbidden thought: This is a girl it will be important to protect.

Finally, still without looking at him, she said, "How are we doing today, Mister Dandridge?" Her brittle tone, oddly flat vowels and that officious "we" broke the spell. Peter's knee throbbed, he knew the earnings from his construction job might be at an end, and suddenly he saw in her a fit target for his frustration.

"Well, I can't answer for the rest of the crowd in here," he said, "but I admit I'm in some discomfort. I thought perhaps medical science could help. Now, if you can find a doctor around here, maybe he could tell me if that's correct. Maybe he could even tell all of us."

She turned to face him, and her level, unblinking gaze punctured his notion of a girl in need of protection. The cheekbone that a moment before had seemed to float in a golden nimbus, now that he could see it paired with the other cheek, looked more like a beveled rampart for her gunmetal blue eyes.

He thought, Whoa, this is a woman it will be dangerous to cross. And somewhere deep inside, though still within his awareness, he knew that for the rest of his life he might need to stand watch on where things stood with her along that continuum between the girl he should protect and the woman it would be perilous to cross.

He noticed, too—though, compared to the lightning-flash just cast on his destiny, it seemed a trivial detail—that the nameplate on her lab coat read "Stephanie Ames, Medical Student." He noticed, too, that she held the clipboard in a claw grip, like a craftsman wielding a power tool.

"I'm afraid I'm as much of a doctor as Baptist Hospital can let out of its doctor box at six p.m. this soon after New Year's," she said. "Especially for a patient who's dumb enough to push a wheelbarrow full of bricklayer's mud along a catwalk with next to zero cartilage in his knee. You've got a hematoma, Mister Dandridge. That's a big glob of blood with nowhere to go. When you did that sideways dance with the wheelbarrow, you ruptured some blood vessels inside your knee. It's not going to get better by itself anytime soon, so I recommend we stick a needle in your knee and draw that blood out."

As he listened to what he would come to think of as her plang-plang tone, the pain in his knee subsided into the soft, distant throbbing of a drum.

"You're not from around here, are you?" he said.

"What makes you say that?"

"Because you keep smushing your vowels."

She was writing something on the bottom page on the clipboard and said nothing until she was done. Then she looked at him, her eyes blue and unblinking.

"The smushing at issue is what you've done to your knee, Mister Dandridge," she said. "We can deal later with my New England vowels."

"Okay," he said. "But let's please do deal with them. They need attention."

This time she cocked her head and gave him a half-smile.

"You have a couple of options," she said. "One is to wait until the full-fledged doctor who's on emergency duty tonight can come tend to you. He's got two patients on his dance card that I know of, and one of them has been shot, so that wait might be two or three hours. That's the best we can do tonight, except in a true emergency. Which, frankly, you're not."

"Option two?" Peter said.

"Option two is you go home, ice the knee overnight and come back tomorrow. It might be a sleepless night for you, but otherwise there's no harm."

"How about an option three?" Peter said.

Again the angled glance and half-smile, and her eyelids crinkled with curiosity. "I give up," she said. "What's option three?"

"Option three is I don't stay here half the night and I don't come back tomorrow, because I need to go to work then. Instead, you pull the blood out of my knee right now, we decide on a time when we can meet to work on those vowel sounds, and I drive home."

She gave him a long look of cool appraisal. Then she left the room. Peter lay back on the examination table, shut his eyes and listened to the jungle-drum throbbing of his knee. When Stephanie Ames returned, a young male doctor with harried-looking, close-set eyes behind horn rims followed her into the room. Behind them came the little nurse, carrying a metal pan, towels, a rolled elastic bandage and a syringe with a barrel that looked about six inches long. This time the nurse kept her eyes down and didn't bother to smile.

"This is Doctor Gilbert," Stephanie said. "He has been kind enough to step in and supervise my work, but we'll need to act quickly so he can get back to his patient."

"Go ahead," the doctor told Stephanie. "This is more in your intended line anyway." He shifted his feet a little at a time toward the door in a way that clearly said he wanted to go.

"A pinch," Stephanie said before she stuck the needle into the side of Peter's knee and guided it into the joint. It hurt badly going in, but the pain stopped when the needle quit moving.

"You can handle it from here, right?" Gilbert said. Stephanie nodded. "You're in good hands," Gilbert said, touching Peter lightly on the elbow. "She's on track to become a first-rate orthopedic surgeon." Then he turned and left the room so quickly that Peter heard his lab coat flap.

"Boy, I'm sure glad you got that close supervision," Peter said. "I needed that reassurance."

"It's the rule," she said, staring at the barrel of the syringe. Peter watched it fill fast with his blood.

"Why do doctors always say 'a pinch'?" he said.

"Would you rather they said, 'a stab deep in your vitals'?"

"It depends," he said. "If you'd said that a half-minute ago, it would have been the simple truth."

Stephanie slipped off the first syringe, handed it to the nurse and fitted another syringe onto the same needle.

"How can you do that without blood squirting everywhere?" he said.

"It costs me a cool three thousand a year to learn stuff like that," she said. "You think I'm going to share that information for free?"

She drew back on the plunger then waited for the barrel of the big syringe to fill with more of his blood.

"I guess to you I seem like an exhibit-grade rube, huh?" he said.

"What do you mean by exhibit-grade?"

"I mean something that's a pure enough example of whatever it is that you could enter it in the state fair and maybe win a prize."

Her nose and eyelids crinkled into that middle ground between wince and smile.

"That comment about your smushing vowels, you know?" Peter said. "Only a rube would say something like that."

She kept her eyes fixed on the syringe, gave the plunger another small tug and then pulled the needle out. The throbbing pain in his knee was gone. She squirted the blood from the syringe into the metal pan, which already held the blood from the first syringe.

"I have no standing to call you or anyone else a rube," she said. "I grew up on a dairy farm."

"A farm?" he said. "I see. That explains the hands, then."

"Huh?

"They look like a farm girl's hands, that's all."

She didn't answer. She held the clipboard in that claw-fingered grip again, as she wrote something on a page.

"I'm not complaining, understand," Peter said. "I could get used to it."

The little nurse started wrapping his knee with the bandage. Her cheeks and neck reddened, as if she felt she'd intruded.

"You should ice that knee at least twice a day, Mister Dandridge," Stephanie said. "Fifteen minutes at a time. Stay off it as much as you can, and keep it wrapped when you have to be on it."

"So I can go to work in the morning, right?" he said.

She kept her eyes on what she was writing. "Not unless you want to be back in here by noon," she said.

"Well, I could bring along some flash cards, then, to help with vowel sounds," Peter said, but Stephanie was already out of the room.

The next day was a Thursday, the next-to-last day of his winter break. He went to work wearing the knee wrap and an old knee brace from high school on top of that. The knee hurt and he moved so slowly that the young mason he was helping—who had to kneel to fit brick onto the rounded outer surface of the kiln—repeatedly ran out of brick, rocked backward and yelled "brick!" in a despairing tone.

Peter checked his knee at the lunch break and again at quitting time and it hadn't swollen much. The mason must have complained about Peter's tardy delivery of brick, because next day the foreman gave Peter a different job: stacking wooden pallets on the blades of a forklift after all the brick had been removed from the pallets. When Peter had stacked the pallets as high as he could reach, the forklift driver would deposit them outside the building. Then he would steer the lift back inside at what to Peter seemed breakneck speed. At quitting time, Peter started to apologize to the foreman, who just gave him a friendly slap on the arm and pointed him to the payroll shed.

On Friday night and multiple times Saturday and Sunday, Peter emptied trays of ice cubes onto an old towel, spread a layer of plastic wrap across his knee to shield it from ice melt, sat in one kitchen chair and propped his heel on another and draped the wrapped towel full of ice across the knee. Each time, as he watched the kitchen clock creep toward the fifteen-minute mark, he pictured to himself Stephanie Ames' steady blue gaze—filled, somehow, with both indifference and profound significance. *I'm just doing this because she wanted me to. If she asked me to do almost anything, I'd try.*

Sunday night Peter called the hospital emergency room from the phone in his family's kitchen. The receptionist told him Stephanie Ames wasn't on duty. No, she said, she didn't know when Miss Ames would be back.

"Can you tell her I called and asked for her?" Peter said. He gave the receptionist his home phone number, and she said she'd leave a note with the emergency staff supervisor.

Peter noticed that his mother, who was reading at the kitchen table, was doing an imperfect job of pretending not to listen. He lightly tousled her hair, then turned her book over to look at its title and the author's name. It was *Cities of the Plain*, by Marcel Proust.

"Gosh, I never knew you read Westerns, Mom," he said.

She closed the book on her finger, drew it back and swatted his backside.

Peter drove back to Raleigh, where his last semester of classes would start next morning. As he followed his headlights' beam, he kept seeing Stephanie's eyes the first time she had looked straight at him. Maybe that's what a good surgeon's eyes need to look like, he thought. Cool. Direct. Prepared for whatever might come.

Six

After Thanh left the soup kitchen, kick-started his Vespa and rode off to his job at the hospital, Peter lingered at the battered metal table. Sitting alone in an atmosphere redolent of lemongrass, peppers and mint leaves, he thought through all that had happened to bring matters to a precarious balance between him and Stephie. Then his mind skipped like a stereo needle on a damaged record, and he knew that whatever it was Thanh was trying to draw him into risked smashing the fragile thing he was trying to build with her.

Peter found he could remember only intermittent patches of time from the months after his blood-bloated knee brought him Stephanie Ames. First came the moments of rising hope, of joy, of passion, of confidence and pride in where his life would lead next, and next after that. Then came the hours when he was torn between the allure of distant danger and the desire to hold fast to all that seemed about to be snatched away from him. And then came two moments of scalding shame. One was on a pier when his friend's halting voice told of the night the ocean's surface had seethed with poisonous snakes beneath the ghastly light of flares. The other moment was in a hallway where there swept past him the exhausted, sheeplike faces of men who had not lived long enough to have much to lose except life itself, and who stood a strong prospect of losing that.

The first of these etched-in-memory moments was his discovery of the letter the night he arrived back at school from his winter break. It had looked just the way an admission ticket to the future ought to look. He had limped from the snow-dusted parking lot into the darkened mailroom on his dorm's first floor. He had dropped the ragged duffel bag his father had given him years before as a whimsical coming-of-age gift, and he had spun the little combination dial on his mailbox door. Then he had seen the letter. It was alone in the box, wedged there diagonally. On a far corner of the envelope he could see the faint red gleam of the embossed return address, and he could make out the words "College of Design."

He had stood there for perhaps a minute, shifting his weight away from his injured knee and hearing the faint sound of voices from the floors above him and the clanging of water pipes in use for the first time in weeks. He knew what the letter would say. It would take him another semester to get all the requirements in place for entry to the master's program, but with that accomplished, he was in. He was too tired to read that or anything else. So he gently swung shut the little door to the mailbox, leaving the letter inside. He stood there a moment longer with his palm against the mailbox door, thinking: How do I get her to see? How do I show her I can make it work? How do I convince her this has to happen? That it just has to?

Next morning he opened the letter and found it was just as he'd expected. And then after a brief blur of days came the call from his mother. The Colombian grad student who was the dorm's resident counselor knocked on his door and said his mother was on the office phone downstairs.

"Doctor Ames is trying to get in touch with you," she said. She drew out the name "Ames" in a way that told Peter she suspected he might find special significance in it. "She wants to know how you're recovering from your work injury."

"It's just Miss Ames, Mom," Peter said. "She's a medical student. She's not a doctor yet. Did you tell her I was fine?"

"I figured it wasn't my place to do that," she said. "How do I know you haven't twisted it again? How do I know you don't have urgent need of further care from soon-to-be Doctor Ames?"

She gave him the phone number he could use to call Stephanie. He gave the counselor a five-dollar bill for a paper cup full of quarters and took them to the pay phone on his floor. It took him four quarters to cover the wait before Stephanie came to the phone.

"I hope I didn't inconvenience your mother, Mister Dandridge," she said in her crisp, professional voice. "We try to do follow-up on all our emergency room patients."

"You're still mangling the queen's English," he said.

"Well, fortunately we have a speech therapist right down the hall, and I can call on her in event of need." Her voice rose a little with annoyance.

"Don't call her," Peter said. "Your vowels are fine as they are. Truly."

"So how's your knee now? I hope you've been icing it and keeping it wrapped."

"Let's forget the knee," he said. "The point of my calling you back is something else."

"Well, look." She sounded far gone in exasperation. "I can't see we have anything more to discuss if you won't answer my simple question. And frankly, I don't see that we have anything to discuss beyond that. I've got work to do."

"All right," Peter said, knowing his own rising anger risked ruining everything. "Got your clipboard propped up where you can write this down so you can file it away in a place where nobody will ever look at it or care? Ready? Well here we go. I kept it wrapped at work, and I iced it a half-dozen times. None of that made much difference. My knee's as near fine as it's ever likely to get whether I wrap it or not or ice it or not. It's ruined what I wanted to do in life a couple of times, once when it knocked me out of football and once when it kept me out of ROTC, and it'll probably knock me out of a few more things before it's done. But a few days ago, when you walked into that room at the hospital, I thought that just maybe my fucked-up knee had made up for all of the things it could ever knock me out of. I thought maybe, thanks to that knee, your plang-plang voice might sometimes be the first thing I wanted to hear and sometimes the last thing I wanted to hear, but it would always be there for me to hear, regardless. But now I figure I was wrong. Maybe the knee has just kind of baited me before it knocked me out of the best thing it could ever knock me out of, which is you. And now I'm about out of quarters, so if you've got any more simple questions, let's hear them. Notice I use the royal plural to cover all of us crowded into this phone booth."

Peter dropped in his last quarter but the silence continued at the other end of the line.

"Just so you'll know," he said, "I've been admitted to the graduate architecture program. It means at least another two and a half years of school here. The draft's not an issue for me, so I can go to grad school. So I guess that's one other favor I owe the knee, if you want to look at it that way."

"I'm glad, I really am," Stephanie said, just before his last quarter's worth of time ran out.

He'd hardly made it back to his dorm room before Gonzalo, the counselor, knocked on his door again. Gonzalo was a slender, smiling man with very bright eyes. He was about ten years older than most of the undergraduates. He had taught biology at a high school in Colombia, and everyone liked him.

"Peter, Stephanie Ames is calling you," Gonzalo said softly.

When they reached the counselor's office in the lobby, Gonzalo let Peter in but didn't step in himself. "Perhaps I should allow you a little privacy," Gonzalo said.

"Oh, that's not necessary, Gonzalo," Peter said. "It's just medical follow-up. Somebody who patched me up at a hospital back home."

Gonzalo leaned his dark, smiling, handsome face around the edge of the door. "Then I wish you and Miss Ames both the very best of health," he said. "Just tap on the door when you're done."

"I called your mother back to get your dorm number," Stephanie said. "I apologize for snapping at you, and for making you run through all your money on a pay phone."

"I think I was the one who burned up most of that five dollars' worth of time," Peter said. "You just asked for a straight-up answer that would have run me a dollar fifty at the outside."

"That brings me to the second thing I ought to tell you," she said. "You got it right a few days ago, when you called yourself exhibit-grade. Now I have to wonder—exhibit grade what?"

"Look, all that I told you a few minutes ago—I hadn't intended to say any of that today, or in the angry way I said it. I wish I'd saved it for whenever I can see you again, if you'll even let that happen. But it's out there now. You need to know it, so you can decide what to do about it. Or what not to do about it."

"Well, that should be an easy call for me, shouldn't it?" she said.

"Abso-lutely," he said, straining to keep the bitterness out of his voice. "You've got work to do, right? So why not just roll your eyes and go do it?"

"Yes, that's the easy call," she said. "But I can't do that, because I mean to be a doctor. Doctors don't get to roll their eyes at difficult patients and walk away."

"I see. So now I'm just a thirteenth wind sprint after you've already done twelve. Real champs always do extra, right?"

"What I mean is a good physician doesn't get thrown off-track when it's clear what a patient needs."

"What this patient needs is for you to know that I fell for you the other day," he said. "Fell way far, real hard and for keeps."

At the distance of more than a year, Peter remembered with particular clarity the long moment when Stephanie, at the other end of the phone line from Gonzalo's little office, said nothing.

"You told me I might make up for a couple of other things the knee had knocked you out of," she said. "Am I just your hedge against bad things coming in threes?"

"You're my hedge against a life without you. That's all."

"Look, all you've seen of me was a med student at the bottom of the holiday-duty pecking order, trying to stay professional after twelve hours of dealing with flu symptoms and a thumb all but severed by a chainsaw and a near-death from poisoned moonshine," she said. "Then in comes the one thing missing after all that: a construction worker who's blown up his knee. You're telling me that's the woman of your dreams?"

"I guess I could tell what kind of day you'd had," he said. "And I knew if I could love you then, when could I not?"

She sighed, then muttered about another patient she needed to check on.

"Look, here's what I think you should do," she said finally, her crisp, professional tone tinctured with the slightest quaver. "Your knee can be stronger, more stable, if you master some simple exercises. They can firm up the muscles above and below the knee, and that can make a big difference. So I want you to meet with a physical therapist, as soon as you can find time."

"I have no classes on Thursdays. Can you set up a Thursday appointment? I could get there by late morning. And after I see the therapist, would you have some time when we could just talk?"

He heard a light, measured tapping sound. In time, he'd come to recognize it as the tapping of a pencil point as she thought.

"You're all just—there on the surface, aren't you, Peter?" she said in a softened tone. "And I've seen too much of the exhibit-grade other thing. All right. I'll be in the student lounge at the med school, starting at three o'clock."

The therapist had little to tell him that he didn't already know about which machines in a well-equipped weight room he should use and how to use them. He had done the exercises sporadically since high school, and he found they helped, though never enough to enable him to play tennis or handball or basketball.

The medical school entrance was across a little courtyard from the hospital. Stephanie sat on a sofa, reading from an enormous medical textbook with anatomical drawings in garish colors. She held a yellow marker poised above the page. She wore a cream-colored pullover sweater and a pleated, plaid wool skirt with diagonal stripes. Some of the stripes were caramel-color and some were a darker, redder color that it took Peter a little while to place. Then he had it: They were the color of the shag bark on a short row of cedars in a country church cemetery two miles from his home. Beneath those cedars lay two of his great-grandfather's brothers, both Confederate soldiers. One, the oldest of four brothers, had died of typhoid in Virginia. The other, a cavalryman, was shot in Maryland during the retreat from Gettysburg.

"I really like your skirt," he said.

"Oh!" she said. Her hand with the marker involuntarily lifted in surprise. She held the marker in that bent-fingered grip, as if it were a dart. "Oh, it's nothing special. I pulled it off a rack in Durham when I was in school there.

"Durham?" he said. "So you're a Dookie?"

"Decidedly not," she said. Laughing, she capped the marker and closed the textbook. "My school was in the other Durham, in New Hampshire. You won't find many Duke-style white-gloved debutantes there, I can tell you."

"Well," he said. "I'm relieved."

Her eyes tilted up at him with a pixie-like gleam. "You mean you'd have to scrape the manure off your image of me if I hadn't gone to a cow college?"

"Something like that. I mean, I see you heading off to the milking shed in the predawn chill. At least once in a while."

Her laugh was a musical bray, a single quick soprano note followed by a drawn-out, alto "haw."

"More than just once in a while, I assure you," she said. She tapped the cushion beside her. "Sit," she said. "I think we have enough privacy here, but if we don't we can go out in the courtyard. It's cold out, but I do cold just fine. Okay with you?"

"I don't care what anyone hears," he said.

"Well, I have to care, because I work and study with the people here," she said. "So if I feel uncomfortable I'll let you know, and then we'll go outside."

He sat beside her and she peered at him in what he would come to recognize as her clinical mode, head tilted slightly back.

"You talked to one of our PTs, did you?" she said.

"Sure. She showed me all the exercises I can do on the machines and several I can do without weights or anything."

"So now you're going to actually do them?"

"Look, let's not rehash the PT," he said. "I've known for years how to do most of what she showed me. For long stretches of time, I've actually done it. And I know I need to get back to doing it, now that I've injured it again."

Her eyes stayed fixed on his, but the clinical distance in them faded, and her voice dropped a little.

"I've thought about what you said on the phone, Peter," she said. "About all of it. And I owe it to you to give it to you straight. I'm twenty-five years old, and you're—what?"

"Twenty-three."

"You're rounding upward by a couple of months," she said. "You're forgetting I've seen your chart."

"Well, I'm seasoned beyond my years. By hardship."

"From your behavior in the exam room, I'd have rounded your age downward to about twelve."

"That was just pain and frustration. I wanted to finish out the job I was doing. I needed the money."

He could see from her slight smile how feeble she found his excuse.

"All right, then," he said. "I just do that with women sometimes. I don't have a lot of looks or accomplishments going for me, so I annoy them. At least that gets their attention."

Her smile turned reflective. "If you knew my history, you'd know why I prefer honest blundering to well-crafted flattery," she said. "But look. I'm a third-year med student, I've already got a lot of debt, and that will keep growing. A week ago you asked me to believe your out-of-the-blue profession of certain strong feelings. I've been working on that. But please answer me this: How foolish would it be for someone in my situation to take up with an undergraduate who's three years, at best, from getting the credential he needs to help support anyone but himself? Who has to spend his school vacations hauling bricks and wheeling bricklayers' mud along catwalks just to—"

"Stephanie, let's pause here while I thank my father for something I thought I'd never have to thank him for," Peter said.

She stopped with her mouth half-open, then rolled her eyes with irritation. "Look, Peter," she said. "No digressions, okay? I'm trying to spell things out as fairly and calmly—"

"And you're doing a fine job of reciting the catechism of the responsible clodhopper son or daughter," he said. "Both of us know it by heart, so there's no point in your going through the whole thing. I can't answer your 'how foolish would I be' question for you. But before you answer it for yourself, you need to have your premises straight. That's what I'm thanking my father for, because he insisted I get just one thing out of college. He thought it would spare me the risk of ever having to do the kind of work his uncle had to do, and who died doing it. Depending on what you make of it, it might spare me a fate that just now seems to me even worse than getting cut in half lengthwise by a sawmill blade. Which would be losing any chance I have of a life with you."

Stephanie's head tilted and her eyes appeared to wander. Then she snorted softly.

"So whatever it is, you don't think it could make much difference?" he said.

"No, no, it's not that," she said. "I'm just thinking what it would be like to be assigned that cadaver in dissection class."

"You'd get a lot of practice suturing," he said.

"A cosmetic surgeon would look at that cadaver and say, 'hey, we can fix that!'" she said. "They make such ridiculous promises."

"Men who are as much in love as I am right now make ridiculous promises too," he said.

The gleam of laughter dimmed slowly in Stephanie's eyes, until once again she fixed him with her calm, clinical gaze. "I've already factored that in," she said.

"Well, this isn't a promise," he said. "Not yet. But call it a good, strong, viable option. My dad said he'd pay for four years of college if I promised to earn a teaching certificate. He said with that, I could always get a good, decent-paying job if I needed it. And I've done what he wanted. I'm certified to teach high school history. Coursework, practice teaching, a strong recommendation from a principal—it's all done."

"I see," she said quietly. "So teaching's your fallback. And you're saying you'd teach and give up your dream of becoming an architect if I said yes to whatever arrangement you have in mind for the two of us. Well, that sounds like a sure-fire prescription for happiness all around, doesn't it? Maybe a cosmetic surgeon could put a smiling face on it."

"I'm just saying it's there if we need it, maybe for a year or two," Peter said. He felt flustered, seeing how deftly she'd outflanked him.

"For a year or two," she said. "Not much chance that could turn into a dream shelved for a lifetime, is there?"

"So you're saying it makes no difference to you," he said. "That I could teach. And that I would do it if—"

"Dear boy," she said. She touched his cheek, and at the distance of more than a year—walking out of the soup kitchen now, exchanging a smile with the proprietor, whose American customers all called him Ed because he was a ringer for a bald-pated, almond-eyed Edward G. Robinson—Peter felt the warmth of Stephanie's fingers flow into his jaw and down his spine. "Of course it makes a difference that you would do that for me," she said. "I just want to be perfectly clear about the odds we'd face, and what sacrifices we might be tempted to make, and which ones neither of us should ever ask of the other. I think you've just identified one."

"Teaching wouldn't crush my soul, you know," he said. "I might even get to the point my dad's at. He says if he didn't have taxes and my tuition to pay, he'd teach for free."

She dismissed what he'd said with a quick brushing-away motion of the same fingers that had touched his face. "I'll tell you one more sacrifice that's off the table," she said. "I mean to become an orthopedic surgeon. Being a woman is obstacle enough in that field, and I'm not going to take on anything or anyone else that's likely to get in the way of it."

Again she fixed him with her calm, clinical gaze.

"You're sending a visual scalpel into my brain, Doc," he said.

"That's because you're supposed to answer."

Trudging out between the concrete stingrays onto the half-mile stretch of asphalt that led to the checkpoint on the street of villas where he lived, Peter remembered this as the exact moment when he knew Stephanie was not going to simply shoo him away. Instead she was setting terms. And he remembered that his heart suddenly seemed so firmly lodged in his throat that he had to swallow repeatedly before he could answer.

"Stephanie, I will never knowingly do anything that gets in the way of your medical career," he had said. "If it ever looks to you like I'm doing that, tell me, and I'll get that obstacle out of your way. And that holds even if the obstacle is simply me."

"All right," she replied, nodding gravely. "You should know, though, that I'm filing that away with your earlier comment about the ridiculous promises men make when they're in love."

"Oh. Well, then, here's another one you can file away. No matter how hand-to-mouth we have to live, I'll never let you go without roses for your birthday."

Her smile looked a little scornful. "Peter, Peter, we've seen each other exactly how many times?"

Peter had thought about her so nearly constantly for weeks that he found himself in near-denial when he realized it was only twice.

"Do you know the phrase—I think it's from dog racing—overrun the rabbit?" she said. "Well, it means you're chasing something so hard and so fast that suddenly you look up and it's gone, because you've run right past it. I think you're in danger of doing that."

Walking alone past the wall of a cemetery the Viet Cong had gotten into the year before, and feeling vaguely excited to think that danger might yet lurk among the graves, Peter thought, Well, thank God I did push it. Not that either of us could have guessed how little time there'd be. Chasing the rabbit too hard, she said. Well, it turned out the rabbit was wearing afterburners that would blast that little sucker up and over the horizon. It turned out I'd have to chase him all the way to Viet-fucking-nam.

Flecks of light seemed to hover above the drainage ditch beside the road. He dropped into a half-crouch and hooked his thumb beneath the strap of his M-16. Before he could lower the rifle, he saw that the pinpoint gleams were moonlight reflected from metal barbs. A length of razor wire had gotten detached from the cemetery wall and sagged toward the ditch. He shook his head. "It's like I caught Rabby's virus," he muttered.

Walking on, he began to laugh softly, remembering how, sitting beside him in the student lounge and having settled matters between them to her satisfaction, Stephanie had been eager to see him gone.

"Time you headed back now, don't you think?" she had said. She stood, smoothing the pleats in her skirt with both hands.

"What? It's not even five o'clock yet. Can't we at least have dinner together?"

"Nope. Starting at five I go on three hours of observational rounds with the top orthopedist we've got here. No way am I going to miss that or be late for it."

"So is this how you slough off unwanted suitors?"

"If I slough you off, Peter, you'll know it. There won't be any subterfuge about it."

"I'll bet you've sloughed off a lot of them. I bet my turn will come."

"Not so many. Some men I seem to scare off without really trying to. Some men—women too—back away from me because I don't suffer fools, gladly or otherwise. You meet some very smart people in medical school who are also really big fools."

"Where do I stand on that measuring stick?" he said.

She pursed her lips and squinted a little. "A little brighter than Jeff Tyson, the guy who mucks out our milking sheds. But you're not a fool, I think. Jeff's no fool either, by the way."

"I hope that's a preliminary opinion," Peter said. "I mean the part about me."

"I'm pretty firm on the not-too-bright part," she said. "That tango you danced on a catwalk with a wheelbarrow load of mortar convinced me of that. I'll await further evidence on the not-a-fool part."

She glanced at her wristwatch. "Bye, now," she said. Without another word or a glance back at him, she walked swiftly to a corridor marked "To Hospital," turned a corner and was gone.

When he called her next day she agreed, with what sounded like a sigh of resignation, to spend a Saturday evening with him later that month. He took her to the movie *Bonnie and Clyde*. As the machine gun bullets riddled Faye Dunaway's convulsing body, he stole a sideward glance at Stephie. Her head was tilted and her lips slightly parted in what looked like absorption, but only that. Afterward they went to dinner at an Italian restaurant she said she liked. They sat in a booth enclosed on three sides by dark wood paneling with carved scrollwork at the top.

"For me, that ending was hard to take," Peter said. "I guess it's different for you. I guess a doctor gets so hardened to blood and suffering that a scene like that just rolls off you."

She gave him a quick, sharp, quizzical look.

"You've helped butcher hogs," she said. "And you told me you went along when your father took beef calves to the slaughterhouse. Right?"

"Yeah. Well, I guess the difference there is the blood doesn't get splashed across a movie screen the size of a semi-truck."

Her probing gaze stayed fixed on his face.

"I suppose I should take your comment as a gallant gesture," she said. "I'll think on it."

He feared that, having skewered him, she might make their parting at her apartment building chilly, formal, perhaps even final. Instead, she turned toward him in the dim light from above the streetside door, seized his upper arms and drew him toward her.

"Remember what I said about not suffering fools, gladly or otherwise?" she said in a harsh whisper. "Well, here are some other things I won't suffer anymore. Empty flattery. Promises that amount to lies. They might give you an edge with the Lula Maes you've gone out with in the past, but they won't work with me."

"But I haven't lied—"

"When I say 'anymore,' I don't mean you. But you do tend to walk up to the brink. Like tonight at dinner, beaming across the table at me with your cornball smile."

"Can't I just say I'm sorry?"

"Don't bother. Now kiss me. Kiss me hard. It'll have to last us a couple of months."

He had to learn to curb his desire to speak to her. He called her every day for a while, until he was warned off by the impatient tone in her voice that grew more pronounced by the day.

"I don't do things by halves," she told him. "Right now I'm doing my third-year surgical clerkship, and I'm sorry, Peter, but everything else gets shoved to the sidelines. That includes you."

He expected her to hang up once she'd said that, but then her voice resumed, in a softened tone.

"Just be patient, buster boy. Remember, I don't do things by halves. When your turn comes, you'll have the whole me. Worn to a nub by that time, maybe. But whatever's left, you'll have it all."

And thank God we got to that part, too, Peter thought, returning the salutes of the two small, barely visible figures at either end of the checkpoint's wood-and-barbed-wire barrier. The timid little Vietnamese soldiers—it seemed to Peter they were always the same two—saluted everyone, of whatever rank. He had never seen them challenge anyone who approached the barrier. Hell, he thought, they'd probably salute a Viet Cong sapper and wave him through.

His villa was set back from a narrow street that ended at the beach. A villa where several officers were billeted fronted the street, and Peter's villa was behind that one. If the night was quiet enough, as this one was, by the time he turned off it to walk the final twenty yards to his villa, he could hear the wash of waves on the sand.

I've got to shut this down, he told himself, annoyed to find he'd actually mouthed those words. If I let it go on, I won't sleep. He had gotten pretty good at blocking memories that served no purpose except to make him seethe with longing and regret. And as he reminded himself of that, suddenly he remembered the way her scent had blended with the acrid odor of the longleaf pine needles that formed a thick, cushiony layer beneath the floor of his too-small umbrella tent.

"Shut it down!" he said aloud, shoving his M-16 into the narrow metal locker in his room. He went into the villa's tiny kitchen, poured himself a rum and Coke and plopped in two ice cubes. He took one swallow of his drink, then threw the rest in the sink so angrily the ice cubes ricocheted to the floor. He went back inside his room, switched on the ceiling fan and sat on his bunk.

"God damn it," Peter said wearily. "Just—God damn it." He could tell there was no shutting them off. He had unlocked the thoughts and memories he'd so carefully kept chained. Then he'd sought to marshal them so they would justify his resentment of Rabinowitz. Instead, they'd become all about her.

Seven

At first, it had looked like somehow, incredibly, it was all going to work. The professor in his principles of architecture class, who liked Peter in part because of their shared status as overachieving bumpkins, got him a summer internship with a small firm in Raleigh that specialized in historic renovations. His professor, who had lost two fingers in a baling accident and had a disconcerting way of baring his long, horselike teeth when he talked, told Peter to ignore the posted job description, which promised a role in preparing construction plans, specifications and schedules.

"You'll be a gofer," his teacher said with that rictus grin. "But pay attention and you'll learn a lot. They'll pay you something, and I'll see to it you get an hour or two of course credit, which means you can stay in the dorm."

With his growing understanding of Stephie's priorities and her abhorrence of waste, especially wasted time, Peter wasn't overly disturbed when she ruled out his suggestion that they spend a Sunday with his family.

"No, no," she said over the phone. She said it so quickly he knew she must have expected he would suggest it at some point and so had kept her answer primed for quick release. "No family visits," she said. "Not to your family and not to mine. Not unless and until you and I get a whole lot further down the road than we are now."

"Okay," he said. "Understood."

He wasn't much concerned either by something his father told him when he'd driven home for a weekend in March. It was a time of year when Peter loved to walk the woods on his family's land, looking for the hint of spring so slight it was best seen out of the corner of the eye, and breathing in the vinegary odor of leaves that snow and rain had rendered into prime mulch. He loved especially to cross the creek in his family's bottomland and look back at the hillside lightly rouged with the purple-pink of redbud. Always when he did that, he remembered what his mother had said one spring evening when she picked him up from school and drove slowly around a final, sharp curve and that hillside, so steep that at a distance it looked almost sheer, came into view.

"I'll bet that's what Juliet's cheek looked like when Romeo spotted it across the room at that masked ball," his mother had said, so softly she seemed to be talking to herself. Then she had chuckled and glanced over at Peter as she steered carefully down the graveled incline to the bridge over the creek. "Of course, like young men always and everywhere, Romeo oversold her beauty considerably," she said. "You wouldn't call that 'beauty too rich for earth,' now, would you? It's just redbud doing what redbud always does."

When Peter got back to the house from his tramp in the woods, his father asked him to help him unload sacks of feed for the chickens and beef calf from the truck and put them in the granary. There were so few sacks in the pickup bed that Peter was puzzled his father would ask for help. When they were walking back to the house, his father said, "What's your draft classification now, Pete?"

"My draft card? It's whatever the student exemption is. I think it's Two-S."

"But didn't they tell you back when you started college that you were exempt on medical grounds because of your knee?"

"Well, yeah. The doctor at my ROTC exam said I was exempt. I even told him I didn't want to be exempt, and he said it didn't matter what I wanted."

"But they never sent you another card? One that showed you were Four-F?"

"No. I figured they didn't have to, since I already had a good-enough exemption as a student."

"But once you graduate, that exemption goes away, see. Under the new draft law, graduate students don't get an exemption, unless they're studying something vital to the national health or safety. I don't think architecture makes the cut."

They stepped onto the big flagstones next to the well porch. Peter was about to open the screen door to the house when his father grasped his arm.

"Let's just talk about this a minute more out here," his father said. "If your mother hears any part of it, she'll have all sorts of questions."

His father was wearing the cap he'd worn as a high school baseball player when he was growing up on a red-dirt farm in Alabama. Nearly all the color had been sun-bleached out of the cap, except for a ring of dark blue around the bottom, next to the headband. Peter's mother had stitched up a couple of torn spots in the cap. Peter had never seen his father wear any other sort of headgear around the farm.

Peter's father dipped his chin so low that Peter could no longer see his eyes beneath the cap's bill. Then he looked up, scratching his temple and squinting. Peter heard the snap of the electrical switch that controlled the well's pump, and then the hum of the motor. His father, still gripping his son's arm, drew him away from the screen door toward the well porch, where the sound of the pump would mask their voices.

"When a war heats up, the rules change for who gets drafted," his father said. "Or they just ignore the rules, because they need bodies. When you got turned down for ROTC, this war was like a little-bitty warning light blinking away out on the far horizon. Now it's blown up way beyond that. Look, you've seen me hobble in from doing chores and soak my feet for an hour at a time? Well, I've got flat feet. I mean all the way flat, heel to toe. They never bothered me much in baseball, but you don't run that far at a time in baseball, and you're not toting a forty-pound pack. No way could I have passed a draft physical in peacetime. But when I went to my draft physical in forty-one, the doctor just told me that if the Army tried to put me in the infantry, to tell them I had flat feet. Then he signed my paperwork and waved me on. They needed bodies then, see? They need them now, too, and they're likely to need more of them now this Lunar New Year attack has shown how stubborn this enemy is turning out to be."

What his father was suggesting was so far from anything Peter had even thought about for the past four years that his impulse was to simply laugh it off as over-anxiety. But he could not suppress a small chill. He'd never known his father to fret needlessly. What if he was right?

"I'm sure flat feet are a bad thing to have, Pop," Peter said. "But I'm not sure that's even a disqualifier anymore. And look at all you were able to do. There's no kind of work around the farm you can't do. Sure, I knew you'd soak your feet after a day out planting or baling, but then you'd always be back at it next morning. I wish this knee weren't a different order of disability, but it is. I'm not hinging my plans on any chance the draft might come after me."

Peter's father seldom made any physical show of affection or concern, but he grasped his son by both arms and shook him, as if he could shake sense into him.

"What I'm telling you, son," he said, "is I think you should do exactly that—hinge your plans on that possibility. And you have a way ready to hand, though I know it's not what you planned or wanted to do. You've got your teaching certificate. Right now, schoolteachers get a draft deferment. Between us, your mother and I have enough contacts in the school system that we might be able to help you find a teaching job here in Newcastle County. Nothing guaranteed, understand. A lot of other young men with teaching certificates are in this same fix, and they're out scouring the market for teaching jobs too. But if you're going to try, you need to put your name in now."

Peter's next thought, once he'd heard his father out, was not of Stephanie or of the track that his architecture professor had laid down for him to pursue a graduate degree. Nor was it of the worry in his father's bleached-looking eyes beneath the bleached-out bill of his baseball cap. Instead, he thought of all the times he had lowered his own eyes and clenched his teeth out of shame and longing as he walked past the ROTC drill field, hearing the high-pitched commands to march and countermarch or the synchronized clickety-slap sound of fifty men each hitting his weapon's breech as the drill team went through its jazzed-up manual of arms. He thought, they might take me after all! They might say I was good enough after all!

"But they did take you, Dad," he said. "And you didn't try to get out of it, did you? You went and did the best you could."

"Well, that's right," his father said, with the kind of sidelong nod that signaled a "but" was coming. "But my best wasn't good enough, and the Army should never have expected it would be. I didn't plead flat feet when they stuck me in the infantry. And I did the best I could once we got to England. We didn't know what we were training for, except that we trained like hell for it. Of course, it turned out to be Normandy. I lost track of how many times we had to jump out of a landing craft into godawful-cold surf and slog up onto Slapton Sands. Three or four times a day, sometimes. And when we weren't hitting the beach we'd make fifteen- and twenty-mile marches up in the Devonshire hills, loaded with full pack and rifle and ammo. And I couldn't keep up. I'd fall maybe a quarter-mile behind, and a couple of NCOs in a jeep would come tilting and swerving downhill at me like a hawk diving at a field mouse, and they'd call me every indecent name they could think of. But I just couldn't. Finally I told them about my flat feet, and they took me to a medical officer, and I took off my boots and showed him. So that's how I became a jeep driver."

"And that's what they should have had you doing from the start, isn't it?" Peter said. "And once they had you doing that, you did it as well as anybody could want, didn't you? And you're not sorry you drove that jeep the rest of the war, are you?"

"No, I'm not sorry about that part. Matter of fact, I'm not sorry about any of it. Not at all. It had to be done, and I'm not sorry I did a little to help get it done."

"Then if I do get drafted, isn't there something I could do just as well as anybody, even with the bum knee?"

The buzzing sound of the well's pump trailed off into a low growl as the tank filled up. His father's eyes had seemed to look inward while he spoke of his bit part in a war long since fought and won. Now his eyes fixed on Peter with a perplexed look.

"I guess I understand your thinking, son," he said slowly. "I understand why you might see some correspondence there, between what I did then and what you might be able to do if you were ever asked to do it. But, Pete, listen: My war was a completely different proposition. Completely different. Here's a term I throw several times a year at my eighth-graders, because it's a fallacy they're so prone to commit. False equivalence. You know what that means, don't you? Well, if you think getting into this war carries as much positive moral weight as getting into that one did, then that's a false equivalence. If that means I was luckier than you in the war I grew up into, then so be it. That's no reason for you to go off and get yourself killed or even just waste your time in a war that never should have happened."

For a couple of weeks, Peter didn't mention to Stephie what his father had said about the chance he might be drafted. He waited until a Sunday when he and Stephie both had time enough for what he had in mind, which was simply to get her on neutral ground and ask what she thought he should do. He drove up from Raleigh in his old powder-blue Chevrolet and picked her up at the medical school. She had told him that on a clear day she could see Pilot Mountain from the hospital's upper floors, and he had asked if he could take her there.

Stephie clomped through the medical school's lobby wearing what appeared to be an Army surplus T-shirt, denim bib coveralls with the cuffs rolled up and tan clodhopper boots worn thin at the toes and shiny at the ankles.

"What I have in the way of hiking gear is all back home," she said when she noticed his stare. "All I've got with me is this gear for four a.m. in the milking parlor. I brought it down here from home as a reminder of what I'm working my tail off to not have to do for the rest of my life."

It was warm enough to roll down the car windows. As they left town and the solitary mountain with its rock-walled dome loomed ever larger ahead of them, Peter told her what his father had said about the chance he might be drafted, and what he thought his son should do about that. And once he was done telling her, Peter knew he had also, without intending to, communicated to her his longing to face the sort of risks his father had once faced, something he had thought would forever be denied him.

She said nothing. Peter glanced at her several times. She looked straight ahead, her blonde hair streaming back from her shoulders. The slight upward cast of her eyes and her parted lips still drew from him an impulse to protect her, though by then he knew that appearance of vulnerability to be deceiving.

Finally she said, "Monadnock."

"What?"

"That's what you've got there, dear boy. Pilot Mountain's a monadnock. A solitary geological freak."

"Well, you're ahead of me there," Peter said. "I thought I'd get to explain to you what that mountain really is. It's an extinct volcano, right? I've seen it all my life from the farm, but I've never actually been up it. You know, for the longest time I thought the name came from the resemblance to the cockpit of a plane, with the big dome the seat back, and the depression the pilot's seat. But of course the mountain got that name long before—"

"From some name the Indians gave it," Stephie said. "Same as our own dear Mount Monadnock in New Hampshire. Could be volcanic in origin, could be other things. All that's certain is it was some process that enabled a solitary rock formation to resist erosion."

"Well," Peter said. "You leave my ego about as flat as a New Englander's vowels."

"Oh, sorry, Peter," she said, tapping his knee with the fingers of her left hand. The slight gesture of apology would have barely registered had she been any of his old girlfriends. Coming from this woman, who seemed to wield the mental powers of Athena, it felt thrillingly intimate.

"I'm really just thinking of what its name might signify, and whether that might lead you in some helpful direction," she said. "Pilot Mountain—I'll bet the Indians believed it pointed to something of more than just geographic importance."

"Now I feel whipsawed, Stephie," he said. "One minute you seem anchored in the hard sciences. Next minute, you're cozying up to the Great Spirit."

"Well, here's one thing that unites science and the Great Spirit," she said. "Death. Whether we dissect it with science or wrap it in mystery, it's always there. Kind of like a monadnock looming over a tribe of flatlanders."

"I can see this is going to be a cheery outing," Peter said.

"No reason it can't be," she said lightly. "For a physician, the first essential is good cheer, or at least firmness of heart, in the presence of death."

The mountain's sheer rock dome seemed to hover above them. He turned off the highway at the sign reading, "Pilot Mountain State Park."

"I give up, Stephie," he said. "What does either a monadnock or whatever it takes to be a good doctor have to do with whether I should angle for a teaching job or take my chances with the draft?"

He had learned not to be surprised by the hair-trigger speed of her responses to questions that baffled him.

"Because I think most of us need to live for some extended time in the presence of death," she said. "Else we never really flesh out— spiritually, I mean. Not to say that's a universal rule. I'm sure some teachers get complete fulfillment from what they do, without ever having a student die on them. But the rule applies to me, and I suspect it also applies to you. It doesn't mean you have to seek death out, challenge it to a duel or something. Else we'd all have to be oncologists. But a good physician needs to have death hanging around somewhere. Maybe just off on the misty blue horizon most of the time, where nobody else even recognizes it as death. But any physician also needs to confront death close-up once in a while—close enough to touch those sheer rock walls, feel the chill."

They passed a turnoff marked "family campground." The road upward ended near the base of the dome. Peter steered into the parking lot.

"Good thing I brought an orthopedist along," he said. "This conversation has been such a mood-lifter I might hop out right here and break into a clog dance. We both know the likely consequences of that."

She laughed her two-tone laugh, and with her fingers flipped her windblown hair backward over her shoulders.

"Stephie, I don't have any death wish," he said. "I just don't want to cheat. If the rules have changed enough to make a million other men who are physically no better off than I am nonetheless good enough to go, then why should I—"

He stopped short, looking into her firm, slightly mocking blue gaze.

"Don't try to con me, Peter, and don't con yourself," she said. "This isn't about just doing your part, and it isn't about a million other men. It's the idea of going to a war that tugs at you. And if they'll accept you in the Army, I'm sure you'll find a way to go to that war. And if you go, what other reason could there be but the presence of death in it? It couldn't be the justice or necessity or even good sense of this war. There's none of any of those. You're smart enough to have figured that out. But death? Sure, there's plenty of that. So if that's what's pulling at you, and if you get the chance to go, then I think you should go. Just don't do anything there you'll regret."

In her face and voice Peter could detect nothing of disappointment or anger. When she had finished, he could think of nothing else to say. They got out of the car, and Stephie briefly studied a giant map mounted on wooden poles. Hiking trails were marked out in dashed lines of blue and red and brown. "Let's do this one," she said, pointing at a brown line that encircled the dome's base like a noose.

She walked ahead of him, handling the uneven trail easily in her worn brogans. Once when the trail brought them flush against the towering dome, she stepped to the far edge of the narrow path and leaned back further still, gazing upward and shading her eyes. Then she moved close to the rock face and brushed the fingers of one hand lightly over the stone's surface. For a moment, she held her fingertips motionless against the stone, as if she sought a pulse. Then she looked toward Peter and smiled the kind of smile that he knew was the only sort he was likely ever to get from her: warm enough in the lips, but with eyes full of cool appraisal. Not with doubt or disappointment or desire for alteration in what she saw. Just with shrewd assessment of what there was in him to see.

"That campground we passed on the road up here?" Stephie said. "You have a tent, right? I'll go home to New Hampshire for a couple of weeks, starting in June. But before I go, can we come up here and spend a couple of nights in that campground? You can do that, can't you, once all your schoolwork's done?"

Eight

Lying in his darkened room in the villa, listening to the faint grinding of the off-balance ceiling fan and the "fuck-you" cries of a gecko tuning up for a night of hunting across the tile patio outside, Peter thought of how, right after that drive to Pilot Mountain, his life had seemed to transform into an almost comical semblance of a black-and-white newsreel on fast-forward.

The speeding-up had started as soon as he got back to campus and switched on his study lamp and the big desktop radio with the cherry wood lattice over its grill cloth. Lyndon Johnson was speaking, and Peter caught the valedictory note in the president's voice. He left his textbook closed and listened until Johnson said he would not seek or accept his party's nomination. And then Peter heard the roar of hundreds of male voices from the floors above and below him and from the other men's dormitories all across campus. For a while he just gazed off into the darkness beyond his room's window, thinking: "So is this really the end of it? Is it really going to be that simple for me now—Stephie, grad school, no need to teach or look for some other hole to scuttle into, the way so many of them are?"

And then Teddy McClearon had called and asked if he could break away for a couple of days to fish for sheepshead and red drum off the bridge and pier at Nags Head. He hadn't seen Teddy since their freshman year together at the university. He knew from other high school friends that, after Teddy dropped out, he had joined the Navy, ended up on river patrol in the Mekong Delta and seen heavy combat. Teddy said he'd gotten an early out from the Navy, as most people did if they returned from combat duty with less than six months left on their enlistments. Peter started to laugh as soon as he recognized Teddy's voice, seeing in his mind Teddy's bulbous nose and pointy chin and constant smile.

"Sure, Teddy," he said. "It's still early season at the beach, right? Can you find us a cheap room down there?"

They went to Nags Head the weekend before Easter. Teddy picked him up in a new, red Dodge truck. It had a white stripe along each side just below window level and a gleaming grill that resembled the smile of some predatory character in a movie cartoon. Teddy said the truck had cost all his Navy savings plus a loan from his dad. He said he was joining his father's lumber business and would start out working on a logging crew.

"He'd put me in the store right away if I wanted that, but I'd rather buck logs for a while," Teddy said. "Maybe that'll help clear my head."

All during their three-hour drive to the beach, gliding past pine forests and freshly plowed fields where cotton and tobacco would soon be transplanted from seedbeds, they spoke of their plans and of friends from high school. Peter couldn't think of a good way to describe his relationship with Stephie, so he said nothing about her. Frustrated at that, he veered absurdly into the sort of joking comparisons he'd made in high school between Teddy's athletic skill and success with girls and his own failures in both departments. Teddy could fire out of a perfect three-point stance and open a hole for a running back against defensive linemen who outweighed him by 40 pounds. He'd been an all-conference tackle, while Peter, before his injury, had been an inept defensive end. What Peter didn't mention, figuring Teddy knew it very well, was that he would have quit football long before his injury if Teddy hadn't been there to shout support whenever Peter made a decent play, and if he hadn't laughed and helped Peter to his feet on the practice field whenever he'd flattened Peter on a fullback sweep.

During the drive, Teddy said nothing about his year in Vietnam, and Peter was careful not to bring the subject up.

They tried fishing for sheepshead near the rocks beneath the Oregon Inlet bridge, but they caught nothing there except blowfish and little drum. Still Peter waited for Teddy to say something about the past year, but Teddy didn't touch the subject except to say he never got to fish the whole time he was in the Navy. The next day was cool and windy, and they spent all of it casting with bloodworms and shrimp from Jennette's Pier. Few fishermen were out this early in the year, and the gimlet-eyed grackles congregated close to Teddy and Peter, stalking the deck and railing on their eerily thin, crinkled-looking black feet. The two men took turns swatting at the birds to prevent them from stealing their live bait from one of the stone cutting slabs mounted along the pier. They each caught a couple of decent-sized red drum, but they had no way to transport the fish, so they unhooked them and threw them back in the surf.

Finally, watching the tide recede in late morning, Peter blurted: "You know, we heard you saw some bad stuff over there. On those boats in the Mekong Delta, I mean. I guess I understand if you don't want to say too much about that."

Teddy shook his head and laughed, keeping his eyes on his rod tip as it dipped and shuddered. Unlike Peter, Teddy never mistook the surf's vast rhythms and eddies for a fish's bite.

"Yeah, I'm trying not to think too much about it," Teddy said. "I tried not to think much about it even when we there. Funny thing, if you let yourself think about the worst parts, it's just like you're right in the middle of it again. Before I caught the chopper up to Cam Ranh Bay to fly home, I spent a night on board our mothership. It was an LST anchored down where some canals converge and flow out into the Mekong River. I got to talking to an old chief petty officer who'd been real friendly to me whenever we got down that far. He'd joined the Navy back in the forties, and he'd been on a cruiser that got hit midship by a kamikaze plane. I told him about some of the things we'd been through, and I told him I guessed they'd fade in my mind after a while. And he laughed and said, 'Don't count on it, son. You'll remember those parts crystal-clear next year, and the year after that. You'll remember them when you're old, and they'll be just like they happened yesterday.'"

Teddy shook his head and gazed out across the foaming breakers. His smile was the same as Peter remembered, the nose and chin drawing close enough to call to mind the Punch figure in a puppet show. But Teddy's eyes were different. It wasn't exactly that all the happiness they used to radiate was gone. It was more like the happiness was somewhere very close by, and Teddy was looking around for it, thinking that at any moment it might turn up. But it wasn't turning up.

"So I just try to think of them as little as I can, since maybe that's all I can ever do," Teddy said.

Well that's that, then, Peter thought, reeling in his line and seeing that the two chunks of shrimp on his rig had turned gummy-looking. He felt annoyed that he'd spent two days guardedly angling for something he now knew he would have to leave undisturbed, hidden in whatever depths of memory Teddy could submerge it. He also felt ashamed of wanting to reel up into sunlight memories that would cause his friend such pain.

For a while they fished in silence. Then Teddy said, "I guess the worst, for me, were the things you knew should never happen, but they did happen because someone was stupid or careless or lazy, and people got hurt or died because of it. The absolute worst thing that happened, because it was just so, so stupid, was the night we broke ambush because our patrol officer got bored. Our boats always worked in pairs, and the patrol officer—he was over both boats—decided we were going to take it easy and rest for the night and not hide in ambush. He figured we could turn in at a little village and tie up where it was fairly secure. Moving once you've set an ambush is a no-no. That's inviting disaster. But about midnight, we started up. And of course the boats make a lot of noise at night, and it really carries. And we went right through an enemy ambush. They let the lead boat through, and I was driving the second boat, and they opened up on our boat. There were so many bullets coming through that I could look at the control panel and read it almost like day, in the light from the tracers. And the forward gunner got shot in the leg, through the femoral artery. Every gunner on a boat sits in a circular steel tub that protects you from your neck to your hips, but it doesn't reach below that. Well, the round that hit our forward gunner must have come through the water and the hull, and it still had enough velocity to tear into his leg. I caught a little piece of shrapnel from a claymore mine, but that was nothing, just like getting hit with a BB. The after-gunner and the mid-gunner didn't get hit—how, I don't know, because all four of us should have been dead with the amount of fire coming into our boat. It was probably because the boat was running wide open. Our speed must have spaced out the bullets enough to beat the odds we'd all get killed.

"It didn't take long to clear the kill zone. Probably fifteen seconds, but it seemed like a lifetime. Once we were in the clear, they called on the radio and said, 'was anybody hit?' And I was boat captain that night, so it was my job to answer the radio. But I was so scared all I could do was open and close my mouth. I couldn't get anything out. I was so scared. I've never been that scared. I finally got out that my forward gunner was hit.

"When I started up again, the boat settled down in the water, and then I realized we were sinking, because there were so many bullet holes in the hull below the waterline. We were a long way from base. And so we just pulled over where we could beach the boat, ran it aground. The patrol officer was on the other boat, and he called for a medevac chopper to pick up our forward gunner. He was already unconscious. His face looked so pale, so pale, and he was a pretty dark-skinned guy. Nathan Aguilar, from Connecticut. We used to ask him if all Portuguese were as dark as he was, and he'd laugh and say not unless they were half Narraganset Indian too. The mid-gunner had done the best he could for him. He'd pulled a rubber tourniquet out of the first aid kit and tied it above the wound, but Nathan had already lost a lot of blood.

"All we could do then was tell Nathan he was going to be okay and the chopper was going to be there any minute. But after a little while we quit even talking to him, and we just sat there and watched him, and we could see he was breathing the whole time he was there with us. And I guess since we knew we'd already scored pretty high on the stupid scale once we'd broken ambush, we must have figured, 'What the hell? Let's go all in for stupid.' So while we were sitting there waiting for the chopper, one of us switched on his transistor radio. It wasn't me, but whoever it was, none of us told him to switch it off, not even the patrol officer. Any VC interested in finishing us off should've known anyway that we were pulled up there on the bank, but just in case they didn't, that radio would have clued them in. And we caught one of those 'history of rock and roll' episodes, and I remember just as clear as yesterday what we listened to. 'Surfer Girl,' a ditzy Beach Boys tune that we used to slow-dance to at sock hops in the gym after football games. The other boat was pulled up abreast of ours and a little offshore, and that crew's gunners stayed on lookout in their gun tubs. But on our boat, we just sat around on the deck, and we watched Nathan's face get paler and paler, and we listened to that Beach Boys song. And I remember how much it sounded like a lullaby. That song might be the last thing Nathan heard in life. And of course it was just an accident it was on the radio when we switched it on. But I think sometimes that playing it might have been the best thing we could have done for him. Finally the medevac chopper came, and there was enough cleared space on the shore for it to land. And they took him to a field hospital, but it was too late. Nathan was the only man killed on a boat I was on, at least while I was on it.

"Once we got our wounded man out of there, we had to figure out how to keep our boat afloat. The boat uses Jacuzzi pumps for propulsion, and you can fit a suction hose down through a cleanup trap on top of the pump and suck water out of the bilges. And so we did that, and we got enough water out of the boat so we could run again. And then we ran it wide open just about all night long till we got to a repair facility. When you run that fast, those pumps do double duty. They propel the boat, but they also keep the bilges clear.

"The one thing we had to worry about was running into another ambush, so we fired off flares all night long so we could see both shorelines. Ever since, Pete, I've wondered just how stupid that was. Because, you look at it another way, we were just telling any VC who were anywhere near the canal, 'Hey, here we are, guys! Come see if you can finish the job on us!' Racing down that canal like a waterborne Roman candle. I think that might actually ring the gong at the top of the stupid scale."

Teddy paused, shaking his head. He reeled in and glanced at his bait. The chunks of shrimp on the rig's two hooks looked surf-worn enough that Peter expected Teddy to replace them, but Teddy merely swung them beneath the pier and made another underhand cast.

"There was just one other time we did that. Fired off flares all night, I mean. And that was almost worse, because of what we saw. We were out at sea then, because we'd been called in to hunt for the crew of an attack helicopter that had been flying air support for some other patrol boats somewhere else in the Delta. The helicopter had been hit by ground fire, and the crew was trying to make it back to its LST offshore. The smart thing would have been to fly it to Dong Tam, where a lot of the Navy's air support was based, instead of out over the water. But that's what they tried to do, and they went down before they could make it to their ship. We fired off flares all night long, but we never saw any sign of the helicopter or the crew. What we saw more than anything else was sea snakes. I don't know whether they feed at night, or whether it was the light from the flares that attracted them, but you could see them all over the surface of the water. It looked like the whole ocean was just boiling with them."

Peter and Teddy packed up their fishing gear with about three hours of daylight left. They ate chopped barbecue and coleslaw across the bridge in Manteo, and for the rest of the drive to Raleigh they talked about logging and hunting. Peter knew nothing about logging and not much more about hunting, but he enjoyed listening to Teddy speak in his soft, high-pitched, modest voice about things he could do well. Peter smiled, remembering the winter morning when he had watched in silent admiration as Teddy, in the basement gun room of his home, loaded the shotgun shells they would use later that day to hunt quail.

When Teddy pulled into the dorm parking lot, Peter climbed out, shut the door and reached back through the passenger-side window to shake his friend's hand.

"Count yourself lucky that you've got that bum knee and you don't have to go over there," Teddy said.

"But I might," Peter said. "Dad thinks they might call me up anyway, unless I find some dodge, like teaching school. Or unless Johnson's pullout from the presidential race means—well, who knows what it might mean for the war."

"I'd say do whatever you have to do to find a good dodge, then," Teddy said. "I never felt like I was doing any good over there. The people didn't want us. They were just afraid of us, even the ones we were supposed to be protecting. And I'd give a lot not to have to carry all I saw and had to do around with me for the rest of my life."

"But if you do have to carry that stuff around, Teddy, why shouldn't I?" Peter said. "How is that fair? I've heard all the arguments against the war. I guess I even agree with most of them. But if guys like you have to carry memories around like—I don't know—like a sack of those sea snakes you talked about, then why should people like me get a pass? Why shouldn't I have to carry around something from that war that it hurts to remember, but that I can't ever forget?"

Teddy said nothing, but he looked downward and shook his head slowly in the light from the truck's dashboard. Finally he said: "Take care of yourself, Pete. Let's do this again, okay?"

The next clip in the speeded-up newsreel that played inside Peter's head as he lay on his bunk beneath the wobbly ceiling fan was of Easter dinner at his aunt and uncle's house. His mother's clan always gathered there for holiday meals, the adults seated at the big walnut table in the dining room, the children consigned to card tables in the parlor. In his newsreel version, the faces and the sounds—the voices and the varying grades of laughter, from his aunt's soft cackle to the earsplitting whoops from his favorite cousin, Polly, and the chorus of appreciation that arose whenever Mona, the cook, entered the room in her black dress and white apron—merged with all the other Easter and Thanksgiving and Christmas dinners he had spent at that table or at one of the card tables. And lying there in the tropical darkness, hearing the geckos' cries and the low, constant buzzing of the motor scooters on the roads toward Nha Cat, Peter felt again, briefly, the suffocation that had crept over him at that Easter table less than a year ago. He felt again his anger toward his father for trying to trap him into a way of life so subtly anesthetizing that he would not even recognize the moment when the last venturesome spark in his spirit had been snuffed out.

He remembered how the voices around that table had slowly trailed off when he blurted that he'd gone fishing at Nags Head with an old friend who was just back from Vietnam. It was as if his words had sucked from the room half the comforting atmosphere laden with rich aromas—of honey-glazed ham, whipped sweet potatoes topped with marshmallows, freshly cut spring grass, his uncle's most recent pipeful of Prince Albert— but it had taken his aunts and uncles and cousins a while to notice.

Peter's father had noticed right away. He looked at Peter sharply across the table. "You mean Teddy, right?" he said.

"Oh, what a nice young man!" his mother had said. "I'm so glad to hear he's home. How is Teddy?"

"He had it really hard over there. He was in the Navy, river patrol. He said he tries not to think of the worst parts."

Peter's father wiped his mouth slowly with his napkin, then dropped it beside his plate. After that sharp first glance, he didn't look at his son.

"So Teddy has changed, has he?" he said.

"I guess I'd say that. Of course, he's just back. I guess it always takes a while to readjust."

"Oh, rabbit hole!" his mother said with an exasperated roll of her eyes. His aunt started to cackle, recognizing her sister's signal that an unwelcome subject must be quickly squelched.

"So he's changed," his father said, still not looking at him. "And not for the better, would you say?"

Peter's mother half-rose from her chair and pounded the table with her palm. "Rabbit hole, rabbit hole!" she said. "I love Teddy McClearon, and I very much want to see him now he's back. But whatever he suffered over there isn't going to cast its shadow over this dinner table. Is that clear?"

The absence of any subcurrent in his mother's voice told Peter that his father hadn't talked to her about what the draft's sharpened hunger might mean for their son. His father's turned-aside eyes told Peter he knew his son hadn't put in a request to teach, and wasn't going to.

From that Easter dinner, the newsreel in Peter's mind skipped to the morning in late May when he'd gone to pick up his diploma at the registrar's office. He had walked up a long, gentle slope past dozens of little white crosses planted on the lawn outside the administration building. A banner that read "Here lies the class of 1968," in hand-painted black lettering, stretched well above head height over the walkway between the rows of crosses. The banner was fastened at either end to poles that appeared to be bamboo, and Peter thought: nice touch.

Then another skip in the newsreel, this time to the arrival of his 1-A draft card in his dorm mailbox. Peter could tell it was his father who had penciled in the forwarding address on the unopened envelope. By itself, Peter knew, the new draft card meant nothing, except that his student deferment was gone.

He'd been able to start the internship right away. As his teacher had said, it was mostly gofer work, but the little firm's lead architect, a transplant from Milwaukee, turned out to be just as engagingly quirky as his specialty, historic restoration, suggested he might be. While Peter fetched copies of property and tax and census records from the 1850s, his boss rambled on cheerfully about how, during the Civil War, the owner of the antebellum home in Hillsboro that he was contracted to restore had slapped his wife to the ground when she tried to protect a defiant male slave. The slave had bared his chest and sneered at his owner, who then killed him with a shotgun.

Peter cautiously told his boss that, as a history major, he had learned to mistrust stories passed down in families, especially horrific stories that lacked firsthand corroboration. His boss laughed and patted Peter's shoulder approvingly. "Exactly right!" he said. "Always look for that authoritative source. Two or three of them, in fact, if you can find that many." Then he had pointed at a desktop tray across the office. "See that purple file folder? Take a look at that. It's from the Federal Writers' Project, interviews with North Carolina slaves. It's the narrative of Dillie Conrad, who was a child on that property in the 1860s. Give it a read and tell me what you think. Bear in mind, those interviews took place in the 1930s, at the height of Jim Crow. Ask yourself: What motive would an eighty-one-year-old ex-slave have for telling a story like that in that era if it wasn't true?"

The couple of weeks after he picked up his diploma had managed to splice themselves at almost full length into what was otherwise a mental newsreel of short, vivid segments. Peter was so punch-drunk with happiness over his summer work, Stephie's promise to him and the near approach of the time when she would keep that promise, he found himself overlooking little things, and some that weren't so little, like shaving or replacing the gas cap when he refueled his car. Now, as he lay on his bunk beneath the ceiling fan, he realized this period of blissful ninny-hood would have lasted up to and beyond the morning when he fetched his camping gear from home and swung by the medical school to pick up Stephie if the second letter from his draft board hadn't shown up in his mailbox. Like the first envelope, it was unopened, and again the forwarding address was in his father's left-leaning cursive. It was a summons to report for a physical exam at the induction center in Raleigh.

"Well," he thought—tamping down his feeling of dread that everything that had seemed about to come together beautifully had fallen within the shadow of an approaching wrecking ball. "Well. Good thing I'm already here for that."

He said nothing to Stephie or his parents about the summons. On the appointed morning, he arrived at the induction center before the glass front door was unlocked. He glanced around at the dozen or so young men, most of them black, standing on the walkway and grass. The morning air already felt latent with the breathless heat that would descend by noon, yet most of the others seemed sunk in a hunched, hands-in-pockets posture better suited to a fall chill. A few of them smoked but kept their eyes averted. No interest in conversation in this crowd, Peter decided. He fixed his eyes on the glass door and its shiny metal doorframe. He admired the simplicity of the door's design, yet it gave him an uneasy feeling. Well, that makes no sense, he thought. But then he realized why: The door frame reminded him of the vertical, sliding metal bars that had pinioned the head of the first beef calf he had raised, on the morning he and his father took the animal to the FCX for butchering. Peter had been twelve then. The calf had ambled into the stunning pen as his father clucked and whistled at it. It had stuck its head trustingly through the opening at the far end. Then the two sliding bars had snapped in tightly behind its ears. One of the two butchers had fired the stun gun between the calf's bulging eyes. His aim must have been slightly off, because the calf just wobbled. A second shot from the stun gun brought it down, mouth foaming, blood oozing from the shallow wound. Then the two butchers opened the bars of the stunning pen and hauled the calf to the cutting room.

As this scene played out in Peter's mind for the first time in years, a black custodian appeared behind the glass door, flipped through his ring of keys and unlocked the door with a great clattering of keys against the glass. None of the other men standing outside showed any interest in being first to enter, so Peter pulled open the glass door and stepped inside.

After enduring the indignities of a military physical exam, he was directed to a room where a doctor sat on a tall metal stool. With his gray hair neatly parted in the middle and his rumpled, double-breasted brown suit, the doctor looked like he could have stepped off a movie set from the

1940s. He flipped through Peter's pre-existing conditions form and asked him how much trouble he had with the knee.

"I have to be careful with it," Peter told him.

"We'll send you down to Fort Bragg," the doctor said, scribbling on Peter's form and tossing it on a stack of other forms. "They'll X-ray it there, and one of their orthopedists will decide how well it's likely to hold up."

So Dad was right about the Spandex standards. Walking out into a midday that had fulfilled the 7 a.m. promise of stifling heat, he knew it was time to call his father and try to heal the breach between them.

But first he called Stephie. When he told her an Army orthopedist would rule on the knee, she quickly asked if he would like her to do anything about it.

"Do?" he said. "There's nothing to do except wait till it's time. They gave me an appointment in two weeks."

"You do have a choice here, I think," she said. She was speaking in her doctor voice, he knew, using the simple, neutral-sounding language she would use with any other patient. "I'm sure we could find an orthopedist here who'd evaluate your knee. The Army and your draft board would probably accept that doctor's opinion. Staff members here say they've done that kind of thing before, and their evaluation has always stood up."

"Well, I hadn't thought about anything like that," Peter said. "What do you want me to do?"

"It's strictly your decision," she said.

"What?" he said. "You're briefing me on this medically assisted draft-dodge, and you have no opinion whether I should take it?"

"It's your decision," she said. "Strictly yours."

"Jesus, Stephie, you sound like an automaton."

"What I'm trying to sound like is a doctor who spells out options but doesn't try to influence the patient's choice."

Peter's annoyance started to get the better of him.

"Well, I think we've already crossed the line there, haven't we?" he said. "On the drive to Pilot Mountain, weren't you urging me to cast aside every thought of mundane, long-lived happiness and go all in for some kind of Wagnerian *liebestod*?"

Stephie laughed—not her two-tone laugh, but a rueful chuckle.

"Try to forget what I told you then," she said. "Focus on what you really want."

"The trouble with that is, you were right," he said. "Going to a war is a big piece of what I want. And there's no good reason to want that—at least not in this war—except a hankering to get close to the death in it. Even if I didn't feel that hankering, I wouldn't want to cheat my way out of going."

She uttered a high-pitched, wordless note of disbelief.

"Cheat your way out?" she said. "You think what happened to it when you did that little two-step on the catwalk was bad? When all you did was rupture some blood vessels in that gap where the cartilage is supposed to be? Well, imagine yourself in a firefight, and the adrenaline's pumping, and you rip that ligament completely loose from the pin. You want to know what would be cheating, Peter? If a qualified orthopedist, Army doctor or whatever, said you were fit for military service without severe restrictions on what you're expected to do, *that* would be cheating."

While Stephie was still speaking, Peter told himself he was done with hesitation and with arguments like those he had heard from his father and was hearing now from Stephie. He had embarked on a course he had thought was forever closed to him. It promised to lead him around darkened corners to places he had thought he would never be able to go, and he found that promise irresistibly exciting. He found it threatful, too, but the threat served only to heighten his excitement.

But my God, what happens then with Stephie! If I have any chance of spending my life with her, and I think I do, how stupid would I be to follow out this course I'm on the verge of locking myself into? How stupid would I be to snuff out my chance with her by pursuing a chimera around those dark corners, only to have it vanish, or else turn and devour me?

Nine

Before they hung up, Stephie told him coolly she was putting their camping trip on hold, at least until she got back from New Hampshire.

"I hope you've got your draft status settled by then," she said. "You have considerable control over that. And I think everyone who's concerned with your welfare, including you, ought to hold you accountable for how it turns out."

When Peter called his home, his father brushed aside his apology for failing to put in a bid to teach.

"I don't think this visit to Bragg will make much difference," his father said. "Just remember that being drafted doesn't mean you lose all control. Keep your eye open for options you could live with. They'll turn up."

His father paused, and in his mind Peter could see that familiar dip of the cap's bleached-out bill and, beneath it, his father's worry-crinkled eyelids.

"But keep this in mind too, Pete. You're likely to feel whipsawed between looking for a job you can handle physically, and saying, 'Aw, the hell with it!' and trying to do this soldier thing full-bore. Things will look different to you once you're in the belly of the beast, drilling and singing out the cadence morning to night. A high-spirited young man in the midst of all that is probably going to start asking himself, 'Well, why can't I do this combat thing? Why can't I, really?' Well, you can't, son, simple as that. If I couldn't do it with something as garden-variety as flat feet, you sure as hell can't do it with that knee. And it's not just that: In this war, it's not worth doing. I don't know how much Teddy told you about what he went through, but I gather he made that much clear. That it wasn't worth doing. It was a mistake."

"Whipsawed" was one of his father's favorite words. In his usage, it meant you were trapped in the force field between two alternatives that were equally attractive or perilous or some blend of both. The word summoned to Peter's mind the "whang-whang" sound made by a long, flexible, two-man saw. But Peter had never felt the word applied closely to him. Now, he discovered, it did.

For the next two weeks, he spent his working hours burrowing away in archives to identify the precise composition of brick and plaster and paint pigments used around Raleigh in the 1840s to build homes for people who could afford the best. He did the same for the varieties of boxwood and flowers those people would have chosen for their walkways and gardens. He brought his notes to his boss, who gleefully pored over them, asking Peter to clarify a point here and there, then drawing up a list of companies that might be able to fill special orders for exact matches of those materials and heirloom plants. Immersed in this work, Peter felt he could never want anything more or better to fill his workdays than to follow out the kinds of questions it raised, questions of client tastes and design and selection of materials. He loved immersing himself in the extra layer of study and care that historical restoration demanded. He felt his life could achieve no greater completeness than by blending work like this with his love for Stephie.

Lacking much interest in anything else Raleigh could offer, he tried to stretch his workdays far enough past sundown to feel pleasantly cooled by the evening air through his car window on the five-mile drive to the campus. By the time he arrived there, his thoughts would have drifted away from his work and fixed instead on those darkened corners, and on his unexpected chance to step beyond them, and on the violence and self-knowledge he might find there.

On the morning he drove to Fort Bragg, the whipsawing between the sunlit life he was leading and the allure of those darkened corners accelerated so drastically that Peter had trouble focusing his attention on the road. He tried repeating to himself his father's warnings: "You can't, simple as that," and "In this war, it's not worth doing." But at the same time, to his overwrought imagination the asphalt highway ahead of his car seemed to bulge and buckle like waters roiled by sea snakes.

After he'd had his knee X-rayed in the giant Army hospital, Peter tried to follow the technician's directions to the orthopedics clinic but quickly got lost. Finally he stopped at a hallway intersection where he saw, approaching from two directions, the shaved heads and dazed, sweaty faces of dozens of recruits being herded along by their drill sergeants. Nearly all the recruits looked to Peter like they were in their teens, and about half of them were black or Hispanic. "How many of these kids will be dead in a year?" Peter wondered. "How many of them—wouldn't all of them—give almost anything for a ticket out of this chute to the slaughter pen? That's a ticket I've been handed, and I can cash it in, if I can just find the right goddamn door."

Finally he did find the door with the number above it that he'd been given in the X-ray lab. But by that time, the whipsaw had swung too far over toward the side of darkness and mystery and danger for Peter to swing it back toward the bright, secure place where Stephie and his parents and the work he was learning to love all beckoned to him. The young doctor wore fatigues with a captain's bars on the lapels. He looked at an X-ray photo, and then he glanced up briefly at Peter.

"Dandridge?" he said.

"That's right."

"All right. Tell me what you can't do."

Peter didn't answer. He remembered Teddy's halting voice, sometimes barely audible above the sound of the light surf rolling in beneath them against the pilings of the pier. He thought of those frightened, sheeplike faces in the hallway.

"Nothing," he said finally. "There's nothing I can't do."

Now it was the doctor's turn to grow silent. He and Peter stared at each other for several seconds. By the time they were done with that, each of them knew all he would ever need to know about the other.

"All right," the doctor said. "Keep your head down."

Ten

Peter half-expected the whipsaw to torment him by swinging back toward the warm, familiar, brightly lighted place on the return drive to Raleigh. Instead, he felt such peace that he was able to enjoy the drive. He rolled down the driver's side window. The outside air resembled the blast from a thrown-open furnace door, but it was laden with a peppery scent so pungent he could envision pitch glistening between scales of bark on the longleaf pines.

He thought of the time his Boy Scout troop had camped in the Uwharrie National Forest. He and his tentmates had swept together a layer of pine needles inside their tent and unrolled their sleeping bags on the needles. Then he remembered he had some empty burlap feed sacks in his trunk. He pulled off on the road shoulder and walked into the forest and scooped pine needles into the bags with his hands.

Stephie wasn't due back from New Hampshire for another week. Peter still didn't know what, if anything, his mother knew about his father's efforts—steady, well-informed but always respectful of his son's right to choose—to steer their only child away from the step Peter had now taken. But Peter did know he couldn't leave his father to face alone whatever fear-fueled anger his mother might unleash. He knew his father would absorb it all without complaint.

When he arrived home the next weekend, his parents' demeanor told him that had already happened. His parents weren't looking at each other. His mother barely greeted him when he walked in the door, and then she turned and went into her bedroom. His father handed him yet another envelope from the county draft board, muttering, "That didn't take them long." This time, the envelope had been torn open. Peter gave his father a questioning look, but his father looked down and said nothing. Inside the envelope Peter found another draft card. It included two puzzling additions on the same line as his 1-A classification. One was an abbreviation in parentheses, "acc." The other was three capital letters, "FQB."

"Dad, do you have any idea what those mean?" he said, pointing at the new coding.

"Ask your mother," his father said, still looking at the floor. "She called the draft board."

Peter's mother came out of her bedroom carrying her purse and her car keys. Without looking at Peter, she said, "I want you to come with me, please." It did not sound like a request.

"Where?" Peter said.

Then she did look at him. She spaced the command as she might have done with a recalcitrant child. "I want you—to come—with me. Now."

He got in her car and she drove, grim-faced, the two miles to Spainhour's Chapel, jerking the steering wheel as she rounded the curves at what seemed to Peter twice her accustomed speed. She parked the car next to the little gazebo in the parking lot of the cemetery that held their Leinbach ancestors.

"Come with me," she said. She opened her car door and walked ahead of him through the gravestones. She stopped beneath the row of shaggy-barked red cedars. Coming up beside her, Peter noticed a third gravestone. It was cut to the same dimensions and inscribed in the same script as those of his great-grandfather's two elder brothers.

"Emanuel Alspaugh," Peter read aloud. "September, eighteen sixty-two. Funny, I'd forgotten there was a third soldier buried here. I wonder if these three were the only ones from around here that their relatives managed to bring back from wherever it was they died."

"Could be," his mother said. Peter, schooled since infancy in the fine shadings of his mother's voice, caught the note of menace behind her faux lighthearted tone. "Or it could just be that whoever planted these paltry little cedars decided this row right here should be reserved for idiots. And then whoever it was who hauled their paltry little bodies back from Virginia decided Samuel Zion Leinbach and Emanuel Alspaugh had earned pride of place in that row. Though let's be fair, Peter: At least those two boys had some excuse. See, they rushed off to fight at a time when the flags were still waving, and you couldn't yet hear the wails of mothers and widows and orphans down every street and country lane. But never mind. Young men who go off to fight for nothing worth winning belong in the idiots' row, simple as that. But then, look!"

His mother glared at him and pointed a trembling finger at the gravestone at the far left of the short row. A ragged seam of cement showed where a corner amounting to about a fourth of the stone had broken off and been reattached. The patch of mortar made the script hard to read, but both Peter and his mother knew it by heart.

"Look at this!" she said. "Younger brother David Henry Leinbach decides to join up *after* his big brother had already died from typhoid. *After* his brother's body had been hauled home—God knows how, maybe in the back of that old wagon we'd hitch Queenie to on your birthday so she could haul you and your snot-nosed little buddies around. *After* they'd buried his brother's already half-rotten body—buried it quick, I'll wager. I'll bet even their mother went along with that idea, once the smell from that box convinced her an overnight wake would put a stink in her table linen she'd never get out. After all that, little David Henry runs off to

Jarvis County and signs up to be—what, a regular soldier? Oh, no! He's going to be a *cavalryman*! A little sodbuster who's maybe been on the back of a horse twice in his life, and a plow horse at that, joins the cavalry! And three months later he's dead. Doesn't that sound to you like a shoo-in for the idiots' row right there? Doesn't that maybe explain why burials in that row ended in eighteen and sixty-three, since nobody was likely to come along again in all the years down to Armageddon who could top those credentials for blue-ribbon idiocy?"

Peter knew what was coming, and there stole over him the same feeling of shame he remembered had lingered for days after the only severe whipping his mother had ever given him. That one was for bullying his four-years-younger cousin. He'd gulled the boy into trying out two pair of boxing gloves that Peter's father had scrounged through school connections. Then he'd punched the boy in the face and made him cry.

"But lo!" said his mother, stepping sideways from David Henry's headstone onto a patch of grass beyond the little row of headstones. "It took just a little over a hundred and five years for another such idiot to sprout from the same soil as grew the last one! Circumstances much the same, and well suited to bring idiocy to full flower. Do we have a war that anybody with brains has figured out—but heck, forget about brains. Anybody with a functioning nose ought to know by now that this war stinks as high as—as those three boxes must have stunk when they hauled them up here in wagon beds and lowered them in the holes and covered them up fast. Do wails of mothers and widows and orphans once more resound? Check. Do we have warning aplenty from those who have come back scarred, if you need that kind of warning? Well, you spent a couple of days at the beach with Teddy McClearon, didn't you? And I had a long talk with his mother. So check that box too."

"Mom, there's a whole other side to the time I spent with Teddy," Peter said.

His mother took a threatening step toward him before he had finished his sentence. "Idiots always have their whole other side, and this is where it lands them," she said, shouting now, and sweeping one finger toward three graves. "And listen: We have one more box to check on the fully up-to-date idiot's qualification form. You get to check this one only if you have some physical problem that ought to disqualify you for military duty of some particular sort, or maybe any sort. Giant carbuncles on your ass, let's say, if you're aiming to be a cavalryman. Or board-flat feet if you're trying to keep up in infantry training. Your father told you about his pursuit of idiot's standing along those lines, didn't he? Well, luckily for us all, he fell a little short. Or let's say, just to pull an example out of a hat, you've had a less-than-sterling surgical job done on a knee you injured playing a sport that a boy with toothpick legs had no business playing in the first place. Come to think of it, just trying to play that sport might have been an early indicator of full-blown idiocy. Well now, to check that box on the form, you have to find some way around that clear physical disqualifier. If you can do that, then that gets you the One-A draft classification you dearly long for, and it keeps you on-track for idiots' row."

She was shaking with rage now. She took another step toward Peter, and she looked threatening enough that he took an involuntary backward step.

"And I'll tell you what," she said. "Let's include an extra-credit box on the form. You get a check mark there if you can get your draft board to add a pair of codes in parentheses after the One-A on your card. They're kind of mysterious codes, but the woman who answers the phone at the draft board office is glad to explain them to you. One of them is the letters a-c-c inside parentheses, and she will tell you in the gentlest tone she can muster, 'Honey, that means he's a-fixin' to be drafted.' Because it means 'accessible,' you see. But the other code—now that's where they separate out the real top-tier idiots. Didn't you tell me you threw your knee out once just jumping across a rain puddle on campus, and you had to gimp around on crutches until the swelling went down? Well, if your knee will do that to you on a little sidewalk puddle and you can still get your draft board to put that code on your card, then let's check your extra credit box, declare you a summa cum laude idiot and reserve you a nice grassy plot on idiots' row. Which is exactly, Peter Dandridge, what I intend to do."

She stood nearly face-to-face with him now, breathing heavily, her eyes bloodshot but tearless. They stood that way for the length of a mockingbird's brief, patchwork song from the pasture across the road from the cemetery.

"Three capital letters," Peter said finally. "Dad showed me the new card, and there were three capital letters, but I don't remember what they were."

She stepped in closer still. "F—Q—B!" Peter felt droplets of her spittle hit his face. "Fully qualified for battle! Does that sound like good, fact-based judgment to you? I don't know what you said or who you said it to, but I'd bet my last dime it was words out of your mouth that account for those three letters on your draft card. Let me tell you something." Her voice dropped suddenly to that gentle tone laced with menace. "You go into the Army, which it looks like you're obliged to do any day now, and you act like you're Mister FQB, jumping out of airplanes or slogging through muck until your knee bloats up and your buddies leave you there in the middle of a rice paddy, with their fond good wishes of course, because they have to hurry back before the helicopter lifts off—if you even train to do any foolishness like that, if you try to act like that FQB holds any rational meaning and I learn of it, I won't wait for you to get yourself killed. I'll reserve that nice spot right over there for you. I'll even go ahead and order a stone for it, because I know we'll need one, and you never know when the price might go up. The only thing I'll need to leave off the stone for the time being, see, will be the date of death. And we won't need any fancy epitaph. No 'Earth hath no sorrow that heaven cannot heal' or any such claptrap. And do you know why? We've already got a perfect, ready-made epitaph, and we'll have it inscribed just as big as there's room for it on the stone. All capital letters. F—Q—B!"

She shouldered past him and started toward the car. For a while he simply watched her rigid back moving past their ancestors' headstones toward the tiny parking area with its gazebo and, beyond it, the white clapboard church with its boxlike, flush-left steeple. What he saw merged seamlessly with the same view of her he'd had time and again through all the seasons of his life. Following her as she passed the stones of her grandparents and rested a hand briefly on her parents' headstone, he could not accept that his relationship with her had forever changed. He called after her, trying to signal with the lightness in his voice that all was as it had always been between them.

"You know, Mom, you're right when you call those cedars paltry little things. I've always wondered why they never got any bigger. You know, we've got cedars at home, down in the woods toward the creek, that are probably less than half as old as those ones back there, but ours are at least twice as—"

"It's because their roots go down into the brains of idiots!" she said, throwing open her car door and craning her neck to glare, red-faced, across the car's roof. "Now get in the car and let's go home."

Eleven

After he'd sat through dinner on Saturday without his mother either looking at or saying a word to him, Peter said he reckoned he'd head back to Raleigh.

"Suit yourself," she said.

Shouldering his duffel, he stepped from the screen porch onto one of the giant stones his great-grandfather had hauled up from the shallow ford of the Yadkin River long before he was born. There were about twenty of the granite stones arranged with the precision of a jigsaw puzzle to cover the space between the porch and the wood-frame structure that housed the well and its electric pump. None of the stones' edges had been altered, yet there was no more space between them than would allow for a narrow strip of moss. As a child, Peter had loved to walk on them barefoot in the summer, even at night, when he risked squishing a slug between his toes.

Before stepping off the last stone and heading for his car, Peter dropped his duffel, knelt on the stone and pressed his palm to its surface. He breathed deeply with what felt like relief. The stone had reminded him that some things that were never supposed to change did, in fact, stay as they had always been. Then, with a sour grimace, Peter ran one finger over the stone, tracing out the letters "FQB."

He heard the screech of the screen door's rusted spring and looked up. His father stepped out onto the stones, let go of the door and then reached back to catch it and ease it shut. Peter guessed he didn't want his wife to know he had followed their son outside. His father said nothing as he stepped past him, but he beckoned to Peter with one hand as he walked on toward Peter's car. Peter followed and threw his duffel bag into the car's back seat. He had put his umbrella tent, a quilt and blankets, cook kit, camp stove, a plastic jerry can and a folding stool in the trunk the night before. He had taken the bags of pine needles out long enough to sprinkle them with water from the garden hose, hoping that would keep them fresh.

"You're going to tell me she'll come around, right?" Peter said, turning to face his father.

"She will, eventually. I doubt it'll be soon. Probably not before you go in the Army."

His father looked straight at him. Peter was glad to see that at least he'd gotten over his sheepish funk.

"What did you tell them down at Fort Bragg?" his father said.

"The orthopedist asked me what I couldn't do, and I told him there was nothing I couldn't do. All he said then was to keep my head down."

A corner of his father's mouth twitched with a quickly stifled smile.

"I see," his father said. "Well, now that I know the question, I could've predicted your answer. I guess I even approve of it. Not that my approval makes it any less a lie. And not that what you told that doctor will do you any good with your mother. Did you tell her what you said?"

"No. She's made it pretty clear she's not in listening mode."

"She has indeed. Neither to you nor me. That helpful person she talked to at the draft board volunteered to her that there had been two previous mailings for you sent to your home address. She confronted me with that information, and I told her I'd sent them on to you without mentioning them to her. You sure you don't want to stay here till tomorrow? Share the bone-deep chill around here and all that?"

"Not unless there's something around here I can help you do. I don't care for her treating me like I'm not there. Like I'm dead already."

Peter expected his father would say something to counter that bleak view of his mother's behavior, but all his father did was lay a hand on his shoulder and remind him to keep his eyes on the road.

Peter covered roughly half the distance to Raleigh in a self-righteous huff. Several times he pounded the steering wheel with the heel of one hand and, in an aggrieved tone, shouted questions such as, "Why isn't it enough that I'm just trying to do what's right?"

Then the dimming, forward-slanting sunlight in the highway's eastbound lane reminded Peter that, despite the reassurance of the stones his great-grandfather had hauled up from the shallow ford, the sun would never again rise on things as they had always been in the home he was leaving behind. By the time he passed Durham, Peter's tone had changed from loud and aggrieved to quiet and supplicatory.

"Please, dear God, don't let me lose Stephie," he said. "Not Stephie too."

Three days later Stephanie called to tell him she was back, having traveled south by train as far as Richmond, then taken the bus. She said she'd spent her time at home collecting cows' first milk after they had given birth, then bottle-feeding it to their calves.

"Why don't you just let the calves nurse from the dams?" Peter asked her.

"Because that's not the industrial model," she said.

She said she had just one more week before her neurology rotation would begin.

"What happened at Fort Bragg?" she said.

"They found me fit," he said.

"With a helpful nudge from the object of deliberation, I'm sure," she said.

"Can we go camping, Stephie?" he said. "Even if it's just for a day or two?"

"So when do you go in the Army?" she said.

"I don't know."

"How does your family feel about it?"

"My mother's not happy."

"You could have avoided this, you know. It would have been so easy to avoid. And it would have been entirely legitimate, above-board, honorable, you name it."

"Can we please go camping, Stephie? Can we go now, before your next rotation starts? I've been working really hard, and my boss has already said I should take some time off."

During Stephie's long silence, Peter shut his eyes, thinking: Please, God, not Stephie too. Don't take Stephie away from me too.

"All right, dear boy" she said finally. "Let's go camping." Instead of the wary acceptance that was the most he had dared hope for, her voice struck the gentlest tone he expected ever to hear from Stephanie Ames.

"God, I love you, Stephanie," he said.

"Wow, she must have socked you pretty hard."

"What? Oh, you mean my mom."

"You've got a full-blown case of oedipal angst. Don't contradict old Doc Ames, now. I've already finished my psychiatry rotation, so I ought to know."

"She said she'd bury me in the idiots' row. She took me to the cemetery where all her side of the family are buried, and she showed me exactly where she meant."

"Well, I've thought all along I'd like your mother. She continues to rise in my regard."

"Oh very funny, Stephanie," he said. "Ha bloody ha." Then he really did laugh, and for a while he couldn't stop.

"That's good," she said. "Exactly what I'd prescribe. I forget who it was that said the best lancet for a purely psychological boil is a good belly laugh. Maybe I was the one who said that. Maybe it was old Doc Ames."

"You know, Stephie, you don't have to do anything you don't want to do," he said. "I mean, when we're in the tent together. If I can just have you there beside me, if I can just listen to you breathe through the whole night, that'll be enough."

In what Peter was learning to recognize as common practice with Stephanie when he'd said something inane, she ignored him.

"Tell me, what is it your mother has done since she learned your draft status that has angered or offended or wounded you the most?"

"Jesus, now you really are playing doctor, aren't you? What makes you think that's not going to anger or wound or offend me?"

"That's of no consequence," she said. "The good therapist takes no account of such niceties."

"Therapist?" Peter shouted into the phone.

"I've got some pretty good psychiatric chops, I believe. I've tested them out on baby calves quite recently, in fact."

"Look, Stephie, if I think I need a therapist, I'll hunt up one who has a shingle and—"

"Who'll charge you fifty dollars per half hour, minimum, while you're getting this one for free, plus you get to bang her in the woods. If you turned down a deal like that, your mom would be right. They ought to plant you in the idiots' plot."

"Well, all right, then," Peter said. "It angers, slash, wounds, slash, offends me that my mom acts like I'm already dead. She acted like that before she went off on me in the cemetery, and she acted like that after we got back home. After a day of that I'd had enough, so I drove back down here."

"I see." For about half a minute, all he heard through the phone receiver was the steady tap of a pencil lead against a desktop. Finally she said: "You're an only child, right? And, if you happen to know this, did your parents hope to have more children, and did that just not happen for them?"

"Yeah. I mean, it wasn't something they ever seemed to dwell on. But both Mom and Dad said over the years they'd wanted more kids."

"I see." Again he heard the tapping. "Well, maybe your mom right now is dealing with her fear of losing you by acting like you're just one more child that ought to be there, but isn't."

"That—" Peter said. He had his breath drawn and his tongue positioned to tell Stephie that she wasn't making any sense when the sense she was making him struck him full force.

"Of course, I have no way of knowing, and maybe you don't either, what the particulars were," Stephie said. "Whether there were times when she thought that finally it had happened again. Or perhaps there was a miscarriage, or more than one. But there must have been multiple times when the child she wanted and could almost see in her arms just disappeared from her view—poof, like that. And if there were enough of those times, she would have worked out a way of dealing with them. And now when, with reason, she fears it might happen again, this time with the child she really did get to hold in her arms, her old way of dealing with that kind of loss is all she has to fall back on. She has to pretend the child is no longer there to be seen. She has to act like he's already dead."

Now there was just silence on the line. He remembered a night before he was old enough for school when he awoke and went into the kitchen to get a drink of water. He had found his mother there. She was standing at the stove, gripping the oven door's handle and gazing upward and sobbing. When she heard him she had turned and forced herself to smile, wiping her cheeks with the back of her hand.

"So what do you think I should do?" he asked.

"I'm not worried about you. Another good belly laugh or two at whatever that scene in the cemetery was like and you're all fixed. One tricky part about being a good physician, I'm learning, is figuring out who's the patient. And it's not always the one who comes to you bawling and holding out his owie to be bandaged. Pretty often it's the one whose owie you can't see."

"Just a guess, but I wonder if I'm playing the less commendable part in that scenario," he said.

"It doesn't mean your owie's not real, my dear," Stephie said. "It just means we slap a bandage on it and shush your bawling and get on to the patient who's going to prove harder to fix. And in this case, assuming we've got a clear picture of her owie, nobody can help fix her but you."

"I see," he said. "And how am I supposed to do that?"

"You must have studied Latin," she said. "So *ad oculos*. Your answer's there in plain view. You have to convince her you won't do anything in the Army that's likely to get you killed."

"You know, Stephie," he said, trying to steer through the mix of admiration and anger she had once again evoked in him, "maybe you should just go back home and hand-feed baby calves. Looks like it's taught you a lot."

"Dairy farming has taught me some things that are good to know. The real reason we hand-feed them, by the way, is it evens out the chances all of them will survive. At some level, the cows may even understand that it's good for their own calf."

"I see. Well, remember how you ruminated on the positive value of nuzzling up to death the last time we drove to Pilot Mountain? And now you're saying I need to convince my mom I'll find a way to be hand-fed like a baby calf for the two years I'm in the Army?"

"That's for you to work out," Stephanie said. "Just keep in mind who the real patient is, who's suffered the deepest wound."

"Well, maybe while we're inside the tent you can help me reconcile the two conflicting lines of advice you're giving me."

"I doubt it. Even a doctor as good as I intend to be can't make life less complicated. When can you pick me up?"

~ * ~

Before he left Raleigh, Peter asked an Army recruiter what options he was likely to have once he was sworn in.

"None," the recruiter said. He picked up a big Styrofoam cup from the floor by his desk and spat tobacco juice into it. "The draft means you take potluck. Now, you sign up for three years and I can offer you choices.

That said, if you go as a draftee, there's always a chance that word will come down the Army needs people with this or that training or aptitude. They may ask you to volunteer, or they might cut you orders and say that's your job. But that's just part of the overall potluck picture."

"I'm certified to teach school," Peter said. "Any chance the Army could use that?"

"Could be," the recruiter said. "Could very well be. I know they're doing language training over in the Nam. But there's no way I could predict."

Peter called home and told his father the truth about his conversation with the recruiter. Then he asked to talk to his mother.

"Yes?" she said. Her flat tone told him nothing.

"Mom, I talked to an Army recruiter today, and he said the odds were really good my teaching certificate would land me in some sort of training job after I get drafted. He made it sound like it was practically a lock."

He heard three muffled squeaks over the phone. He guessed that she had her hand over her mouth. Then she said in a voice that suddenly sounded immensely tired, "I'm glad, Peter. I'm glad. Thank you for letting me know."

After he hung up, Peter walked off campus to the nearest liquor store. He bought a fifth of Jim Beam and got five dollars in change. He took the whiskey to his room and quickly drank more than half of it. Then he went to the pay phone on his floor and called Stephanie.

"Have you made definite plans?" she said.

"Just one, actually," he said. "I plan to make love to you until you beg me to stop."

"My, my. And I thought all I had to do was lie there and breathe."

"That was my first offer. You missed your chance at that one."

"Well, don't make promises you can't keep," she said. "I've never been known to beg."

He fumbled the little stack of three quarters he was ready drop into the phone's slot, and he swore while he tracked them down on the tile floor. As he fed the coins in, the receiver slipped from his shoulder and banged his knee, and he swore some more.

"Promise I can't keep, huh?" he said. "I've already made one of those today. There's no way I could promise it, even though I did promise it to my mom, just so she wouldn't go on thinking I'd end up like those two they hauled up there in the wagon and dumped them in the ground and covered them up fast. Am I making any sense?"

"Not a lot," she said. "How much have you had to drink?"

"About two-thirds of a fifth of Jim Beam, whatever that amounts to."

"Good way to finesse your problem, right? You'd better get to the point before the full effect of that much liquor kicks in and you pass out."

"Okay. What time early tomorrow can I pick you up?"

"Pick me up at noon by that little courtyard outside the med school entrance," she said. "And remember I said noon. You're not going to be in any shape to drive early tomorrow."

~ * ~

Next morning he felt surprisingly good until he got on the highway and the gong-like vibration that the sunlight set off in the backs of his eye sockets grew so jarring he had to pull off at the first rest stop and throw up. By the time he got to the second rest stop he felt good enough to try vending machine coffee. The coffee lay atop the burbling remnants in his stomach like the blackened crust on a lava flow, but it all stayed put.

This time Stephie wore shorts and good hiking boots with padded rims above the ankles, and she had a red bandana pulled over her hair and tied in back. She wore a knapsack that was so frayed and sun-bleached it reminded Peter of the baseball cap his father always wore around the farm. When Stephie climbed in the passenger seat, she unslung the knapsack and parked it between her feet on the floorboard.

"I've got sandwiches if you feel up to eating something," she said. "Just white bread and banana, with mayo."

His stomach gave a warning burble. "Maybe later," he said.

As they drove out of town, Peter fixed his eyes on the distant mountain, shrouded in a blue heat haze. After a while, he realized his silence must seem sullen.

"So you've got pretty good psychiatric chops, huh?" he said.

She gave her head a theatrical toss, ending with a brief, diva-like elevation of her nose. "Oh, how can I deny it?" she said. "I just hope I was right, or close enough to it to be of help. I'm no shrink. Just a would-be sawbones."

"I think you were right," Peter said, hearing in his own voice a resignation bordering on misery. "And it does help, as therapy. I mean, for my mom. But it sure as hell complicates what I'll have to try to do once I'm in the Army."

He described what the recruiter had told him and how he had distorted that information in the hope of comforting his mother. As always when he drove, Peter had moved the seat to its farthest-rearward position. Glancing toward Stephie as he spoke, he saw she was sliding downward in the seat, until her knees touched the dashboard and her head rested nearly halfway down the seat back. He had never seen or imagined Stephanie Ames in a slouch. Seeing her that way both excited and unnerved him.

She steepled her fingers above her stomach, still with that angling of the knuckles.

"And now you've got to try to make that hopeful fiction come true, and you might not be able to do that," she said. "Complicated for you, for sure. But what else could you do? You did the right thing, Peter, even if it's just the palliative thing."

They were close enough to the mountain then for Peter to distinguish the sheer rock face and the tree-feathered crest.

"So why medicine, anyway?" he said. "I mean, why did you take it up? And why, you know, here?"

"Why medicine?" She began to lightly tap her fingertips together. "Because I like fixing things. I figured if I could fix a milking machine, I could fix knees and elbows and shoulders. They aren't all that much more complicated, but they matter a whole lot more to people than milking machines do to anybody but a dairy farmer. And I was good at math. And there was the example of my great-granduncle, who could have used a lot of skilled fixing, which just wasn't available in his day. So those three things: wanting to fix people, being good at math, and Elisha Coddington, amputee extraordinaire."

"Yeah? Did you know him?"

"Oh, no. He died long before I was born. But I kept running across photos of him. There was a big, sepia-toned pair of them in our family doctor's waiting room. I have no idea why any physician would want patients to sit there and contemplate those, but there they were. One of them shows this little stump of a man with empty sleeves and pants legs and big, lugubrious eyes and a beard down to where his knees would have been if he'd had any knees. He's just sort of hanging there from a metal frame with padded pieces that run under his arms. The other photo shows him in his Union Army uniform, outfitted with artificial arms. I remember his beard reminded me of one of the dried-out tomato plants my mother would hang upside-down in our root cellar in October. God, those were awful pictures. But, you know, they made me wonder from an early age, couldn't I maybe do better with somebody in that fix?"

"Wounded in the Civil War, right?" Peter said.

She snorted, audibly and with enough force that he felt tiny moist droplets strike his bare forearm.

"Veteran for sure, but so far as I know, he came out of the war with all limbs intact. But then he had the poor judgment to sign on to reconstruct an un-reconstructible tract of south Georgia swampland. He had the further poor judgment to strike up an amorous liaison with the sister of a local un-reconstructible. As he should have expected, a whole gang of them ambushed him while he was riding home from a tryst. You almost have to admire the devilish clarity of what they had in mind. They aimed to send him back north as an object lesson in the perils of what he no doubt regarded as a patriotic calling with certain perquisites. They shot him multiple times in each of his knees and elbows. They shot him with such precision that amputation was pretty much an afterthought. He lived on into his nineties, just down the road toward Pelham from our place. Dear old great-granduncle Elisha, New Hampshire's beau ideal of the quadruple amputee."

Peter was going to tell her he wasn't dumb enough to buy that tale, though it was a pretty good one. But he held off when he saw her head was slowly shaking, as at some remembered grief. Her eyes betrayed no hint of mischief.

"So that's the why medicine?" he said.

"Not just medicine," she said. "Orthopedic surgery. Someday we'll be able to replace elbows and knees even on somebody as badly damaged as Elisha Coddington. Then no one in that bad a fix will have to live a life like his, dependent on charity and medical textbook publishers and country doctors on the lookout for waiting-room photos that might cheer patients up."

"Cheer them up?" Peter said. "But you said they were awful."

"Sure. But patients could look at those pictures and realize that, no matter how bad they felt, things could be worse."

"And then, why here?" Peter said. "So far south, I mean? Is it because the South is where old Coddington got shot up?"

"No, just the usual good reasons," she said. "A degree from the Boyd Hayden med school means something, especially in orthopedics. And they made it affordable for me to come here. So there's no very exotic reason."

Stephie drew herself upright again against the seat back. She untied her bandana and shook her hair until it streamed straight back in the wind through her window. When she half-turned her head toward Peter, strands of her hair flew so wildly about her face that she cupped one hand above her eyes and squinted at him, as though from a distance.

"Unless, of course—oh, how would some wild-eyed Romantic poet put it?" she said. She lifted her nose. Her theatrical pose was back. "Unless, my dear, years and years hence, my sojourn in the southern wilds will prove to have been all about you."

Twelve

Months later and half a world away, whenever Peter thought back on that day and night with Stephie on the mountainside, it was with shame, laughter, raging desire or a debilitating mix of all three. It didn't seem to matter whether he thought of it just as a single day and night or as a culmination of the half-year since he had first encountered Stephanie Ames in a hospital emergency room. Whether he took the longer or the shorter view of it, all he could see was cascading error on his part, and grace, sound judgment and tenderness on hers.

Peter had hoped for a close approach to backwoods camping. Instead, each site in the campground contained a raised, level surface of sand and pea gravel framed by landscaping timbers, and a sign declaring tents must go there and nowhere else.

"Don't you southern boys like to boast you lost your virginity with some smoking-hot Lula Mae in the tall weeds where only the young and the lusty and the pit vipers dare go?" Stephie said. "Well, it looks like you'll have to lose yours with prim little Stephie in a sandbox."

"What makes you think I have any of that to lose?" he said, and he tried to arch an eyebrow in a way he hoped would convey strength and confidence. He realized later he must instead have resembled one of the puffed-out blowfish he and Teddy had reeled in from Jennette's Pier and thrown back into the surf in disgust. Yet Stephie, in her way, honored his bid for credibility. She tilted her head and gave him the gaze of cool appraisal that he was still learning to prize as the most finely calibrated means he would ever have for measuring his own worth.

"We'll know soon enough about that," she said, smiling. "Won't we?"

He spread a groundcloth on the sand-and-gravel tent pad and dumped the longleaf pine needles onto it. He spread them enough to form bedding for two and laid the flattened sacks over the needles to hold them in place.

"That plus the quilt will make it soft enough," he said. "We did it this way when I was a Scout and we went camping down east where there's nothing but pines. The odor of those pine needles, that's something I just love."

They pitched the umbrella tent atop the pine needles. Peter unrolled the quilt inside the tent and asked Stephie to test the bedding.

"That'll work," she said when she climbed out. She raised her right hand in a three-fingered salute. "Scout's honor."

They hiked a trail that wound upward from the mountain's base. It circled the dome in the same tight loop they'd hiked in the spring, then ended with a steep, tricky descent that seemed to be mostly jagged rock. Before they were halfway down, Peter was limping and counting cadence by muttering "F, Q, fucking B." He picked up one short piece of downed timber after another until he found one light and smooth-surfaced enough to serve as a walking stick. Stephie stopped several times and waited for him to catch up, but she said nothing about this evidence of his unfitness for things his draft card claimed he was eminently fit for.

When they got back from their hike, he filled up his plastic jerry can with water from a spigot near the campground entrance. He opened a packet of dehydrated chicken à la king and cooked that and a pot of rice on his two-burner gas stove. By the time he was done cooking, his hands were shaking so badly that he spilled some of the chicken and rice as he spooned them onto two metal plates. Stephie sat on his folding camp stool and watched him with a smile of mocking tenderness.

"Feeling lightheaded?" she said. "Well, you haven't eaten anything since last night, have you? It must be that."

While they were eating, he frantically ran over in his mind all the advice regarding amorous behavior he had gotten from men his own age. He remembered with particular clarity a point that Cameron Duvall, their star running back, had harped on. A half dozen of the senior players had gotten together after the football team won its first home game after opening the season with an away loss. Peter had already had his surgery by then, and he wore a thigh-to-ankle cast, but that just sharpened his desire to be in on all team events. They gathered behind a tobacco barn around a little fire made with hickory slabs left over from curing season. They had pooled their pocket money and bought three bottles of sloe gin. The wretched, syrupy stuff packed enough of an alcoholic punch to fire their adolescent imaginations and libidos.

"Ru-uub that belly," Cam had told them, demonstrating with one hand the proper slow rotation. "When she tells you that's as far as she wants you to go, just ru-uub that belly. Keep on ru-ubbin' that belly. Ask her how far she feels like going then." Peter had planned to test Cam's method when he had the opportunity, which had not come with any of the girls he dated in high school or college. He had never gotten beyond being grudgingly granted access to nipples at a drive-in movie.

Peter had brought only the one folding stool with his other camping gear. Stephie had asked if he wanted to sit on it, but he had told her, falsely, that his knee felt better when he was standing. He was eating from the metal plate and mentally reciting, as if it were something from a user's manual, Cam's advice about how a girl whose belly was sufficiently rubbed would lose all restraint, when he looked across the campsite at Stephie. She was finishing the last few bites of her dinner, lightly scraping the bottom of her plate with the edge of her fork. She paused once to flick a wisp of her hair backward with her fingers to keep it out of her chicken and rice. When she was done, she looked off through the trees and seemed to listen to the slow, winding-down song of cicadas. The upward tilt of her eyes and the mild sadness in them told Peter that her thoughts were ranging in time, and that in her generous habit of mind she encompassed his history and future as well as her own. He reached once more for the adolescent fantasy of a female body overmastered by his passion, and supine beneath his controlling hand, and he found it had vanished like a snatched-away child's toy. He knew he would have to confront on terms that she, not he, would determine, this woman who knew all his limitations, all his penchant for plowing toward disaster despite red-flashing warning signs, and who yet was still here—very much right here—awaiting, as she had more than once told him with her noncommittal smile, "further evidence."

He began to hear a metallic drumming. It took him several seconds to figure out that his hands had again started to tremble and that the spoon he held in one hand was striking the metal surface of the empty plate he held in the other.

Stephie looked at him with that gently mocking smile. "Hey, mister tambourine man," she said.

"Well, I guess I'd better wash all this up before it gets dark," Peter said.

Stephie stood and, without a word, poured water from the jerry can into the pot he had used to cook the rice. She squirted detergent into the pot from a plastic bottle and lit a burner and placed the pot on it. She took Peter's plate and spoon from his hands and dumped those and the rest of the cooking gear he had used into the pot. Then she took his hand and pulled him toward the tent.

"You first," she said, pulling aside the tent fly.

"What if it boils over?" he asked.

"The dishwater?" she said. "It won't. You'll be out here again long before that could happen."

Peter's alarm must have shown in his face. Stephie threw her arms over his shoulders, and instantly he felt suspended—weightless and stripped of all senses except that of smell—in the blended aromas of mature, receptive female and chicken à la king.

"What old Doc Ames has in mind for you is a carefully sequenced course of therapy," she said. "The first treatment will likely leave you capable of some such menial chore as washing and rinsing dishes. Subsequent treatments, however—" She looked at him down that expanse of cheekbone so like the glacis of a fortress, and for the first time Peter saw a glimmer of ferocity behind the cool blue rationality of her eyes. "Subsequent treatments may not."

Long after Peter had stumbled out of the tent and washed and rinsed the cook kit items and stumbled back inside in a blissful daze, Stephanie paused partway through a therapeutic session. Peter felt he was floating on a cloud redolent of pine needles and of her panting breath trapped within the hair that draped his face. "I wonder," she said. She resumed her application of therapy for some amount of time—Peter had long since lost his ability to judge the passage of time or any interest in doing so. Then she stopped again. "No, I need to know this," she said. "Hand me the flashlight."

"Wha—?" Peter said stupidly. "You want—flashlight?"

Stephanie reached over his head, found his miniature flashlight and switched it on. The beam of light swept across her face and hair, and Peter felt a moment of astonishment at how much this passionate creature who had materialized from the darkness inside his tent resembled Stephanie Ames. A blanket lay bunched at their feet, and Stephanie drew it upward as far as his chest. She told him "back in a minute" and plunged downward beneath the blanket. Later, when Peter tried to sort out what had happened, he figured something in her training had told her she should grant a male patient this degree of privacy.

He felt her grip the part of himself she had lately been attending to in a very different fashion. She bent it back against his abdomen.

"Stephanie, what in the hell are you doing?" he said in a hoarse whisper.

"Hah!" she said. "Our dermatology text said men sometimes get those things there. And, son of a gun, here one is!"

"What?" he said, lifting himself on his elbows. "Here what is?"

"A sebaceous cyst. Right behind the head of your peckah. It's compact, very near the surface of the skin. Should be easy to get rid of."

"A what? And right behind my what?"

"Sebaceous cyst," she said from beneath the blanket. "It's like a zit, but the stuff inside it looks more like camembert cheese. And it's on your peckah. Isn't that what you southern men call it?"

"My pecker? I've got a pimple on my pecker?"

"Yep. You're a medical marvel. Listen, reach back with your left hand until you find the zippered bag against the wall of the tent, and then hand it to me," she said.

"No! God no, Stephie. You're not going to perform some kind of surgery on me with a flashlight and a pocket scalpel or whatever it is you've got in that bag. There can't be anything that urgent about getting rid of a zit."

Her fingers clamped tightly enough to force from him a sharp intake of breath. "Hush, and quit wiggling," she said. "All I need from that bag is an alcohol swab. Once I have that, this should take about five seconds."

He felt around behind him in the darkness, found the oblong zippered bag and pushed it toward her beneath the blanket. He heard the zipper open and a small tearing sound, and then he felt the cool dabbing with the swab.

"A pinch," she said.

"Good God, Stephie!"

A tiny fraction of his flesh felt caught in a powerful pincers, but in a few seconds, as she had promised, it was over. Again he felt the cool dabbing of the alcohol swab. Stephie emerged from beneath the blanket with the flashlight in one hand and what looked like a small white cylinder balanced on a fingernail of her other hand. She unzipped the tent fly and flicked the tiny cylindrical thing out into the darkness.

"What in hell did you use on me just now?" he said. "Forceps?"

"Fingernails," she said. "This saves you the embarrassment of going to a doctor, who'd have likely done exactly what I did."

She closed the tent fly and switched off the flashlight and lay down beside him, pulling the blanket up over them both.

"Is there anything I ought to do about it?" he said. "I mean, I don't know what I did to cause it."

"There's nothing you need to do," she said. "They're benign. But maybe it's a good idea to wash that area well from now on. So, let your motto be 'flip it and scrub.'"

"Sweet Jesus, Stephie, where did that claw grip of yours come from?" he said.

"Hand-milking," she said. "I could give you a demonstration of my milking technique if you like."

"You did that a few minutes ago," he said.

"Let's see if I can make it up to you," she said. "How about this, then? And this?"

When finally they peeled apart, lathered with the acrid sweat of lovemaking, Peter laid his forearm across his eyes. As his passion cooled and the sweat on his breast turned clammy, he felt he was tipping over some verge. The plunge toward despair came so suddenly it revived that morning's nausea. He shook his head, hearing the crunch of pine needles beneath the tent floor.

"Damn it, Stephie, this wasn't supposed to turn out this way," he said.

"You had it scripted very differently, didn't you?" she said.

"You bet I did. And it didn't include spending two years as an Army typist or mail clerk or something else menial but safe so my mother wouldn't order me a headstone with everything filled in except date of death."

"Well, if I were really being sententious and doctor-like, I'd tell you that when things fail to turn out the way you've scripted them, then change the script."

Peter peeked out from beneath his forearm. Stephie had raised herself on one elbow and propped her cheek on her hand.

"Oh!" Peter said. "Yes, I see! Scales fallen from eyes. All better now."

Peter could feel rather than see her tolerant smile, offset by the shrewdness in her eyes. "I wonder how far back in your life it goes," she said. "This tendency to become so mesmerized by a story line that you actually try to live it out. And if you can't do that, because you lack whatever fact-base the story line requires, then you count it as a catastrophe. Tell me, were you a very good football player?"

"No. I loved football, but—no. I wasn't at all good, really."

"Yet you count your injured knee as one of the great setbacks of your life. As if without it, you would have gone on to great athletic success."

"It wasn't just that, or even mainly that. Without the knee injury, I could have done ROTC—"

"Which would have led you to roughly the same point you're at now. You've been stamped with the coveted three letters—what were they again?"

"FQB. Fully qualified for battle."

"So, you're cleared for any sort of military duty, and all that remains is for you to choose—assuming the Army allows you some choice—between greater and lesser degrees of danger. The woman to whom you've sworn lifelong devotion has just inducted you into the society of the well-fucked. For lagniappe, she's smoothed out the sleek lines of your peckah. Yet you feel this has all turned out in the worst way possible. And why is that? Just because it veered from the story line you'd sketched out when you were fifteen?"

"What I wanted was, if I had to put everything else on hold for two years, I could honest to God go to a war," he said. "Now I've promised my mom I wouldn't. So I give that up, give you up, give grad school up, give up this job that I lucked into and now almost feel I was born to do. Bing bing bing goes the personal-choice slot machine. All lemons."

"I think you're short one bing."

"Bing, then."

"Oh, you'll get to the war," she said. He could feel, rather than see, that she was nodding gravely in the darkness. "You'll find a way, without breaking your promise. And I think you should go, since you want it so much. But beware of story lines, Peter, whether they're your own or someone else's. Check the fact base before you commit to any of them. Macro-scale, you can count this whole war as a ghastly example of failure to do that. Micro-scale—tell me, did you believe what I told you about why I set my sights on orthopedic surgery? I mean, that story about my great-granduncle, Elisha Coddington?"

"I liked it a lot. It shows you've got a whole different thing going on in a part of your brain. Different, I mean, from the slicing and dicing of clinical information that goes on in the rest of your brain."

"I see," she said. "You're talking about my flawless recollection of historical detail. Good, I'm glad that registered with you."

He laughed. "No, Stephie," he said. "I mean a part of your brain that's stocked with the kind of wooly stuff you'd find in a Flannery O'Connor story."

"And what if I swore my story was true? What if I said that I take offense at your cynical reception of it?"

"I'd say you were just miffed because you couldn't sell me a phony bill of goods."

"And what if I said that story was my entry at a med school Christmas party, where the competition was for the best 'why I want to be a doctor' story, and first prize was dinner for two at Vincenzo's?"

"Then I'd ask who got to share the dinner with you, and I'd be miffed it wasn't me."

"Well, it wasn't Gilbert, if that's your worry. Anyway, I wasn't ready to invite you anywhere for any purpose in that time frame, if you remember."

"That's all right," Peter said. "I think I'll take a night in a tent with you over the eggplant parmesan at Vincenzo's. That's a close call, though."

"So it looks like you've got a functioning tall-tale filter," she said, and once again he sensed rather than saw her grave nod. "Remember to use it. I suspect that shamelessly false stories abound among men ten thousand miles from home. They may feel immune from fact-checking—which they probably are, at that distance. They may think they can gain a lot from getting a lie widely accepted, even if what they want most is to convince themselves that they're something they're not. So use your filter. Watch out for the ardent desire of tale-tellers to be believed. Watch out too for your own desire to believe a tale that seems just too good, too urgently demanding of belief, to be a lie."

Stephie lay down again with her back to him. She adjusted the blanket, tugging one side of it her way but then patting across his chest to make sure he too was well covered. He heard the pine needles crackle as she settled into them, and then a long, exhaled breath.

"Do you wish we'd brought pillows?" he asked.

"No, I'm fine. Sleepy time now."

"Hey, Stephie? Do you know what we're having here?"

"Yes," she said, a little sharply. "We're having a late-night conversation about four hours before milking time, and I really don't do well at those."

"Pillow talk," he said. "We're having our first pillow talk. Without pillows."

He listened to her breathing. That's what I'd told her was all she'd have to do, he thought. Just lie beside me and breathe.

And listening to her breathe, and awash in the mingled aromas of pine needles and of this mysterious, passionate creature who was also, somehow, Stephanie Ames, Peter fell asleep.

Thirteen

Lulled by the thrumming "fuck you" cries of the geckos outside the villa and by the faint, rhythmic clanking of the wobbly ceiling fan, Peter was asleep, barely, when his roommate, Dan Beauchamp, returned from the night's movie and switched on the ceiling light. Peter sat up, rubbing his eyes and groaning.

"Oh shit," Dan said. "Hey, I'm sorry. I thought you were asking a question. You said something about a mistake."

Dan stood in the doorway, shifting his weight slightly from foot to foot, as he did whenever he felt he'd made some blunder. Peter figured the habit was a holdover from childhood, and he always instantly forgave Dan for whatever he'd done or said.

"It's all right, bud," Peter said. "Mistake? Oh, yeah, I was thinking about something my dad told me before I left home. Something about a medal he got when he was in the Army."

Dan switched off the light. He grabbed a towel from a coat hanger on his locker door. "When I get back, I'll leave the light off I and won't make any noise," he said.

"Okay, but that'll still cost you three Hail Marys. Plus a prayer of contrition for leading nuns astray."

"Get it straight about the number of nuns, okay?" Dan said.

"I remember it was in the single digits," Peter said.

"Yeah," Dan said. In the light that filtered in from the hallway Peter saw that Dan lifted one fist in feigned belligerence. "The single-est of all the digits," Dan said. He went down the hall toward the shower.

Almost as soon as they moved into the same room at the villa, Peter had felt a deep liking for Dan. He also felt he thoroughly understood him. Consequently, he had little interest in learning much more about him. Rabinowitz, whom he understood not at all, interested him far more. Peter valued Dan especially because of the one thing they shared: love for a woman and bitterness and fear because of the possible consequences of their separation from her. Dan was from Youngstown, Ohio, and his wife had dropped out of an Ursuline Sisters novitiate there to marry him. She was having a difficult pregnancy. After Dan learned of her obstetrician's insistence that she enter the hospital a week before her due date, he had hit the side of his sheet-metal locker multiple times, throwing it out of alignment with the clasp on the door, which made the door impossible to lock.

"At least you had the good sense to use the heel of your hand," Peter said after watching Dan assault the locker.

"Well, you do as much AAU boxing as I did, you learn to protect your hands," Dan said. Then he hit the locker again, this time with his knee.

After Dan left for the shower room, Peter lay back down and tried to drift close enough to full sleep for his father's voice to return. His father had driven him to the draft board office in town early the morning he was to be sworn in. They rode in the old Dodge pickup his father used as a farm vehicle.

~ * ~

Peter's mother had stayed home. After their embrace, she had gripped his elbows, held him at arm's length and, smiling up at him, had summoned up a game the two of them had played in his grade-school years. When she would come into his room to kiss him goodnight, she would ask him to quote a line from something he had read that reminded him of her. Then they would switch roles.

This time, she cued him to the game by giving her answer first.

"Here's my line for you, dear boy," she said. 'You might find recent events cast some light on it. It's from Othello. That play, you know, offers so many insights into both love and distortions of it. Ready? 'I humbly do beseech of your pardon, for too much loving you.'"

She hurried on, leaving Peter no time to respond. "And wouldn't you know, that's Iago speaking!" she said. "Distortion for sure, though not the one I attach in offering it to you. Quick now! What line from Shakespeare would you pick for me?"

Peter chuckled softly. "Oh, that's pretty easy, Mom," he said. "I think of that one just about every time I see you walk into a room. It's from Antony and Cleopatra: 'Age cannot wither her, nor custom stale her infinite variety.'"

The ride in the truck with his father telescoped backward in Peter's mind into the years of early-morning trips they had made to the roller mill to buy feed for their chickens or hogs or beef calf, or runs to the FCX to get their fresh eggs candled and graded. The truck was nearly as old as Peter. The steering column had what his father called the "shimmy-shakes," and the junkyard transmission his father had bought the previous year leaked fluid badly. Wincing in the sunlight that suddenly flooded the cab as the truck started down the long slope past a neighbor's cow pasture, Peter thought: This could be the last time I will look out through this grimed-up window, feel my spine twisted by these broken-down springs, smell the effluvium of the farts this truck seat has absorbed since before my feet could touch the floorboard.

As the faint clanking of the ceiling fan above his head blended with the rattle of the steering column in his father's truck, Peter remembered it was just after they had turned from their farm road onto the highway toward town that his father began to tell him about the day when slapstick error had saved him from a lifetime of regret.

"Do you remember, Pete, those times you asked me about that medal, that Bronze Star, you found in the desk? Remember I'd always say it was a mistake, or it was just luck? I never explained to you what I meant by that, never gave you any details, did I?"

"Yes sir, I sure do remember," he had said. "And no, you never explained."

"Well, it was both those things, for sure. It was a mistake to give me that medal. But what happened to account for it was pure luck—good luck, the sort you want to follow you around in a war. If you saw my behavior throughout that whole episode, you'd laugh your tail off, because it was ridiculous. That's one reason I just never cared to talk about it. But the whole thing, including the ridiculous part, added up to a tremendous stroke of luck, because of the bloodshed it averted and the grief and guilt it spared me. So I've always counted that medal as a sort of lucky charm. And if I'm ever going to fill you in on what happened, now's the time. Maybe it will do you some good where you're going, wherever that turns out to be.

"What led to it happened in August of forty-four, but it was almost half a year later, when we were camped in Thionville, France, that I learned I'd get a medal for it. The captain told me at roll call one morning that something that would look good on my uniform would probably catch up with us by the time we got to Germany. Now, if I ever deserved a medal for anything, it was for what we were doing right there in Thionville, so I figured the medal would be for that. We were building a camp for people who were getting freed from the places the Nazis had herded them into. Forced labor camps—or worse, as we found out soon enough. Places like Buchenwald, I mean, though we didn't yet know about those places, the death camps. Well, I had pretty good carpentry and plumbing skills, and I put in some fourteen-hour days knocking together barracks for the poor, desperate, beaten-down people who were pouring across the border out of Germany. Remember that story I used to tell about the Polish woman, and how I'd swipe loaves of fresh-baked bread from the chow tent and hide them under my helmet and take them to her, and how she'd slice that bread wafer-thin and serve it like it was cake? She was sheltering herself and her two little kids in an abandoned building outside our perimeter. A lot of the guys found ways to get rations to people like her, who were literally starving. After we got the barracks up and the people moved into them and the Red Cross started feeding them, there wasn't any more need to smuggle food to them like that.

"What we tried to do for those people in Thionville was the best thing I got to do in that war, hands-down. All that infantry training I flunked out of, all the days we had to wade through that godawful cold surf to hit the beach at Slapton Sands, and then turn around and climb back into those LCIs and do it again—all that was worth it for the privilege of helping poor, hungry people like that woman and her little children. If I'd gotten a medal for that, I'd figure I deserved it. Hell, I might have even put it in a frame and hung on a wall in the living room, and then you and Mom would yawn every time somebody asked about it and I started bragging about how I got it. But I didn't get it for that. I got it for something that had happened way back during the breakout in Normandy, something all I felt about was embarrassment and relief that I hadn't killed men who'd already been shot up and just wanted to surrender.

"I'd ferried an artillery major to the division command post in the rear, and I was headed back out to the forward area, where it was my job to stand by for any officers who needed quick transport to points up and down the line. Now, the forward area at that time was moving ahead several miles a day, and once I got to where my little transportation unit had been when I left it, I had to ask directions from an ambulance driver who was taking some wounded to a field hospital. By then we'd broken out of that hedgerow country, where usually you couldn't see what the terrain looked like for more than fifty yards in any direction. I saw what I took to be a short cut down a farm lane, because I figured it must connect to the larger road I was on, which I could see winding up a hill maybe a half-mile off. Well, that lane ran down into a little swale, and when the jeep came up out of that swale it made a lot of noise. Around a curve up ahead I could see a stone wall about shoulder-high, and behind that a little farmhouse built from the same yellow stone as the wall. And behind the wall I saw about a half dozen men from the shoulders up, and one of them wore a uniform shirt with shoulder boards and a couple of the others had on German helmets.

"Now, I know I've told you about that gun rack I'd rigged up for the jeep. I soldered some lengths of rebar together to make a frame about four feet tall, and attached a hook near the top of it on each side, and then I bolted that frame to the back of my seat. I could hang my M-1 on those hooks with the strap pulled tight, so the rifle couldn't flip off in rough terrain. If I ever ran into an ambush I could just hit the brakes and reach back over my head and I'd have my weapon ready to fire in a few seconds. I practiced doing that until I figured I had it down to minimal time and no wasted motion. And of course, when I saw those heads and those helmets behind that yellow stone wall, I figured the time had come. I braked hard enough to shut down the engine, and I pulled the rifle over my head like I'd practiced, and I drew a bead on the one with the shoulder straps, the officer. I remember thinking it was strange they just kept standing there without bringing their own weapons into play, but I was too caught up in my gun rack drill to stop and think through what that might mean.

"Well, there was one necessary element I'd never practiced, and that was releasing the safety. On the standard-issue M-1 the infantry carried, the safety and the clip latch were in different spots, and they operated in entirely different ways. But the troops who just kind of buzzed around the front lines without running dire mortal risk, people like clerks and cooks and jeep drivers, they didn't get that heavy-duty, thirty-aught-six M-1. They got the M-1 carbine. It was a nice little weapon, very lightweight, but on that carbine it was easy to confuse the safety and the clip latch, because they were both little buttons in front of the trigger guard, one button just ahead of the other.

"Course, once I'd drawn a bead on the fellow with the shoulder boards and reached with my finger for the safety release button, what I hit instead was the clip release. Those carbines had a banana clip that hung down below the breech, and the clip bounced off my leg and fell on the floor of the jeep with a big clunk. And now I had an unloaded weapon. The jeep had no doors that I could duck down behind, so there I was in a panic scooping up the clip and fitting it back into the carbine and expecting any second to have my head blown off by those Germans behind that wall. Well, once I got the clip back in and clicked the safety release button—the correct one this time—and sighted down the barrel, those Germans were still standing up behind that wall, but now one of them was lifting up a crutch, and another one was raising up an arm to show me it was bandaged from the fingertips to the elbow, and one of the ones who must have had a helmet on before was pointing at a big bandage on his head, and the one with the shoulder boards was flapping a little piece of white cloth. Trust a Nazi officer, I suppose, to make sure he had an almost-clean handkerchief handy to signal 'we surrender' should the need arise.

"And right then it bore in on me why those German soldiers were there, and what kind of awful thing I'd almost done out of fear and lack of time to think my way through to the reality of what I saw. Because a bullet, you know, never allows you that kind of time. The Germans had been using that little farmhouse as a field hospital. After our army broke out of that hedgerow country, we advanced so fast the Germans started leaving behind everything that would impede their combat capability, and that included their own wounded. So these wounded men had just been waiting there for American soldiers to come along, trusting they'd do the decent thing, the thing the laws of war called for: We'd see to their safety and medical care. And what I'd seen behind that wall was simply that trust in play. Hell, they must have thought when I pointed my rifle at them that I was just following military protocol. They probably figured a lot more American soldiers were headed up the lane right behind me and would come in through the gate in the wall and start triaging them and figuring out which ones could walk and how many ambulances they'd need for the rest. They probably thought that while all that happened, I'd go on sitting there in the jeep, sort of keeping them covered, just for the form of the thing. You see? Misperception on both sides, and it would have turned into tragedy if my fingertip had just found the safety release button instead of the clip release. I'd have blown that officer's brains out. And then the rest of them behind that wall would have gone for what weapons they had, and they did have some. Either they'd have shot me or I'd have shot more of them, or more likely both. I still don't like to think about it. It still gives me chills.

"Well, when I saw what the real state of affairs was, I put my weapon back on safety and got out of the jeep. I hung that carbine back on the rack and left it there, which was against training, but after what I'd almost done I just didn't want to have to touch the thing I'd almost done it with. I walked up to the gate in the wall, and one of them came over and unlatched it and waved me through. I could see that the one with the shoulder boards, the officer, was peering back down the lane and then frowning over at me and then looking down the lane again and then frowning harder at me. He'd expected, you know, that a whole company of American infantry would be following me up out of that little swale, so that he'd get to surrender to a captain at least. Now he was getting the picture that, if a surrender was in order, it would have to be to a private who couldn't even operate his weapon properly.

"One of the other men there spoke pretty good English. Later on he told me he'd picked it up before the war when he was a longshoreman in Hamburg and would hang out in beer halls with crewmen from English ships. He said the officer had volunteered to stay behind, claiming his rank would give him leverage to make sure the other wounded men got humane treatment. But from the way the fellow looked at me when he told me that—kind of conveying a wink, you know, but without really winking—I concluded the officer had simply had a bellyful of war. I figured he must have welcomed his wound, plus the chance to wave that little pocket handkerchief, as an honorable enough exit from it, at least in appearance.

"There were about a dozen other men inside the farmhouse who had more serious wounds, and two who were already dead. The flies were everywhere, a lot of them just walking around on those men's bloody dressings because the men didn't have the strength to shoo them away. I didn't see any extra bandages anywhere. I told the English-speaking guy I'd take him and the officer in my jeep to find somebody with enough rank to get a medical team in there as soon as possible. And that's what I did. The officer rode in front with me. He looked pretty old for a first lieutenant, which is what his shoulder straps said he was, and he wasn't making any further eye contact with me, maybe because he felt mortified at being ferried into captivity that way by an enemy private. The other guy wedged himself into that little space in the back, where he could have easily lifted my carbine off the rack if he'd wanted to. I didn't even have the presence of mind to take the ammo clip out of it until we were about a mile down the road. When I thought of that, I pulled over and got out and made sure I punched the right button and caught the clip as it popped free, and the guy in back just laughed a little and nodded, like he was pleased to see I'd gotten it right this time.

"We hadn't gone more than three or four more miles down the route that the ambulance driver had told me about before I found our transport company's tents. So that *oberleutnant* finally got the satisfaction of surrendering to a fellow officer, our captain. The English-speaking fellow was able to guide some corpsmen and an ambulance driver back to the farmhouse to take care of those wounded men. And I figured that was the end of that, and I was just desperately relieved I'd gotten through it without bloodshed, entirely by luck, of course.

"I didn't know better until the medal finally caught up with me. By then the war was over, and we were billeted in high comfort in Bad Tolz, in Bavaria, in a big *kaserne* that up until a couple of months earlier had been the SS officer candidate school. That's when I found out the captain's medal recommendation said I'd single-handedly captured sixteen German soldiers, including a first lieutenant."

Peter remembered that, when his father reached this point in his long-withheld story, the truck was approaching the big hill with the city limits sign at its foot. High above the hill's crest ran a row of aircraft warning lights atop metal spires that at a distance looked tinsel-thin. Peter had felt since childhood that the lights' continued presence at that height with such frail support testified to some sort of faith.

"So you can see, can't you, why I held off on telling you what lay behind that medal, beyond saying it was both a mistake and pure luck?" his father said. "I figured the whole story would probably just confuse you. But now, heading off to where you're headed, maybe you can get something useful from it. In a war—maybe outside a war too, but more so in a war—you need to be prepared for the lack of connection between what you try to do and what comes of it. A lot of people think war is like a game, where if you act in a certain way between the lines on the field, you can have a reasonable expectation of the outcome. But a war isn't like that. You need to watch out, too, for the lack of connection between what you think you see and the reality behind it. Just like I thought I saw a deadly threat behind that wall, and was completely wrong. And all I had to set me straight was the blindest of blind luck."

As the truck rolled down a tree-lined avenue through what had once been a tobacco baron's estate—heading for the single-story building where inductees stood before a flag and took the oath—the pavement ahead of the truck slowly faded into darkness. Peter, lying in his bunk, frowned with closed eyes. It mattered urgently, he told himself, which of two defective mechanisms, the steering column near his bad knee or the ceiling fan above his bed, was making that rattling sound. Then, just before he tipped over into deep sleep, he realized his mistake. Nothing truly mattered, he knew, except for what he was seeing now and the unseen presence at his side. He stood looking outward through a wide window high above the city. Someone warm and safe and beloved stood beside him, but he didn't turn to see who it was. Instead he gazed off toward the winking aircraft warning lights and the faint blue outline of the distant, solitary mountain.

Fourteen

Of the months after the bus to Fort Bragg disgorged him and the recruits it had picked up at a half-dozen other county draft board buildings en route, Peter could remember little about the strictly military part except disappointment. He remembered how promptly the Army fulfilled his father's warning that it would prove "profane beyond belief." He remembered with a mix of resignation and gratitude that he'd been able to deliver on those shot-in-the-dark promises he'd made to his mother.

The full-pack road marches, crawling beneath live machine-gun fire and middle-of-the-night guard duty shifts hadn't risen to the level of hardship set by the two-a-day football practices, often sandwiched around a couple of hours of hay-baling, that Peter had endured in high school. But about halfway through his nine weeks of basic training, word came down that college graduates could interview for teaching jobs at the Vietnamese air academy in Nha Cat. One of their two drill sergeants read out the notice at morning muster. It said those selected would teach Vietnamese officers and enlisted men the specialized English that would fit them for military training in the States. Peter interviewed with a fifty-ish civilian from the Defense Language Institute who told him the teaching was all "direct-method," meaning teachers used only English in the classroom. He said the only preparation they would get was a five-week course in methodology, plus a little orientation in the do's and don'ts of Vietnamese culture.

"Once you finish basic, you'd probably be in a holding pattern for more than a month before the next training class starts up," the man said. "That could work to your advantage."

"An advantage in that much dead time?" Peter said.

The man had a salt-and-pepper mustache cut flush with the corners of his mouth and the raffish smile of a man with something up his sleeve. He looked down into his coffee cup and tilted it to see how much coffee remained. Then he looked up again at Peter.

"You're a draftee, right?" he said. "If you come home from the Nam with less than six months left on your enlistment and a clean service record, normally the Army will give you an early discharge. They don't need your job specialty anywhere in the States, and it's not worth the Army's nickel to retrain a troop with so little time left to serve. Once you finish instructor training, you can expect a couple of weeks' home leave before you ship out. Normal tour in Vietnam for all branches except the jarheads is one year, but you'll have some discretion. You can probably get your rotation date set a few weeks beyond the one-year mark. Over there, the Army is getting the only good use they're ever going to get from you, right? Why wouldn't they let you stay on for a little extra time? Right? So do the math."

Peter did the math. "When do I have to let you know?" he said.

The man swirled his coffee. The trickster smile stayed fixed and his eyes narrowed a little.

"You're just what we're looking for," he said. "Strong college record, certified to teach. For us, the crème de la crème would be a guy with an ESL degree, but damned few of those turn up in Army basic training. So I'd say that if you sign this form right now, you're a lock." He edged the paper toward Peter's side of the desk and tapped a forefinger against the signature line.

"And how about if I wait?" Peter said. "What if I learn tomorrow that they need volunteers for a field I'm more interested in?"

"Like what?"

"I don't know. If I'm going to Vietnam, maybe I could get a little closer to the real action than being stuck in a classroom."

"Sure you could," the man said. "They need helicopter door gunners. I saw a poster this morning that said they have openings. Of course, you'd have to pass a flight physical. And you might want to check the mortality rate for door gunners before you sign on for that."

"Yeah, I'd like to check on that," Peter said. "So can I take a little time to do that, and maybe let you know in a few days?"

The eyes narrowed to a squint. "Like I said, you're just what we're looking for. But I'm here to sign up eight firm commits, right? You'd be the fifth to commit if you signed up today. Would I have any slots left if you came back in two or three days? I can't promise you that."

"All right," Peter said, trying to think of all the ways the options might play out. "Let's say I do sign this form, but down the line another opportunity opens up. Could I still switch?"

Beneath the salt-and-pepper mustache, Peter saw the glint of teeth, and the man's tone of voice shifted from wily to annoyed.

"My friend, this is the U.S. Army," he said. "At any given time, you've got about a quarter million little marbles bouncing around in a thousand roulette wheels, and who's to say which slot any of those little marbles will tumble down into? All I can tell you is that, of the men I've signed up as language trainers for Vietnam, so far as I know, every mother's son of them has ended up in that assignment."

Cerberus, Peter thought. Guarding the entrance to the underworld. Letting faint, shivering shades like me pass in, but letting none out. He signed the form volunteering to teach English in Vietnam.

Fifteen

When he glimpsed swirling dust motes through his half-open eyelids and heard the familiar sound of empty cardboard boxes being kicked around a concrete-walled room, the sound raised in Peter's mind questions—also familiar—about that room's distance from the one where he was just waking up and who or what was kicking the boxes.

"Holy shit, B-52 strike, and it's not even seven o'clock!" Dan said from his bed across the room. "Spooky must have stumbled onto something last night he couldn't handle, so he called in the big boys."

Peter opened his eyes fully and focused them on the wobbly ceiling fan.

"Hey, Pete, you awake?" Dan said in a near-whisper. Even groggy from sleep, Peter felt touched, as he always did, by Dan's fear he'd made some blunder. Peter glanced across the room at his roommate, who was sitting up on his mattress.

"'Here's death, twitching my ear,'" Peter said. "'Live,' says he, 'for I'm coming.'"

Dan's bedsprings creaked as he flopped back down. "What's that from?" he said. "Mother Goose?"

"Search me," Peter said. "It's the motto I picked off a list of options when I was a high school senior. It ran with my picture in the yearbook."

"Think we're following death's advice?" Dan said.

"If marking time counts as living, then sure," Peter said.

Peter heard a rapid tapping on one of the shutters over his window.

"Good God!" Dan said, swinging his feet to the floor. "Could that be death twitching our ear?"

"That's exactly what it is," Peter said. He unlatched the green wooden shutters and carefully swung one of them outward. A girl of about eight, wearing a blouse with a ring of red stars embroidered over the heart, stood on the screened porch outside his window, grinning at him. Her black hair was tied with pink ribbon into puppy ears and she was missing several front teeth. Her dark eyes gleamed with intelligence and mischief. Peter and the girl jabbed index fingers at each other and called each other fat—*"Mâp! Mâp! Mâp!"*—though neither was remotely fat. Then she turned and ran out the porch door, taking care not to let it slam. Her sandals slapped on the concrete patio. Peter knew that when she reached the street, she and two other children would climb onto a motorbike driven by a woman who taught at their school in Nha Cat. There skimmed lightly across his mind the thought that, if death ever did arrive at his window in the form of a beautiful child, he would open it as swiftly and gladly as he had just done for Huê.

Watching her as she rounded a corner of the officers' villa, Peter reminded himself, with a pang of jealousy, that however much Huê valued Dan and himself as playmates, she shared a deeper bond with Rabinowitz. More than once she had mimicked Peter by putting on his fatigue cap backward and his glasses upside-down, then slouching along the patio wearing a doltish grin. But she never mocked Rabinowitz. If Rabby emerged from his room at the far end of the villa and cast a meaningful glance in her direction, she would break away from whatever else she was doing and hurry off to sit beside him on a step outside the screen at his end of the porch. Rabby would appear to speak to her lightly at first, but then he would seem to outline for her some action plan, using dramatic gestures to clarify it. He would point at Huê, pump his arms as if he were running at top speed and then point at his room.

Once Rabby had brought some photographs with him onto the porch. As he was trying to explain to Huê something in one of the photos, he stood and made a motion of throwing something upward. Peter could tell it must be something substantial, since Rabby used both hands to throw it. He raised his hands to show that some obstacle of considerable height stood in the path of his toss. Then he shuffled quickly to the far side of the invisible obstacle, and pantomimed a gentle, two-handed catch. He went through this sequence multiple times, making the motions of tossing and catching more dramatic each time, then pausing to gauge the child's reaction. Huê's uncomprehending smile remained fixed. Finally Rabby put his hands on his hips and stared down at her, frowning. Then his frustration crumbled into laughter, as if he recognized that whatever importance this toss-and-catch held for him, it was impossible to convey it to a child—or perhaps to anyone.

Later, Peter had asked Rabby if he was sharing with Huê a secret rescue plan.

"An at-need rescue plan," Rabby said. "One I promised her will always be there."

"And what about the up-and-over part?" Peter said. "Please tell me you weren't explaining to her how the gecko cleared the fence."

"Don't be an ass, Peter."

"Good, I thought not. Well, was that a part of your at-need rescue plan she just couldn't get?"

Rabby stared at him for a while without answering.

"That was different," he said finally. "That was once a much-needed rescue plan. And, no, she couldn't get it. And you know, Peter, you wouldn't get it either. It worked well, though. Once."

"Well, was there some common element, then? I mean, that made you want to tell her about those two rescue plans back to back?"

Rabby's head bobbed slightly several times in what seemed an effort to stifle anger.

"Yeah," he said finally. "Razor wire."

"What? You mean barbed wire?"

"I mean razor wire with barbs sharp enough to inflict death by a thousand cuts on anybody who thinks he can climb over it or through it."

"But you hate barbed wire, Rabby. Christ, you had me bury two pieces of it because you hate it so much."

"Yeah. But to everything a season and a time. A time to bury barbed wire, a time to string it across your doorsill."

"You boggle the mind, Rabby."

"And you, Peter, display a failure of imagination. All too typically, I might add."

~ * ~

Peter remembered all of this as he and Dan pulled on their fatigues and took their M-16s and ammunition clips from their lockers.

"Arrogant S.O.B.," Peter muttered. "He's always got to get in a demeaning dig."

"Who does?" Dan said.

"Rabinowitz," Peter said.

"Oh, I don't know about arrogant," Dan said. "Sometimes I think Rabinowitz carries a heavy load."

"Yeah, sure. Our resident man of sorrows. Until he gets tired of that role and resumes the glide path to comfort and riches."

Peter and Dan headed for the street. They would not have a chance to eat until ten o'clock, when a food truck from the air base would pull up near their classroom building and they could buy sandwiches and coffee.

"Here it comes already," Dan said. Peter could see the sweat beading on Dan's forehead.

"Hot season clamping down," Peter said. "You know, some candy-assed poet once called April the cruelest month. And he'd never even seen April on the South China Sea."

It took Peter a moment to realize Dan was no longer beside him. He turned and saw Dan had stopped several paces back and was staring straight ahead.

"What the fuck?" Peter said. Dan gave him an annoyed glance and nodded toward the street, silently mouthing the word "there."

Peter saw an American station wagon ease up outside the gate of the compound across the street. He knew it as a CIA compound because everyone who lived on the street or worked at the air academy called it that. The station wagon's appearance left no room for doubt about the CIA connection. Apart from its fake wood paneling, the car's body was a lackluster swamp green, a color that reminded Peter of the axle grease his father used around the farm. Through the car's tinted windows he could see several heads wearing caps with bills. Another head, in a rear seat between two of the hatted heads, had a shock of spiky black hair.

"You ever see anyone go in or out of that compound?" Peter said.

"Never have," Dan said. "Well, yeah, but just the guards."

"Me neither," Peter said. "Here I'd been giving them high marks for secrecy. Then they drive up in that behemoth. The only way they could make it any more clear would be to have a sign on top, flashing 'CIA' in red letters."

Three Americans wearing civilian clothes climbed from the car. Two of them dragged out the man with spiky hair, a Vietnamese in a checked shirt with a black blindfold knotted at the back of his head. The Americans muscled their prisoner through the cast-iron gate and up the walkway to a two-story villa that had sienna-colored walls and a red tile roof. The man's hands were tied in front of him and his arms were pinned to his sides by a black cord that encircled his body above his elbows. After a helmeted Vietnamese guard bolted the gate from inside, Peter saw through the gate's bars that the two Americans, who were much taller than their prisoner, flipped him around and dragged him backward to the villa's door.

"Well," Dan said after the gate's bolt slammed home. "Looks like April might be a cruel month for that dude."

The station wagon, empty except for the driver and a man in the front passenger seat, slowly pulled away. Once through the checkpoint, the driver turned left on the intersecting road toward the air base. Peter saw, on the road shoulder ahead of the station wagon, a figure wearing a crush cap and wraparound sunglasses and straddling a parked motorbike. The station wagon eased to a stop beside the motorbike. The man in the passenger seat lowered his window, and the one on the motorbike leaned in to talk. After about a minute the car pulled ahead and the figure on the motorbike—insect-like with its giant black lenses instead of eyes—headed off in the opposite direction, toward the air academy. Peter saw the two little guards at the checkpoint salute as the man on the motorbike sped past them.

"Well, that could explain a lot," Peter said.

"That was Lieutenant Pham, right?" Dan said.

"Yeah. I'll bet he was parked there watching the spooks make their delivery, just to make sure it all went down."

"So Pham's a CIA informant, you think?"

"You've seen the crap he gets away with at the academy, right? Kicking recruits, pulling kids out of our classrooms? You heard about his toying with barbed wire shackles, right? He's just a lieutenant, for Christ's sake. Yet his commander does nothing to rein him in. Even Jesperson handles him with kid gloves. There has to be some reason. Would it surprise you if the CIA was able to put pressure on both Duong and Jesperson so a good intelligence source gets to go on rolling in whatever counts to him as clover? Especially if that clover is a complete so-what to the CIA? If all he wants is a nonstop open season to torment the people we're counting on to fight this war so that you and I can go home and—I don't know—lead more nuns astray?"

They crossed the street and stood by the CIA gate to wait for the next shuttle truck. Watch it, Peter reminded himself as they waited. This is not your business. Seven more months, big bird fly away. That's your only business. Or eight months, with extension. Then home free.

"As long as we're speculating—" Dan said.

"Let's not," Peter said.

"No, listen. Your connections add up, sort of. Do you see any connection running through the events of just this morning? I mean not just that blindfolded dude they dragged in there and Pham up the street watching it all, but that early morning B-52 strike too?"

"Oh, well, let's just step over there and rap on the gate and ask for a moment with the station chief and pop him that question," Peter said. "I'm sure he'll cut two-stripers like us in on a mere top secret slice of information like that."

~ * ~

Peter got to his classroom a quarter hour before his students would arrive. He always tried to do that. He wrote on the blackboard key terms from the dialogue he'd use in his first class. It was a conversation between a Huey helicopter pilot trainee and his instructor. The instructor tells the student the Huey's guidance system is called "the collective." The student asks why it's called that. The instructor says it's because you can use the collective's handle to do almost everything needed to fly the helicopter. Twist the part that looks like a motorcycle grip and the engine and rotor will speed up. Lift the handle and press a foot pedal and the helicopter will rise and hover. Once airborne, you can use the collective to drop the helicopter's nose and attain proper climb speed. Finally the instructor says, "See how many things the collective can do for you?" And the student answers, "I sure do! That's a lot!"

Peter wrote the terms "collective" and "motorcycle grip" and "rotor" and "pedal" and "hover" and "climb speed" on the blackboard. All the while, to the tune of "This is the way we go to school," he chanted through his clenched teeth: "This is the way we win the war, win the war, win the war. This is the way we win the war, without much risk of a gut wound."

Each day he would take up a new dialogue. When class began, he would read the dialogue slowly. Then he would repeat key terms while circling the room, to give each student a close view of his lips and tongue. He would read the dialogue line-by-line and have the students repeat it.

Finally he would have the students pair up and read the dialogue without prompting. To drive himself through this brain-numbing routine, Peter had tried, with some success, to be altruistic. If he thought mainly of himself—of getting through his year with a minimum of hassle and an unblemished record—he would intersperse the dialogues and drills with instruction in Beatles lyrics. If he focused instead on shielding his students from the likelihood of getting killed, he could plod on class after class, day after day, with the prescribed lesson plan. Whenever his focus slipped, his students would remind him of their stake in it. They would tolerate at most a ten-minute exegesis of "Hey, Jude" or "Yellow Submarine" before one of them would point out, "But teacher, we need to study for test."

On this morning, Peter's students had started to file in when Rabinowitz arrived on the last shuttle truck. Rabby's rust-splotched M-16 had a too-loose strap, and the rifle clattered against the wall of the truck bed as he climbed down. Through his classroom doorway, Peter saw the kind of narrowed, sidelong cast to Rabby's eyes that meant he found something vexing. Hoping to shoo Rabby off by ignoring him, Peter started chalking an extra word, "twiddle," on the blackboard.

"Did you catch the live-goods delivery this morning at the villa across the street?" Rabby said.

"Don't you have a class to teach?" Peter snapped. "I certainly do."

"Little birdie says there've been two late-night sightings of Pham over there. Gate opens, in he slips. Most recent entry was two nights ago. No witness to time of exit."

Peter's hand paused at the second 'd' of 'twiddle.'

"Birdie a credible birdie?" he said without taking his eyes off the blackboard.

"Two silver bars," Rabby said. "One of the captains in the villa next to ours."

"Well, crap," Peter said, slamming the stick of chalk down in the metal tray that ran the length of the blackboard. The chalk shattered, and the soft chatter of the students in the desks behind him ceased. Peter stared stubbornly at the list of keywords on the board.

"What makes you think I need to know any of this?" he said.

"Because somebody has to. As they say in the old schoolyard game of tag, you're it." Rabby turned away toward his own classroom. "I'll catch you later at the food truck, then," he said.

"Well, I don't think I'm hungry," Peter said. "Enjoy your soggy tuna sandwich."

For the next two hours, Peter taught on autopilot. He had grown steadily more adept at doing this whenever he had some preoccupying concern, such as the news his widowed grandmother had suffered a stroke but refused to let his parents bring her up from Alabama to live with them. For a time, what weighed on him most had been a jolting message from Stephie. In his five months in-country, Stephie had written him once every two or three weeks. In all but one of those letters, she gave only a crisp summary of events. Finally he had understood this was of a piece with her intolerance for chatter, and had willed himself to quit fretting about it.

Then came a letter that spelled out the history of her involvement with the man Peter had previously known only as the one he was so very unlike. He knew this unlikeness was the first, and for a while the only, reason Stephie had felt attracted to him at all. She'd written the letter in the same matter-of-fact tone as her letters about the responses she was getting on internships, or how her family's dog had lost a hind leg after getting run over by a brush mower hitched to a tractor. In this new, out-of-the-blue letter, she said she'd been a college senior slogging through advanced chemistry when the man teaching it came on strong to her. He told her he was on loan from Cornell, filling in for a professor on sabbatical. He told her he knew a couple of people in Cornell's medical school who could give her a thumbs-up on admissions. And, oh, by the way, his family had a getaway cabin in Vermont.

"He certainly looked the part of the Ivy League up-and-comer," her letter said. "Right down to the hound's-tooth jacket with leather elbow patches."

When the man disappeared after fall-term finals, all she could learn from the chemistry office at Cornell was that he was no longer on faculty there. A Cornell student government staffer tracked down a female chem major who told her he'd been denied tenure and had left town.

"She was brassy enough to ask if I was familiar with the décor in that cabin in Vermont," Stephie wrote. "She welcomed me to the club. She said his wife left him after finding out she was just another club member too."

Stephie said she learned the club included others at her own school. One of those women gave her the phone number of a doctor in New York who'd do abortions.

"It was a couple of weeks before I was sure I didn't need one," Stephie's letter said. "But if I had, I'd have gone. No hesitation. Do you remember how, after you told me how you felt about me, that I'd have to decide what to do or not do about it? Well, now you have to decide that too."

Peter found the letter so unsettling that, having read it, he'd threaded a new cloth patch through the slotted end of his gun-cleaning rod before he remembered he'd just cleaned his rifle. But the only reply he ever made was to instruct his mother two weeks later to have a dozen roses delivered to Stephie on her birthday.

Peter found he could allow his mind to work even on matters as highly charged as this without losing more than a slight edge in class. This was especially true when the task at hand was something as cut-and-dried as modeling the words of a dialogue and drilling his students until they could repeat it.

Once he'd shooed Rabby away and started the lesson, Peter quit trying to process what Rabby had told him about Pham's midnight visits to the CIA villa. Without his willing it, his mind leapt instead to the last time he'd seen Stephanie. It was in the students' lounge at the medical school, the day before his parents drove him to the airport for the first leg of his flight to Vietnam. He had seen little of Stephie during his two weeks of home leave before he shipped out. It had been October, and for all but a few days of his leave time she was away, interviewing for internships in orthopedic surgery at Dartmouth and Tufts and Vanderbilt. In the scant time she spent back in Weston-Carmel, she worked furiously to catch up in her classes. Before his final day of leave, he had seen her only once, when he took her to dinner at Vincenzo's. Otherwise, he had stayed home and helped his father winterize the plumbing. They had dug up the copper water line between the well porch and the house, disconnected it and then reconnected it a foot deeper in the soil, so it wouldn't freeze, as it had the previous winter.

On the evening before he left for Vietnam, he had sat beside Stephie on the same sofa where he'd first awkwardly spelled out his plan for a life together, and where she had let him know that, while that plan would never work, she was open to the possibility of finding one that might.

This time, when he sat beside her, she had looked at him in her frank, unblinking way, and for a while said nothing.

"I know this isn't what you wanted," she said finally. "And it's not what you had a right to expect. My spending so little time with you while you're home, I mean."

"I had no right to expect anything else," he said.

"No, you did have a right," she said. "But these little windows of opportunity to interview at top hospitals—if I don't act on them, they'll slam shut. And they won't open again."

"I've had a few recent lessons in the perils of letting windows slam shut," he said. "You told me some time back you don't do things by halves. I take that as a promise, and I want you to keep it. Just promise me one other thing as well."

Her eyes narrowed. Then her lips curled in amusement.

"I bet I know what that is," she said.

"In the next tiny sliver of time, whenever that might come, that you can make that hundred-and-eighty degree turn—"

"Yes, I promise," she said.

"—and devote the whole package to your humble servant for maybe, oh, a couple of hours, or maybe three hours if one of us lasts that long, and maybe you could even bring a little of your medical expertise to bear somewhere in there."

"Oh, shut up," she said, and she kissed him. It was a very light kiss, but she held it in place long enough for her breath to transport him back to their darkened tent on the mountainside.

And then she drew away, and suddenly her steady, unblinking gaze was back. And he read its meaning as clearly as if she'd used the words. She was ready to honor the thing she knew he had to do, and she expected him to go now and do it. She had already told him she couldn't go with him to the airport when his parents drove him there next day. And he had thought then: Maybe, after all, this is the best there is to be gotten from a war. Not any scars or medals. Not any self-knowledge of a deeper sort than you could likely delve down to in peacetime. Not any memory so searing that you can't bring yourself to talk about it, but that at least gives you the satisfaction of knowing it's yours alone. Maybe the best thing a war can bestow is a moment like this, when you and somebody you love look into each other's eyes and understand what each of you has got to do, and then you turn your eyes aside calmly, knowing you both will carry out that trust.

But to have had moments like that, and to have come away from them feeling clean and ready for all they seemed to promise, and then to end up like this, as a sort of schoolmarm in jungle fatigues—that was what caused Peter to rage, as he did now, on that entirely separate track in his mind, without any lapse in his rote drilling of students in the pronunciation of "collective" and "rotor" and "climb speed."

Instead of lobbing grenades, we lob vowel sounds, he thought. What's the closest I'm likely to get to hand-to-hand combat? Probably teaching them to distinguish "snakes and spiders" from "snacks and speeders." Hey, if I can get a whole class to do that, shouldn't I at least get a Bronze Star?

But then he thought of the steam from the bowl of soup wavering before Thanh's glistening eyes like the sulfuric vapors in the Sibyl's cave, as Thanh told him that Pham had come from the North, and that the other

Vietnamese junior officers disliked him as intensely as the American instructors did. Yet Pham enjoyed a privileged status with both Vietnamese and American commanders—and why was that? And he remembered how Thanh had turned in the soup kitchen doorway to remind him to tell this to his friend, because Rabinowitz needed to know. Well, then. Given this morning's strong-arming of that trussed-up, spiky-haired unfortunate outside the CIA villa, and assuming what Rabby heard about Pham's midnight visits to the villa was correct, wasn't it likely Thanh's information could clarify the little they already knew? And didn't that mean Rabby did need to know it?

When Peter had reached this point on one mental track, on the other, real-time track he found himself leaning to model vowel sounds for the trim, smiling, straight-backed major who had faced down Lieutenant Pham.

"Eeeh—aaah," Peter said, his lips forming a faux smile on the first vowel sound and an oval on the second. "Pe-dal. Pe-dal."

"Pe-eh—da-al," Major Hung said. The sprinkling of gray hair at his temples glinted like steel filings in the sunlight through the window as he nodded with each syllable. "Pe-dal."

And on that other track in Peter's mind, he heard the tap-tapping of Stephie's pencil. Then he imagined her voice, measured out as carefully as when she tried to unknot the mystery of his mother's threat to bury him in the idiots' row.

"You see, Peter, this little man has it within him to wade on and on through this tedious, childlike task, and then to step through that doorway and behave like a soldier. Isn't that what you've longed for—the chance to prove you could do that too?"

When the siren atop the language school's orderly room issued three staccato bleeps to signal the end of the first class, Peter shouldered his rifle and walked the two short blocks to the food truck. It was parked on a strip of pavement that led to the rows of sheds—each walled with mosquito netting and surrounded by sandbags—that served as barracks for the Veenaf cadets and for the lower-ranking students in the language school. Each morning the food truck brought pastries and sandwiches from the air base mess hall. The driver was a Vietnamese man whose smooth, expressionless face and sleek hair made the Mafia-esque nickname Guido seem a natural fit, so that was what the Americans called him as he handed over their cinnamon buns and coffee and took their military scrip at the truck window. A second and routinely longer line of men waited to make their purchases from a girl whose eyes, so like the luminous brown eyes of Natalie Wood, had earned her the nickname Natalie. Her finely articulated fingers reminded Peter of the slender, segmented branches of the redbud trees behind his home, where tiny purple blossoms would sprout each April. Peter spotted Rabinowitz near the head of Guido's line and mouthed the words "just coffee" to him. Normally, once men had made their purchases, they would step under a corrugated steel awning that served as an open-air break room, but Peter waved at Rabby to indicate they should walk back toward their classrooms.

Rabby handed him the coffee and peeled the waxed paper from his own purchase, a tuna sandwich. His rifle's too-loose strap slipped from his shoulder. When Rabby lifted his elbow to catch it, the top half of the soggy white-bread sandwich, deprived of the waxed paper's support, flopped over onto his knuckles. "Crapola," Rabby muttered. He turned his hand to position the flopped-over portion of the sandwich horizontally and crammed most of it into his mouth.

"Rabby, that was magnificent," Peter said. "Only a Princeton dining club could have prepared you to handle that with such aplomb."

Through the gap between two buildings, Peter glimpsed the guard post and swirls of perimeter wire, and he heard the caterwauling of a funeral procession.

"There are two or three of those a day lately, aren't there?" Rabby said, chewing.

"What, funerals?" Peter said. "I haven't kept count. Maybe a lot of people are dying. I hear there's still a war on."

Rabby licked his fingers. "Have you watched one of them lately?" he said.

"Funeral? Not since the day we were out there and screwed around with the gecko."

"Well, I pulled guard duty again last week. And you know what? Two funerals in three hours. Both times, there was an extra box in the wagon. One of them looked like the box you spotted, the one you said could be for small arms or ammo. But the extra box on the other cart was different. It was plenty big enough for a body. They'd painted it bright red, but with just one coat of paint. You could see through the paint it had 'U.S. Army Medical Corps' stamped on the side. Looked like the container for some sizable piece of equipment, like an operating table. And both times there were young guys bringing up the rear who didn't look like grieving family. No mourning bands on their heads. And you know what? One of those guys bringing up the rear both times was the same one that caught your eye when you and I were out there. The one with that bone-white scar."

This time Peter could not simply wait out the wave of alarm. It swept him up in its cold churning.

"And there must have been more just like the ones you and I witnessed," Rabby said, still calmly. "Funerals, I mean. With extra boxes and what look like extra young men trailing along, who might have something to do with whatever happens to those boxes inside the cemetery.

"Sweet Christ, Rabby," Peter said. "You're saying they're burying enough small arms and ammo in that graveyard to—"

"No, no, no," Rabby said, shaking his head. He carefully unwrapped one corner of his remaining half-sandwich. "I'm not saying that. Not yet, anyway. I'm just trying to identify bits of evidence that might add up to some pattern."

"You can't do that!" Peter said, grabbing Rabby's forearm. Rabinowitz made an oddly graceful ducking motion to preserve the balance he was trying to give the sandwich. "Haven't you reported this?

God damn it, this isn't something you can puzzle over for your private amusement."

Rabby shot him a resentful side-glance. "I wrote down exactly what I saw," he said. "I printed 'confidential' in all-caps on the envelope and handed it in at the orderly room. I checked by next day, and the E-Five at the desk said he'd already handed it to the colonel. Sound like enough? Now, if I knew where the trip-switch was for the alert siren, I suppose I could throw that."

Peter exhaled with relief. "No, that's enough," he said. "God, why didn't we think to report this when we saw that ammo box in the wagon?"

"Good question," Rabby said. "I think at the time you were distracted by concern for a lizard."

"Well, nothing bad has happened, has it? And now the matter's out of our hands."

Rabby squinted at him. "You say that like the greater good lies in dodging responsibility for any shit storm," he said.

"Yeah. I guess to that extent, I've acquired the military mind."

"But I'm free to go on collecting puzzle pieces, right? Good. I tagged you with some information this morning. From the way you reacted, I suspect you've got some information to tag me back with. And, who knows, it all might fit together."

"Well, you know Lieutenant Thanh, right?" Peter said.

"Sure. Mister Meds and Band-Aids. Day after Pham tried out his barbed-wire shackles, I hunted down his two victims. The kid he'd handcuffed had an infected wrist. Thanh cleaned it up, gave him some antibiotics. Thanh was a med student in Hue, you know that?"

"Yeah. He said that during Tet a year ago, six of his classmates were shot and dumped in a ditch," Peter said.

"Huh." Rabby was still paying close attention to his half sandwich, slowly unwrapping it and biting off an exposed portion as soon as it started to sag. "Wonder how Thanh could know that in such detail and live to tell it," he said.

"No idea, but that's what he told me," Peter said.

"Huh. Doesn't Thanh have a second job, at a hospital downtown?"

"Yeah, he works a night shift there. Well, for some reason, Thanh worries about your welfare. He's afraid you'll get your nuts crushed when you take on Pham's team in soccer. You're playing them next week, right?"

"He's worried what Pham might do to me?" Rabby gave a dismissive snort. "Well, thank him, but tell him I honed my defensive capabilities playing rugby on the Jersey shore. Anyway, it's just a game. Practice on the beach tomorrow, by the way. Want to give it a try?"

"Answer's still no," Peter said. "Thanh's concern doesn't seem limited to soccer, though. He thinks you need to know Pham comes from North Vietnam—Haiphong—and that he's been in the South just two years. Thanh sees some connection there with the special status Pham enjoys here. And maybe you know this piece already, but this morning Pham was up the street, watching the spooks deliver a trussed-up, wiry-haired little guy to the CIA villa. Pham talked to the driver after the delivery. Dan and I saw that on the way to work."

Rabby listened to all this with seeming indifference, slurping down two final bites of his sandwich. "Double agent, then, do you suppose?" he said.

Peter stopped and stared at Rabinowitz, who glanced casually back at him. Then Peter shook his head and laughed.

"God, let me guess," he said. "You're with CIA counterintelligence. They sent you over here undercover because they suspect their dingbat field crew in Nha Cat has been taken in by a North Vietnamese double agent. And, let's see, said double agent poses as a junior officer who torments air force recruits. Good so far? Your job here is to blow his cover and pin down which side he was with before the other side doubled him, and whether he got doubled once and then redoubled, and how one side or maybe both sides did the doubling. And of course your cover is you're a humble Princeton law student who landed the crème de la crème of all

Army Reserve placements, but responding to a wild hair, you requested a TDY assignment to Vietnam. Now how could it have taken me this long to figure out something as in-your-face obvious as that?"

Rabby chuckled and licked a final dab of tuna from a thumb.

"Pete, maybe you're sort of right about the what-I'm-supposed-to-do-here part," he said. "But you're wrong about the back story. No CIA taint there. It's way stranger than that. Sometime when you've got an hour or maybe six, I'll spell it out for you."

Rabby half-turned to head on toward their classroom building, but then he paused again, cocked his head and squinted at Peter.

"You know, Pete, I'm not the only one who feels a wild-hair sort of calling here," he said. "And I doubt I'm the only one who has a complicated back story to account for it."

"*Calling?*" Peter said. The incredulity he'd packed into the word crumbled as soon as he remembered why he had left his classroom and headed, as if by forced march, down to the food truck. He'd known then that he was risking further entanglement. And now, sure enough, it had snared him.

"Callings are for preachers and doctors," Peter said.

"No, they're just as much for streetwalkers or language instructors or high-grade double agents," Rabby said. His laugh contained an unaccustomed sour note. "Sometimes they're for out-and-out nutjobs too."

"To that I'd say, present company very much included," Peter said.

He saw that Rabby's eyes had the same sidelong, preoccupied cast he'd seen in them that morning. Then he noticed Rabby's sidelong glance was directed at him.

"I'm sure there are good reasons I chose you to tag," Rabby said. "Though if you asked me to spell them out, I couldn't. And now, without much wanting to, you've tagged me back. That's what a calling does, see? It calls, you follow, and whether you welcome it is pretty much beside the point."

Other instructors were starting to pass them, headed from the break area back to their classrooms.

"Oh, I feel a sudden calling!" Peter said. "I feel called to teach a dozen Vietnamese in ranks ranging from sergeant to major how to speak English just poorly enough to get recycled through the class level they're already in, but just well enough to avoid flunking out and getting sent out in the field, where they'd likely get killed. That's the calling I feel. Now how about you?"

Sixteen

The checkered soccer ball hung spinning in the sea breeze above the beach. Rabinowitz plowed after it, his torn black sneakers throwing gouts of sand against the pale, simmering sky. His green jersey with "United States" in white lettering across the front had turned a two-toned black with sweat.

The breeze carried the ball up the beach toward a scrub palm. In the tree's paltry shade, five little whores squatted drinking thick, black, cold-brewed coffee out of tumblers and passing photographs. The whores came to the beach each morning and washed their hair in a big stainless steel garbage can. Then they would brush each other's hair until the whole shimmering sheath, down to their hips, would respond to the slightest twitch of the head. They knew they could do things with their hair to Americans that they could never hope to do with their bodies. Wringing out their wet hair, they looked like ten-year-old children who had drenched each other at a pajama party.

Rabinowitz, his ponderous, streaming face set with a savage leer upward toward the ball, hurled two other players aside by their shoulders, tripped over a fruit seller's basket, careened with one arm outstretched, and tumbled backward—huge, pink-fleshed and hirsute—among the tiny, screeching whores.

By the time Peter could run down from the picnic shelter behind the beach where he had sat watching the soccer practice, the whores had gotten over their alarm and were pinching Rabinowitz and refusing to let him up. One of them held his head in her lap by the hair and showed him photographs. Down the beach, the other soccer players stood laughing and shouting obscene suggestions to the whores. The fruit seller, an old woman wearing a conical straw hat, gathered up her scattered melons and bananas.

Peter looked down over the shoulder of the whore who cradled Rabby's head. Her clothing was spattered with coffee. She held a photograph of what Peter took to be herself and the other whores kneeling in a temple before a Buddha with rows of smoking candles in front of it. The hold she had in Rabby's hair bent his head to the side. His eyes shut, Rabinowitz grimaced. Peter was reminded of the suffering of saints in woodcuts.

"Welcome to our shore, spaceman," Peter said. The whores looked up at him, tittering and showing their teeth like little, nervous, crop-toothed ponies. "Thanks for introducing us to the subtle courtship ritual of your planet."

"Peter," Rabinowitz said. His eyes were still shut, and despite his panting he sounded oddly drowsy. "Make these people let me go. I understand your amusement. But I would like now, please, to go about my business."

"About your Father's business?"

One of Rabby's eyes opened in an annoyed squint. "I recognize the poorly chosen Christian allusion," he said. "Now what's it supposed to mean?"

"Poorly chosen, huh? Well, I was just reaching for something to sub for your term, 'calling.' You need to pop up and chase a ball along the sand because your calling requires that, right?"

"Sort of. Yes. With, as I see, no help from you."

Rabinowitz tried to lift one leg. A whore sprang at it and clutched it joyfully. She pressed her chin against the kneecap and squeezed her eyes shut, as though the leg were a splendid, furry doll.

"Sorry, pal," Peter said. "You're theirs. You fell from the sky. Their claim would stand up in any court anywhere. For a fee, Harlowe and Rabinowitz will tell you the same."

The whores quit pinching Rabinowitz. Their screeches gave way to a melancholy cooing over his pink, reeking flesh, mottled with white splotches where they had pinched it.

"You've got to practice your game because your calling requires you to go *mano a mano* with Pham on the soccer field. Right? Neither side allowed barbed wire sidearms."

Both Rabby's eyes opened wide. The whore holding his head made horns of her first and little fingers and poked playfully at his eyes and made a suggestive sucking sound. Rabinowitz twisted his head and stared angrily past her hand at Peter.

"Pete, drop the idea that sly digs about barbed wire are ever going to strike a note that's acceptable to me or helpful to you," he said. "Okay? You got that?"

"Well, excuse me," Peter said. "I hadn't realized I was the one who'd foregrounded barbed wire as a subject of concern. But, oh my! I guess I was forgetting I was the one who buried those pieces of wire. But, oh my again! I guess I was forgetting you were the one who asked me to bury them good and deep."

Rabby grasped the hand in his hair and gently forced it to release its hold. The fruit seller shouldered the flexible pole bearing her balanced baskets of fruit and padded away up the beach in a scarecrow glide.

Peter shook his head and clucked his tongue sympathetically. "My, my, shouldn't this tender interlude tell you something?" he said. "Falling from the sky or falling through the center of the earth, as we all did, makes you equally a spaceman here, Rabby. A calling, your Father's business, whatever you want to name it—you think you can achieve it by falling on Pham?"

With a final, petulant wriggle that sent two whores skittering out of range of his flailing tennis shoes, Rabinowitz twisted free. He scrambled to his feet and stood swaying like a chained bear until he spotted the ball near the row of concrete-filled jet fuel drums marking the perimeter of the American beach. Then he glowered at Peter. The whores, gabbling and screeching again, threw fistfuls of sand at him, but Rabinowitz shielded his eyes with one hand and kept frowning at Peter.

"Fall from the sky?" he said. "Fine, look at it that way if you want. You like being stuck up there in the firmament, remote from earthly concerns? Fine. Take care you don't fall out of it too."

Rabinowitz lumbered toward the ball and nudged it into motion. Its checkered scales slithered across the sand with a light, sinister crackle. Rabinowitz shambled drag-footed after the ball and kicked it high into the bleached and simmering atmosphere, where its gleaming scales hung swirling.

Seventeen

Over his five months in-country, weighted by the tedium of his work, Peter's mind had sunk into a stupor that he found not entirely unwelcome, since it helped pass the time. Until Rabinowitz showed up and ruined this soporific rhythm, Peter's stupor was punctured only occasionally, in one of a few ways. One way was by rage at this futile hiatus in the life he had planned and trained for, a rage heightened by knowing he'd had chance after chance to avoid it and had turned his back on them all. Then there were the moments when he was struck dumb by beauty. It might be something he had seen every day for months that suddenly astonished him—something as mundane as a flowering vine clinging to a chalk-white villa wall. Or it might be a ballad sung in a stylized, quavering tone, heard through radio static. Listening to it, suddenly he would know, without having understood a word, that the song expressed the singer's love for her village. Her voice would paint in his mind the shadowed doorways of the thatch-roofed dwellings, the dike with a footpath along its crest, the paddy fields and beyond them the gleaming black backs of grazing water buffalo. Or the beauty that suddenly held him rapt might be a certain distant, slender figure in a fluttering *áo dài*, her black hair glistening within the shadow of her parasol. He had glimpsed her several times from his evening vantage point on the villa rooftop, each time thinking: It isn't fair, really, that so much beauty should surround me in a place I want so badly to escape.

He found a third sort of release from his mental numbness in the clarity that often came to him in the hour before full darkness. Increasingly, it was this clarity he craved. He could find it only when the sun had slipped behind the scrub-covered mountains that ringed the bay and its alluvial plain. It was in search of this hour of clarity that most evenings, barring foul weather or the wail of the security siren, he would skip the chow run to the air base and instead eat a bowl of pho at the Vietnamese soup kitchen inside the academy's gate, then walk the half mile to the street where the American instructors lived. He would climb the rust-coated rungs of the rickety metal ladder on an outer wall of the concrete and stucco villa he shared with Dan, six other privates and the sergeant who lived with Huê and Hien, the child's heart-stoppingly beautiful mother. As part of Peter's evening ritual, he would carry up a glass of rum and cola poured over two cubes of ice from the tray in the villa's fridge. Two cubes was the rule, since the fridge lacked a second ice tray. Sometimes Peter would also carry up one of the draftsman's pads his mother had mailed him, and a pack of colored pencils, and he would sketch the buildings that lined his street and those on a street about a quarter mile distant.

Several Vietnamese officers who worked at the academy lived on that more distant street, in homes of high-grade plywood and corrugated metal roofing their American fellow staff members had built for them on weekends. Laughably, the work qualified as a civic action project. Peter had signed up for it once. He'd assumed the poster's call for "volunteers to build homes for families in need" likely meant they'd help people move out of the shantytown just beyond the air base fence. He'd long wondered why those families—refugees from the bombing and shelling farther inland—had built there in the first place, and why they were allowed to stay. They lived in shacks of scavenged lumber shingled with flattened, multicolored tin cans that in the midday sun gave a glittering, carnival-like appearance. The shacks were bunched next to the jet fuel storage tanks, where they'd be blown to bits if a VC mortar crew hit a fuel tank. Peter thought that if he could help get those people out of harm's way, it would give him something worth taking away from this place—a small-scale version of what his father had brought home from his work on the refugee camp in France. If he could not have the thing that Teddy had—the thing a man would try to forget and could not—then at least he would have something worth remembering, something that would hold its value down the years.

When he had returned to his villa after writing his name on the signup sheet in the staff room, Peter had asked Rabinowitz if he'd sign up too. When Rabby muttered something about his lack of mechanical skills, Peter touted his own ability to teach Ivy League know-nothings how to recognize the business end of a hammer. Then Rabby had stared at him with what Peter later realized had been a knowing look.

"No thanks," Rabby had said at last.

"Oh. Well, then," Peter said. He had waited until Rabby was out of earshot before adding, "Fuck you too then, buddy. Fuck you very much."

The next Saturday morning, after he hopped in the back of the shuttle truck carrying the civic action volunteers, Peter had expected the truck to turn left toward the air base when it reached the head of the street. Instead, it turned right toward the academy. When the truck pulled up at the work site, Peter saw a man standing by a parked Vespa who wore the shoulder boards of a Veenaf major. The man, whom Peter recognized as one of Colonel Duong's aides, was the prospective owner of the home the volunteers were building. He bestowed a broad smile on the Americans. Then he mounted the motor scooter and left.

Throughout his five-hour stint, Peter worked with a controlled fury that drew puzzled stares from the NCO who acted as crew chief. Peter realized the whole project—building homes for Vietnamese officers on this street—served as pretext for a check mark in a "civic action" box on the advisory team's to-do list. He knew, too, that if anything, it widened the gap between Vietnam's citified elite and its war-ravaged peasantry, a gap that civic action was supposed to help bridge.

At first he said nothing to Rabinowitz about his disillusion with his day's labor, but somehow Rabby guessed.

"I could've told you, Pete," Rabby said. It was on their morning ride to school aboard a shuttle truck. "I checked the fine print. New homeowners were supposed to be service members with large families. I heard Jesperson had a cow when he found out they'd all be officers on Duong's command staff."

"Well, yes you could have told me, couldn't you, old buddy?" Peter spoke in the kind of scorn-laden whine, much heard in the rural South, that he had grown up detesting, but that he could turn on when he chose. "But you didn't."

Sometimes, weeks later, sitting on the villa rooftop in the evening, Peter would gaze at the half-dozen identical corrugated metal roofs, and he would shake his head at his foolishness in falling for that ruse. But on that same street there was an older house he loved to sketch. It engaged both the artist and the aspiring architect in him. Its mottled yellow stucco resembled the walls of Tuscan villas. The veranda seemed to him a happy afterthought of the builder, who'd made no prior load-bearing provision for it, yet must have felt its aesthetic rightness would sustain it.

At other times, Peter would simply contemplate his own narrow street. It was lined end-to-end with flat-roofed villas like his own—beachside relics of a vanished colonial empire. He could see its full length, from the strip of white beach sand marked off by rows of olive-colored fuel drums to, at the far end, the checkpoint where the street dead-ended against the wider road running from the academy to the American air base. One spindly, lost-looking Vietnamese private in an oversized helmet stood at either end of the checkpoint's barrier.

The sunlight would deepen from saffron to bronze. Finally, when the sun's rim dipped behind the mountains, it would shift to something else entirely. Peter never lost his sense of surprise, the momentary catch of breath, when the last rays of direct sunlight vanished. Everything that daylight had melded into a sort of garishly colored, simmering stew—features of the landscape, buildings, human figures—suddenly stood forth each with a distinct identity. It was as if, Peter thought, a bell jar had been clapped over the street and all the air sucked out. Thoughts and feelings that all day had surged through his mind in an undifferentiated stream sorted themselves too, into the trivial, the significant and the possibly dire.

After he got back to the villa from watching the soccer practice and losing patience with Rabinowitz, Peter climbed to the rooftop and sipped his rum and cola. His time at the beach had taken up most of the hour he liked to spend on the roof. He'd been up there for only a few minutes when the sun disappeared, the bell jar plopped into place and it struck him with the force of revelation that the two little guards at the checkpoint up the street would likely die in any Viet Cong ground attack.

A ground attack aimed at the only worthwhile target, the CIA compound across from Peter's villa, would have to roll in at the head of the street. From his rooftop vantage point, Peter could see that a couple of mortar rounds lobbed from inside the cemetery could easily take out the checkpoint. There were other Americans billeted on streets near the air base perimeter, but none of those streets had a checkpoint. Peter had never heard an explanation from anyone in a position to know, but it seemed obvious that the only good reason to have a checkpoint on this one street would be to give the CIA agents and their guards a few minutes of advance warning.

Day after day Peter had trudged home past the checkpoint, noting with weary indifference that the pimply, scared–looking faces of the soldiers at either end of the barrier always seemed to be the same two. But now, with the sun gone, there swept over him a wave of the feeling he sometimes had for his students, when he thought how their lives were being borne who knew whither by the crosscurrents of this misbegotten war.

"Poor little buggers," Peter said. "Canaries in the coal mine."

During his evening hours on the rooftop, Peter rarely let his eyes linger on the intricately colored little structures inside the cemetery wall. Everything else within view he could understand and, in some measure, embrace, but not those ... he wasn't even sure what to call them. Tombs, he supposed, though they looked more like outlandish dollhouses. The cemetery wall stretched for nearly a quarter mile along the far side of the road leading to the academy. Beyond the wall, the tombs were crammed together so tightly that, like Rabby, Peter wondered how they found room for new burials. And now, studying the cemetery more closely than ever, Peter wondered where the boxes of mortars and grenade launchers and ammunition were being buried, and whether any Viet Cong attackers would likely blow a breach in the wall or simply climb over it once they had taken out the checkpoint.

He had begun to wonder whether Viet Cong who hit the jackpot of a CIA compound would bother to sweep up the available chump change—a few dozen American technical instructors—when he heard someone clatter up the ladder to the rooftop. It was Rabinowitz.

Peter could see that since leaving the beach, Rabby had paused only long enough to swap his torn sneakers for flip-flops and grab a can of beer from the fridge. Sodden with sweat, Rabby's green jersey swung from his torso like chain mail as he climbed the last rungs. Peter knew Rabinowitz must have come to the rooftop simply because he knew that he, Peter, was up there. On fine evenings, other men might come up, especially if a Spooky gunship was pouring down minigun fire beyond the mountains. Whenever someone already on the rooftop shouted down the news of a Spooky sighting, Peter, too, would usually climb up to watch. But Rabinowitz was no fan of combat-related spectacles. Besides, Spooky wouldn't come out until full dark, and it was at least a half-hour short of that.

At first Rabby seemed indifferent to Peter's presence. He pulled an aluminum-frame folding chair from the stack of them leaning against the cistern's concrete wall. In his weariness, Rabby knocked from its nail the fine-mesh fishnet that the villa's NCO, Sergeant Winfrey, kept there to dredge insects and other gunk from the rainwater inside the cistern. The cistern's top was screened with small-gauge chicken wire, but bird and rat droppings would fall through the wire and bugs would get in through cracks in the concrete. Water from the cistern flowed into the villa's sinks and showers. Peter kept his mouth and eyes shut when he showered, smiling sourly as he thought of how that might prove the closest he would get to a tale of personal hardship in a combat zone.

Rabby returned the net to its nail and muttered "crapola," still as if he hadn't noticed Peter.

"Doesn't merit an oy vey, huh?" Peter said. He felt surprise and shame at his sudden desire to needle Rabby and, if possible, drive him away.

"Oh, no," Rabby replied evenly. "Far from it." He unfolded his chair beside Peter, dropped into it with a sigh and propped his sandaled feet on the low parapet at the roof's edge.

"Like so much in life, it's a matter of degree," Rabby said. "A first principle of law—language too, I'd say. Know how much firepower you can bring to bear, and understand which targets merit the full weight of it."

"Like a faggoty-looking lieutenant merits your kicking him in the nuts?" Peter snapped. "As a 'necessary first step,' I think you said, toward fulfilling this calling you can't even spell out? I can tell you one thing you'll take a step toward if you attack a Vietnamese officer. An Article Fifteen. But then, maybe you don't sweat small stuff like that. Maybe a blotched service record will mean nothing to you, back in the world. Maybe it wouldn't even count as a blotch, in the Madison Avenue Machine Gun and Polo Club, or whatever your by-invitation-only reserve outfit calls itself. I wouldn't know. I never got the invitation. I never had my name on a brass doorplate, either. I don't know what the world looks like from the Harlowe and Rabinowitz office suite."

For at least a minute, Rabby said nothing, and he didn't look at Peter. Here it comes, Peter thought—without any clear idea what it was likely to be. He took a nervous sip from his rum and Coke.

"Do you have any idea what my name means, Pete?" Rabinowitz said softly. Then, answering himself in the same barely audible voice, he said, "No, of course you don't. Couldn't."

Is that all he can muster? Peter thought. He snorted so hard that droplets of his drink spattered his glasses.

"Well, let me take a whack," Peter said, laughing. "I'm sure it means different things to different folks. Let's see. To some clients, it must mean an estate plan so airtight that no castoff spouse can crack it. To others, it probably means a lawsuit that lodges so many claims only a fool would spend what it cost to disprove them all, so the defendants throw up their hands and settle."

While Peter was speaking, Rabby's head rolled slowly backward, and he shut his eyes. There was just enough sunlight left to glisten from his black ringlets.

"Thanks, I guess, for endorsing the firm," Rabinowitz said. "But I meant what the name means. Like, from back in time. But never mind—"

"Well, sure I know," Peter said. "In Warsaw or Danzig or whatever the hell part of Poland your ancestors felt compelled to clear out of, it meant son of the rabbi."

Peter felt his own words hang motionless in the rapidly cooling air, until finally Rabinowitz, still in that soft voice, said: "Odessa, actually."

"Odessa?" Peter said, quickly sifting through his scant knowledge of Jewish ethnography and drawing a blank. "I thought Rabinowitz was strictly a Polish name. In Ukraine, wouldn't it be—I don't know—Rabinovych or something like that?"

Rabby lifted his head, opened his eyes and gave Peter a look of mild surprise.

"Pete, you're exactly right," he said, still in that quiet tone. "Exactly right. You know, for a man whose range of professional, personal and may I say ethical concerns would fit on a pissant's eyelid, you sometimes display an impressive breadth of knowledge."

The barb would have caused Peter to flush with anger had Rabby uttered it an hour earlier, before the bell-jar effect of approaching darkness brought on its sorting-out of his thoughts and emotions. As it was, Peter felt content to merely feign rube demeanor, rubbing the back of his neck with one hand.

"Well, ya' know, city boy," Peter drawled, "on those long summer days of my upbringin', after you'd picked down the last row of snap beans, sometimes there just wasn't nothing better left to do than, ya' know, set in the shade with a glass of sweet tea and a thick tome on the history of East European Jewry."

Rabby threw back his head and uttered a single "Ha!" Compressed into it, Peter realized without wanting to admit it, was a warmth of heart that escaped Rabby at unguarded moments.

"So," Peter said. "How did your great-grandfather or whoever it was, get from Danzig or the shtetl or wherever he started out all the way to Odessa?"

Rabby looked off toward the mountains' faint lingering silhouette. He drank the last of his beer and positioned the can carefully between the edge of the parapet and the sole of one flip-flop. He crushed the can, let it fall to the rooftop and stared at it for a moment. Then he looked off again toward the mountains.

"It's complicated," he said.

Eighteen

Sitting in the rapidly cooling evening air on the rooftop, waiting for any light Rabinowitz might shed on the complications surrounding his ancestors' trek from Poland to Odessa, Peter heard a mosquito's whine. He spotted one of the green plastic cups containing citronella candles that the men kept on the rooftop to make any lengthy stay there tolerable. He placed the candle on the parapet, and Rabinowitz handed him a matchbook.

"Actually, I mean my full name, Pete," Rabby said. "How the first name got paired with the last."

"Pardon?" Peter said.

"Look—how many Jews do you know named Tony?"

Peter stared at Rabby's hulking frame as the absurdity of the question sank in. When he finally spoke, he tried to file the hostile edge from his voice.

"Rabby, I suppose I knew you had a first name. If I knew what it was, I wouldn't have thought one thing or another about it. Now, if you'd told me your name was Tom Pete or Joe Bob or some other backcountry name common among my childhood friends, I'd have thought, 'hmmm, now how did that name get paired with Rabinowitz? Does that mean pinheads everywhere end up with the same names, even if they're Jewish?' But Tony?"

This time Rabby's single snort of laughter seemed more distracted than heartfelt. He lifted the edge of his T-shirt. Without looking down at the pack of cigarettes wedged in the waistband of his shorts, he tried to fish one out. He fumbled the cigarette and it fell to the concrete rooftop. Rabby's hand hovered in the air for a few seconds, then dropped to the arm of his chair. His eyes shuttled as if he were studying the line of the mountains' crest as it merged into darkness.

"Antonin," Rabby said at least. "It's Antonin. Actually more a French name than Polish. Though for a long stretch of time, French names were much in vogue in Poland. But whether French or Polish, it is, my friend, most certainly not Jewish. Now, how do you suppose a goyish name like Antonin found its way into a family of Polish Jews? And why do you think it's stuck there, in both its masculine and feminine forms, for two generations?"

Peter gave up trying to keep the acid out of his voice.

"Look. I'll concede that, aside from your family name, I don't know how any name got attached to any human, animal or mineral in Poland at any time, ever. So save time and cut to the story."

"We-ell," Rabby said. His head lolled backward with his eyes closed. In the flickering candlelight Peter saw a pranksterish smile cross his face. "It's the story you want, is it? Not just the Q-and-A. Not the canned version, but the story? Well, the question then becomes how far back do we—"

"Hey, hey!" Peter said, his eye snagged by downward-angling streaks of light over the distant mountains. They streamed from a slowly circling point in the sky toward a fixed point on the earth below. It was as if a giant lariat were being slowly twirled by a hand on the ground. All that could be seen of the lariat was a connecting rope that consisted, Peter knew, of minigun rounds, with every fifth round a glowing red tracer.

"Hey guys!" Peter shouted, loud enough to be heard by anyone on the patio between his villa and the one that served as an officers' quarters next door. "Spooky's out tonight!"

Peter strained to catch the sound of gunfire, but the lumbering aircraft was too distant to provide a full sound-and-light show. The first time Peter saw Spooky, soon after his arrival in Nha Cat half a year earlier, he had assumed from the aircraft's snail's-pace circling that it was a helicopter. Later, while he was riding in the bed of a shuttle truck during a lunchtime run to the air base, one of the other men had pointed to an aircraft parked on the tarmac. Except for the tan-and-olive camouflage paint, it looked to Peter like an outdated, propeller-driven passenger plane. That, the other man explained, was Spooky. It was a military adaptation of the old DC-3 airliner, chosen because it could slowly circle a fixed target hour after hour. Spooky could keep it up all night, if commanders wanted to rain down death for that long on a patch of ground the size of a baseball diamond.

No matter how many times Peter saw Spooky, and no matter the revulsion he felt when he caught other glimpses of the war's hideous face—a hooch maid's wail when she learned her husband, an infantryman, had been killed, or an Army sergeant's gleeful description of the "ears-for-beers" game he and his men played out in the boonies—still, his pulse quickened and he felt the same deep thrill whenever he watched the gunship at its slow, silent, mesmerizing work in the distant darkness. Somehow, the certainty of death within the target area added to the purity of that feeling. It was, Peter understood, as much a response to beauty as what he felt when he glimpsed the distant figure in her fluttering áo dài. But the girl's beauty was merely that; it had no dark substratum. Spooky's beauty, he felt, was heightened by its lethal underpinning. And, feeling again the impulse to plunge as deeply as he could into this war, he would think: I could have been out there, manning one of those miniguns. Damn it, I ought to have been out there.

Hearing a metallic clatter from the wall where the ladder hung, Peter turned to see who else was climbing up. Three figures stepped one after another onto the rooftop. It was too dark for Peter to make out their features at that distance, but he could see a bristly protrusion from the upper lip of one of them. He knew that must be one of their villa mates, a Louisianan named Emmet Doucet who cultivated a mustache of grander dimensions than he could get away with stateside. By the time the three men reached the cistern wall to get lawn chairs, Peter was able to make out the captain's bars sewn into the lapels of the other two. Both, Peter knew, were Air Force officers who lived in the villa across the patio from his. He recognized one as a navigation instructor at the academy. He was very tall, and his high forehead—stubbornly pale despite the tropical sun—and his large, luminous eyes always reminded Peter of Boris Karloff.

The other officer, a much shorter man, Peter knew only as someone who had twice drawn his attention by behavior that at first struck him as priggish but that, once he pondered it, he had grudgingly admired. The first time was during a marathon showing of porn films at the officers' villa. All ranks had been invited. Peter had gone over about midnight. The room was so packed he had to stand outside a door and could see only a narrow slice of the screen. He settled for standing on tiptoe to survey the faces in the room, all of which seemed frozen in a slack-jawed stupor. Then this little officer stepped through a door in a far corner and wedged his way through bodies that were packed in so tightly he had to hold his toothbrush and toothpaste tube above his head with one hand. He didn't glance at the screen and was clearly intent only on getting to his own room. The second time was at a showing of the film "M.A.S.H." in Colonel Jesperson's staff room. The timing of the little captain's exit made it apparent he took issue with the depiction of hijinks by medical officers at a field hospital in Korea. But, just as during the porn extravaganza, his face showed no ire or condemnation. It just looked like he'd decided there was somewhere else he'd rather be.

Doucet unfolded his lawn chair beside Rabinowitz. The two officers stood for a few moments farther along the wall toward the ladder, gazing off toward the distant, circling gunship.

"He's only firing one minigun now," the navigation instructor said, leaning toward his companion and speaking in a near-whisper, as if concerned he might tip off the enemy. "Maybe he's trying to flush them out before he cuts in with the other two guns."

Peter noticed the quickened pace of Rabby's breathing, and from it he realized that Rabby had started to seethe.

"Remarkable display of gallantry, don't you think?" Rabinowitz said in a loud, mock-jovial voice. "And bear in mind, they're entirely unprotected from those spear-wielding peasants below, save by aircraft armor, flak jackets—and oh yes, the distance of several thousand vertical feet."

Doucet chuckled and spun between a thumb and forefinger the whiskers above one side of his mouth. It was a nervous habit, and it gave his mustache a perpetual uneven appearance, pointed at one end and frayed-looking at the other. Peter liked Doucet for his quirky disavowal of all things military, and for what he took to be a bayou-bred mixture of merriment and pain in his small, sparkling eyes.

The Karloff look-alike captain turned toward Rabinowitz and seemed to weigh how to respond.

"Well, the term peasants might fit, but for sure they're not carrying spears," he said. His voice was calm, explanatory, not unfriendly. "Shoulder-fired SA-Sevens, more likely. Without as much suppressing fire as they're putting down now, an aircraft moving that slow would be a sitting duck."

"Certainly, it's worth waiting to see if the merchants of death pay out in yet more handsome coin," Rabby said. He had dialed down the edge and volume of his voice, but there was no mistaking his sardonic intent.

"Now those—what to call them?" Rabby said, "Those knights of the circular death-dance. Their idea of valor would have seemed very strange to my namesake. Who in fact, Peter, was born in a shtetl. You're right about that part. Though as I told you, it's complicated. She grew up, lived her whole life, by a very different idea of valor. Died in full possession of it. I suppose you could call it the last full measure kind of thing. But actually, no, you couldn't call it that. Because for her, valor couldn't have meant anything measurable. For her, it had to be something high and bright that perhaps you could reach up and touch just once in a long life. If you could do that, then your life would have been worth living. For her, valor was entire and indivisible. You couldn't parcel it out.

"Now, for those fellows out there—if valor means anything to them, it's not only measurable, it can actually be counted. You can measure it by the number of hours under enemy fire, the number of minigun rounds fired, the number of bullet holes in your fuselage, the estimated number of enemy killed. All those numbers will probably go down in a log book in a debriefing room by the flight line tomorrow morning. Once the numbers reach a sufficient sum, they'll add up to a citation, maybe a medal, certainly a step toward promotion. And Antonina—Antonina would have understood none of that."

"Antonina?" Peter said. "Your ancestor, the one you're named for, was a woman named Antonina?"

Rabby laughed briefly, without mirth. "There's one of us now in each of two generations since Antonina was killed," he said. "My dad's sister— Aunt Nina, the crazy, half-Catholic kibbutznik. And then me."

"Wait—killed?" Peter said. "Antonina, the one you're named for, you say she was killed?"

Rabby sighed. "Gunned down, saber in hand," he said, a theatrical flourish in his voice. "Whether she was shot by Greek sailors, Russian dock workers, Cossacks, there's no way of knowing. My great aunt was there and saw it, but she was just five years old, and she wasn't sure what they were. Odessa was an ethnic mixed bag, and once a pogrom got going it was hard to sort out who did which bit of killing."

Rabby's story had snared the two captains' interest. They slid their lawn chairs closer to Doucet's. The Karloff one leaned into the faint circle of light cast by the citronella candle.

"Let me get this straight," he said. His voice was still polite but it had a skeptical edge. "Your ancestor, this woman who was killed. She was a

Jewish woman in Odessa in—around the turn of the century, I'm guessing. And she was armed with a saber?"

"The year was 1905," Rabby said. "October, to be exact. Yes, this happened in Odessa, and yes, Antonina swung a saber. Moreover, she used it to good effect. But she wasn't Jewish. In her sector of the world, it would be hard to imagine anything more decidedly not Jewish than a Polish noblewoman."

"What?" Peter said. His mind spun through surprise, confusion and the impulse to laugh before it came to rest on denial. "You're telling us your Jewish great-grandfather skedaddled all the way from Poland to Odessa only to hook up with a Polish baroness or something once he got there? You're telling me I ought to be able to look at you and discern a blond, blue-eyed ancestry? Oh, c'mon, Rabby!"

"Look, Pete, did I not tell you it's not that simple?" Rabby said. His voice had a peevish, lecturing tone. "You threw it up to me that it might not be in my personal best interest to take on Pham—that I run some risk in trying to stop a petty sadist from inflicting on our recruits what amounts to, well, torture. Torture that's likely to bring on sunstroke. Not to mention the broken ribs and the ruptured nuts he dishes out on pretty much a daily basis. Nor the torment he had in mind with those barbed-wire cuffs. I made the mistake of telling you my name was a clue. And now, speaking of outcomes I'd rather avoid, you leave me the choice of either telling you as much of the story as I can—the bits of it I know, hoping they might give you an idea of the whole thing—or standing accused of lying. So?"

"So?" Peter repeated. "So what?"

"So shut up and listen!"

Rabby carefully lifted one foot from the rooftop's parapet. He drew it slowly upward while peering intently at his ankle. Then he swatted a mosquito that had braved the cloud of citronella smoke to land there.

"We have just one photo of her. Possibly taken at the dacha of one of her Russian benefactors. She's already old in that photo. About seventy, I'd guess. She's standing not quite in profile but with one shoulder angled toward the camera. The colors in the photograph are all a sort of pastel blush. I don't know enough about photography in that period to tell whether the colors were in her face and clothing or added after the fact. Still, I feel pretty confident about her eyes. Gray, like Athena's. Peering down at the camera with that backward tilt of her head, as if mild disdain were her M.O. She's wearing the kind of gown you'd expect to see on a woman who still enjoyed the patronage of men of wealth. There were still some number of such men, even when she was old. Because she'd been discreet, you see. Once she entered that phase of her life—she was already twenty-eight when she realized it had become necessary—her beauty and her bearing quickly won her several benefactors, patrons, whatever you want to call them. But unlike other women who took that path, she never played off one against the others. She'd always apprised herself of where the boundaries were, and she never overstepped them. The men remained grateful to her for that, and I suppose they were willing to do many sorts of favors for her because of it, even when she was old. But she never asked for much. For herself, she only wanted the means to pursue the life she had chosen: suitable clothes, a good, small house with a parlor, a carriage and team, entrée to the circles where she could not only look the wives of her patrons in the eye but could actually smile at them. There was only one larger favor that Antonina ever sought from the men. It might have been pretty difficult to deliver, but to their credit, they did deliver it for as long as it lay within their power. And—I guess you could say to her great good fortune—it did lie within their power for exactly as long as it took for her to reach the point she'd been aiming at all her life."

He shook the last cigarette from his pack and Peter lit it for him. While Rabby had been talking, the tracer streams from Spooky's miniguns had disappeared, then reappeared further north. Now, instead of a single stream of tracer rounds, there were at least two. Peter guessed that onboard spotters had pinpointed a more promising target, and Spooky had shifted position and opened up with more of its three miniguns.

"You could think of that point Antonina was aiming at—I prefer to think of it—as the intersection of two arcs," Rabby said. "Arcs of moral commitment, both aimed at the preservation of life. Arcs that leave a lighted trail even at the distance of a hundred-thirty years." He waved his lit cigarette out toward the circling aircraft, invisible above its tightly focused streams of tracer fire. "Arcs that couldn't be more unlike those murderous vectors out there."

"Oo-ooh, geometry!" said Doucet, chuckling. "Arcs and vectors! Spooky's got a circumference going on out there too, Rabby. You better find a way to work that in."

Rabby went on as if he'd heard nothing. "One was the arc of charity," he said. "Her father had committed himself and her both to that as soon as she was born. So you could say she didn't choose that one. But she did become sole possessor of it at age twenty-seven. That happened on the day she ran from her father's shipping agency—that's where she was spending all her days then—and found her father and Meir Rabinowitz standing back to back in the doorway of Meir's house. Her father was holding his cavalry saber. Meir must have been armed with some ready-to-hand weapon: a meat cleaver, maybe, or a pitchfork. When my great aunt Dalia was old enough to listen and understand, Antonina told her about that day. She said both men were bloodied, and one of Meir's earlobes was dangling by a shred of skin."

"Earlobe?" Peter said. "This ancestor of yours had a hacked-off earlobe?"

The Karloff captain shot Peter a glance of pure annoyance.

"He did indeed," Rabby said. "Dalia told me Rachel made some effort to stitch it back."

Peter shut his eyes and shook his head. "This is it, isn't it?" he said. "This is that six-hour back story you warned me about. God, how could I let myself get suckered into this?"

The Karloff captain burst out in the kind of modulated roar that Peter had learned to recognize as one hallmark of an effective officer. He pointed a finger first at Peter, then at Doucet.

"You will both of you kindly—or not kindly, I don't care—shut the fuck up and let the man continue!" the captain said. The roar ceased instantly when he spoke to Rabby.

"This woman's father and Meir Rabinowitz were standing there bloodied, you say?"

"Yes, both cut up," Rabby said. "They'd been fighting off a gang of drunken Greek sailors who were celebrating Holy Week by roughing up Jews. That was about all that particular pogrom amounted to. There wasn't much actual killing that time. When Antonina moved to take the saber from her father's hand, she saw that his arm hung limp. Then she saw how one eyelid was half-closed and how his whole face on that side sagged. And when he stared at her as if he didn't know who she was, she knew he couldn't make good anymore on the pledge he'd made for both of them when she was born. She knew she'd have to make good on it on her own."

"Aren't you short an arc?" Peter said acidly. "You said there were two, and one's charity. The other one's got to be valor, right?"

Rabby sighed. "Pete, you want the story? Well, quit getting in the way of it. As I said before, for Antonina, valor wasn't something you could claim as your own—something you could capture if you just charted the right trajectory. Valor was something that maybe you could reach up and touch once in a long life, but it didn't belong to you or to anyone. It was too high and too pure for that. The other arc—the one Antonina knew, as soon as she took that saber from her father's palsied hand, that she'd have to follow to the day she died—was sacrifice. She'd make any sacrifice needed to protect Meir Rabinowitz, his wife, his children, even all his descendants insofar as she could affect their destinies. She would do that even at the cost of her reputation. Even at the cost of what most people would call her virtue. Even at the cost of her life. And she paid that cost. She paid with all three."

"And those first two prices she paid, her reputation and her virtue," said the navigation instructor. He had pulled his folding chair close beside

Doucet's. It struck Peter that their two faces in the citronella candle's flickering light resembled the Greek masks of comedy and tragedy. "Are you saying she became a—"

Rabby cut him off. "Antonina became one of the most desired and famed courtesans of her place and time," he said. "And given that we're talking about a go-to resort city in Tsarist Russia in the middle of the nineteenth century, that's clearing a pretty high bar."

"Well then," the captain said. "Doesn't that make her a, you know, a—"

"A prostitute?" Rabby snorted. "If you were a man of means or noble blood or even ordinary discretion, you wouldn't have dared to call her that in Odessa in that era. And if you'd ever seen her, you probably wouldn't have thought it either, given her beauty and the aura of nobility that seems to have struck every man who ever laid eyes on her. What men of power and wealth felt for her is quite clear from her correspondence. My father's family salvaged most of the letters those men had written her. Brought them to America two years after she was killed. Prostitute? If the mere question of payment is the issue, consider the coin she required. As I told you, she never wanted for housing or clothing or access to the highest tiers of society. But marriage would have secured those things for her as well. What marriage could not secure for her, but life as a woman loved passionately by some of the most powerful men in Odessa could, was what amounted to a protective cordon around the household of Meir Rabinowitz."

Nineteen

On and on Rabinowitz unscrolled his story of bravery and loyalty that overleapt centuries-old barriers of caste and hatred and fear. He waggled his sandal-clad feet, propped on the concrete parapet with what looked like keen satisfaction when his tale took improbable but well-crafted turns. Several times he waved the glowing tip of his cigarette like an orchestra leader his baton. It was as if, Peter thought, Rabby was conducting an intricate musical passage in mocking counterpoint to the stupifyingly slow gyrations of the gunship, with its downward-angling streams of tracer fire forever converging on a single patch of earth where, as the eye might convince the mind, nothing might ever again live. The same tale told by a different Jewish voice might convey a broad humanity that had stayed stubbornly intact past pogroms and deportations, even past the sortings into those who could work and those fit only for obliteration. But this voice, Peter fumed, could hardly be a farther cry from one with such earned moral weight. This was Rabinowitz.

"But those connections, of life to life, start in Poland," Rabby was saying. "And starting there—the first thing, the essential thing if you're ever going to see Antonina clearly, is to catch a glimpse of her mother. Of her father, too, of course. But the mother comes first, as mothers tend to do, I suppose, for their daughters. But the mother I can see only dimly. Very tall and not given to smiling, in my image of her. An unvarying expression of fearless appraisal. Not scorn, mind you—just calm, gray-eyed appraisal. Antonina, of course, had no memory of her mother, though I'm sure she had a clearer image of her than we could ever have. It's probably useful to picture the mother and father both on horseback. I suspect Antonina herself thought of them that way. It was on horseback that they would naturally have fit into her dreams, given the parts they'd played in the revolt, and especially in their escape from Warsaw. Her dreams must have lingered on the single stone cross standing by itself in a tiny fenced plot. It had to be well away from the huddled gravestones of the shtetl cemetery. The people there needed to leave their own cemetery room to grow without ever coming too close to a Christian grave. Her father had told her how the people had found space for a grave, and how they'd found, too, enough space in their mistrust of all things Christian to put a cross on it. And in dream she must have followed her father and Meir as they rode on through the snow, her father with his cloak drawn tight across his mouth and knotted at the saddle pommel, breathing downward onto his newborn child's head, hoping that would keep her from freezing. Riding on that way until they reached the next shtetl, and the next. What?"

As Rabby was speaking, the Karloff captain leaned in still closer, pressed his palms together and wordlessly, very slowly, moved his steepled fingers in a line from left to right. Rabby looked at the captain with a puzzled frown. Doucet started laughing.

"He means he thought you were on board with the plan to tell it straight," Doucet said. "You tell a story like my maman. Throw all the puzzle pieces out on the board and say, 'Here you go, Boo-Boo! Have fun now!' Maman gets you so tangled up in the who did what where and with whom the year before Great Aunt Mathilde fell off the trawler and drowned, you don't know where you're at."

"Well, it sounds like your maman understands that any story told true to life is just that, puzzle pieces on a board," Rabby said testily.

Doucet twisted a corner of his mustache and either smiled or winced—it was always hard for Peter to tell which. "Remind me, man—what is it you're gonna be back in the world?" Doucet said. "A lawyer, right? Ask a jury to follow along while you spell out why they ought to award Great Aunt Mathilde's relatives triple damages because—"

"All right, all right," Rabby said. "Where to start, then? Well, at the risk of confusing matters further, we have the matter of identical names. So there were two Antoinettes. One was Antoinette Tomaszewska, a teenage girl who took part in a cavalry charge on Russian troops. She was one of a handful of Polish girls who did something of that sort in the revolt. And at least in legend, she did such a convincing job slashing left and right that the male cavalrymen toasted her after they'd all galloped back to their own lines. Trust the nineteenth century Polish gentry, I suppose, to have something of a respectable vintage on hand to toast with and fine glasses to drink it from right after a cavalry charge. So, that's Antoinette number one, Polish heroine of the fighting in 1831.

"Antoinette number two was Antonina's mother, Antoinette Tarnowski. Not a figure of legend, except that she became one to her daughter. Certainly a brave woman, though. She followed her husband, a career soldier named Konrad Tarnowski, throughout the campaign. Then, once the revolt was crushed, she escaped with him, and with Meir Rabinowitz, through Russian lines. So, here we go: events of the story all neatly lined up, whatever that might do to its heart and soul. I should tell you frankly that I don't have any better authority for some of it—most of it actually— than my great aunt. But her word is enough for me. I don't know how else to explain all the other parts that I'm certain of, right down to that moment seventy-five years later when Tarnowski's daughter tottered through a doorway and brought the blade of his saber down on the throat of one of the Greeks or Cossacks or whatever that drunken, murderous gang happened to be. Now—where was I?"

"You were giving us the quick and dirty on Antoinette number two, and then you veered off-course by about a century," Peter said wearily.

"Right," Rabby said. "So, two Antoinettes. It seems that at some point during the nine months that the Poles held out, Count Tarnowski, who was a cavalry officer, actually encountered Antoinette number one. It wasn't at the moment she led that fabled cavalry charge. Still, she made a strong enough impression on him that he could describe her, years later, to his daughter in terms that made just as strong an impression on her. And as my great aunt remembered the stories that Antonina told her when she was little, a single female figure seemed to ride through all of them on horseback. At some points, this figure—her name was always Antoinette—was standing in the stirrups with her raised saber flashing in the sunlight and her horse outpacing the rest of the troop until it collided with the Russian cavalry. At other points, Antoinette and her husband rode side by side at a fast canter as their regiment decamped barely ahead of enemy pursuit. At still other points, the woman and her husband rode slowly through a darkened forest in a thick fog, while a third figure led them on foot.

"Now, proceeding still in linear fashion, that third figure: Meir Rabinowitz. Individually not a person of historical significance, but part of a group that—note the immense sacrifice—gave up their beards for the privilege of fighting the Russians. Some Polish Jews, even today, take pride in remembering them. Meir Rabinowitz, a hick kid from a shtetl about a day's ride east of Warsaw, was one of about two hundred fifty students at the Warsaw Rabbinical School who volunteered for the Polish army around the end of 1830. And there were other young Jews, hundreds of them in fact, who wanted to fight. After some harrumphing about whether to allow Jewish blood to mingle with the blood of Poles on the battlefield, the Polish commanders decided Jews could enlist, provided they shave off their beards. Jews who refused to shave could only serve as a home guard.

"So off came Meir's beard. Some of the students were as young as fifteen and probably had nothing yet to shave. Meir was about twenty-three, so he might have sacrificed a pretty lush growth. I suppose the citizens of Warsaw got treated to the unaccustomed sight of beardless rabbinical students mastering countermarch and by-the-left-flank commands outside their windows that winter. Drill was all that Meir and the others could do at first, because the army didn't yet badly need them. That was a heady time, I'm sure. Volunteers poured in from every sector of Polish society, from gentry like Tarnowski to the rakers of pigsty muck. Together with the regular soldiers, but still minus the Jewish volunteers, they added up to enough of an army to bloody the Russians' noses several times running.

"It's a forgotten war today, but for a time the Poles did well enough, and the tyranny they were fighting was brutal enough, that crystal wine glasses were being clinked in drawing rooms in Paris, London, even New York and San Francisco, in toasts to the Polish patriots. Nobody came to their aid, though. The balance-of-power nervous Nellies in Berlin and Vienna and Whitehall saw to that. When things got desperate, the Polish commanders finally made good on their promise to absorb beardless Jews into regular units. And the Jewish students did well enough in the scrum of combat that Count Konrad Tarnowski, for one, started to see past differences of class and religion. With him, and I'm sure with some others, it was at first just the familiar story: Another man's mode of addressing God seems less offensive when both of you are getting shot at, especially if the other guy stands next to you and shoots back at the enemy. Meir Rabinowitz ended up fighting pretty much side-by-side with the count. And Meir must have been more than just a pretty good soldier for a Jew. He must have been pretty good by any standard, because Tarnowski latched onto him, made him a sort of adjutant. And something else that turned out to be important: Regardless of army policy, Tarnowski couldn't care less about the whisker length of a man who could fight. So his soldiers kept their bayonets either sheathed or fixed on their muskets, rather than whetting them and shaving once a week. And the beards started to grow back, on Meir and the rest who were old enough to sprout them.

"By late summer, the Poles had been driven back on Warsaw. Most of what was left of their army was looking for the nearest border they could cross with some confidence they wouldn't be pitched right back over it to the tender mercies of the Russians. For the Jewish fighters, of course, no such border existed. There were a lot of Jews next-door in Prussia who felt quite comfy in what they perceived as their assimilated status—it would be another hundred years before Jews in Germany got un-deluded about that. But in 1831, the Prussians, including a lot of those assimilated Jews, were just as interested as the Russians were in keeping those scruffy Polish Jews confined to what they called the Pale of Settlement. And the Pale ended at the Prussian border. So there was nowhere west of Poland for the rabbinical students to go.

"For a while, those young Jews had been dispersed throughout the army, but by the time the Russians closed in on Warsaw, the rest of the army had pretty much melted away. That left Meir and the other Jewish soldiers as a marooned remnant, and for a few September days they fought on against the Russians through the same streets and alleys where a few months earlier they'd drilled with broomsticks and axe handles instead of weapons.

"And Tarnowski stayed on and led them. I doubt he'd shucked off all the centuries-old bigotry—at least not yet. Given the trust he'd placed in Meir Rabinowitz, Tarnowski was probably destined to wind up leading that bunch of no-longer-beardless young Jews in the last-ditch battle of a doomed campaign. He was a professional soldier, after all. And he had to know that if this wasn't the end of life for him, it was at least his last chance to lead men in battle.

"He tried to send his wife to a place where she'd be as safe as he could make her anywhere in Poland. She was pregnant, maybe four or five months along by that point, but so far she'd refused to leave him. She and a few Jewish women were bandaging wounds, using whatever cloth they could scrounge or tear from their own clothing. But finally Tarnowski sent her off to the estate of some elder kinsman. That wouldn't have taken her very far—just a day's ride or so outside the city. But since the kinsman had taken no part in the revolt, the Russians had no cause to blacklist him. So Tarnowski hoped that would be enough to make her safe.

"Of course, he was right to try to send her away. There was nowhere anymore that could be called behind the lines, no camp where he could leave her in any semblance of safety. This was just street fighting now, and if she stayed near him she'd be as likely to be cut down in a volley as any of those young Jews who were firing and falling back block by block. So he sent her off on the horse she'd ridden throughout the campaign. He sent along several of his youngest soldiers, all of them unarmed, to escort her on foot. Perhaps he hoped the Russians would decide they had more urgent things to do than detain a gentlewoman and a half-dozen unmounted, unarmed teenagers.

"That left him with just his three or four hundred Jewish fighters to worry about. They included that home guard bunch, who probably weren't much of an asset. But what was left of the original two hundred fifty had more than proven that they deserved skilled military leadership, and he knew he could provide it. That was enough for him. He showed them how to deploy with the best chance of catching their pursuers in enfilading fire. He showed them how to secure a line of retreat. What he could not provide them, of course, was any clue what they should do once the Russians had them trapped with their backs to the Vistula. Once that happened, there'd be nothing more he could do for them, except surrender rather than see them slaughtered. And he couldn't expect his fate to be much better than theirs. He'd already passed up the chance to abandon his men, find fresh horses and gallop with his wife to the Prussian border. Probably the best he could hope for was that his wife would remain safe with his kinsman, and that he'd be sent into exile. And except for what he had no way to expect or even imagine, he'd have been right. Once the Russians crushed the revolt, they sent about twenty-five thousand Polish rebels, including titled gentry like Tarnowski, into exile in Siberia. If that's the way it had played out for him, Antonina's mother might have lived, and Antonina would have grown up on a great-uncle's country estate, and she would never have met her father. And nobody named

Rabinowitz would have been saddled with the name Antonina or Antonin, or with the expectations that come with it."

Rabby's sudden silence struck Peter as timed and staged for theatrical effect. Rabby patted across the waistband of his shorts until he remembered he'd already emptied his pack of cigarettes.

"Anybody got smokes?" he said.

"Look next to your chair," Peter said. "You dropped one there."

Rabby looked left, then right. Then he leaned forward to peer beneath his chair. "Aha!" he said. He gingerly lifted the cigarette and brushed off its filtered end with a forefinger.

"So good of you to notice, Pete," he said happily. Peter handed him the matchbook and he lit the cigarette. "Well, gentlemen," he said. "Shall we call it an evening?"

Peter decided to call his bluff. "Fine with me," he said.

Rabby blew a smoke ring. Drifting and fading, it briefly framed the streams of tracer fire that poured down from the invisible, circling aircraft in the distant sky. Then, placing both hands on the aluminum arms of his chair, he started to lift himself upright.

"Whoa, whoa, whoa!" the Karloff captain said, making such a vehement tamping-down motion with an outstretched hand that the palm slapped Rabby's knee. Peter couldn't restrain his snort of laughter when Rabby instantly dropped back into his chair.

"Look, I know we can't go on all night, but it's still just ten o'clock," the captain said. "There's no need to leave the story hanging right there."

"Sure there is," Peter said, still laughing. "After all, that's how Scheherazade made it through to the next night, then to the next and next. Look, sir, this is just his ploy to get us to hear him out, whether now or later on. He figures we're likelier to swallow the whole wild-assed tale if we beg him to go on with it. Once he's back in the world, he'll probably tell his high-priced lawyer dad how he sold this cobbled-together yarn about ancestors who never existed to four dimwits—pardon me, sir, but I'm just anticipating what he'll say—sold it to four dimwits on a rooftop in Vietnam. And then the two of them, father and son, will probably split a bottle of very good, very high-priced scotch and laugh themselves cockeyed. And then they might split another bottle while they calculate how long it's likely to take them and how many dimwitted juries they'll have to fool before Rabby can buy himself a summer home in the Hamptons."

Before he had half-finished this tirade, Peter wondered with mild alarm where within himself it was coming from. But by the time he was done, he was enjoying the disoriented look on Karloff's face and the squinting gleam of either merriment or pain in Doucet's eyes and the furious twirling Doucet was giving his mustache. Rabby, though, seemed unfazed. With his head cocked slightly toward Peter, he took slow drags on his cigarette.

"Look, sir, it just doesn't add up," Peter said, intent now on goading Rabinowitz. "Why should we believe any of it is true?"

"First of all," Rabby said evenly, "because it is. And second, because it has to be."

"Well, I'm not sure whether to call that a tautology or just bird crap," Peter said.

"It has to be," Rabby repeated. "Because without what you call wild-assed tales that link lives together down the years—without that, all we're left with is what's out there. All we're left with is Spooky, endlessly revolving in its small but very convincing circle of hell. And Spooky's circle has no Dante to spin a story—a wild-assed tale, as you'd have it—to give it meaning. Nothing within that circle connects with anything else, except lead with warm bodies."

"Well, to that I will offer a qualified amen." The voice was as lacking in tone and resonance as a plucked, untuned banjo string. It took Peter a moment to realize it was the other officer who had spoken, the captain who sat in the shadows beyond Karloff's shoulder. Although the man was billeted in the villa next door and Peter had seen him often on the grounds of the academy, he couldn't remember ever having heard him speak. In fact, on those two occasions when the man had captured Peter's attention, his very silence had strengthened the impression he had made. Now that

Peter had heard the voice, he put it together with what he remembered of the man's demeanor, thinking: cow college ROTC; hill country origin, somewhere along the arc from West Virginia to north Mississippi; hard-shell Baptist, or maybe some stripe of Pentecostal; solid smarts, yet unable to work free of that doctrinal cage.

The officer who had spoken stood abruptly and stepped forward beside his companion, then reached between his knees to yank forward his folding chair. It took Peter a moment to dredge up the memory the man had touched. It was a long-ago visit he had made with his schoolteacher father to a farm deep in the Carolina countryside. The man who had greeted them on an unpainted board porch had invited them to "pull up a cheer"—and had done so himself, in the same abrupt way as this man. The officer placed his hands on his knees. His knuckles looked like they belonged on a man who had milked cows at dawn and unharnessed mules at sundown.

Rabinowitz cast a languid glance toward the captain, who responded with a quick smile wide enough to crinkle the corners of his eyes. Watching this wordless exchange, Peter thought, Well, I'll be damned. Jewish patrician PFC condescends to hayseed Protestant captain. God bless America, I guess, for making this possible.

"Sir, I see I'm playing to a tough crowd," Rabby said. "So thanks for the endorsement, however partial."

"Not partial," the captain said, making a hatchet-chop with one hand for emphasis. "Not partial as regards your main point. I mean both the 'is true' and the 'has to be' parts of that. Where I part company with you, Private, is on the notion that the men in that gunship are trapped in some circle of hell."

"I wouldn't say trapped in it," Rabby said. "I'd say spinning it out like a spider spins a web, because that's what they're programmed to do. But either way—"

"Or that they're creating one." Again the captain gave the hatchet-chop for emphasis—a gesture, Peter thought, he might have picked up watching some hotshot revival preacher.

"What do you think war is, Private? It's well and good to talk about reaching up and touching a chalice of valor. And yes, we need stories, like the one you're telling, about people who actually do it. And, yes, some number of those stories have to be true. And you can't allow any space between the 'has to be' and the 'is.' That's a built-in precept of the faith I hold to. But who in a real war gets a chance to touch that chalice you talk about? What part of a war is not, at bottom, a matter of connecting lead with warm bodies? In war, it's always a question of what the bodies would do if the lead weren't there to prevent them doing it. Now, odds are the people on the ground out there—or more likely, safely underground out there—will, if they get the chance, come down out of the mountains tomorrow. They'll kill a village elder or a schoolteacher or somebody else the local VC have fingered as an obstacle to getting the collectivist, atheistic doctrine taught pure and complete. Does the gunship crew out there know they can prevent that? No. Do they know that if they do prevent it, things will somehow work out for the better? No, of course they can't know things like that. That's the small-scale version of what they call the fog of war. And nobody ever glimpsed a hovering chalice of virtue in the fog of war."

Rabby moved one of the citronella candles closer to the two officers. Then he stretched out his elbows and yawned. Peter thought, with a mounting feeling of alarm, does he really mean to pack it in? Will we have to live through another night of this?

"I have to tell you gentlemen I'm glad you're here to challenge my logic and my facts," Rabby said. "Mind, I don't concede my position that what we see out there is a circle of hell. I'm sure you both know what an imprecise art aerial targeting is, especially when you're trying to pinpoint something in daylight and then blast it to smithereens in darkness. But still, all you say is well taken, well taken. Now—shall we call it quits for tonight?"

Peter burst out: "Oh, hell, get on with it, Rabby! And get done with it!"

Rabby stared, expressionless, at Peter, then looked at the three men to his right, who sat silent and expectant. Rabby flicked his still-lit cigarette over the parapet and it spun away in the darkness.

"With some dispatch, then," he said, steepling his fingers, "First, though—sorry, but I must ask one of you to remind me—"

"Jewish brigade guys running out of city blocks to defend," Doucet said, holding his fist to his mouth to mimic an out-of-breath news announcer. His small, dark eyes danced in the flickering candlelight. "Antoinette off to stay with husband's uncle. Count don't know whether to fight it out or pull on sheepskin boots for the trek to Siberia."

"Right, right," Rabby said. "At least, Tarnowski thought Antoinette was going to the uncle's estate. She went along with that idea to the extent of riding off on the horse she'd ridden throughout the campaign. Probably those half-dozen Jewish kids trotted alongside her. But if she had any intention of going through with this plan, she'd dropped it by the time she got east of the city and could see how strung-out the cordon of Russian soldiers there was, and how thin it was at any point. That convinced her that, with speed and surprise, she and her husband could break through it. Perhaps she ordered her escorts not to bother further with her but instead to save themselves, to hurry off to their own homes.

"Or maybe she said nothing to them, but just turned her horse and spurred it until she'd outdistanced them. For sure, she wasn't going to let a bunch of Jewish teenagers interfere with what she believed was a workable escape plan. She might never have picked up a saber, let alone swung it like that other Antoinette. But remember, she'd stuck with her husband through the whole campaign, and it had taken something close to main force to pry her apart from him to the distance she'd just ridden. Maybe she was willing to leave him to his fate, if that was what he wanted—and he did want that—if they both thought that was the only way to save the child she was carrying. But she was damned if she'd leave Konrad Tarnowski if she saw a good chance to save all three of them.

"But by the time she caught up with her husband, Meir had gone her one better. He'd figured out a way to save all the rest of them too. Though that's likely giving him too much individual credit. The same idea must have popped into the head of every one of those young Jews as the Russians drove them closer to the river. All Meir did was give voice to it, present it to Count Tarnowski in the form of a plan. You see, the Russian attack on Warsaw came from the west, which offered the soldiers in Tarnowski's little brigade the kind of life-saving option that just days earlier would have seemed entirely out of reach. You might call it the Br'er Rabbit option. You know that old plantation tale, right? 'Please, Br'er Fox, don't throw me in the briar patch!' Well, Tarnowski's bunch was being driven back toward the west bank of the Vistula. And what lies on the Vistula's west bank? Why, not just the rabbinical school but the whole Judenviertel, Warsaw's Jewish Quarter.

"After two days of fighting on the city's outskirts, the Polish commanders and their gentile troops decided there was nothing of their revolution left to save but their skins. Whereupon they skedaddled for the Prussian or Austrian borders. That left Tarnowski and his Jewish brigade as the only meaningful resistance—only it probably overstates the case to call it meaningful. The Russians were simply mopping up. There was just this one little band left to deal with. It did show an annoying knack for holding up their advance toward the river. Still, it was just an annoyance. And then it disappeared. And the prevailing sentiment on the Russian side must have been simple relief. What could the Russians have done, anyway? Sort through the dozens of students at the rabbinical school—let alone the thousands of young male Jews throughout the Jewish Quarter—to see which ones had the kind of black-powder cheek burns you were likely to get from firing a musket? Go household to household to ferret out the ones with wounds? Good luck getting a Jewish mother to provide any clue where she'd hidden either her own or some other Jewish mother's wounded son. Round up beardless Jews? If the Russians even knew about the no-beards rule, it was a non-factor now, since Tarnowski had never enforced it.

"So by the time Antoinette found her husband, his brigade was gone—reabsorbed, with his blessing, into the Judenviertel. That made the question of whom to save even more clear-cut than she'd expected. Except for one thing: Meir Rabinowitz was still there. Meir, you see, didn't intend to leave Konrad Tarnowski. And Count Tarnowski didn't intend to abandon Meir Rabinowitz. That much was clearly understood by the time the three of them held a hurried, end-of-game council of war.

"And when Antoinette told her husband and Meir her breakout plan, Meir had a ready answer to the what-next question. He wasn't a Warsaw Jew, but his village—shtetl, they called those little Jewish towns in the Pale—was less than a day's ride to the east. And east, they determined, was where they'd have to go, with Meir's shtetl as their first stop. How much further east they'd need to go, they didn't yet have any way of—"

Peter half-rose from his chair. "Hold it, hold it, hold it!" he said, waving one hand. "Rabby, let me count the ways you're not making any sense! You said that, for people like Tarnowski, the only chance of safety lay to the west, across the border to Prussia or Austria. Right?"

"If there was any way for them to get there, yes," Rabby said. "And for Tarnowski and Antoinette, by this point, there wasn't. By this time, the Russians' whole army was massed west of Warsaw, except for the thin cordon of troops to the east that Antoinette was convinced they could break through."

"All right," Peter said. "So we take escape to the west off the board. The only other option that you've talked about was some in-country safe haven, like the estate of this kinsman that Tarnowski wanted his wife to ride to. If that would do for her, why wouldn't it do for both of them?"

Rabby's eyebrows lifted in what Peter took to be silent acknowledgment that the question was a fair one. "Think on it a bit, Pete," Rabby said. "Sure, the Russians were likely to leave Antoinette alone at the kinsman's estate, even if they discovered her whereabouts and knew she was the wife of a rebel officer. But those assumptions didn't hold for Tarnowski. He wasn't part of the high command, but the Russians had to know he'd taken an active part in the revolt. If his kinsman took him in, Tarnowski would at best be doomed to a life in hiding. The Russians in that era weren't anywhere near as methodical about eliminating people they saw as a threat as the Nazis would be in the next century. Still, at some point, they were likely to draw up a checklist of known revolutionaries who weren't already accounted for as dead, captured and shipped to Siberia, or known to have escaped to the West. And as they got down to the T's on their list, the estate of a known kinsman would be a place they'd check. And if they found Tarnowski there, it would mean exile not just for him but for his elderly kinsman as well. And there was no way Konrad Tarnowski would ask a kinsman to take that kind of risk."

"All right, then," Peter said, trying to tamp down the annoyance in his voice. "Fine. They can't make a dash for Vienna or Berlin. And, noble soul that he is, the count won't ask his uncle or cousin or whatever he was to put him up. So Tarnowski's solution to this dilemma is what? To trust that he and his wife can blend in with Polish Jews? To think that a couple of fair-haired, upper-crust Poles who are each of them probably a half-foot taller than any of Meir's folk could just smile and wave if, say, a troop of Russian cavalry should pass through this shtetl? Jesus, Rabby! A jury of kindergartners wouldn't buy that yarn."

Peter would have left off that final insult if Rabby had not turned away from him while he was speaking and tried to cadge a cigarette from any of the other three men who might have one. None did. Peter suspected Rabby had turned his back on him simply to goad him, since Rabby was really not that heavy a smoker. Rabby slumped back in his chair and shook his head.

"No, no, blending in wasn't any part of it—couldn't have been," he said. "The breakout idea was Antonina's, but what came afterward was strictly Meir's plan, and it was up to him to make it work. He must have made it clear to them from the first that it would be achingly slow. Day after day they'd have to hide in miserable conditions, and night after night they'd travel on horseback from one village to the next, always through woodlands and fields, always staying clear of roadways. And I'll grant you that Tarnowski would have been a fool to buy into it if a half-year of fighting, and especially the last few days of really desperate fighting, hadn't convinced him that Meir Rabinowitz was a man who could find or create a way where none seemed to exist.

"Meir also knew his own world—the world of Jews in the Pale—well enough to have an endgame in mind. He knew that winning that endgame meant they had to reach some city that offered an escape route westward for a Christian couple who needed it. Obviously, a port city would fill that bill. It also needed to be a place where a young Jew like himself would find his prospects limited only by his ambition and ability. It had to be distant enough that no one there would be likely to recognize them, but it also had to be a city they could reach without leaving the Pale. They needed to be able to get there by heading east, since east was the only direction they could go, at least initially. Take all those requirements together and you're left with just one option: Odessa."

Peter snorted. "Makes perfect sense!" he said. "At the very time every other Pole with some means and connections and good sense is working hell-for-leather to escape to the West, your ancestor persuades these two to run straight down the gullet of the Russian bear. And you know what, Rabby? I'm even inclined to believe it! In fact, this part of it might swing me around to buying the whole story. And do you know why?"

Rabby looked sidelong at Peter, and for once he had no ready answer. "No," he said finally. "Why?"

"Because it's such a goddamn perfectly Rabinowitz-ish thing to do!" Peter said. "How many American men would you suppose, just this year, have tried everything from suddenly discovering Jesus has called them to the ministry, to sleeping with a bar of soap wedged in an armpit to drive up their blood pressure, to—I don't know—maybe promising to marry the butt-ugly daughter of their draft board chairman, all to avoid getting drafted and shipped to Vietnam? And here, present in our midst, we have a rare specimen who didn't need to bother with any of that! No indeed, because he got invited to join a reserve unit whose colonel, by sheer coincidence, is a member of the law firm where this noble lad's father is managing partner.

"And yet, is this pinnacle of good fortune enough for our hero? Why no, not quite! Because it lacks the one element that it's perfectly, and one might assume purposely, configured to avoid. It lacks shipping orders for Vietnam! And so special arrangements must be made. The Army must understand its pressing concerns now include dispatching one Private A. Rabinowitz to a tour of duty that promises just enough hardship and risk that the 'chalice of valor' he prattles on about won't turn into a laugh line. Now, getting the Pentagon to cut a set of orders like that might not be all that demanding for a top-of-the-line law firm like your dad's. But it is unusual. And asking that orders like that be cut just for one interested party is somewhere beyond unusual. Demented? Arrogant? So, yes, I'm ready to believe your ancestor looked this Polish count in the eye, pointed east and said, 'there lies the route to something like freedom and prosperity!' Because that scenario has a strong enough streak of self-serving perversity in it for the family likeness to show."

After Peter stopped talking, Rabinowitz looked at him for a long moment. Then he said: "Self-serving? Think of the matter as something like the Underground Railroad turned topsy-turvy. How could you call it self-serving if a slave conspired to spirit his slavemaster and the slavemaster's wife across six hundred miles to save Massah and Missus from some duly adjudicated legal consequence? If they got caught, wouldn't the slave's prospects be pretty much limited to a rope and a sycamore tree?"

"Just tell the rest of it, Rabby," Peter said, shaking his head. The other three men were laughing. "Just get them to Odessa and either all safely dead or far enough toward it that we can see the point."

"Well, then," Rabby said. He propped his feet again on the parapet and waggled them with apparent self-satisfaction. "Imagine yourself, then, a Russian junior officer in charge of a segment of the cordon that's supposed to prevent any breakout by Polish rebels. The cordon's thickly manned west of Warsaw, because the Russians figure any chance of escape for the rebels lies that way. But you're sitting on a camp stool east of the city, and where you are, the cordon is a flimsy, pro forma thing. It's nearly dawn on an October morning. Your troops are strung out so thin to your left and right that you can't see any of them in the mist. You can't see anything in front of you either, as you sit there blinking and yawning and trying not to nod off and tumble off your camp stool into the muck. And then, from somewhere ahead of you, you hear the splash of cantering hooves. A little after that, you see the tall figure on horseback, holding a drawn saber and heading pretty much straight at you. And behind that one comes another rider almost as tall as the first, but this one is wearing bloused-out skirts and appears to have something about the size of a small pumpkin growing out of one shoulder. Maybe you have enough presence of mind to call out an order to halt, but all these two riders do in response is spur their horses to a gallop, and that leaves you barely enough time to stumble off to one side to get out of range of the saber. By the time they draw abreast of you, before they get swallowed up by the mist again, you can see the one waving the raised saber is a man and the second rider is a woman, and what had at first looked to you like a pumpkin jouncing along on her shoulder is the head of a third rider, and he's hanging on with his arms around a part of her that appears to contain one more passenger. And if you're from somewhere well back in Mother Russia, maybe you've never even seen a Jew before. So looking at this hanging-on rider's face, with its dark, scrunched-up features and what looks like little black coil springs covering its cheeks, instead of yelling 'halt' again or reaching for your pistol, you just stand there, getting all splattered with mud flung from the horses' hooves, and you mutter to yourself, 'now let's just decide right now you never saw this, because nobody would believe you if you told them, and nothing could be done about it if they did.'

"All it took was that one quick dash, and then it was more than just the Russian cordon that Konrad and Antoinette had broken through. They'd ridden straight out of the roles they'd played all their lives, the same roles their ancestors had played since roughly the fourteenth century. They would have died still playing those roles and never even imagined themselves as anything else, if they hadn't trusted Meir enough to make that breakout ride in the direction he'd chosen. They'd ridden out of the fog as Polish landed grandees, but after they'd passed the one or two befuddled Russian soldiers who likely got a glimpse of them, they rode back into the fog as something else. Or rather, as nothing else—not just yet. They rode back into it—the count, Antoinette, their unborn child—as displaced persons whose new identities would have to be created out of whatever was going to happen to them next, and next after that. And insofar as all those next-afters depended on any single agent, they depended on that little Jew with the freshly sprouted coil-spring beard who was hanging on with both arms wrapped around Antoinette's six-months-pregnant belly. Because they were in Meir's world now, and only Meir could orchestrate whatever of safety and whatever of new ways of thinking and feeling his world might provide them.

"There weren't going to be nearly enough next-afters for Antoinette. There must have been enough of them, though, before she died, that she could at least see that there was no way to reach back to her old life, and no good reason to want to. That the old ways of thinking and feeling and acting amounted to a death-grip of the past, and it was worth any amount of terror and suffering, worth even the sacrifice of her life, to ride free of them. Provided, of course, that she could pass on to her child the value of that sacrifice. And of course, there was no way she could know things would work out that way—that is, that she would die, her child would live and the moral capital the mother had accumulated by her suffering and death would pass on undiminished to the child. But back before they set out, back when Meir told them what they faced—a ride of six hundred miles, moving from shtetl to shtetl, staying away from main roads and traveling mostly by night—Antoinette must have realized how slender the odds were that both she and her child would survive it. And I believe she just silently accepted that. Remember, all she had to do to obtain the best odds for her child and herself was do what her husband wanted: take shelter with his kinsman and leave him, Konrad, to the fate of a soldier who stood by a losing cause. And she had been about to go along with what he wanted, right up until she saw that all the Russians had in the way of a containment barrier was—well, the equivalent of those two little Arvin troops at the checkpoint up the street, who look like somebody plucked them off a playground and plopped helmets on their heads and handed each of them an M-16 but neglected to tell them what it was for. You can almost see Antoinette's little lip-curl of disgust, can't you, when she saw one pitiful excuse for a soldier over here and another one way over there? Seeing that, it couldn't have taken her more than a second to comprehend and reject the weight of shame she would pass on to her daughter if she rode on, rather than turn back and convince her husband that some sort of shared future was just one short dash on horseback away.

"That gallop through the Russian cordon stripped away the identities Konrad and Antoinette were born into, but it had pretty much the opposite effect on Meir. It vested him, for the first time in his life, with the full weight of his identity as a Jew."

Rabby stopped talking. There had been no change of pace or emphasis in his voice. It just stopped. As he had all evening, Rabby kept gazing off into the night sky, where Spooky had moved to a new target further west. Only the tops of the tracer streams remained visible beyond the mountains.

The little captain cleared his throat. "Full weight of his identity," he said. "I think I understand. You don't mean his identity as a young man steeped in Torah, a man on track to live about as successfully as a man could hope to live in a little Jewish town in Poland in that era. A man who marries well, succeeds his father as rabbi, grows old honored by his neighbors. A man esteemed even by Christians roundabout. You don't mean all that, or not just that. You mean identity as a Jew in the ancient sense, don't you? You mean a man who had to give up everything he had always known and everything he'd ever aspired to because God called him in a still, small voice. Because God, or conscience if you want to call it that, told him to take a new direction. That's it, isn't it?"

At first Rabby gave no sign of having heard. Then his head snapped upward, as if he'd been jolted from a reverie.

"What?" he said. "Oh, yes. I mean, I guess I meant all that. Or I would have if I'd thought it through. God, conscience or whatever it takes to make a Jew do the quintessentially Jewish thing."

The officer's jaw clenched, and his face—as best Peter could judge in the faint candlelight— appeared to flush with embarrassment.

"Well, I thought that was what you were waiting for," the captain said. "I thought you were giving us time for it to sink in, and you wanted us to let you know when it had."

"I see," Rabby said. "No, actually, I was trying to figure out how to get past the part I don't know. The part that happened in Meir's shtetl. My great aunt Dalia told me that was the part her grandfather always carried with him. She said that, watching him, even as a child she could figure out that much. She said it was that part—what happened in the shtetl after he arrived there that day with Konrad and Antoinette, and before he left it forever—that he could never either talk about or forget."

Twenty

The words jolted Peter like a gut-punch. Then he started to laugh.

"Please, Rabby," he said, still laughing. "Please tell me whether you just said, 'part he couldn't either talk about or forget.'"

Rabby waggled the fingers of one hand to signify Peter had it more or less right.

"Well, correct me if I've misremembered," Peter said, "but hadn't Meir just taken close enough part in an honest-to-God war for gunpowder to singe those coil-spring whiskers you spoke of? Can't we assume he'd seen men shot down and coughing blood in the street? So how is it that whatever happened during a pit stop in his hometown could eat at him worse than all he'd just been through—eat at him so badly he could neither talk about it nor forget it?"

As he was still shaping his questions, Peter remembered the glazed, frightened look that had stolen into Teddy's eyes that afternoon on the pier, and the way Teddy's mouth had worked before the words would come, because Teddy had been hearing the bullets rip through his boat's hull and seeing the ocean seethe with snakes in the ghastly light of flares. And suddenly Peter hated Rabinowitz for both summoning that memory and violating the sanctity of it.

"You're just lying," Peter said. "God, I don't know why we should listen to any of this. You don't know squat about the things a man can't talk about or forget. You hear me? You don't know squat!"

"What we could stand to hear less from right now is you," the Karloff captain said. "First you tell him to hurry on to the end of it. Then you keep butting in and trying to shut him down."

"But he's—look, sir, it's worse than lying. He's playing us for—"

The smaller captain, leaning around his fellow officer's shoulder, cut Peter off.

"I think we've already allowed for the possibility that Private Rabynovych might, let's say, embellish the sketchy facts that have come down to him," he said in his flat, banjo-string tone. "Even so, it seems to me the whole story holds enough moral weight to justify sacrificing an hour of sleep to hear him out."

"But please," Karloff said to Peter, "please don't ask us to tolerate an extra half hour just to listen to you bitch. Now go ahead, Private."

Doucet leaned in toward Rabby and spun one hand at an accelerating rate.

"Sure, sure, Emmet," Rabby muttered. "*Vite, vite, plus vite*! All right, then. Meir's identity as a Jew. I guess he could never have felt the full weight of that until he had to choose to give it up. He'd made that choice back in Warsaw, but that wasn't enough. Before it could count, he had to make it again, facing his own family and the people of his town. They'd all assumed, you see, that he would live the life implicit in his name: son of the rabbi. Which he might or might not have actually been. I never knew, because Dalia never told me, because Meir had never told anyone. But no matter: he'd been chosen. And the town just assumed—no, that falls short of what his people expected. 'Assumed' admits the possibility of an alternative, and they could never have imagined that someone chosen for a life so honored and so essential to every other life in his town would simply decline to live it. 'Of course!' they thought. Of course he'd rejoice to find the life of a rabbi in his native town was open to him. And not only that. Because of the bravery and skill he'd shown as a soldier, his townspeople were ready to top all the honor due a rabbi with a dollop of even greater honor than a novice rabbi could ordinarily expect. So of course he'd accept that honor, for the sake of all the people of his town.

"And then he had to find a way to tell them no, he would not. And he had to try to explain to them why. He had to tell them—due respects, Captain, but he couldn't just tell his townspeople something about a 'still, small voice' and then walk away. Some of them were his own flesh and blood. If he wanted to make any sense at all to them, he had to point to some other flesh and blood that he could argue was also, in some sense, his. And all that he could point to in an effort to make that case were, first, the Polish nobleman who had taught him the soldier's art, who had begun treating him as an equal and, toward the end, had treated him almost as a brother or a son. Second, he could point to that man's wife, who had a chance to escape with her unborn child to a sanctuary among her own kind, but had instead chosen the course of love and loyalty and mortal risk. And now all three lives were in his hands.

"That would have been the best Meir could hope to do, in the way of explaining. Whether he actually did it, I have no way to know. For all I know, once they were rested and adequately provisioned, Meir might have awakened the count and Antoinette in the dead of night and led them out of town without any explanation to anybody."

"Or he could have just told them he was doing what good rabbis are supposed to do," the little captain said in a firm, pan-flat voice. "He was teaching. He was just teaching on a higher plane than they were accustomed to being taught."

Rabby brushed what seemed to be an imaginary mosquito off his thigh. "What makes you think that?" he said warily.

"Oh. Well, heh-heh." The officer made a tossing-aside gesture with one hand. "Oh, you can ignore that. Comes out of my faith tradition."

"Actually, I can't ignore it," Rabby said. "How else to make sense of that gap, that silence about his last days in his town? And then all the rest of his life after that, and the count's, and Antonina's. If they weren't teaching—whether or not anybody was paying attention to what they taught—then what was all that about?"

Then the storyteller tone and demeanor snapped back into place.

"Well, proceeding at Emmet's preferred pace—*vite et plus vite!*" Rabby said. "You already have most of the rest of it. The parts I know, that is. Because they were the parts Great-aunt Dalia knew. Great-aunt Dalia knew them because Antonina lived long enough to tell her. And of course Dalia didn't need anyone to tell her the final part, because Dalia was there to see it during the worst Odessa pogrom, the one in October 1905.

"But it all needs fitting together, doesn't it? With informed speculation to sub for the missing pieces. So. *Plus vite!* October 1831, Meir's shtetl. The count and Antoinette and Meir hunkered down there until Meir figured the weather and Russian troop movements made it safe for them to move on. It was six hundred miles to Odessa. There was no way to get there but on foot or horseback, and they could travel only at night. Which meant they'd have to travel through the winter, and the baby would be born en route.

"The three of them had already passed into legend among Warsaw's Jews. That legend preceded them at every stage of the trek to Odessa. Word traveled fast among Jews in the Pale. It had to. The Jews there depended on it for their economic health, which was pretty robust in those days. The Pale was a conduit for all sorts of imports that Russians in the heartland craved, but those goods couldn't come in above board because of inane protectionism. Fine products from France? Goods like jewelry, cognac, watches, tableware, mirrors, leather boots? Forget it. Russians were supposed to either make do with shoddy Russian-made goods or do without. So those things had to be smuggled in, and Jews in the Pale stepped in to handle the smuggling. Russian customs officials were happy to look the other way. So Jews in the shtetls developed efficient, concealed lines of communication. Which equipped them to handle not just contraband goods but human contraband, too, such as three refugees from a failed revolution.

"So Meir didn't have to worry about planning a workable route, or about getting advance permission for a stopover from each little town along the way. Once the Pale's communication network picked up that Odessa was their destination and they wanted to get there with the least possible risk to those who helped them, the network generated their travel plan as efficiently as a mainframe computer could have done. The same simple elements would govern every stage of that plan. It was a lot more dangerous to harbor a known rebel than to transport something like a French-made silver snuffbox, so the rules for handling contraband goods wouldn't be strict enough. There could be no concrete, traceable sign of collaboration or aid—nothing in writing, no escort between one shtetl and the next, no loaned animals. A shtetl couldn't even give them transportable food if its freshness could tip off a Russian patrol that it must have come from a town no more than a day's ride back.

"So, one shtetl to the next. Often sleeping in stables, probably. Maybe sometimes staying in the home of some couple who could look forward down the years and ponder the value of telling children and grandchildren, 'they stayed right here with us—we sheltered them.' Moving only at night, guided by landmarks Meir was coached to recognize.

"And they almost made it. Of course, there's no way to know whether Antoinette would have been any more likely to survive childbirth in Odessa than in the shtetl where Antonina was born."

"Please, God," Peter burst out, knowing but not caring that he'd draw another rebuke. "Don't let this child be born in a stable!"

Again the captain made a casting-aside gesture. "Oh, that doesn't matter," he said.

"Peter, I don't know if it was in a stable," Rabby sighed.

"And it doesn't matter!" the captain said.

"No, it doesn't," Rabby said. "What matters is what Meir asked of the people in that shtetl, and what they did about it. And it wasn't the count who asked them. That's important too. It was Meir."

"You mean the cross on her grave, don't you?" the officer said. "And you mean what matters is that it was a rabbi—even if he was unordained, a shavetail at best—it was a rabbi who asked them for that? Because it contradicted anything they'd imagined a rabbi might ask. He made it clear to them, didn't he, that there could be no transgression when what they granted was a gesture of love?"

"All I'm sure of," Rabby said slowly, "is it was Meir who asked for the cross. And somewhere they found a stone mason who could chisel it out. And they found a place for her grave, well away from all the other graves, as it had to be. Any question about that was settled around the eleventh century. As far as I know, it's still settled: no non-Jewish burials in a Jewish cemetery.

Peter saw his opening. He recognized the malevolence behind his impulse to take it, and he took it anyway.

"Well, thank you Rabby!" he said, slapping his knee. "At last you've given us what we need!"

"Yes, of course," Rabby said wearily, waving one hand repeatedly past his ear as if a mosquito were hovering there. "You mean exhibit A. The concrete, verifiable detail. Or the absence of one."

"Exactly!" Peter said. "Now, surely you can tell us the date of the National Geographic issue that contains a photo of this stone cross in such close proximity to a shtetl cemetery somewhere in southern Ukraine? I'll bet your family even has that photo framed on a mantel in their modest eight-bedroom home in Westchester County."

Karloff thrust his face forward in what remained of the light from a guttering citronella candle.

"Look, Private, I don't know what grounds you have for what's clearly a deep and bitter disagreement with this man," he said to Peter. "But whatever they are, please pursue them further on your own time, not ours."

There was a tense quaver in the little captain's voice. "Oh, he's dredging up the old, old fallacy," he said. "If you can't produce a sliver of the true cross, see, that proves the gospel's a cockamamie tale."

Rabby shook his head. "No, the question demands asking," he said. "It's incredibly tantalizing, still, to think that the cross is still there, perhaps hidden by vegetation near the crumbling gravestones of a Jewish cemetery. But where? The odds weigh against finding it, absent some guide who knows where it is.

"My father gave it a try, though—probably the best try one could make under the circumstances. Those being the aftermath of the war in Europe. He was with the JAG Corps. At war's end, he was billeted at a former spa in Bavaria, Bad Tolz, in what had been an SS officer candidate school. He tended to a legal officer's usual duties: disciplinary proceedings, arbitration with local civilians. Ho-hum stuff. Then he got tapped for something more interesting.

"The Nuremberg prosecution wasn't a JAG show, but the prosecutors did look to JAG lawyers for what Dad called 'third-tier' help. That included monitoring the selection of witnesses outside the American zone of occupation. Only the occupying power got to screen potential witnesses in each zone, you see. When Dad was growing up in New Jersey, his family spoke a mix of Yiddish and Russian. So he was a natural pick to be sent to the Soviet zone—with the Soviets' approval, of course. It probably didn't hurt his chances, at least with the Americans who did the choosing, that he was Jewish.

"So for half a year he sat in on the Soviet interrogators' sessions with people who'd survived camps like Treblinka and Sobibor. All he was authorized to do during those sessions was listen and take notes. But he got pre-clearance from the Soviets he worked with to ask about one matter, once they'd finished their own questioning. He made it clear to them that his questions had nothing to do with potential trial evidence, and that he only wanted to talk to people who had lived in southern Ukraine. He wanted to know if they knew anything about a shtetl where a Christian cross marked a grave outside the Jewish cemetery.

"Well. As we might correctly infer from Peter's derisive comments, in six months of traveling around Poland and eastern Ukraine with the Soviet interrogators, my father heard nothing about such a place. He got to pose his questions to dozens of camp survivors, but except in one case, he either drew a complete blank or he made people angry.

"The only witness, he said, who seemed to show a glimmer of recognition when he asked his questions was a woman who'd lost the ability to speak. The Soviet interrogators brought her in because they'd heard that, at one of the camps—Treblinka, I think— she'd seen a guard cut off her husband's ear and beat him with an iron pipe, then force him into the gas chamber. Since then, she hadn't spoken a word. The two Russian interrogators did their best to see if she might be good for some sort of testimony. But she just sat there pretty much inert while they recited to her a description of what had happened to her husband, as well as other things she might have witnessed, until they got exasperated and gave up.

"After that, Dad didn't expect much from her. But in the background sheet the Soviets had drawn up on her, he'd seen she was Jewish and she'd been born near Vinnytsia, a town a couple of hundred miles north of Odessa. So Dad sat down at a table across from her and asked if she'd ever seen or heard of a shtetl where a cross marking a Christian burial stood near the Jewish cemetery.

"Up to that point, Dad said, the woman had looked dazed, as if she couldn't even hear the interrogators' questions. But when he asked about the cross near the Jewish headstones, her eyes suddenly fixed on his and her breath started coming in short gasps. And then she reached across the table and squeezed his hand, hard. He said he asked his question again, slower this time and with more detail: Had she ever seen or heard of an unmarked stone cross near a cemetery where all the headstones were covered with Hebrew script? She kept looking straight at him but in an unfocused sort of way, as if she were seeing not him but something beyond him. And he said her breathing quickened until she was almost panting like a dog. And this frail little woman gripped his fingers and pulled until he heard his knuckles crack. He said it was as if she were trying to pull him into whatever it was she was seeing. But she never said a word."

"So she must have known, right?" the officer said, with a hopeful inflection that was almost a whine. "She had to know or remember—something?"

"Actually," Rabby said, "my dad decided the woman's reaction had nothing to do with the content of his question. He figured her suffering in the camps had unhinged her to the point that statements of fact meant nothing to her, while even a slight show of empathy meant everything. The two Soviet interrogators had questioned her pretty harshly, like prosecutors at a trial, while my dad had spoken gently to her, in the manner of someone sharing a secret that only he and his listener could understand.

"Besides, even if she'd heard of the cross—even if she'd seen it and yet couldn't tell him where it was—what was he supposed to do? Petition the Soviet command to let him spend a few weeks roaming the Vinnytsia and northern Odessa regions in search of a Jewish graveyard with a cross in the tall weeds somewhere nearby? Think about it. That could lead to something worse than a simple nyet from the Soviets. It could lead to an involuntary discharge from the Army—honorable, no doubt, but on the unspoken grounds of temperamental instability. Not a promising starting point for a young attorney planning to launch a career in the midtown Manhattan shark tank.

"So he gave it up. He filed a report in Nuremberg on the six months of interrogations he'd witnessed. Then he got his travel orders cut and shipped out for the States."

"I see," the smaller captain said with a sigh. "Well, sometimes a story gains in power by having to remain just a story, doesn't it? No—strike the word 'just.' When it has to remain a story, sometimes that's an affirmation of its truth."

"Sure," Peter muttered. "Absence of evidence is the best proof of all."

Twenty-one

"Hey, Rabby," Doucet said. "I bet you five dollars you still ain't done with your yarn by the time Spooky packs it in for the night. Take me up on dat?"

"Hell, Emmet," Rabby said. "You're suggesting I just hand you five dollars." He swept his hand toward the portion of the mountain range where the gunship had poured down minigun fire since shortly after sundown. "Spooky's long gone," he said.

"*Au contraire!*" Doucet said. He turned in his folding chair and pointed northward, beyond the dim lights of Nha Cat. Spooky's distant ring of tracer fire was barely visible through the humid, fetid atmosphere above the city. "Old Spooky must've topped off her fuel tanks before takeoff," Doucet said. "Spotters down yonder must've radioed her, 'Hey, Spooky! Come up here for lagniappe! Target of opportunity! *Laissez les bons temps rouler!*' Now she's likely to dance all night."

"I'll take you up," the little captain said. "That's a bet I prefer to lose, frankly. I've got to hope Private Rabinovych's chronicle of life outlasts what he calls a dance of death."

Rabby yawned. "Pardon me, Captain," he said, "but I intend to win this for you. No more digressions. So: Antoinette died, and they buried her beneath an unmarked stone cross. The baby survived. A wet nurse was found. Beyond that—here's where the genius of that Jewish communication network in the Pale really kicked in—wet nurses were lined up in advance nearly the whole rest of the way to Odessa, with Rachel as the last, the bombshell—"

"Rachel?" Peter said.

"—so the baby would never have to go more than a single night's horseback ride without a chance to breastfeed. Meir was mounted now, on Antoinette's horse, so they were able to move faster from one village to the next."

"Rachel?" Peter said, trying and failing to tamp down his aggrieved tone. "What Rachel?"

"I got a strong hunch," Doucet said, "that there ain't but one Rachel."

"I haven't mentioned Rachel yet?" Rabby said. He propped both feet on the roof's parapet again and gave them that happy waggle at the ankles. "Rachel was the last in the lineup of wet nurses, and she was the power hitter. They might even have fetched her in from another village, knowing she had enough beauty and focused willpower to swat down any reluctance on Meir's part. She brought along a newborn daughter of her own. That was a plus. See, it would prevent any confusion over primogeniture, assuming in due course she presented Meir with a son. Her husband had died in a freak accident. He'd been roofing a synagogue, and some of the tile slid out from under him, and he fell off the roof and broke his neck.

"Meir never had a chance, probably. By the time he and Tarnowski rode in before daylight and dismounted and stamped the snow off their boots and stepped into a stable or some other place that was warm enough for Konrad to unwrap the baby and hand her to this new wet nurse, nuptial arrangements had already been made. So my great-great grandmother Rachel became the only mother that Antonina would ever know."

"And the father, the battlefield leader—he went along with all this?" Karloff said. "He just handed over his child, a single night's ride from where his wife lay buried beneath a stone cross, to be raised by a Jewish woman?"

"Raised?" Rabby said. "No, that wasn't an issue. Not yet, anyway. Once Konrad pulled away whatever rough cloth the women at the last shtetl had bundled the baby in and he'd handed her to Rachel and Rachel had stepped behind a stable wall, or perhaps just turned aside, and the baby had latched on, that breast milk became the whole point. That is, how to keep it available as long as needed. And if Rachel's designs on Meir were clear from the first, then there must have been lengthy eye contact between Konrad and Meir. And since Konrad had the habit of command, we shouldn't imagine that the look he gave Meir was pleading."

"I see," Karloff said. "You mean it was more in the nature of, 'You know what you gotta' do, soldier!'"

"Nor should we picture any defiance in the look Meir gave him," Rabby said. "More likely, it contained about as complex a mix of messages and feelings as you can pack into a few wordless minutes. Meir must have looked a little resigned, but even more elated. Having walked away from one sweet marriage deal back in his hometown, here he had on offer an even better one. Granted there was no dowry, but neither were there any hovering in-laws. Plus, unlike her biblical namesake, this Rachel offered him proof positive of her fertility, in the form of one of the two infants now latched onto her nipples."

Peter sighed. The small captain threw back his head and laughed.

"But Meir needed to convey at least one more message," Rabby said. "And that one had to filter through his mixed feelings of resignation and elated surprise. That final message had nothing to do with Meir himself and everything to do with Konrad Tarnowski. It was a question: 'Are you sure?'"

"You mean—yes, I see," Karloff said. "You mean, 'Are you sure you want this?'"

"Correct," Rabby said. "Because remember: This whole bass-ackwards plan of escape—moving with agonizing slowness, shtetl to shtetl, hundreds of miles to the east and south—was aimed at getting Tarnowski and Antoinette to a warm-water port far enough from Poland that nobody was likely to challenge them when they tried to buy tickets on a steamer bound for Trieste or Venice or Ravenna. From any one of those destinations, it would have been a short hop to Austria, where dozens of Konrad's fellow officers from the Polish revolt were living in exile. They would have pooled whatever resources they could spare to take care of a fellow officer and his family who, after all this time, had managed to join them by such a bizarre, circuitous route. Meir's part in this scheme would be to wish them well, wave to them as their steamer headed off toward the Bosporus, then figure out how to construct a new life for himself as an Odessan.

"Now, standing there in a stable—or maybe it wasn't a stable, maybe it was a room with a curtain that Rachel could duck behind to suckle those two baby girls—Meir had to tell Konrad, using just his eyes: 'Yes, I will marry this woman, as you want me to do. But you're still free to go, as soon as we reach Odessa. I know, too, that you feel your freedom to do that is slipping away. I know you already feel an ankle-chain binding you to that plain stone cross back there in the snow. And I know you're about to feel a shackle close on the other ankle because you think you're forcing me to marry this woman, when the fact is, given the chance I'd probably marry her even if you were in Vienna or Siberia. So if you don't want that second chain riveted on, find a way to let me know it. You and I will thank this woman for nursing your child, and I'll skip past the trap she and the people here have set, and we'll ride on. We'll find another wet nurse, and another, for as long as the child needs one. You don't need words. Just tell me with your eyes.'

"But Tarnowski didn't tell him that, either then without words or later on with them. Maybe that first chain was enough. Maybe it bound Tarnowski so tightly he knew he'd never break free of it. Maybe he already felt the second chain and welcomed it. So if he and Meir came to any shared understanding while those two infants tanked up at Rachel's breast, it was simply to reaffirm the commitment they'd made back in Warsaw: that neither of them would abandon the other. The difference was that, back then, it had only meant for as long as they faced imminent danger. This time, it meant for the rest of their lives."

"Ah, my," Peter sighed. "Gods and heroes. Even a sublime matriarch with gushing teats."

"So, on to Odessa!" Rabby said hurriedly, before Karloff, who had raised an index finger, could again chastise Peter. "*Plus vite*! Maybe Meir had some prearranged point of contact there. More likely it was Rachel, whose home was just a day or two's ride north of the city, who knew somebody who knew somebody in Odessa who could take Meir and Tarnowski in for at least long enough to fulfill the ninety-day rule. She couldn't remarry, see, until her late husband had been dead that long. The object being complete clarity about which husband had begotten which of her children. That's just Jewish law, but it also suited Meir's and the count's particular case to a T, since it gave them that much unencumbered time to fashion the breadwinner roles they'd now have to play.

"Rachel must have told Antonina—because Great-aunt Dalia told me, and she could only have gotten it from Antonina—that Rachel laughed at Meir when he insisted it would be too dangerous for Tarnowski and himself to travel that last leg to Odessa by daylight. That might have been the first of the many times Rachel laughed at Meir. In my family, the sound of her laughter has sort of resounded down all the years since her time. 'What?' she must have told him. 'Skulking in the dark? Why?' Because, for her, Odessa and its tree-lined boulevards and its views of white-sailed boats tacking across the harbor was a city best seen in brilliant sunlight. All Meir knew yet about Odessa was what he'd heard back in Warsaw: that it was distant enough that political refugees could probably live undetected there, and even if they couldn't, the city's polyglot mix of people would simply shrug and go back to their main concern, which was making money. All that was correct, but it undershot the mark. Odessa was still a relatively new city then, built by royal decree. Its climate and sandy beaches quickly made it a year-round resort for Russia's aristocracy. Plus about a third of Odessa's population were Jews, and unlike in the Pale, they could play an unrestricted role in the city's economy. That all added up to make Odessa, at least for a few years, the most cosmopolitan, tolerant city in imperial Russia. Having come of age where she did—sort of in the city's penumbra—Rachel had good reason to laugh at Meir for thinking they could safely approach it only under cover of darkness."

Once again Doucet leaned toward Rabinowitz and spun one hand at an accelerating rate.

"Okay, okay, Emmet," Rabby said. "*Plus vite, et encore plus vite*! Telegraphic style, then." He tapped two fingernails against his front teeth in an arrhythmic semblance of Morse Code.

"Arrive in Odessa, spring of eighteen thirty-two. Tarnowski plugs into small network of Polish businessmen, signs on with a shipping agency. Owner, a Pole, might know of Tarnowski's role in Polish revolt but either approves of it or doesn't care. Meir seeks rabbinical duties. Odessa's chief rabbi says, 'You completed the full course in Warsaw, right? Our synagogues jointly support a yeshiva. How about teaching there?'

"Living arrangements: Meir and Rachel find lodgings in Jewish quarter. Tarnowski takes a flat two blocks away, lives there with Antonina once she's weaned. When he's at work, he parks the kid with Rachel. Sends kid to Catholic school once she's school age. But Tarnowski supplies the part of her education that lodges deepest in her mind. It serves her as both compass and rudder for the rest of her life. At home at night, he tells her stories. One's of the legendary Antoinette Tomaszewska, the sixteen-year-old who dropped out of convent, strapped on armor and fought the Russians. He uses his cavalry saber to show the child how that Antoinette charged into the Russian ranks, slashing left and right. He tells her about the young Jews who defended Warsaw, and how that other Antoinette, her mother, stayed with the dwindling band led by her husband until he forced her to leave. How even then she refused her chance for safety and instead came back at a gallop, insisting her plan of escape would work, provided he and Meir didn't dither away the window of time. How she braved the cold, the fear, the strange faces and strange words of the people in the little villages during their trek toward Odessa. How she died having seen her child lifted up before her. How she lay buried beneath a plain stone cross. How her father looked back as he and Meir rode away from that village and saw, by starlight, the cross capped with snow."

Rabby's voice trailed off. His sandaled feet were still propped on the parapet. He waggled one at the ankle, briefly and slightly but with what Peter read as muted self-satisfaction.

"You already have the rest," he said abruptly. "But keep in mind the glue that binds it all together: that unspoken pledge, man to man, Jew and Christian, each never to abandon the other. A pledge that in time devolved full-force on Antonina.

"The count sent her to Catholic school for probably as many years as girls were allowed to attend. He'd become manager at the shipping agency, and he had nothing better to spend his money on than his daughter's education. Meir became headmaster at the yeshiva. Of course, Ilana couldn't go there, but Meir and Antonina, and the count too, teamed up to conduct a Sundays-only crash school for Ilana. It's likely she was the only twelve-year-old Jewish girl in Odessa who could read and write in both Latin and Hebrew. So, on one level, these two men, Tarnowski and Meir, sank into what must have been dull bourgeois lives. But on another level, that bond between them gave their lives and their children's lives a quirkiness that could also, depending on how outsiders viewed it, turn dangerous.

"So, just in from Western Union." Rabby administered another set of telegraphic taps to his front teeth. "Eighteen fifty-nine. Antonina's been working for her father about ten years. In the run-up to Easter, gangs of toughs roam the city, threatening to kill Jews. Happens every year in Holy Week, but this year a mob, mostly Greeks, swarms through the Jewish quarter, smashes windows, beats any Jew out on the streets, breaks down doors, pulls people out so they'll have more of them to beat. Tarnowski and Antonina are at the shipping agency by the port when someone tells him about the mob. He says nothing about that to Antonina but calmly tells her to mind the store. Then he climbs the two hundred stairs up from the harbor at what for a sixty-odd years old man amounts to top speed. Stops by his flat to grab the saber and heads for Meir's house. Finds Meir there armed with the nearest thing to hand that could pierce or cut—a pitchfork, or maybe a meat cleaver. The two of them take position in Meir's doorway just as the mob comes howling up the nearest alley. At first the Greeks hold back, not knowing what to make of this tall, gaunt, blond, blue-eyed man standing there with a saber in his hand, back to back with a stubby little bearded Jew. Sailors or dockworkers in the mob recognize Konrad from the port and try to steer the others onward to some target less complicated and less capable of defense. But then perhaps the battle rage rises in the old Polish war horse and he shouts some dare or insult or even makes a one-man sortie. And the mob surges in, and Konrad and Meir swing and thrust and give as good as they get, or even a little better, until at last they're standing there alone, panting and bleeding, while the mob draws away and surges on into the next street. And Meir, with an earlobe dangling, says something like, 'We still know how to do this, don't we, Captain? We still know how to make 'em pay.' But Konrad doesn't answer. And then Antonina is there, because someone finally told her about the rioting. And Meir turns and looks into what he expected would be the old ice-blue fire in his commander's eyes, but one eye is hidden beneath its drooping eyelid, and in the other eye the fire has gone out. And then Meir watches Antonina slowly lift the saber from her father's hand."

Rabby stopped, drew breath and exhaled slowly. There was no ankle-waggle this time. One of the citronella candles was out. As the evening cooled, the land breeze had swept the rooftop clear of mosquitoes' hovering flight formations.

"I don't suppose any of you gentlemen would be so kind as to fetch me up a cigarette from your own reserves?" Rabby said.

Karloff uttered a tongue-click of frustration, then tapped the face of his wristwatch with a fingernail.

"It's nearly midnight!" he said. "I think we reached a pact here, Private, some time back. And your part in it was you were going to finish up as quickly as possible. Our pact contained no provision for smoke breaks."

Rabby gave a start of what Peter, with a snort of disgust, read as feigned surprise.

"It's that late?" Rabby said. "Well, of course you're right, then. I'll press on, press on. As I said, you already have all the major pieces. It was a stroke, of course. Apparently it damaged the count's memory and speech, because he was no longer able to work. And I suppose it was impossible for a woman to go on working in a business like that with no male relative present. So Antonina stopped working at the shipping agency. Meir took in the count to live with him and Rachel and Ilana. Meir would have done that without any recompense, but Antonina insisted on covering all her father's costs. And she moved into a place of her own. Not just another flat, but a small house, in a fashionable part of town where aristocrats from Moscow and Saint Petersburg had their dachas. Of course, the big change left out of that accounting was the one that made it necessary that Antonina have her own house, far from the Jewish quarter."

"Sure," the little captain said. "You mean—well, whatever a woman had to do to signal to men of that cut of society that she was, you know, available."

"But you should understand, it wasn't that my great-aunt tried to suppress that information," Rabby said. "She had to explain things in a way that would make sense to an eight- or nine-year-old kid, which is what I was at the time. She probably said something like, 'Antonina was a beautiful and intelligent woman with a noble bearing, and when she finally started going out in society, men vied for the privilege of becoming her friends and patrons.' Now what's so damn funny about that, Emmet?"

Doucet was cackling so hard he almost collapsed his lawn chair.

"Suppress?" he said. "If Great-aunt Dalia explained it any more exactly, she'd need an anatomy chart!"

"Well, I'm glad I was allowed to grow into that kind of knowledge," Rabby said icily. "Which you no doubt acquired in a bayou canebrake by about age six."

"And that setup," Karloff said, "Antonina's star ascendant as a courtesan, Tarnowski well cared for, Meir's family shielded from further mob violence—all that stayed in place for how long?"

"Care for her father dropped out pretty quickly," Rabby said. "Tarnowski died within a few years. Meir died about 1880, Rachel soon after that. If anything, their deaths just upped the pressure on Antonina to keep protection for that one Jewish household intact. It didn't help, either, that Odessa was changing. The old tolerance withered away, and the cold Jew-hatred that lies deep in the Russian soul crept in. Great-aunt Dalia said Antonina told her once that, in her youth, the scent of the acacia trees on Odessa's boulevards smelled to her like the breath of freedom. Then Antonina told her she hoped that someday, somewhere, Dalia would find a scent that smelled like freedom to her. It was clear to Dalia that for Antonina, Odessa's acacia blossoms didn't smell like freedom anymore.

"By the time Rachel died, Ilana was long since married. Like every other Jewish family, once pogroms became a recurring threat, Ilana's household had to hunker down within their own four walls and hope the angel of death would pass them by. Her husband, Isaac, had replaced his father as yeshiva headmaster. Isaac's status, plus the lingering memory of the donnybrook in that doorway during Holy Week in 1859, made his household a prime target for the next mob that would bubble up from Odessa's ethnic stew when religious frenzy and economic resentment brought it to a boil.

"Sometime in the late 1890s, not long before Dalia was born, Antonina moved in. She was in her sixties then—still beautiful, I'm sure, but she must have realized it was time to quit the kind of life she'd lived for better than three decades. She must have foreseen that soon she could no longer elicit desire and envy, and would instead become the object of pity. But mainly, I think, she moved in with Isaac and Miriam because she thought they might someday need her badly, and when that happened, they'd need her close by."

"I guess she fell on hard times," the smaller officer said. "I mean, after she no longer had those clients. What you call her benefactors."

"Oh no, she always had them, at least in the role of benefactors," Rabby said. "And she had as much wealth as she would ever need to live on her own. It was just that she had no more need for the moderately lavish, very private quarters a successful courtesan required. Her two sons were grown men who needed nothing from her—never had, in fact."

Karloff jerked forward in his chair as if he'd been poked in the back. He wore a frown of dismay.

"Sons? Where in the damn's hell did they come from?" he said. "For Christ's sake, Private, don't take us down another side trail at this hour."

"Oh, I didn't mention her two sons?" Rabby said. Peter noted the brief, self-satisfied waggle of the ankle. "No need to linger on those. Her benefactors helped her there. A couple of them took the boys in, almost from birth. They saw to their education and social standing. One became an admiral. Came to disgrace for his less than stellar performance in the war with Japan. The men who took them in—their fathers, we can assume—sent her occasional updates on the boys, at least when they were young. I don't think she ever communicated directly with her sons. And I don't know if they ever knew the facts of their birth."

Karloff squinted skeptically. "So she treated them as just a minor occupational hazard?" he said.

"Oh, I'm sure not minor," Rabby said. "But it was something her benefactors, by prior understanding, could make go away. She must have selected those men—her benefactors, patrons, clients if you want to call them that—with great care. She had at least a half-dozen of them over the years. They supplied her with all she could need in the way of material support. But what she needed from them most, and what for thirty years she had gotten from the ones who wielded the most clout, was a guarantee of safety for the household of Meir and Rachel Rabinowitz. But by 1905, those old guarantors of protection were either dead or out of power. She had long ago reached an understanding with the commander of Odessa's military garrison, and she took care to renew it each time a new commander came in. She would arrive at the new one's office by appointment, dressed in her finest silks I'm sure, and fix him with that calm, gray-eyed gaze and ask him if the promise given years ago by one of his honored predecessors still held. And they always said yes. She did have that much of a guarantee, but she had never yet had to put it to the test. So she must have felt that the only reliable protection she could give the home of Isaac and Miriam was the kind her father had given it a day or two before Easter in 1859, when it was still the household of Meir and Rachel. She'd have to be there in a doorway, with nothing to wield against an attack but her own flagging strength and her father's saber.

"So she moved in. She asked only for a single room, and she had a private entrance built into it, at the rear of the house. The door between her room and the main part of the household she kept locked, and seldom used it. She wanted to make sure she wasn't a bother, I suppose. I suspect she also foresaw a time when a separate entrance, not visible from the street, would help her make good on her vow of protection.

"Her move into that tiny room, I'd say, completed her physical alignment with the cloistered life that, in her mind and heart, she'd lived all along. The kind of life Antoinette Tomaszewska, that sixteen-year-old girl that Antonina knew only from legend, had put behind when she left the convent and joined the Polish cavalry. A life of poverty, chastity and obedience. For more than thirty years, Antonina had to shelve poverty and chastity to make good on the obedience part. Now they all lined up, and she must have felt at rest, in a way. But wary, too. Which is why, in what might otherwise have passed for a nun's chamber, she kept that saber handy and well-sharpened."

For the first time, Peter heard a note of hostility in the little captain's voice. "Before you tie too neat a bow on Antonina's approach to sanctity through self-sacrifice," he said, "I'd like to hear how you square that with her choice to surrender her two children."

Rabinowitz nodded once, gravely. "All I can tell you is there was nothing chosen about it," he said. "I mean the life she was leading, and had to go on leading. Because that life ensured her the means—and, more important, the influence—to keep that protective cordon around Meir's family intact. To put it crudely, her beauty and her bearing weren't enough if she wasn't also available when one of her benefactors happened to be in town. And if she followed through on motherhood, if she tried to raise her children, her availability would just be occasional, and always fraught with secrecy and deception. In other words, a relationship with her would be just another sordid affair, and no man who could afford a real courtesan would put up with that. I don't think she ever hesitated about handing those infants over to men she knew would bring them up in privileged surroundings. Because, at least in her mind, the essence of the vow passed on to her by her father was that it trumped bonds of flesh and blood."

Karloff began tapping the face of his watch again, holding it up first toward his fellow officer, then under Rabby's nose.

"Okay, *plus vite encore*," Rabby said. "Sometime after the turn of the century, she moved in. All appurtenances of her old life gone—the small, very private house, all its furnishings, the carriage and team—all gone, except the one outfit of fine silk. And the saber. And her necklace with that outsize crucifix. As it turned out, all three of those things proved essential. The silk finery in securing armed protection when badly needed. The saber and crucifix in buying just enough time for that help to get there."

For a few seconds, Rabby chewed his lip. "You've got to understand," he said, "that what happened to the Jews in Odessa in 1905 didn't just spring unbidden out of the black soul of Mother Russia. The Jews themselves had a hand in it. They jumped the gun badly during Holy Week, when Jewish men patrolled their streets armed with pistols and knives and whips. A Jewish self-defense league even printed up leaflets urging women to carry vials of sulfuric acid to throw in attackers' faces. You couldn't call that readiness campaign a provocation, exactly, since in years past attacks on Jews had become routine during Holy Week. But that year, nothing like that happened. Short-term, you could say that showed preparedness pays. Longer-term, it stored up bad blood among the kinds of people—dockworkers, day laborers—who'd look for ways to teach a lesson to Jews who dared prance around packing heat.

"But that self-defense campaign might also have saved the lives of Miriam and her two youngest children. I suspect it was what prompted Antonina to add an extra layer of preparedness when she visited the new commander for the Odessa military district that spring, when the leaflets about carrying guns and knives and acid were being handed out. Apparently, she had never needed to say much to each new guy in that position. All she had to do was remind him the guarantee was there and ask if he stood by it."

"Yeah, I've seen how that kind of thing works," Karloff said. "Some General What's-his-nitzky could have been smitten by her forty years back, and it's your ass if you don't deliver today on whatever promise he made back then."

"Well, this time, Antonina asked for an extra layer of protection," Rabby said. "When this stately old lady in her fine silks walked into the office of the new guy, Alexander Kaulbars, she probably sized him up quickly. She was a past master at that, with men of his class. Kaulbars might have felt pretty dejected at the time. Maybe even a little physically sore, too. During a Russian retreat a few weeks earlier, he'd fallen off his horse and injured his ass, which the Japanese had already soundly kicked at the Battle of Mukden. He was a disgraced military leader. He could have compared notes with Antonina's son the admiral on what that felt like. Yet here this distinguished-looking woman was bowing and addressing him as 'Your Excellency.' And not in a sycophantic way, because her calm gray gaze told him she was incapable of falsity. What she asked, beyond the renewal of a pledge that had held for decades, seemed so modest. It was just a specific arrangement for emergency response. So he said 'of course.' If she ever sent word by some agreed-upon means, he'd immediately send a squad of soldiers to the address covered by that longstanding protection agreement. And one more thing she told him. I'm sure it helped fix those details in his mind. It was no longer just a family named Rabinowitz that lived at that address. She lived there too."

"And the means?" the smaller officer said. "How would she send that summons?"

"My guess is she promised some kid in her neighborhood a tidy sum to serve as her runner when she handed him the message for Kaulbars," Rabby said. "Or maybe she had quick enough access to a telegraph office that she could message him that way. Anyway, that plan was in place by Holy Week. It might have helped her credibility with Kaulbars that she didn't send him some cry-wolf summons then. Nor did she send him one in June, when the Potemkin and its mutinous crew steamed into the harbor, and the army opened fire on rioters there, and—in good old Russian leap-of-logic fashion—word spread that the bloodshed was all the fault of the Jews.

"By mid-October, hell was breaking loose, and it kept escalating. Still no summons from Antonina. This was the year, understand, that brought Russia up to the brink it would finally plunge over in 1917. Labor strikes, mutinies, attacks on police and soldiers. In October, the Tsar issued a Manifesto granting certain civil liberties. When the text reached Odessa, it set off dueling demonstrations between people who welcomed it—Jews, students, workers—and loyalists, ethnic Russians who'd bow as low to the Tsar's portrait as they would to an icon of Christ. You can picture their displeasure when left-wing students, Jews among them, tied portraits of the Tsar to the tails of dogs, and the dogs ran through the streets and ripped the Tsar's likeness to shreds with their fangs. For a little while, the cops and soldiers kept control, in finger-in-the-dike fashion. Still no word for Kaulbars from Antonina, though I'm sure she wasn't his top-of-mind concern at that point."

Doucet began making the accelerating spiraling motion with his hand again. This time, Rabby snapped at him angrily.

"Oh, hell, Emmet," he said. "This was an immense human catastrophe, and it directly affected the lives of everyone in my family down to this day. And I'm not going to boil it down to an undergraduate's cheat sheet."

Karloff touched Doucet's elbow in what Peter took to be a sign of appreciation for the hit Emmet had taken, but also an order to let Rabby proceed uninterrupted.

"Next day, the loyalists marched from the harbor up toward the city center, where shots were fired from surrounding buildings," Rabby said. "A kid carrying an icon fell dead. Apparently, that was like flipping a switch, because it threw the passions of that crowd into default mode, and the cry went up, 'Kill the Yids!' Which some hundreds of them proceeded to do. And unlike the day before, soldiers and cops either stood aside or took part in the killing and looting. In other words, a full-blown pogrom, though unlike the smaller-scale violence that Jews had for years suffered during Holy Week, it was hard to see it coming.

"Certainly Isaac hadn't seen it coming. Else he wouldn't have led most of his older students, including his son Yosef, downtown to take part in pro-Manifesto demonstrations that day. A lot of men from Jewish households must have made a similar bad choice, because there weren't nearly enough of them around to defend their families when the mobs reached their streets, howling for Jewish blood.

"From her back room at Isaac and Miriam's house, Antonina must have heard that howling at a considerable distance. Either that, or perhaps something in the confluence of time, memory, the way the October sunlight slanted through her window, the ordinary household sounds beyond the locked door to the family's sitting room—something in all of that signaled to her that this was the very day she'd been destined for, and the moment was approaching when she'd have to act, and she'd better prepare for it quickly.

"If it was a written message she sent Kaulbars, she must have already had it addressed and sealed when she left the house. Rather than coming through the sitting room, she left through the back door and came around to the front, probably to make sure it was safe to open that one. When she knocked and Miriam opened the door, all that Antonina told her was, 'I'm going out. Stay inside and keep this door locked, and don't open it for anyone except Isaac. I'll let myself in by the rear door when I get back.' And then she was gone. She must have gone at least far enough toward the city center to hear the mob's hullabaloo. Probably she noticed that the Christian households had all placed a cross or an icon in a front window or nailed it to their door, so that the mob would pass them by. Perhaps then she wondered if that outsize crucifix at her breast might have been enough to fool the mob's scouts or outriders. But she must have known that possibility was too slender to count on, assuming, as she had always assumed, that the memory of what happened in Meir's and Rachel's doorway in 1859 had lingered on ever since in the collective mind of would-be Jew killers.

"So she hurried on—a tall old woman in a plain house dress, but still with that straight-backed bearing, and with the color mounting in her cheeks from the October chill, and from the sense that now every step she took, every word, every use she made of her hands had to precisely fit a role scripted for her before she was born.

"And then." Rabby waved a hand slowly in front of his eyes. "Then, for a little while, I lose sight of her. Could she have made it to the nearest telegraph office, sent the message to Kaulbars and still made it back before those killers—some of them spattered with the blood of the children they'd butchered just a few houses away—showed up at Miriam's door? Or had she prearranged with some fleet-footed youngster, possibly a Christian kid who'd have less reason to fear being spotted on the street, to carry that sealed envelope to Kaulbars' headquarters and deliver it directly to his hand? However she got the message to him, she cut it close on timing. She might not have even made it back before the mob arrived. She would have followed a back alley, since her private door opened onto one. On her way back, she might have passed a house a few doors from Isaac's while the mob was at work there. If she did, she must have gotten some notion what was going on inside from the collective howling of the killers and the mother's crazed shrieks. Wonderful, isn't it, how even in the matter of murder, the creativity of the human mind seems nearly boundless? That group had chanced on a woman alone with her six children. The mob had a rope. They found an exposed beam beneath the ceiling. And voila! Stroke of genius! They looped the rope around the woman's legs and hung her upside down from the beam. While she dangled there, they butchered her six children and laid them out on the floor beneath her. Laid their bodies out symmetrically, don't you know, like a six-pointed star. Then they left her there that way. Alive.

"A locked door doesn't stand much chance against a mob that has tasted blood. Especially if they've tasted it in a fashion certain to satisfy whatever deep artistic yearnings might reside in a mob. Without bothering to knock, they stove in the front door of Isaac and Miriam's house with a section of railway track they were toting around for that purpose. Little as she was then, Dalia still has a clear memory of all that happened once they got in. She remembers her mother shrieking and begging, and little Avram crawling across the floor and reaching up with a grin—Dalia calls it a stupid grin—to tug on the trouser leg of one of those men. Can you imagine? Tugging on the pants leg of a man who had come to kill them all! What a little shit that kid must have been, that Avram!"

Rabby's teeth bared in a furious grimace that, as swiftly as it came, was gone.

"But of course he was too little," he said. "He shouldn't be blamed, should he? Of course not. And even Dalia remembers that the men themselves didn't immediately look bent on mayhem, though she saw the guns and knives and the blood on the shirts of a few of them. Perhaps they were temporarily sated from their last blood meal. Dalia said they just seemed intent on getting down to business, like workmen come to make a repair. The oddest thing, it seemed to her, was the way one man walked slowly around the room looking at the ceiling while the others just stood and watched him. Finally, he got up on a chair beneath a half-exposed wooden beam, and he started chipping away at the plaster above it with what looked to Dalia like a big iron nail—probably a railroad spike. When he started chipping a hole over the top of the beam, it jolted the rest of them out of their torpor. Dalia remembers hearing the phrase, 'slit them open,' but mostly the sound they made was just a wordless howl. Dalia felt a man grab her by the shoulders, and several men wrestled her mother to the floor, and someone in the crowd at the doorway tossed them a rope that had a loop tied in each end.

"The men got a loop around one of her mother's ankles. They were trying to pin down Miriam's other leg and yelling at the man on the chair to hurry it up with the hole above the beam when Dalia bit the hand of the man holding her and tried to pull free. She had almost made it, she said, when she heard the lock click in Antonina's door. She couldn't tell whether anyone else heard it, but to Dalia it sounded like a thunderclap.

"Then Antonina kicked the door open. Dalia said that as Antonina stepped forward, her eyes didn't look distressed or frightened. They didn't look anything except intent, coolly measuring distance and the angle the blade would need to take. She raised the saber with both hands and brought the blade down on the neck of the man who was chasing Miriam's flailing ankle. She must have got him cleanly through the carotid, because Dalia saw a spurt of his blood hit the other one in the face. Antonina would have gotten that one too, if someone in the doorway hadn't gotten off a quick shot that stopped her. And then a volley of shots sent her backward through the doorway she'd just stepped through.

"That volley knocked her to the floor with such force, Dalia said, that for a second, her big gold crucifix on its chain hung in the air, wobbling like a wounded bird before it dropped onto her breast. Then, Dalia said, the mob's howling stopped just like—and here she'd make a sharp twisting motion with her hand, meaning it was like switching off a radio. And she said the man on his chair quit chipping away at the plaster above the beam, and he looked at the corpse with the crucifix on its breast, and then he stepped down.

"And then…" Rabby chuckled. His chuckling sounded too hollow and went on a little too long, Peter thought, to spring from actual amusement. "You know, if they'd gone through with what they intended, it would have been a comedown for them anyway," Rabby said. "In this household, there were just two children, whereas in the last one there were six. But once an artist discovers his true métier, he sticks with it, you know? He does his level best with whatever materials come to hand, be they six in number or just two. But this crucifix cast the matter in a different light. Besides being artists, these were men with sincere ethical concerns, of their own special kind. They must have discussed whether inadvertently killing Christians on the way to intentionally butchering Jews constituted what you men of the military profession might call acceptable collateral damage. No doubt one of them had removed the crucifix from Antonina's corpse and wiped the blood off it and held it up while all of them, with their ropes and guns and knives at the ready, pondered that question. And that discussion must have lasted long enough for the dozen or so soldiers that Kaulbars had dispatched to arrive and give an attention-getting bayonet prod to the backsides of the rearward-most of that gang of murderers and thieves. Considering their respective numbers and weaponry, the best the soldiers could hope to do with that bunch of pogromists was persuade them to move along and practice their chosen art form elsewhere. They succeeded at that. And the one who lifted that ornate gold crucifix on its necklace from Antonina's body succeeded in making off with it. Proving, I suppose, that even if those killers did try to murder selectively, they were equal-opportunity thieves."

"What about Isaac and his son?" the little captain said. "Did they make it home safely?"

Rabby winced. "O-ooh, painful subject," he said. "At some point after that handful of soldiers drove away the mob, Isaac and my grandfather, Yosef, got home. Possibly word had reached them and the other Jewish demonstrators downtown that the flames of hell were licking at their families' doorsteps. I don't know exactly what happened when

Isaac and Yosef arrived home, because nobody in my family has ever talked about it. If anyone, even by accident, said something suggestive of that topic, my grandfather would get up and leave the room. I do surmise from hints Dalia let drop that it involved some weapons-free physical attack by Miriam on her husband and elder son.

"So there you have it all," Rabby said, tapping the heels of his hands lightly, once, against the aluminum arms of his lawn chair. "Some loose ends, quickly told. Remember Meir's intent, his pledge, was to get Tarnowski and Antoinette to a jumping-off point, where they could find passage to a place of refuge? Well, after all those years, it worked out the other way round. Antonina had given Isaac instructions that, when she died, he should contact one of her patrons. The man was a relatively minor local official—which is surprising, given the much higher tiers of officialdom and aristocracy that most of her benefactors had belonged to. Plus he was several years younger than Antonina. She would have been in her fifties before he was even assigned to Odessa. My conclusion: He must have loved her passionately, loved her for what she was at least as much as for her beauty, which would have been sharply diminished before he ever laid eyes on her. She knew she could trust him with her final wishes. She wanted him to hold securely all her assets, and upon her death hand them over to the two people she named as her heirs. Both were Jews, of no blood relation to her: Isaac Rabinowitz and Ilana Kopelman. It wasn't a fortune, exactly, but it was more than enough to cover passage to New York for Isaac and Miriam and their three kids. Isaac thought—correctly as it turned out—that he had an opportunity to sign on with a startup yeshiva in Manhattan that would blend religious instruction with a secular high school education. Ilana's portion enabled her and her children and grandchildren to emigrate to Palestine. Where, incidentally, a few years later, one of Ilana's sons helped found the first kibbutz. And that's the same kibbutz where Nina, my nutty half-Catholic aunt—but that, truly, is another story.

"Also, Antonina wanted this guy who held her assets to arrange a funeral Mass and burial next to her father. Catholics say Mass is celebrated, don't they? She wanted hers celebrated in Polish.

"So. *Finis*! Captain, sorry, but it looks like you win the bet you said you'd rather lose. Emmet was right. Spooky means to boogie all night long."

The gunship had moved back down the mountain range. It was firing sporadically now, and only along a short arc, as if its gunners were striving for pinpoint fire on a small target. Peter thought he caught the sound of the aircraft's engines, and he guessed it was directing fire at something a little beyond a Korean infantry post in the hills south of the air base. Peter had visited the post once at the invitation of a Korean sergeant. The soldiers were living in dugouts covered by tarpaulins. Peter remembered the pet monkeys leashed to the support poles beneath the tarps, and how quiet the men were as they cleaned their weapons before heading out on night patrol.

Doucet waved a five-dollar military scrip note above his head. The captain barely glanced at it as he snatched it and stuffed it in a breast pocket.

"So you feel this woman gave up—well, everything, including her life, so your family could survive?" the officer said.

Rabby was silent for so long that Peter took it as his way of saying he was simply, finally, done. Then Rabby said:

"Torah teaches that everything in life has a deeper meaning, and that this double meaning is often a paradox. You'd be hard pressed to find anything that mattered that Antonina didn't give up. On the other hand, you could say she gained everything that mattered—to her."

"Yes," the captain said. "'Whoever shall seek to save his life shall lose it, and whoever shall lose his life shall preserve it.'"

"Between the moment she brought her blade down on the neck of the one who was chasing Miriam's ankle and the moment the others shot her, she knew she'd finally done it," Rabby said. "She'd achieved the apotheosis of the two Antoinettes and she'd proved herself worthy of them both. She'd reached up and touched that chalice of valor, without ever having forsaken her commitments to charity and sacrifice. No matter how much it cost her in humiliation, in having to live in what her faith taught her was mortal sin. In silent grief at having to give up her two children. In loneliness. In having no one of her direct lineage to carry on her name or even remember who and what she was. No matter any of that. She had done it."

"And the name," the captain said, leaning forward in his lawn chair with his big-knuckled fingers interlocked, almost in a pose of prayer. "That was our point of entry into this whole story, wasn't it? The passing of her name to the firstborn now in each of two generations—is that just a way of honoring this woman? Or does it lay some special obligation, some burden, on the bearers of that name: your aunt, and now you?"

Rabby chuckled, stretched his arms and yawned.

"Yes, I think my name's pretty special," he said. "And yes, I think I ought to try to live up to it, in small ways, here and there. But live into it large-scale? No, I don't think I ever could do that."

"Bing-bing, it's O one hundred hours!" Karloff said, standing suddenly. "Thank you, Private. Now I think duty summons us all in one direction only, and that's to bed."

Standing, the smaller captain put a hand on Rabby's shoulder.

"God bless you, my friend," he said. "And, you know, maybe to live up to that name, you just need to live a while longer, and you'll find a way." Both officers collapsed their folding chairs and propped them against the wall of the cistern. Peter bit his lower lip, wary of reviving Karloff's ire.

"There's something else," he said.

The officers, already halfway to the ladder, stopped and glanced back. They were already outside the candles' wobbling circle of light.

"Look, everybody knows what happened at the CIA villa last week, right?" Peter said. "About that VC suspect, assuming that's what he was, getting delivered there and hustled inside. Has there been any follow-up? I mean, any sign, any word of why they brought him there or what they did with him?"

Peter heard a long, slow expiration of breath and knew it came from Karloff.

"If you assume the bars on our collars mean we have some inside channel to that villa across the street, Private, you couldn't be more wrong," the captain said. "Nor at this hour do I have the slightest interest in speculating about that."

The other officer started to chuckle. "Well, I can pass on a little staff room scuttlebutt," he said in his banjo-twang voice. "Source was supposedly some guy in the Army motor pool who shuttles Special Forces types out to the docks in Nha Cat. Special Forces keeps a watercraft there for quick-hit missions along the coast or on close-in islands. This fellow's answer to the question you just asked was supposedly, 'Only the fishes know for sure.' Now, take a grain of salt with that, or maybe a whole shakerful. That's the kind of thing you'd expect to hear, you know, from somebody who just enjoys creating an air of mystery."

"And—and—you were saying, staffroom scuttlebutt," Peter stammered. "Has there been any of that about, you know, anything that might be related to what you heard? Like small arms getting smuggled into Nha Cat and maybe buried somewhere?"

"Haven't heard that," the captain said, his voice still patient, genial, countrified. "The only other tidbit I heard—and it supposedly came from the same source in Army motor pool—was the Special Forces people he works with said they had one more rat left to catch, and they were figuring out how to bait the trap. Now, if you've heard something about buried weapons, you should report it. If the colonel thinks it's worth checking, he can kick it over to intel. Bear in mind, though, rumors of buried arms are probably the oldest bugaboo in the history of warfare."

In a moment, Peter heard the officers clattering down the rickety iron ladder.

"*Merde*!" Doucet said. "Spooky's done packed it in! If you'd padded it out five more minutes, I'd of won my bet!"

"No, no, Emmet" Rabby said. "Look out there."

Peter looked where Rabby was pointing and saw that the gunship had resumed its hypnotic stitching-out of a full circle of tracer fire, this time above mountains in the middle distance.

"*La danse macabre continue encore*," Rabby said.

"*Merde* anyway," Doucet said. "One way or the other, you lost me the five." He collapsed his folding chair and took a step toward the cistern. Then he stopped and tilted his head back at Rabby.

"So we ought to start calling you Tony, right?" he said.

"No, no," Rabby said. "I just wanted you to know the name was there, that's all. Using it now would just cause confusion."

"Then—look, *dit mon la verité*," Doucet said. "This whole story you're telling us, you didn't make it all up, right? Cause if you did, man, you've still got my respect. Where I'm from, a lawyer who can lie that good is gonna for sure go far. If he's either Baptist or Catholic, maybe even the governor's mansion in Baton Rouge."

"Like I said, Emmet," Rabby said. "Everything I told you about my ancestors either is true or it has to be. And the 'has to be' parts just bridge gaps in the 'is.'"

"Well, that's good, because I was wondering," Doucet said. "I majored in geography at college, you know? That coursework was mostly crip, but some of the stuff I remember real well, especially things that didn't line up with what most people believe. And one of the things that stuck with me was from a course in geography and climate. I'd always thought winter everywhere in Russia was bare-ass cold, just like Siberia. And I learned it's not. In fact, down around the Black Sea, in that area where you said the count had to breathe down on his newborn baby's head to keep her from freezing—well, I learned the wintertime temperatures there aren't that different from where I grew up. When I was little, my *maman* used to walk with me out to the end of our gravel road in the wintertime when it was still dark and cold in the morning. She had to catch the bus into town every day so she could park me with *mémé* and go to work at her checkout job. And at nighttime, we'd come home the same way. And *maman* never said anything to me about having to breathe down on my head to keep me from freezing."

Rabinowitz began wagging his head side to side in a way that, to Peter, signaled oncoming, closely targeted drollery.

"Well, the first thing to say about that, Emmet, is you weren't a newborn, and Antonina was," he said. "The second is that, by the age of two, you were probably getting a big enough daily dose of pepper sauce to keep your physiological engine humming during a Louisiana cold snap. The third and slightly more serious thing to say about it is—look, in your geography and climate studies, did you ever come across references to a period called the 'Little Ice Age'?"

Emmet started twirling the edge of his mustache with two fingers. Even in the faint starlight, Peter could see the pained glimmer of his eyes. "Sure, I heard of that," Emmet said.

"Well, we can probably assume the nighttime temperatures in February 1832 along the route Meir and Konrad were traveling dropped considerably below whatever higher figure you saw cited for southern Ukraine. And the fourth thing to say is: Look, is it contagious, this virus of doubt?"

"Oh, I think Emmet came by it the old-fashioned way," Peter said. "By comparing the fable-like aspects of your story with the facts of the known world. He matched up a telltale marker in your story with an instructive bit from his own experience, and he finds—*Voila*! There stands the fabulist unmasked! Whether the fabulist was cynical or compulsive, I can't say for sure. In your case, I prefer to think the latter. And I say all of this as one who, right now—and I think I speak for all of us who heard your tale—would prefer to believe it's true."

"Then I recommend you accept it all as true, on grounds of that preference," Rabinowitz said. "Because you won't find any other grounds to prove or disprove it."

Rabby was silent a long time. Spooky circled on, half its orbit hidden by a distant mountain. A halo of tracer fire hung askew from the mountain's peak. Finally Rabby began to laugh, very slowly, still looking toward the gunship. For a long time he laughed like that, in barks of humorless laughter that alternately built and waned and were so widely spaced that his laughing consisted more of silence than of sound: "HA—ha—ha. HA—HA—ha—ha—ha." Then he stopped.

"So on grounds as paltry and irrelevant as..." He shook his head. "Tell me, gentlemen: Did either of you ever in your lives hear of another Jew named Antonin?"

Twenty-two

When the final bell had rung on Friday and Peter's students, a new class of warrant officer cadets, had gone out chattering about the soccer match, Peter leaned out the window to beat his eraser against the wall and saw Rabinowitz plodding past toward the shuttle trucks.

"Hey, you headed home?" Peter said. "Is the soccer match off?"

"Not a bit of it, my man," Rabby said. He had his thumb hitched beneath his rifle's sling. His fatigue cap was perched far back on his head, and his ponderous face with its drooping lower lip was bent toward the pavement. "I'm going back to the villa to suit up."

"Here," Peter said. He put his hand on the window ledge and vaulted out. When he landed, he felt a warning twinge in his knee. Gingerly, he jogged to catch up with Rabinowitz.

"Let me keep that thing for you," he said. "You tote it like it was a keg of nails."

Rabinowitz half-turned his head and scowled. "What sense does that make?" he said. "I'm going to throw the damn thing in my locker."

"You know the regs, Rabby. It'd be just like the team chiefs to check during the game to make sure we had our weapons by."

"Yeah? You think I care?"

"Look, will you give me the gun? It's likely to rust away before you can get home with it anyway."

Rabinowitz irritably shrugged the rifle free. He caught it with one hand as it fell and tossed it behind him without looking. Peter had to lunge to catch it.

"The clips too," Peter said.

"Officious goddamn nervous Nelly," Rabinowitz muttered. Getting rid of the rifle altered his plodding not at all. He flipped first one clip, then the other over his shoulder, and Peter caught them.

Men headed back to the villas were climbing into shuttle trucks parked between the soup kitchen and the stingrays. Peter shouldered Rabby's rifle and pocketed the clips.

"Hey, Pete," Rabinowitz said. He stopped and squinted back at Peter with what looked like mistrust. "I ought to tell you—this game might not play out the way you expect."

"Yeah?" Peter said. "Well what is it I expect, if you're free to disclose that information?"

"I have no idea, but whatever it is, the game's not likely to turn out that way," Rabby said. "Don't let that throw you. Think of this soccer game—think of it as just a piece of a longer game, a higher-stakes game. Okay?"

"Absolutely," Peter said. "I'll think of it as just a little piece of the big game that's going to get one Private A. Rabinowitz back to the Harlowe and Rabinowitz office suite in minimal time, with some good stories to tell. Some of which might even be true."

Peter went back to his classroom to get his own rifle. He slung a rifle on each shoulder and carried a set of clips in each side pocket of his fatigue blouse. He wedged his books under one arm. The four clips, swinging in the pockets of the loose blouse, scourged his thighs and dragged at the muscles of his shoulders and back.

"Hardship in a war zone," he muttered. "Just a grunt suffering hardship in a war zone."

He felt a hand touch his elbow, and he heard Thanh's voice.

"Ho, Dan'ridge! You go to see play football or you go for hunting VC in the moun-taine?"

Peter did not know why the sight of Thanh's harried-looking gaze should prick him with unease.

"The other rifle belongs to Rabinowitz," he said. "The rusted one. I'm keeping it for him during the game. Sure, I'm going to the match. You?"

Thanh looked up at him steadily with the small, round eyes that reminded Peter of the lustrous shells of roasted chestnuts. Thanh carried what looked like a binoculars case, suspended from a shoulder strap. The front of Thanh's crush cap rose absurdly high above his compact, oval face. Peter had been looking at Thanh for a while before it struck him that it was absurd for the two of them to be stopped, standing there, wordlessly looking at each other.

"Well?" Peter snapped. "Are you going to the game, or not?"

"Have care for your friend," Thanh said. "Pham is very good with playing football and with, what you call, the fighting that you do not for all the time see."

"With karate. So what does—"

"Yes, yes, but different," Thanh said, his voice rising with the effort to explain. "It is not what you think when I say karate. I tell you this is fighting for playing football and it is with the feet and hands you do not maybe see."

Oh, shove your little smug patient worried smile, Peter thought.

"What do you think I can do about it?" he said. "Blow Pham away during warm-ups? Maybe I could use Rabby's own weapon. Sure. More fitting. Let Pham waste away of rust poisoning."

Thanh's smile waned, but beneath the sheer khaki cliff of his crush cap his eyes kept their unintimidated luster.

"I do not say what you should do," Thanh said. "I do not know what is happening for you can do. I say only this: Have care for your friend."

"Yeah?" Peter said, furious at being saddled with Rabinowitz again. "Well, you go have a tender care for a rice snake, Thanh."

Peter started to turn away, but again Thanh put a hand on his arm.

"Did you remember, Dan'ridge, what I tell you? That Pham is from the North?"

"Oh, now, how could I ever forget that," Peter said acidly, "given how relevant it must be to the outcome of a soccer match. Look, I told Rabby you'd said Pham came south from Haiphong a couple of years ago. And I told him you found it remarkable that Pham had won prima donna status here in that amount of time. Did I get all that right?"

Thanh nodded slightly, once. "And did he say, maybe, he being more careful? Not today only, but being careful all of time, with Pham?"

"Rabby said nothing about being careful. It would be completely out of character for him to say that. What he said was something about Pham being a spy. No—what he said was that maybe Pham was a double agent. Actually, I don't think he said straight-out he meant Pham, but it seemed pretty clear. Double agent—that would be like a spy for both sides, right? I think that's what it means. Actually, I don't know what it means. Coming from a Jew who claims he's named for the daughter of a Polish countess, it probably just means he's delusional."

While Peter was still mired in this senseless ramble, Thanh started nodding more deeply, with what looked to Peter like satisfaction.

"Now I think he is being careful more time, all of time," Thanh said. "Maybe you, too, Dan'ridge. Maybe you, too, will be careful all of time about Pham."

"You bet," Peter said, turning away again. "Careful's our watchword. Eggshells wouldn't crackle under our feet."

Peter still felt a twinge in his knee, but weighted as he was with one rifle on each shoulder and ammo clips in both side pockets of his blouse, he at least felt physically in balance. Then he felt something else was out of balance, and it had to do with Thanh. Peter turned and squinted back at the trim little man in the absurdly tall crush cap while a breeze drew a light veil of pink dust between them.

"Why are you still here?" Peter said. "Isn't it past time for you to go to the hospital?"

Thanh gave the sort of high-pitched giggle that Peter recognized as a polite vocal tic usually empty of further meaning.

"Oh, today, yes, today only I stay here for a little more time," Thanh said. "Today I will visit a patient very close to here, and then I will go to the hospital."

"Are those field glasses you've got there?"

Another giggle. "Yes, field glasses!" he said, lifting his arm and patting the case. "One of my patients here at the school, Major Loc, made me gift of field glasses. He said he had extra field glasses and he asked if I could use. Now I can have a hobby, watching for birds!"

"Or you can watch the soccer game and make a clinical study of Pham's fouls against Rabinowitz," Peter said. "Why don't you stay and do that?"

"No, no, now I must go and see a patient at his home. Very close by, but now is when I tell him I will see him. You know this saying, Dan'ridge? Make it your habit to help, or at least do no harm? That is the best teaching for doctors. So. When I can do no more good in one place, then it is time I should go to the place where maybe I can do good."

"Yeah, I see," Peter said. "You figured you could do more good sticking around here to stoke concerns about Pham than checking on a patient or helping deliver a kid. That's so admirable I might tear up."

A group of students passed between Peter and Thanh. Two of them had been in one of Peter's previous classes. He barely glanced at them, hoping they'd hurry on so he could study Thanh's face a little longer. But the two students paused to greet Peter at length, and by the time they passed on toward the soccer field, Thanh was gone. But no—Peter saw him near the door of the soup kitchen. Thanh glanced back in his direction. Then he walked quickly down the row of parked motor scooters, mounted his Vespa and steered it out between the concrete stingrays. He had the strap of the field glasses case slung around his neck.

They had chalked the dirt soccer field. Students and American instructors from the language school and the air academy stood two and three deep along the sidelines. Peter saw a pair of students at one end of the near sideline flail at each other with all of their thin, green-clad limbs, like battling insects. Their sparring seemed to him to signal a rising charge of unfocused anger in the crowd around the playing field.

Several of the American players, wearing shorts and the stenciled jerseys they had mail-ordered for the match, stood in a ring in front of one goal and awkwardly passed a ball, their feet raising spurts of pink dust. The Vietnamese players, some in shorts or swim trunks and some wearing fatigues, passed a ball fluidly down the other half of the field, running in long, gliding parabolas, their knee-swiveled legs askew like skiers' sticks as they positioned to kick.

Peter had seen Pham play soccer enough to recognize him by the thighs smoothly sheathed with muscle and the deft, skipping, weaving dance up to where the ball spun twenty feet to one side of the net; the elbow-wrenching kick; the prim pinch of the lips as the ball caromed wide off the tubular metal bar. Pham didn't wear his wraparound sunglasses, but it didn't seem to make much difference. The wide-set, flat-looking eyes had the same insect-like effect.

Peter moved up to the sideline beside another language instructor, a lank Georgian with a concave chest and an acne-pocked face.

"I sweah, Pete, if somebody was to bet me ten dollars I wouldn't pick that little mothah up, I'd do it," said the Georgian, Carlton Beshears. "But I'd get me an eight-foot hoe handle and buy the stoutest clothesline and rig up the damnedest snake pole you ever saw to do it with."

Peter heard the grind of truck gears. A gray shuttle truck, its nose down-tilted by sudden braking, rolled between the stingrays. A soccer player in a fluttering jersey stood on each running board. The truck jolted aside off the street and rattled toward the field. The sand thrown beneath the chassis by the wheels made a crackling sound like an approaching brush fire. There were three players in the cab, and Peter saw the clustered muzzles of rifles between two of them. He didn't see Rabinowitz. The truck swung around and skidded to a stop behind the net at the end of the field where the Vietnamese players were warming up. Two players jumped out of the canopied back of the truck. Then Rabinowitz climbed down.

"For the sweet Lawud's sake," Carlton said. "What's the matter with him?"

His head down, Rabinowitz plodded up the far side of the field. To Peter, Rabby looked no worse than he often did when the heat had worked him over.

"You figure he's foxin' 'em?" Carlton said.

"How in hell would I know?" Peter said. "You think I've got a hotline to the inside of his skull?"

Pham stood at midfield, his foot atop the ball, rocking it, his delicate chin poised in a way that was not quite a smile. When Rabinowitz reached quarter-field, Pham flicked the ball out to his right. Then he danced around ahead of it, the smooth bulges of muscle above his knees winking as he danced. When Pham was running sideways, parallel to and a little ahead of the ball, he planted one foot, sending a spray of dust toward Rabinowitz, who was still plodding, head-down, a few yards away. With his other foot, Pham kicked the ball to a player who was drifting up from a corner of the goal.

"Jee-haws-a-phat!" Carlton breathed. "Alphabet better kick some zippertail now, or he won't have enough face left to shave."

There wasn't a hush, just a muting of the desultory crowd sound. But Peter could tell from the tongue-clicking nearby that Carlton was right—that Pham's act ensured every Vietnamese there would perceive the match as a matter of face between Pham and Rabinowitz. The wind picked up most of the spray of dust and dispersed it in a drifting pink veil above Rabby's head, but enough of it reached Rabby's face to force him to stop and spit and wipe his eyes with the bottom of his jersey. Pham jogged back toward the field's center circle. Rabinowitz watched him, seemingly without surprise or anger.

"When's Alphabet plan to nail him, Pete?" Carlton said. "How's he plan to do it? Lawud, I got to get ready to whoop."

"Look, what do you think I am, Angelo Dundee, that I can call his round?" Peter said. "The last word I got was that he's going to yank out a menorah and bastinado Pham to death. I haven't got the faintest notion what he's going to do. It's not my business. And, God damn it, his name's Rabinowitz. Say it."

Carlton smiled a skeletal smile, a smile refined through generations of parched hominy and plow-wrenched joints to an essence of spectral patience. "Rabinnerwitch," he said. Carlton blinked. "I just thought you were his special buddy, that's all," he said. "I thought he might of told you."

The crowd's separable voices hushed, then fused into what sounded like a low moan, and Peter knew the game had begun.

Students clustered along the sideline at midfield. Behind them stood Americans, centurion-like with their peaked caps and their rifle muzzles at their shoulders. Peter shoved in between two taller men and saw, over the bobbing heads of the Vietnamese, Rabinowitz barreling from a back position toward a scrimmage at the midline. His head lowered, Rabinowitz ran with the lumbering grace of a charging elk. Peter searched for Pham within the swirl of scything, dust-enveloped knees and elbows before Rabinowitz vanished into it and the ball flew out in a straight, rising line like a marble slung from a centrifuge. When the scrum broke, Peter saw Pham bound twice sidelong away from it. Pham looked back into the dust, then turned to pursue the ball. In a few moments more, the dust had cleared enough for Peter to see Rabinowitz standing, one flexed arm and leg thrust forward, in an attitude of motion. It was the way a big animal might stand if it were hit on the run by a bullet of too small a caliber to fell it.

"Ooooh, tsk tsk tsk!" Peter saw that the students in front of him were also watching Rabinowitz, and that it was at whatever had happened to Rabby they were clicking their tongues. "Ooooh, numbah one, very strong, I think so."

Rabinowitz, shaking his head slowly as though he were refusing a great favor with due regret, tilted forward and began to jog with his body bent stiffly from the hips. As he passed in front of Peter, his eyes stayed fixed on the ground, and a white line of spittle rimmed the vermillion pouch of his lower lip.

"Rabby, come out of there!" Peter shouted.

Rabby paused at the sideline, frowned at Peter and said in a panting near-whisper: "Things have changed, Pete. We've got to let this play out now. Just stay clear of it, okay?"

"Things have changed?" Peter said. "What in hell is that supposed to mean?"

"In a word, it means I'm the cheese."

"You're cheese? You're the big cheese? You're the Limburger? Look, take yourself out of the game and let's talk about what kind of cheese you are."

But Rabby had already jogged away toward midfield, where the Vietnamese players were working the ball with short, teasing kicks past the Americans' galumphing efforts to steal it.

"Rabby, come out of there now, before he hits you again," Peter shouted. But Rabinowitz merely lifted a hand in a wave of weary dismissal.

All right, get coldcocked, damn you, Peter thought. Get yourself an Article Fifteen. Go home in a doggie bag, if you can carry it that far. You've courted this ever since you got here. And damn you, Rabinowitz, who am I to deprive you of it now?

Peter saw that the students in front of him had turned and were staring at him shyly. Their eyes looked both luminous and dusky, high within the shadows of their long-billed caps.

"Man, you spooked them," a voice beside Peter said. "You've got them thinking Rabinowitz is a ventriloquist. He gets his nuts clipped, and you bawl like the calf that got gelded."

Peter didn't answer. He watched Rabinowitz run toward where the ball, steered by pawing cuffs from Pham's little clublike feet, turned out to be when he got there. This time there was no excuse of dust for failing to see the blow. Pham kicked the ball just far enough to one side to be free of having to attend to it for a moment. Then Pham crouched, the way a cat might crouch on a railroad tie with its head swiveled upward toward the light of a hurtling freight, holding that pose until the last possible instant, then springing to safety across the track.

Pham lifted one foot just enough for the leg to hang suspended from the knee. What Peter saw then was not a blow exactly but a stitch, like the stitch of a sewing machine needle that anyone can see in the aggregate but no one can swear to have seen in its separable units. Then Pham veered away, cuffing the ball, leaving Rabby standing transfixed, as though upon a thought of great importance. Rabby seemed again like a bullet-stung elk or even, in the suggestion of vast bulk in which a momentary sag or teeter makes one aware of the enormous collapsible skeleton, like an elephant this time. Rabinowitz made a sound, too, not with the blow but after it. It sounded like a big, hurt animal's deep-chested cough or groan: "hu-unf."

"I'll be damned," an awed voice near Peter said. "It's a good thing nobody was making book, because I'd have bet on Rabinowitz. I'd have figured that by this time you could mix Pham with a little flour and milk and call him chipped-beef gravy."

"It's almost like Rabinowitz planned it this way," another voice said. "It's like he's inviting it. Maybe he figures he can take Pham's best shots so that nobody can say he didn't have provocation, and then nail the little fucker the first time he gets careless about how quick he moves in for that little knee-chop."

"Ma-an, are you crazy?" the first voice said. Peter didn't hear the rest. He was moving again, down the sideline toward the American goal. As he wove through the crowd with the stocks of the two rifles banging against his buttocks and the clips clattering in his pockets, he could tell his own perceptions were verging on the hallucinatory. Ahead of him, against a red and refraction-bloated sun, students stood in spindling silhouette, and the sentinel Americans' shadows appeared vastly elongated. Peter didn't watch the field, but he could tell from the seabird-like cries of the

Vietnamese players that they were working the ball near the Americans' goal. Peter's wrist scraped the bare corner of a cartridge clip. He lifted the edge of his fatigue blouse to look at the hole, and he saw that the rest of the threadbare cloth along the pocket's bottom was ready to give way. When he reached the playing field's end line, he saw the American goalie, cursing, slouch behind the net and free the ball from it with a savage kick that tore the netting loose from a stake. Peter watched Pham's prim little pony-trot back upfield. Only then did he realize that he was trying to get close enough to Pham.

"You'd better start *calling* this *game*, motherfucker!" someone yelled as the referee, a Vietnamese sergeant who was a technician in the language school's tape lab, ran along the sideline. The little sergeant's eyes rolled like the eyes of a frightened calf running along a fence line during an electrical storm.

After the Americans had begun to curse and threaten, the referee did call Pham for a foul. But it was already too late then to stop the ugly mood, or to salvage any chance for Rabinowitz. Rabby no longer pursued Pham. Gasping and hobbling, his jersey black with sweat and so weighted with it that the shirt swung from his torso like chain mail, Rabinowitz had strength enough left only to heave himself now and again into Pham's path.

"Come to me, Pham," Peter once got close enough to hear Rabinowitz gasp. "I've got a barbed wire licorice stick for you, Pham. Come get it stuck up your ass." Rabinowitz would loom up in front of Pham like a cave and Pham would come dodging and fluttering up to him like a moth until, at the moment the moth would have vanished into the cave, there would be that jerk or stitch and then a freezing, the moth frozen for an instant in the cave's shadow, and then Pham would veer skittering away. Rabby's bottom lip would droop and his eyes would narrow, but the rest of his face would be as devoid of pain or any other feeling as an open-mouthed, slit-eyed mask cut crudely out of wood. Then he would make that sound, neither quite a cough nor a groan: "hu-unf."

Peter elbowed his way to the sideline, then waited until Rabby was close enough that he didn't have to shout.

"Rabby, will you come out of there now, before he finishes you?" Peter said.

Rabby's head hung to one side. He spoke just loudly enough for Peter to hear. His voice sounded almost casual, like the voice of an actor stepping for a moment outside his role.

"Look, Pete, I've got to play this out to the end," he said. "Otherwise it might not take."

"Play what out?" Peter said. "Damn it, Rabby, this all has to do with some double-agent fable you've pieced together, doesn't it? And, oh my, it just has to be true, doesn't it? Has to be, because you want it to be."

Rabby turned wearily away and heaved himself into a jog. Then Peter saw Pham tapping and tapping the ball upfield with his deft little feet. The ball's scales slithered crackling through the dust.

Peter shrugged off Rabinowitz's rifle and laid it on the dirt. He put down his books beside it. He unslung his own rifle and pointed it toward the ground and cocked it and clicked off the empty chamber.

"Holy shit, man," a voice said. "You going to blow the bugger away?"

"Going to give Rabby his chance, that's all," Peter said. He grasped his rifle's breech with both hands and held the weapon across his chest like a pugil stick. He waited until Pham had passed, cuffing the ball like a cat cuffing a mouse that it doesn't intend to kill for a long while yet. Then Peter ran onto the field.

He heard the voices rise behind him, felt the blast of fury in them. He watched the backs of Pham's knees to gauge the direction Pham would take. He knew his own knee, with its ruined ligament and lack of cartilage, would make pursuit hopeless if Pham should become aware of him and dodge.

Peter saw that before he could get to Pham, Pham would get to Rabinowitz. He saw the momentary freeze within the shadow, saw the flash, like the instant the spark leaps the gap in a welding torch, of the blow, saw clearly and heard the shot with the knee high inside Rabby's groin. Then Peter was aware of passing Rabinowitz only as, when passing a mountain at night in an automobile, one is aware of the massive, inert felt presence. Peter followed Pham's sprint toward the American goal as he would follow the ultimate reach of his headlights in a fog. He felt his pocket tear and the ammunition clips, falling, bounce from his thigh. He saw the soft sheen of the blued metal spinning away.

"Kill him!" a voice shrieked. "Kill the son of a bitch!"

Peter knew he could not have caught Pham if Pham had not heard the voice too. Pham tilted back his compact torso like a balking pony. The crouching American goalie crept forward in the gloom like an octopus oozing from its lair. Pham swiveled his head. "Ha!" he said.

It took Peter a moment to recall when he had last felt the surge of elation he felt as he closed the gap between himself and Pham. It had been the only time he had made a solo tackle in a football game, and his tackle had prevented a touchdown. It was late in the fourth quarter of a home game that his school was losing badly. The stands were emptying, and scrub players—himself included—were in for both sides. It was a third-down play on his team's two-yard line. He read the play correctly as an end-around, and he got deep enough into the backfield to make the tackle before blockers could seal off the runner. His tackle had made little difference in the game's outcome, but ever since he had been chasing the feeling it gave him—chasing it and forever falling short. Now, having chased it to the other side of the world, here it was again.

I'm not out here because of Rabinowitz's fable, Peter thought. I'm out here because I'm snared in my own fable.

Pham ducked and made a tight, fishhook dodge, raking the ball back and away, but it was too late for him to pivot clear before Peter was on him. It happened too quickly for Peter to stop and square off and occupy Pham with the rifle until Rabinowitz could catch up, as he had hoped to do. Holding the rifle across his chest and lifting it sharply, Peter felt but did not see the weapon strike, knew that Pham was going down but not where, thought for an incredulous instant that he himself was past and clear. Then, feeling that his leg from the knee down had been painlessly snatched away—a sensation of giddy impossibility as awful as the cymbal-crash of pain that would follow—he knew that Pham had seized his ankle.

"Get him quick, Rabby, he's down!" Peter shouted as he fell. He hit the ground with such force that that for a moment he lost track of where he was. He heard a metallic striking sound, and his first thought was: Ginger? Because the sound resembled the yawps his mother's little half-beagle dog would make on a late fall evening, when the chill air clipped all sounds to half-length. Then he knew he was lying on his shoulder with the breath knocked out of him, and staring into a pall of pink dust. He knew the metallic clacking was the sound of the butt and muzzle of his rifle striking the ground as the weapon spun end over end away from him. He knew that what had briefly seemed a pleasant warmth suffusing his left side was the fierce pain of his unsocketed knee.

"Oh, dear Jesus," Peter moaned. As he bent convulsively toward his knee, Peter saw Pham lying in the dirt, propping himself on one hand and pressing the other hand against his throat, coughing with his tongue sticking out. So I got him in the neck, Peter thought. Beyond Pham, Peter saw Rabinowitz on his knees, swaying a little. Rabby stared at Pham, then shifted his gaze to Peter and began to slowly shake his head. Peter shut his eyes and grasped his shin and pulled until, with a sensation like a searing, monstrous tickle, the shin bone popped back into its socket. With his eyes still shut, Peter heard booted feet running and voices shouting words that waves of pain would not let him distinguish.

He wondered: What'll the charge be? Something like assault on a Vietnamese service member, with allowance made for provocation? Article Fifteen—maybe no worse than that. Though that's plenty bad enough. But I got him. I got the little bastard. Nothing can take that away from me now.

Peter no longer heard men running, but instead a massive shuffling. He opened his eyes and saw what they were doing to Pham. A swarm of instructors moved to and fro in front of the American goal, kicking and cursing. Between the canvas-covered ankles, Peter saw Pham spinning in the dust as the boots struck him. He could see that Pham had his arms folded around his head to shield it. Suddenly Peter understood that the men kicking Pham—all fellow instructors, all men of generally mild demeanor—were acting, just as he had acted, out of months of pent-up rage, unleashed by Pham's pinpoint use of his feet and knees and elbows to hobble Rabinowitz.

Peter saw students running toward their tents or barracks, stopping to glance behind them, then running on. Except for those doing the kicking, most of the Americans who had watched the game were still on the sidelines. Among them, Peter spotted several officers, none of whom made any move to break up the assault on Pham. At the corner of the field nearest Peter, he spotted the Air Force captain whose luminous eyes and high forehead had reminded him so strongly of Boris Karloff. The captain's name, Peter had since learned, was Tomczak.

"Sir, can you please help break this up?" Peter called. "Just a loud-enough order ought to do it." It was clear that Tomczak had heard him. Looking at Peter, the captain folded his arms and slowly shook his head. His expression—somber enough at any time—contained more of sadness than rejection.

Far off, beneath the palm trees that shaded the American training team's headquarters building, Peter saw a lank, hatless figure step from the doorway, shade his eyes and peer toward the field. After what Peter took to be time enough for Colonel Jesperson to tell a fight had broken out between Vietnamese and the Americans under his command, the figure turned briskly and strode back into the building.

Peter used his hands and his right leg to crawl toward his rifle. He propped himself on the weapon and rose carefully. Using the rifle, muzzle-down, as a cane, and feeling his knee wobble in its socket, Peter limped toward the mob that was kicking Pham.

"Stop it, you people!" Peter shouted.

He recognized the pitted skin on the back of a scrawny neck. He grabbed Carlton by the shoulder and spun him around. In the twilight,

Carlton's eyes had the glowing, bloodshot hue of the eyes of tracking hounds.

"Eeee-haw!" Carlton said.

The dozen or so other men engaged in kicking Pham backed away from him slightly, as men baiting an animal might do to give it the illusion that escape is possible. Pham obliged them. Still with his hands and arms shielding his head, he rolled to one side, sprang to his feet and charged blindly ahead. Carlton jerked free of Peter's hand and joined two other men in heading off Pham's dash. The three of them drove him to his knees by pummeling his back and neck. Peter hobbled toward them with his makeshift cane, and again he grabbed Carlton's shoulder.

"Stop it!" Peter yelled into Carlton's death's-head face. "Make them stop it! My God, do you want to kill him?"

"Man, after what he done to you and Alphabet?" Carlton said, and he jerked his shoulder free. Peter, thrown off balance, fell forward but thrust out the rifle and caught the firing grip. He toiled erect, hearing the boots hit Pham.

Something demonic bludgeoned the air about Peter's head. By the time he was upright, he saw that the men who had been kicking Pham had dropped to all fours or stretched themselves flat on the ground. Pham had risen to his knees and was pinching his bleeding nose in the tail of his shirt. When the bludgeoning sound stopped, Peter realized it had been a burst from an semiautomatic weapon. Far off, Peter heard another sharp bang, which he recognized as the backfiring ignition of Major Duong's Citroen. Then he heard the first guttural moan of the flight line alert siren.

Off to one side, Peter saw that a column of what looked like white smoke had risen into the twilight. At the column's base stood Rabinowitz. Rabby popped a clip free from the rifle he had just fired skyward. As the white column toppled and dissolved, Peter felt grains of it strike his face. He dry-spat: chalk dust.

As best he could amid waves of pain, Peter tried to piece together what had happened, and what might yet happen. He thought, Rabby found

241

his chalk-clogged rifle where I parked it. Then he found the clips that fell from my pocket when it tore. Interesting, isn't it, how that worked out? Rabby started this, and then he was the only one with the presence of mind to stop it. What is it they call that? Orchestration?

As Rabinowitz approached him, Peter could see he was saying something, but the alert siren drowned it out. That Rabby remained ambulatory at all seemed to Peter baffling and offensive. Peter tried to account for it while also trying to shift weight onto his rifle from his rapidly bloating knee, and trying also to lip-read whatever Rabinowitz was saying. At first, he could hear nothing through the surrounding dome of shrill sound. Then, as the alert siren wound down, he heard Rabinowitz say: "Definitely not part of the program, Pete. Now we just have to hope the other pieces fall into place."

Then he heard Doucet's voice, wavering like the voice of a man veering between laughter and nervous collapse.

"Hey, Pete, that was the closest thing to a banzai charge I ever saw outside a movie theater," he said. "Didn't you get the word?"

"Word?" Peter said. "Word about what? That Pham was supposed to get away with knees-and-elbows butchery?"

Peter felt someone slide a hand around his waist from behind, then lift to take pressure off his leg. It was Captain Tomczak.

"Yep, that's pretty much it," Tomczak said. "Reasons for the order not made clear, except that Special Forces made an urgent request. Now, if you want to know why Special Forces should take a vital interest in a soccer game between teams of strictly rear-echelon types, you'll have to ask them. All we were told was that if we saw blatant fouling on the field and one or more American players getting the worst of it, we were to stand aside."

"Told?" Peter said. "Who did the telling? Who got told?"

"The colonel briefed us in the staff room this morning."

"'Us?'" Peter said.

"Officers, and a few others who he said had a need to know."

Suddenly Peter felt too furious with Rabinowitz to even look at him. "Goddamn you, Rabby," he said.

"The only other clue the colonel gave us," Tomczak said, "was that Special Forces had their shorts in a twist about a theft report turned in by Army ordnance."

"God damn you, Rabinowitz!" Peter said, glaring at Rabby. "You set me up for this, didn't you?"

Rabby appeared not to hear him. His eyes kept switching toward the road that ran toward the villas and the air base.

"Time to get him off the field, don't you think, sir?" Rabby said.

"You thought if you kept me in the dark, it would brighten the spotlight on your own role," Peter said. "Then you could just sweep my carcass out of the way."

"Okay, listen fast," Rabby said, with a flash of Princeton-honed arrogance. "Those caskets we thought might be weapons boxes? Army ordnance reported a couple of weeks ago that several empty crates used for arms shipments had gone missing. Word came back through Vietnamese channels that somebody had spotted those boxes stacked against a back wall at the hospital downtown. The hospital's the point of origin for a lot of the funeral processions that end up in that cemetery. You got all that?"

Rabby's eyes kept switching toward the road, as if he expected something to appear there.

"You weren't intended to play any part in this," he told Peter, "and the quicker you disappear, the likelier it is the pieces will fit together like they're supposed to. And that you won't have to bear all the blame if they don't."

The distant siren went into a dying fall, and Peter heard Duong's Citroen backfire and expire somewhere nearby. Tomczak tightened his hold on Peter's waist, handed Peter's rifle to Doucet, and drew Peter's right arm across his own shoulders. "You, Private," Tomczak told Doucet. "Lift his leg and keep it elevated. Ready? Here we go."

"Go?" Peter said. "Go where?"

Ave Antonina

Michael Jennings

"Air base infirmary," Tomczak said, "where let's hope they ship you off fast. Dollars to doughnuts what set off that air base alert was a call about a nut case running onto the field and attacking a Vietnamese officer with a rifle."

With Captain Tomczak lifting from his right and Doucet holding up his left thigh, Peter felt himself spun toward the near sideline. As he turned, he saw the Vietnamese commander climb from his bare-framed Citroen and lift a big first aid kit from the floorboard. Then Duong waddled, dewlaps quivering, toward Pham. He carried the heavy first aid kit so low it seemed to glide like a caravel upon the dust. Pham had tossed aside his bloodstained shirt and was staring at the Americans who had attacked him. There was a red welt on the side of Pham's neck where the rifle had struck him. Now that the odds had shifted against him, Pham still looked as calmly intent on inflicting harm as he had when they were all in his favor.

Once Tomczak and Doucet crossed the sideline, Tomczak paused to shout that he needed a shuttle-truck key. He said "please." Then, after nodding in a cadence that Peter read as counting off several seconds, Tomczak bawled out his name and rank and demanded a shuttle-truck key. Promptly a set of keys sailed over the heads of the men nearest him. Doucet caught them one-handed.

"They're numbered," someone shouted. "Four keys, four trucks."

Peter made an occasional toe-touch with his right boot as Tomczak and Doucet lifted him and hurried toward the shuttle trucks. "What about you, sir?" Peter said. "I mean, if I'm gone from the scene and they learn you're responsible, could they nail you and Doucet for—"

"Fuck that," Tomczak said. "Nobody's going to take issue with an officer taking an injured man for treatment. I think I begin to see the shape of this thing now. You might even have played a useful role in it, unintentionally. But, big picture, the best thing now is to get you out of the way."

After they'd eased Peter onto the truck's seat, he saw the green station wagon with the faux wood side-paneling pull slowly between the

244

stingrays. Doucet climbed into the truck bed and Tomczak started the engine.

"Yep, right on cue," Tomczak said, idling the truck while the vehicle turned left onto the soccer field. Peter could make out four heads in baseball caps behind the car's tinted windows.

"Watch for Pham to put up a fight when those guys take him into custody," Tomczak said. "But that could mean either he's in on the game plan, or he's not."

It looked to Peter like the main resistance came from Major Duong. All four doors of the station wagon opened and all four American agents got out, and one of them approached Duong and spoke to him briefly. The American appeared to speak with calm insistence, while Duong seemed bewildered. Then Duong started to flail his arms, and he edged around to position himself between the American and Pham. Another of the men in sunglasses and a dark blue baseball cap approached the Vietnamese commander from behind and together the two Americans—each about a half-foot taller than Duong—elbowed him aside. The other two agents moved in swiftly to grab Pham by the arms and muscle him into a rear seat of the station wagon. Pham pulled backward and twisted a little, but it was all done too quickly for anything that could be called a fight.

Peter wondered why Rabinowitz hadn't shown any interest in this confrontation. Then he realized Rabinowitz wasn't there. Finally he spotted Rabby beyond the sideline. Rifle slung from his shoulder, Rabby was plodding toward Jesperson's headquarters building. He wasn't even bothering to glance behind him to see how events he had helped set in motion were playing out.

Peter thought, It's like he has no role in this part of the script, so he can just casually amble offstage.

Three of the CIA men climbed back in the station wagon. The fourth stood by the open front passenger door, nodding and speaking to Duong in what Peter took to be a final effort at conciliation. Doing the little he could to restore lost face, the Vietnamese commander abruptly turned away from the American, picked up the first aid kit and waddled back toward the bare chassis of his Citroen.

"This whole thing's a charade," Tomczak said. "But who's supposed to be taken in by it?" He looked at Peter, his big, somber eyes almost eclipsed in a puzzled squint.

"Somebody who might not be here to witness it?" Peter said. Gripping the steering wheel, Tomczak leaned back and exhaled slowly. "All right," he said. "Let's *di di mao*."

He let the clutch out too fast. In the rear-view mirror, Peter saw Doucet reach for a hand-hold on the edge of the truck bed to halt his slide toward the open end. Through the dust raised by the wheels, Peter saw Rabinowitz again, standing next to Jesperson outside the headquarters building.

Tomczak turned toward the air base. His unfamiliarity with the truck made for a jerky ride. Peter laced his fingers beneath his swollen, throbbing knee. He could make out in the rearview mirror only a faint outline of buildings in the distant city. In the same direction but much closer, he could see several two- and three-story buildings.

A little later, it occurred to him that someone on an upper story of one of those buildings could get a clear view of the open ground where the soccer game was played. All you'd need would be a pair of field glasses. But by then, the on-call doctor at the air base infirmary had cleared him for transfer to the Army hospital at Khoang Trong, and Tomczak and Doucet had left.

Twenty-three

In his first night at Khoang Trong—after they put his leg in a cast and told him that if he needed surgery, he'd be dead last on their priority list—Peter badgered the night nurse to help him find a telephone. On both turns through the ward, she swept past him like an oblivious wind-up toy.

Finally he slept. He awoke to a tapping sound and a voice that made music of his name: "Private Dandridge?"

Waking, he realized fingers were tapping his cast.

"I've figured it out," he muttered.

A nurse in fatigues stood at the foot of his bed. She was black, and her Afro was so compact and sharply cut that for a moment he mistook her hair for a helmet. The name sewn above the pocket of her fatigue blouse was Cottingham. She wore rimless glasses with round lenses that magnified the weary patience in her eyes. She had medical paraphernalia—cotton swabs, gauze, tape, scissors, surgical clamps—stuffed in the breast pockets of her blouse or pinned to their flaps.

"Private Dandridge, we need you to get up now," she said. Her voice took a soothing downward turn at the end of his name, and instantly he liked her. "We've got combat casualties coming in, and we're going to need the beds of everybody who counts as ambulatory," she said.

A second nurse stood by his bed. She was white and her mouth had been awkwardly and garishly lipsticked. She held a pair of crutches. Peter saw she was a first lieutenant and her name was Pedersen.

"These are yours," the lieutenant said, handing him the crutches. "Get up now, and I'll show you where to go."

"Sure," Peter said. The other nurse, who wore the twin bars of a captain on her collar, lifted his cast carefully over the edge of the bed.

"I'm sorry we have to do this," she said, "but it looks like with these men coming in, we'll be about three beds short."

"It's fine," Peter said. "I've had a lot of experience hopping around in a cast."

"I'll bet you have," Cottingham said. She laughed slowly and stroked his shoulder. Then she turned away and headed up the ward.

"You know how to use them, then?" the Pedersen said, handing him the crutches. Peter sensed the disapproval in her clipped voice.

"Oh, I can dance on crutches," he said. "I can ski downhill. It's a shame we don't have snow here or I'd show you."

"You got it playing soccer, did you?" she said. "Well, the men we've got coming in this morning didn't get hurt playing a game."

Peter turned on his crutches and looked at her. She had Nordic-looking blue eyes set so wide apart there was something cartoonish about them. Her straw-colored hair was pulled straight back. He wondered why she bothered to smear lipstick on her unsmiling mouth.

"That's right," he said. "I might have been drunk when I played that game. Maybe I was high on dope, too. I don't even remember whether it was soccer or badminton. You know, it's a good thing we've got nurses like you to expose malingerers like me."

He followed her outside and down a concrete walkway, swinging on the crutches. The sunlight glancing from brilliant white sand made him wince.

"We've got two hooches we use for overflow," she said. "They're plenty good enough for people with sports injuries."

"Are those wounded men here yet?" he said.

"They're being helicoptered in. Their firebase got hit."

"How many wounded?"

"No idea. First they'll go there." She pointed to a long, low building ahead of them. "Triage. Unless too many wounded come in at once and we have to do some triage in a ward. Or unless they're already in body bags. Then they go straight from the helipad to the mortuary fridge. You'll hear that in a minute."

"Hear it?" Peter said.

"There's something wrong with it, I think."

Peter glanced through the open door of the triage building as they passed it. He could see a row of what looked like pairs of metal sawhorses, spaced so a stretcher would fit on each pair. The fluorescent lights were on and medics were rolling hangers for drip bottles into place. As he followed the nurse up the walkway, he started to hear a wavering buzz.

"You hear it now?" the nurse said.

"Yeah," he said. "Compressor. They'd better replace that before it goes completely bust."

"I don't think the people who work there day and night need you to tell them what's wrong with it," she said without turning around. "I'm sure they know already."

"I'm sure they do," he said. "But I thought I was just talking to you, not them. My mistake."

She said nothing more but walked ahead faster, and he swung along faster on the crutches to keep pace. He could see ahead a long row of tin-roofed buildings. They were hooches, he guessed, for enlisted medical staff.

"Look, is there any way I could use a phone?" Peter said. "I need to call my orderly room back in Nha Cat. It's important. Security-related."

She turned so abruptly that he almost swung into her.

"You're kidding, right?" she said. "You're kidding that I'd take time to find you a phone when we've got incoming casualties?"

He choked back his anger long enough to read in her face how much she hated what she would have to see and do when the wounded men arrived.

"I wasn't kidding," he said. "But I know you need to get back. I'll ask somebody else about finding a phone."

When she opened the door of the hooch, Peter could see that all four bunks were unoccupied. "Take your pick," she said, turning away without looking at him. "If there's a rocket attack, that's your bunker over there. Enlisted chow hall is down that way."

Peter watched her rigid back as she hurried down the walkway. He turned to look at the hooch door and saw "Ward C, Annex 1" stenciled in black across its top. Then he noticed the nurse had started to run toward a swirl of white sand outside the triage building. Medics carried two stretchers through the miniature sandstorm kicked up by the medevac chopper. The nurse caught up with the medics in time to take an IV drip bottle from one of them who was holding it above a stretcher. The nurse put her other hand on the wounded man's arm, and she leaned to speak to him before they passed through the door of the triage building.

He watched as more wounded men on stretchers were carried into the building. He counted seven men. The nurse had said it was a firebase that got hit. Next time it could be us, he thought. Suppose that show at the soccer field speeds up plans for an attack. Then tomorrow it could be casualties from our street that get ferried up here. It could be Dan or Doucet or Rabinowitz headed into triage on a stretcher and getting pelted with white sand by the rotor wash. It could be one of them wondering why the last face he sees in life has an angry red smear across it.

Twenty-four

Peter swung around on his crutches and headed up the avenue of hooches, away from the triage building. Goddamnit, he thought, there's got to be somebody here who can patch me through to Jesperson's HQ.

He spotted the words "Orderly Room" above the door of a wooden building on stilts. Peter swore as he struggled up the steps. The smooth-faced desk sergeant, who had been sleeping in a tilted-back chair, jerked forward and stared in mild alarm at the out-of-breath patient in sweat-splotched, light gray hospital pajamas who swung through the doorway on crutches.

"Can I help you, sir?" the sergeant asked. In the absence of any insignia on Peter's pajamas, the young sergeant had assumed he was outranked. Peter decided to leverage that. He said he needed to be patched through, pronto, to the American command shack at the air academy in Nha Cat.

It took a while. When the duty officer at Colonel Jesperson's headquarters picked up and the desk sergeant handed over the receiver, Peter had to identify himself by name and rank. That drew a nasty look from the desk sergeant. All Peter learned from the duty officer was that the colonel had ordered that no one should discuss matters pertaining to the soccer game.

"Dandridge, huh?" the duty officer said in a tone of rising annoyance. "You're the one who crushed that zip lieutenant's voice box, right? What you did, Dandridge, is the sole reason for that don't-discuss order. Now you double down by putting me as well as you in violation of it on a non-secure phone line."

Then the officer hung up, but his words had been enough to quell the panic-driven pounding in Peter's ears. Peter knew then that the only thing of substance he had to offer, the tip about the field glasses, wouldn't have made much difference. Maybe whoever scripted the closing scene at yesterday's soccer game didn't know or care that it was Lieutenant Thanh who would sound the alarm for the Viet Cong once he saw Pham dragged into that swamp-green station wagon and driven off between the stingrays toward the CIA compound. But he, they—whatever configuration of military and CIA brainpower was dictating strategy—had figured out that somebody involved in the burial of weapons in the cemetery would witness Pham's arrest and would sound that alarm. And he, they, were content to wait until the baited trap was sprung. And that was enough to quiet Peter's mind as he thanked the desk sergeant, who was again tilting back in his chair and staring at Peter with his hands clasped behind his head.

"Fuck you," the sergeant said, rocking a little in the chair. "If you ever show up here again and try to order up an in-country phone call, I will personally kick your ass down those stairs. And I will enjoy hearing that cast hit every step on your way down."

"Sarge, I'm sorry," Peter said. "Listen, I'm ninety-nine percent sure that something—that something I just learned I can't talk about is—is happening, or anyway going to happen."

The sergeant made an incredulous head-roll. Peter marveled, briefly, at the power of Army life to induce bitter cynicism in the young.

"You impersonate an officer, you order me to make a phone call on an insecure line, and you expect me to buy a cover story that you can't talk about?" the sergeant said.

"I never said I was an officer," Peter said.

"I said impersonate, dickhead! You came as close to strutting in here as your cast and crutches would allow. Now get the fuck out of here."

Peter headed back toward the overflow hooch. Past his panic now, he swung slowly on the crutches, his eyes fixed on the long, diminishing row of dark, lumpy-looking bunkers ahead of him. Set in the brilliant sand, they resembled identical hovels hewn from dark stone. The heat waves shimmering above their sandbag-covered roofs added to the illusion that they were all the same bunker, replicated endlessly.

When he opened the door of his hooch, he saw men on the two lower bunks. One man had his face to the wall and seemed to be sleeping. The other had stripped off his hospital pajama top and was sitting on the edge of the bunk holding a tiny barbell in one hand. The sidelong grin he gave Peter tightened into a wince as he slowly lifted his arm to shoulder height with the barbell held straight out to the side. As he lowered the weight the wince dissolved, and he grinned up at Peter again as he placed the weight on the floor.

"Hey, bro, bottom bunk's yours," he said. "House rule, you know? Man with cast and crutches gets the bottom bunk."

Peter would have expected such a deep, resonant voice only from a man bigger and more barrel-chested than this one, who looked plenty strong but on the small side.

He said his name was Mo Sommerville. He quickly volunteered that his was not a war wound either.

"Four years of college football and nothing worse than a hamstring pull," he said. "Then I ship to Vietnam, get drunk in the EM club, lean back against what I thought was a wall but turned out to be a door with a concrete floor on the other side. So I fall through the doorway, reach back with one hand to break my fall. And bam. Torn ligaments, maybe shredded cartilage in the shoulder. Doctor here took one look at my X-rays and said I'd probably punched my ticket for surgery in Japan and a medical discharge. He said they'd give physical therapy and rehab a try first."

"Does that hyper-empathetic nurse know how you got hurt?" Peter said.

"Flo? Sure. She makes it her business to find out. So she's been on your case already, has she? It's not like she's all sweetness toward the ones who got injured in combat, either. Check how much attention she pays Harold, the guy with his arm blown off."

"Flo?"

"It's for Florence Nightingale. They must've started calling her that long before I got here."

Mo said he was assigned as a radio humper to an infantry platoon but he'd hurt himself before he got assigned to a unit. Peter asked if he felt lucky.

"Lucky? Do I feel lucky? I feel like a complete, stupid shit, is what I feel like."

After a while Peter and Mo Sommerville went to the chow hall, then to the enlisted men's club. Neither of them had any military scrip, but an orderly bought them each a beer when they told him they'd been bounced from their ward to make room for incoming casualties. The orderly had just gotten off duty in triage, and he said they might be stuck in overflow for a while. He said another medevac chopper had come in behind the first one. There were twelve wounded men in all, he said, and three body bags that went straight to the mortuary.

After they left the EM club, Peter asked about their hooch-mate's injury. Mo said he didn't know what it was.

"He was the same way back in the ward," Mo said. "He just lies there and stares at the wall."

"Well, that's great," Peter said. "We're a complete blue-ribbon outfit, then. Two malingerers and a psychological basket case."

When he climbed into his bunk that night, Peter could hear Armed Forces Radio playing in a nearby hooch and the rattle of the mortuary fridge's failing compressor. He wondered how often the bodies in the cooler got flown out and whether the three that had arrived that day were still in the cooler and what would happen to them if the compressor suddenly quit. Then he remembered the angry snub Rabinowitz had given Doucet during that rooftop Spooky-watching session. Rabby had been going on and on with his convoluted tale, and Doucet had tried to hurry him along, and Rabby had snapped that he didn't intend to boil down what he was trying to describe to fit an undergraduate's attention span. An immense human tragedy, Rabby had called it. Well, Peter thought, an immense human tragedy is unfolding all around us right now, in every direction except maybe straight out to sea. How is the story of a Polish noblewoman's sacrifice a hundred years ago supposed to help us cope with that, except as a mocking diversion?

When he closed his eyes, Peter saw a line of dark, lumpy hovels marching off toward the horizon in a landscape of barren sand. As he drifted toward sleep, he understood that the identical hovels went on and on beyond the most distant one he could see, and that they never led anywhere and never meant anything.

Twenty-five

When Peter awoke next morning, the man in the other lower bunk was sitting on the edge of his mattress and staring at him so fixedly that Peter was reminded of a hawk on a fencepost.

"I'm hungry," the man rasped. He was thin and wiry-looking, and he had a strip of sunburn across his forehead. Perched there as if ready to spring, he did not look at all catatonic.

"Can you bring me something to eat?" he said.

Peter raised himself on his elbows. "And why, exactly, should I do that?"

"I need to stay off my feet," the man said. "My feet are still numb."

Peter noticed the flesh on the tops of the man's feet looked scaly. "Yeah?" Peter said. "How'd you get up here from the ward, then?"

"The nurse said they had to make room for casualties. She asked me to try to make it this far, and she said she was sorry."

He linked his fingers beneath his right knee and lifted the foot clear of the floor and carefully waggled it at the ankle.

"After I walked up here, my feet felt like they were on fire, but today they're completely numb again," he said.

256

He lifted and waggled the other foot, staring at it as if it were something alien and distasteful.

Peter swung his own leg in its cast clear of the mattress and reached for his crutches at the foot of the bed.

"I reckon we can bring you some breakfast," he said. "Mo, you awake?"

On the way to the chow hall, Peter told Mo Sommerville he'd revised his opinion that their hooch-mate had suffered a psychological wound.

"He's just old-fashioned chickenshit," Peter said. "But I guess this proves humanity, including the Army, does inch forward."

"Yeah?" Mo said. "How's that?"

"A hundred years ago if he'd told his officers he was hungry but couldn't walk, they'd have fed him hardtack for his last meal, then set him on a barrel and had him shot."

"Well, I don't know that he's faking it," Mo said. "All that sleeping—I think he couldn't sleep because his feet wouldn't let him, so they gave him enough morphine to knock him out for a couple of days. Besides, who are we—I mean, you and I—to sit in judgment?"

"Which is exactly why you're going to bring him scrambled eggs and bacon and coffee," Peter said. "Sorry I can't help you with that."

When they got back to their hooch, the numb-footed soldier was gone.

"Maybe they shot him after all," Peter said.

But in a few minutes the pale young man came back. He wore what looked like blue plastic slippers, and he winced at each step.

"I had to piss," he said. "I had to make it that far."

When Mo said he was supposed to use a pulley machine in the gym, Peter went with him. They spent that day and the next shuttling between the enlisted men's club and the gym, where they killed time watching half-court pickup basketball and critiquing men who sparred in a boxing ring.

Peter kept thinking: *Maybe it's tonight they'll hit. I wonder whether they'll climb over the cemetery wall, maybe a few at a time and off to one side, hoping nobody will spot them, or blow a hole in the wall and all swarm through at once. I wonder if Special Forces has beefed up our street's checkpoint by posting their own people in it, or if they're leaving those little sheep-faced Vietnamese out there for their decoy value, knowing those two will be the first to die. And whatever the setup is and whatever's about to happen and however it's going to turn out, why do I have to be here and not there?*

After they'd spent two days in the overflow hooch, the medical staff had cleared enough space in the ward to bring them back. By then, Peter was so on edge he was taking it out on the numb-footed soldier, whose name was McLemore.

Two orderlies came through their hooch doorway and slowly lifted McLemore to his feet.

"Be careful you don't make him walk so much you drive the numbness up into his nuts," Peter told them. "You do that, man, you've sterilized him for life."

A wounded glance or even a whimper from McLemore wouldn't have surprised Peter. What he got instead was the heel of McLemore's hand in his chest.

"That's pretty funny," McLemore said, giving him a light shove. "You know what's funnier, though?" He shoved Peter again, this time hard enough that Peter lost his balance on his crutches and fell backward onto his bunk. On his way down, the back of his head hit the edge of the upper bunk.

"Now, that's really funny," McLemore said. "On a one-to-ten scale of not funny to funny, that's about a ten."

One of the orderlies helped Peter up. The other one went through a sort of manual of arms of indifference, first scratching his neck and then letting his eyes roam the hooch's plyboard ceiling, as if he were searching for a fly. Mo just stared at Peter and shook his head.

Each orderly slipped an arm under one of McLemore's arms and around his back. They practically carried McLemore like that all the way to the convalescent ward, as Peter swung along behind, wondering woozily if the clang of his head again the bunk rail might serve as a sort of starting gun for whatever would happen back in Nha Cat.

But more days went by, and nothing he wanted to happen happened. Mo shipped out for surgery in Japan. McLemore would cry out in the middle of the night, and whichever nurse was on graveyard shift would bring a pan of warm water so he could soak his feet. Each time a medevac chopper arrived with fresh wounded, Peter asked if they were from Nha Cat, and the nurses said no. The major who occasionally glanced at the chart hanging from the foot of his bed told him the cast had to stay on two more weeks. When it got quiet enough at night, he could hear the rattle of the mortuary's faulty compressor. The blinds rattled up every morning and down every night. He came to believe that if sewn-together bamboo strips were capable of mocking laughter, that was the sound they'd make.

He began to take out his frustration on Flo by asking her questions that verged on insubordination.

"Hey, Flo. I heard there's a new medal for sports injuries in a combat zone. Could you check on that for me, please?"

"Hey, Flo. When Goliath got KO'd by David's slingshot, would you call that a sports injury?"

"Hey, Flo. I've been lying here trying to remember: Who was it said the Battle of Waterloo was won on the playing fields of Eton?"

"Hey, Flo. Did you know Rasputin's assassins had to poison him, shoot him three times and throw him in a frozen river before he'd stay dead? Now, would you call that a triathlon?"

"Hey, Flo. You know, that's really sweet music you make raising and lowering the blinds. I bet you play the marimba in your spare time."

He would have relented if Flo had ever looked at him, even with exasperation, as he reeled off this nonsense. She did pay a little more attention to the one-armed man Mo had told him about. The man's bed was across the aisle and closer to the nursing station. The pleading look in his eyes always intensified when a nurse circled the ward. Captain Cottingham, the head nurse for convalescent care, always paused to speak to him, and sometimes she even got him to smile. Once Peter saw Flo massage the man's stump, but aside from announcing what she was doing, she said nothing to him. Routinely, the most the amputee got from her was a wordless glance as she marched on toward the nurses' station like an automaton with a garish red mouth.

The more Peter tried to needle Flo, the longer and more piercing became the looks he drew from Captain Cottingham. Finally, and chiefly to hasten a final reckoning, Peter stepped over the line with Flo in a way he figured she would find intolerable.

He waited until a night when Flo was on graveyard shift. When she approached his bed during the first of the two turns through the ward the night nurse had to make, he sat up so abruptly that she gave a little jump backward.

"Oh, sorry, Lieutenant," he said. "It's just—I've been lying here wondering whether you've ever worn fluorescent lipstick. Did you ever hear that the wounded men Florence Nightingale cared for in the Crimea took to calling her 'the lady with the lamp'? Well, they did. And do you know why? It was because when she made her last round late at night, she would carry an oil lamp, and they could all see her face. And that was a real comfort to them. And I think it would be such a comfort to the men in this ward if they could see the illuminated outline of your beautiful lips moving through the ward late at night, like, you know, a ghostly emblem of compassion. So would you just consider that, Lieutenant? It would mean so much to men who have learned that they could always, *always* rely on your care and compassion, shining for them like a lamp in the darkness. Sorry if I alarmed you, Lieutenant. God bless you, and good night."

"I'm going to write you up, Private Dandridge," she said.

When he heard the blinds rattle up next morning, Peter started in on his morning litany of curses at his luck and at Rabinowitz before he even opened his eyes. When he did open them, he saw Captain Cottingham pacing back and forth at the foot of his bed. Her eyes, magnified by her circular lenses, stayed fixed on him each time she changed the direction of her pacing. Peter was reminded of an owl's ability to hold its head motionless as it pivots its body on a limb.

"Private Dandridge, I know how impatient you are to get back to your unit," she said finally. "That's a good thing. And when impatience gets frustrated, it tends to boil over, and if anybody's standing too close to it, they might get scalded. And that's an understandable thing."

The medical clamps of various sizes pinned to her fatigue blouse jangled a little as she paced back and forth at the foot of his bed.

"Captain, you can cut to the chase," Peter said. "Everything she told you is true. I was rude and insubordinate, and it wasn't even spur-of-the-moment."

"Oh, I'm not talking just about Lieutenant Pedersen, or just about her and Specialist McLemore," the captain said. "You see, I heard about that little tiff you had with him too. Apparently you thought his foot problem was just an act. Now, that'd be a pretty smart trick if he could get away with it, wouldn't it? Especially when some men go to all the trouble of shooting off a toe. But I'd like for the two of us to speak more broadly. You see, I like to try to get at the root of things. Seems foolish to just tamp down symptoms when what you need to do is treat the disease. You think about it, that's about as dumb as sitting on your back porch and swatting flies all summer long, when just over the fence there's a big pile of garbage where the flies are breeding like—well, like flies. Just get rid of the garbage, and you've cured your fly problem, see? Then with the flies gone, you can sit out on your back porch and think of something else to complain about. Like, for example, you could complain about having your boyfriend or your girlfriend off in Vietnam when you'd rather they were right there with you on the porch, so you could both come in out of that sticky heat and go in the bedroom and switch on the window unit and get down to business. You know, I'd like to think my boyfriend and your girlfriend do complain about that. If I calculate correctly the time difference between Vietnam and Chicago and wherever in the South you come from, it's just possible they're both complaining about that right now. Now, when I say it's possible, I'm assuming my boyfriend's on the back porch with nothing and nobody but a beer to keep him company, which he'd better be. And I'm assuming you've got a girlfriend, which for a good-looking young man like you I take to be a given."

"Is there a first name your boyfriend is supposed to be whispering to himself while he drinks his beer?" Peter said.

"Doreen," she said. She stood still long enough for two drawn-out, owlish blinks, then resumed her pacing. "But let's stick with our proper subject here. Let's talk about the things you don't know, and how they might change some of your opinions if you knew them. Now about Specialist McLemore: Did you know he was a forward artillery observer? No? Well, I didn't think you did. And do you know what a forward artillery observer has to do? He gets sent out ahead of his unit, and he has to wade through the little canals that run between rice paddies, and he has to find some patch of ground that's high enough he can stand on it and see if the artillery rounds from his battery are landing where they can kill the enemy, or whether they're likely to kill women and children and old people instead. And then he has to radio back to the gun crews to do one of three things. They should keep firing on the same coordinates, fire on new coordinates that he's calculated, or cease firing, either because of the threat to civilians or because he sees nothing worth blowing up. Now, did you know any of that? And do you understand that sometimes an artillery unit might stay on the move for days or weeks at a time, and a forward observer like Specialist McLemore will have to stay out ahead of it, and that means he might have to slog through those rice paddies and irrigation canals day after day? And do you know what happens to your feet when that paddy water with all that bacteria in it keeps squishing around in your boots and you never have time to pull your boots off and let your feet get dry? Your feet get covered with sores, and pretty soon what the soldiers call jungle rot sets in, and you start to lose feeling in your feet. If you don't get some intervention right then, which Specialist McLemore was either smart enough or lucky enough to do, the flesh on your feet starts to die and rot. Then you're looking at amputation, maybe just of some toes, maybe of the whole foot. Now, if you do get treatment before your jungle rot takes a turn for the worse, it takes a good while to get better, and the getting better goes in stages. Little by little the numbness goes, but what takes its place is some awful pain when that dead flesh sloughs off and live flesh starts to grow back in. Now, did you take any of that into account before you made that smart-alecky comment about the numbness in Specialist McLemore's feet creeping up into his private parts?"

Peter had shut his eyes, the better to savor the counterpoint between the soothing curlicues of her voice and the stark description of life in combat she was asking him to accept as applying to McLemore. He opened his eyes again when he realized she was waiting for an answer.

"No," he said. "I didn't take that into account. I didn't know anything about it."

He glanced toward McLemore's bed. It was at the far end of the row of beds against the ward's opposite wall. McLemore was leaning back against the side of his bed, bracing himself with his elbows on the mattress while he soaked his feet in a basin of water on the floor. He'd spent plenty of time in the sun, all right, Peter thought. Even the crewcut blond hair on the back of McLemore's neck had been burned to the coppery hue of a piece of cheap, tarnished jewelry.

"You seem to know an awful lot about his history," Peter told the nurse. "I'm impressed."

"Never mind about that," she said. "What's important is what you didn't know, so you made up a history for Specialist McLemore and assumed it was true. And you don't know anything about Lieutenant Pedersen's history either, do you? So you made up one for her, and you pestered and picked at her because you never considered she might have a real history completely different from your made-up one."

"I never thought about her history," Peter said. "If I had, I probably would've concluded she marched fully formed out of the devil's toyshop."

"Re-ally, Private Dandridge?" Captain Cottingham said, chuckling softly. "Re-ally?" The drawn-out, musical way she pronounced the word and the way she tilted her head and peered at him suggested this was supposed to be part of a private code between the two of them. "Now, what if you'd known that Lieutenant Pedersen had a brother who was a Marine, and that a couple of years ago, when she was still in nursing school, her brother was killed up near the DMZ? What if you knew that was why she decided to join the Army and try to go to Vietnam, so she could take care of men who got wounded fighting? What if you knew she never even thought until she got here that men in a combat zone get hurt or sick in lots of other ways, just like they do anywhere else?" Captain Cottingham chuckled again, softly and briefly. "What if you knew she just finds that offensive, that they would dare to do that?"

Peter was watching Captain Cottingham's face. Her eyes behind the round lenses seemed to him to grow larger and softer, and beyond her the beds and the men in them appeared slightly blurred.

"What about the lipstick?" Peter said. "Something tells me you're going to set me straight on that too."

She chuckled again, but her eyes narrowed a little, as if she realized he had her number.

"Re-ally, now? You're holding it against her that she wears lipstick?"

"Well, you don't wear any," he said. "None of the other nurses do. And it's not just that she wears it. She smears it on. She always looks like a wolverine fresh from its last blood meal."

"Re-ally, Private Dandridge!" she said. Her guttural tone signaled a mix of disapproval and amusement. "Re-ally, now. Well, wouldn't it change your opinion if you knew that when she was little, she had surgery to correct a harelip, and it left a little scar in her upper lip, and she uses lipstick to hide what happened there? I'll grant you, maybe she overdoes it. But wouldn't that make her seem a little more human to you and a little less like a wolverine?"

Peter knew what Captain Cottingham wanted him to feel. He found he was no longer capable of feeling that way.

"Look, ma'am, I shouldn't be keeping you here when you've got rounds to make," he said. "I appreciate all you've told me, though. It's given me a lot to think about."

"Oh, I'm not here on rounds," she said. "I'll make those later. Right now my concern is all about you. I've got to decide what to do about this report Lieutenant Pedersen has given me, you see? And her report includes what those two men who fetched you down from overflow told her about the demeaning comment you made to Private McLemore, and how he reacted to that. Now, I have to send her report forward, but when I do that, I want to attach my own statement to it, you see? And I want to be able to say that the language you used to Private McLemore and the lieutenant was based on misunderstanding, on false assumptions you'd made about both of them. Now I need you to help me with that, Private Dandridge."

Peter was relieved that the captain's eyes had returned to their proper size, and that he could again see clearly the men in their beds across the ward, and that he knew what he had to do next.

"So what you'd like me to do is tell you how much I regret getting it wrong about McLemore and Lieutenant Pedersen, and go down there and shake his hand, and I guess make some face-to-face apology to the wolverine. Right?"

She laughed quietly. The array of forceps and clamps on her breast jangled a little. "I wouldn't get in the habit of even thinking of her by that name, if I were you," she said. "I know you men call her Flo, and I'd just stick with that."

"Look, I'm not going to grovel to McLemore," Peter said. "I'm square with him already. He cured me of any misconception I had about him when he shoved me and clanged my head. As for the lieutenant? Whatever hang-ups she has are the hang-ups she has. Any apology I made to her would just make her feel justified, and the next patient who fits my profile would pay the price for that."

"I see, I see," the captain said, nodding and blinking. "Well, let's look for some middle-ground solution. Let's think on that."

"Or let's not," Peter said. "Look, is there a possibility that if I'm a bad enough actor here, I might get shipped back to my unit sooner than I would otherwise?"

"Well, I couldn't honestly tell you I've never heard of basing medical decisions on patient misbehavior." She laughed a little. "But you're going to be up and out of here in ten days anyway."

"But it can happen?" he said. "And forget about ten days. How about tomorrow? Couldn't you say I was undermining good order and discipline on the ward, and that ought to outweigh any benefit I might get from a week of physical therapy once the cast comes off? Look, my unit back in Nha Cat is going to get hit by the VC, if it hasn't been already. And if it hasn't, then I need to be there when it does."

"And what good could you do back there in the shape you're in?" she said. "And why would you want to run toward trouble two ways at once? Getting a reprimand on your service record—that'd be one way—and maybe getting shot while you try to hobble out of a line of fire?"

"I can't disentangle that puzzle for you," he said. "I can't even disentangle it for me. But I've got to be there when it happens, if I can. So please send that report forward in the same form you'd have given it if we'd never had this conversation. Or, better yet, just put in the report what actually happened. Say you confronted me with perspectives on McLemore and the lieutenant that differed totally from mine, and I told you I preferred my perspectives and regarded yours as artfully crafted crap. Crafted with my best interests in mind. I understand that."

Captain Cottingham was looking off to one side and absentmindedly stroking the shin of his good leg through the light blanket that covered it. Her face gave no clue he had offended her. He was struck afresh by the likeness to a helmet of her massive Afro hairdo with its severe edges above her forehead and below her ears.

"You know," she said slowly, still stroking his leg, "you might have found us that middle ground we need. You might even have hit on a way to recruit the ally you'd least expect."

She told him this was her second tour of duty at Khoang Trong Hospital, and she knew she'd have the ear of medical officers there if she ever needed it.

"And you say you've got to be there," she said. "I think I understand what you mean. But, just between us now, what if I represented you as saying your presence at your duty station might prove essential to its defense?"

"I'd call that classic military doublespeak," he said.

"All right." She gave his good knee a final pat.

She started back toward the nursing station but turned when Peter said, "Captain, one more thing."

"Yes?"

"You started off saying you were going to trace my symptoms back to the disease. The symptoms, I guess, were my getting crossways with McLemore and Flo. What's the disease?"

"Oh," she said. "Freeze-frame syndrome. You're the worst case I've seen in a while. You look at a person at a given moment or in a given situation, and then: freeze frame. You decide what you see in them then is all they are, and all they ever could be."

Twenty-six

It seemed to go quickly and well after that, right up until it all went disastrously wrong. Later that morning, Captain Cottingham told him Flo had withdrawn her report after she learned he wanted to get back to Nha Cat in time to help fend off a VC ground attack.

"Hey, Captain?" Peter said as she headed back toward the nursing station.

"Ye-e-es?" she said in a voice laden with mock suspicion. She half-turned and gave him a sidelong glance.

"I just wondered if you could give a message for me to that boyfriend of yours back in Chicago," he said.

"Ye-e-es? Well, first you'll have to tell me what that message is, and then I'll have to decide."

"Tell him a smart-mouthed private on your ward said all he ought to have out on that back porch is a six-pack of beer, plus a fly swatter if he needs one. Tell him I said you were a keeper."

She kept the sidelong glance in place a while longer. "I'll think on it," she said.

That afternoon a medical officer ran a little circular saw down the length of Peter's cast and pried it off. Then he tested Peter's knee by bending his foot to one side, then the other, and each time slowly driving the knee back against Peter's chest. "Not bad, for a knee with zero cartilage," the doctor said. He handed Peter an illustrated pamphlet of instructions for the same exercises Peter had done, off and on, for years. Peter threw it in a trash bin as soon as he got back to the ward.

He knew as soon as he was awakened next morning by the fierce clatter of window blinds being opened that it was Flo's hand on the ropes. The two junior-ranking nurses seemed to vie to complete this job as fast as possible. Flo held an edge in the sustained racket she produced.

Soon she came back to his bed with a set of military orders in her hand. The lipstick was slathered on as usual. He could tell from her eyes and the way she walked and the offhand way she held the orders that she wanted to keep this low-key and brief.

"Captain Cottingham got these cut for you," she said, dropping the orders on the mattress by his shoulder. He picked them up, saw they were in triplicate and read the phrases "authorize immediate return to duty" and "transportation by military aircraft by the most feasible route."

"Thanks," he said. "And please thank the captain for me."

"See that right there?" the nurse said, flicking a fingernail against the typed line authorizing transportation. "That means you'll hopscotch back to Nha Cat. You might ride in a bucket seat up to Da Nang on our C-47 supply shuttle, then a different aircraft down to Cam Ranh Bay, then a third one up to Nha Cat. Or you might have to fly down to Tan Son Nhut and work your way up from there. It'll probably take you two days to get to Nha Cat, maybe more. So you might want to take your blankie."

"This blanket?" he said. "You sure you can spare a blanket?"

"Somebody told me once it can get cold at night at Da Nang," she said. She flipped up the edge of his blanket and looked at his knee, wrapped in an elastic bandage. "You sure you can walk on that without crutches?" she said.

"As long as I'm careful and keep the bandage on, I'll be fine," he said. "I've had plenty of experience doing that."

She flipped the blanket back down. "Well, the blanket's on offer," she said, turning away. "Take it or leave it."

Peter watched her head back up the aisle, knowing he ought to say more to her. But what? Sorry your brother got killed? Sorry you were born with a harelip? How do I even know Captain Cottingham was telling the truth about those things, rather than just trying to talk me around to where she didn't have to let Flo's report stand as written?

His fatigues and boots were in plastic bags under the bed. He put them on and took the blanket. An orderly he'd befriended called to get the departure time of the next shuttle to Da Nang, then drove him to the flight line to catch it. When he got to Da Nang, he was told the best they could do was get him to Cam Ranh, where there were flights and ground convoys up the coast to Nha Cat. He spent a night in the terminal at Da Nang with the blanket pulled to his chin, and next afternoon he got a seat on a shuttle to Cam Ranh. When he arrived, he waved a copy of his orders at a flight clerk, who told him there were no regular flights to Nha Cat.

"That's not what they told me in Da Nang," Peter said.

"Well, whoever told you that in Da Nang must have decided you weren't his favorite turd after all, so he could afford to shit you," the clerk said.

On his third day in Cam Ranh, the flight desk clerk told him if he flew back to Da Nang he could probably hitch a ride from there to Nha Cat on a flight requested by Special Forces. So Peter caught the shuttle back to Da Nang, spent another night there beneath the hospital blanket and at dawn carefully climbed the steps into a twin-engine plane with "Air America" stenciled in slanted lettering near the tail. The men on board wore tiger-stripe fatigues with the sword-and-thunderbolts shoulder patch of Special Forces. Most had M-16s propped against their seats, with yellow safety sticks protruding from the muzzles. All the seats on the right side were taken, and Peter asked if someone would move so he could stretch his left leg into the aisle.

"I'm only going as far as Nha Cat, if that makes a difference," Peter said.

"No difference," a man wearing a first lieutenant's bar said, heaving himself to his feet. "That's the end of the line for all of us."

A couple of the other men turned to look at Peter as he eased into the seat.

"Wound?" one said.

"No, just a bum knee," Peter said. "I spent two weeks in a cast in Khoang Trong. Now I need to get back fast to Nha Cat."

More heads turned. "Why's that?" the man said. "They get hit again?"

"Again? What do you mean by 'again'?"

"Again means like time number two."

Several of the men laughed.

"Time number one was a few days ago," the lieutenant said. "We're supposed to help beef up defenses there, you know? Kind of like the cavalry riding to the rescue after Fort Apache has burned to the ground."

"Oh, it wasn't that bad, from what I hear," another man said.

"Not good, though," the lieutenant said. "Not good anytime Charlie can mount a direct attack on a CIA compound. Not good anytime Americans and Arvin take casualties in what's supposed to be a secure area."

Peter said nothing more until the plane had taken off. He leaned his head against the window by his seat and shut his eyes as the plane rumbled down the runway. So it's over, and I wasn't there, he thought. And goddamn you, Rabinowitz, it's your fault I wasn't.

When the plane was airborne, he opened his eyes and saw beneath the plane a village of thatch-roofed houses next to a canal. Hard against the dry-land side of the houses were several round wicker trays used for sun-drying rice. The trays looked filled to overflowing, and they were crowded together between the houses and a perimeter of concertina wire. They have to cram it all in there behind the wire to keep the VC from stealing it, he thought. You won't catch those people demanding that somebody take away their barbed wire and bury it.

"I didn't know it had happened yet," Peter said. "I just knew an attack was coming, and I had to get back. And now I'm too fucking late."

"Hah!" the lieutenant said. "That makes about thirteen of us. But everybody in Nha Cat was saying they knew what was coming and could handle it by themselves, no problem. Special Forces, CIA, Arvin, Korean infantry—they were all on the same page about that."

"Something went wrong, then?" Peter said.

"You could say that. As I understand it, they expected there'd be just one point of attack, a checkpoint outside a cemetery where the VC had somehow set up a weapons cache—weapons buried in there among the graves. Well, Charlie did come over the cemetery wall, all right, but it turned out his plan was three-pronged, not single-point. Point two was an assault on a company of Korean infantry stationed on a hilltop just south of the American airbase. The VC hit the Korean camp with enough numbers to prevent the Koreans from hopping on helicopters that were held ready at a helipad up there to ferry them down to the backside of the cemetery. The idea was the Koreans would deploy around the cemetery, pin the VC inside it, then go in and wipe them out. That's pretty much what happened during Tet a year ago. Now, you might ask why our master plan didn't account for the possibility that Charlie might have learned from that experience. And I could not answer that question for you.

"So right there you have what a good ground tactics instructor might call a compromised plan of defense and counterattack. But the *pièce de résistance* for the VC was their third point of attack, one that was wide open. See, about ten days ago, one of the seagoing boats we had under supposedly secure guard in Nha Cat harbor was stolen. Our esteemed colleagues in Nha Cat assumed Charlie had it, and they expected Charlie would use it to stage some tit-for-tat version of the quick-hit raids we carry out with boats. So where, oh where should we look for them to try that? Hmmmm? How about five clicks south of the harbor where they stole it, on an undefended beach at the seaward end of the same little street that has the checkpoint and cemetery at the far end and the CIA compound in the middle?"

"Oh, Jesus Christ," Peter said, pounding his fist against the little window by his head. "That's our street! And they didn't even post a guard at the beach end? How many casualties were there? Were any kids killed or hurt?"

"Whoa! Whoa!" said the lieutenant. "Hey, like I said, we're just the cavalry, summoned late and from afar. We're lucky if we get briefed on broad outlines. The only figures we've got for casualties are four Arvin, one Veenaf, two ROK and one U.S. service member killed. Plus at least forty enemy killed. No word on civilian casualties."

A blast of morning sunlight struck Peter through a window across the aisle and he shaded his eyes with a hand. "Just one more thing," he said. "Is the dock for those boats near a Vietnamese hospital?"

"Why, yeah," the officer said. "The hospital's on the next street up from the dock. Why?"

"I know somebody who works at the hospital," Peter said. "That's all."

For the rest of the flight to Nha Cat, Peter gazed out the window in silence. About a half-hour out of Da Nang, the plane flew over a river valley hemmed in by small, scrub-covered mountains half-shrouded by tufts of cloud. The mountains, conical with fluted sides, looked as nearly identical as if all had been poured from a mold. Beginning flush against the foot of the mountains on either side, paddy fields in shades ranging from emerald to dun stretched to the river's banks. Capillary-thin canals connected the paddies.

Watching wisps of cloud dissolve as they drifted over the paddies, Peter thought, I'm about to leave this beautiful place, aren't I? And I'll have to leave it without ever having run much risk of dying here. And that was what I wanted most, wasn't it? Not to die, but to run the risk of it. Even if that amounted to no more than a few hours beneath the shadow. A shadow that Teddy lived under for so long that, even now, whenever he casts a fishing lure into glittering sunlight, that shadow falls over it.

Peter remembered what Stephie had said the first time he drove with her to Pilot Mountain: that your spirit never fleshes out until you walk close enough to death to touch those sheer walls, feel the chill. And who, now, on his quiet street where until then the war had entered his life only as a nighttime light show or as the distant drumroll of a B-52 strike—who had been engulfed by that shadow? And whose fault was it? For the men on this plane, what had happened on that street amounted to just another instance of military planning gone awry—FUBAR, in the military lexicon. Fucked up beyond all reason. These men had neither the need nor the capacity to pinpoint the lapses of intelligence-gathering and clear thinking that produced this particular case of FUBAR. But whatever that total picture looked like, Peter knew his own demented charge onto the soccer field, ending with the uppercut he had delivered to Pham's throat with his rifle butt, was part of it. It had altered what came afterward, perhaps in some important way. Maybe even in some deadly way. He would never know. And that was going to be what he would carry home from the war. That would be the thing he could neither bear to think about nor forget.

When the plane taxied to a stop in Nha Cat and the boarding ramp dropped from its belly, a jeep hitched to a two-wheeled trailer pulled up beside it on the tarmac. There were three blue-helmeted air policemen in the jeep, and two of them jumped out to help the Special Forces men unload several metal boxes from the plane's baggage compartment and place them in the trailer. Peter recognized the boxes as the kind used to transport heavy weapons, such as machine guns and grenade launchers. They were the same sort of boxes, he thought with a knife-twist of guilt, that—painted to resemble caskets—had been carried multiple times in that rattling wooden cart right past an American guard post and buried in the cemetery.

The jeep driver sat slumped over the steering wheel until all the passengers had deplaned except Peter. Then, as Peter haltingly descended the four steps of the boarding ramp, a broad smile spread across the driver's face and he stepped onto the tarmac.

"Hot damn, you finally made it!" he said.

Peter glanced back over his shoulder to see if the man might be talking to someone else.

"You're Private Dandridge, right?" the policeman said, shaking his head as if there was something hard to believe about Peter's appearance. "First time I've been ordered to give V.I.P. treatment to a private," he said.

Peter hobbled to the jeep while the driver extracted a portable radio from behind his seat and punched in a number. "This is Sergeant Eric DeLaney, Air Police," he said. "The guy the colonel was waiting for is here. Yeah. Dandridge. Just stepped off a flight from Da Nang. Want us to bring him over to…? What? All right, we'll have him in the guard shack."

He turned to Peter with another puzzled look. "I can't tell whether they think you're high-value or whether they just want to throw you in the guardhouse," he said. "Not my affair."

The two others climbed in back and they headed to the terminal with the boxes of heavy weapons in tow. At the terminal, DeLaney motioned for Peter to stay in his seat. The others jumped out, unhitched the trailer and hauled it clear of the jeep. Then DeLaney drove Peter to the guard shack at the entrance to the flight line. He said the Air Police had checked for him on every arriving flight for the last three days.

"Ever since the VC got into that little street that runs from the checkpoint to the beach," he said. "Hear about that yet? They killed four or five Arvin at the checkpoint, but what seemed to get everybody's shorts in a twist was the two they killed on a rooftop. One was a Veenaf officer. You'd see him riding a Vespa sometimes on the beach road. Wore sunglasses that wrapped around his head so tight he looked like a bug. I think the other one was a teacher at the air academy. Moskowitz or something. Some kind of -witz. Liebowitz? No, that's not it either. Damn."

DeLaney pulled up at the guard shack and Peter got out. He stood between the jeep and the little wooden building while DeLaney stepped inside and spoke to the guard, who stole half-fearful glances at Peter through an open window.

Peter tried to remember why he was there, but for a few moments he could not. What he remembered instead was a day when he had stood beside narrow-gauge railway tracks with the sun drilling through his fatigue cap, looking down into a pair of aviator's sunglasses. That had been the time he found Pham forcing students to stretch in pushup position over a ditch. When Pham challenged his right to intervene, it had been the heat that momentarily rendered him unable to think clearly. What was it this time?

"They're dead," he muttered. "It's Rabby, and the other one's got to be Pham. And he said they were killed on the rooftop of a villa. Ours? And why on the roof? And...and...that rattletrap compressor in the mortuary. Isn't that where they'd send him if he was dead? And he's dead, so that's where he's got to be now, isn't it?"

DeLaney came out of the guard shack with the air of a man freed from a small but nettlesome burden. "You can step in there out of the sun if you want," he told Peter. "Technically, you're in detention. We had to set up a chain of custody as soon as you stepped off the plane."

In a few minutes, the station wagon that served as Colonel Jesperson's staff car pulled up at the gate. Jesperson, who was alone in the car, got out and approached Peter in a loose-limbed amble. Jesperson raised and dropped his own offhand salute before Peter's hand had reached the bill of his cap. When the colonel saw Peter's hobbling gait, he opened the front passenger door for him.

"Two reasons, really, that I figured I ought to come by myself to pick you up," Jesperson said as he drove up the beachside road toward the checkpoint. "One is to let you know in confidence that I have to go through with this detention thing, however bullshit it might appear in a fair-minded view. Reason for that is also twofold. And here I go complicating matters, but bear with me. We need to maintain best possible relations with Major Duong. Beyond that, we have to repair Duong's standing and our own with the Veenaf high command. And they are royally pissed by the spectacle of an American private dashing in from the sidelines in the middle of a soccer game and swinging his rifle stock into the throat of a Vietnamese officer. That lick you gave Lieutenant Pham must have crushed his voice box, judging by what filtered back from the CIA efforts to interrogate him. And, bullshit or no, I'll have to follow up with some formal punitive action. I won't go beyond an Article Fifteen, but that's nothing to celebrate."

"Forget about that," Peter said. "Tell me, was it Rabby? What happened to Rabinowitz?"

The rasp always present in the colonel's voice sounded all but smoothed away, as though with fine-grained sandpaper.

"Well, that was the other reason I figured I should come fetch you," he said. "I knew you and Avram were close. I know that when you ran out onto that soccer field, you were aiming to protect him. And I thought I should tell you personally that Avram was shot and killed on the rooftop of your villa. The circumstances were confusing, but they appear to be pretty much of his own making."

"Wait a minute," Peter said. "Avram? Did you say Avram?"

Jesperson cast a sidelong glance at Peter's open-mouthed stare. "Yes," he said. "Your friend, Private Avram Rabinowitz."

"Did he have another name?" Peter said. "A middle name, maybe?"

"Matter of fact, I do know, since I had to sign the report on this whole sorry incident. It was Meir. His name was Avram Meir Rabinowitz."

"Well, doesn't that …" Feeling Jesperson's sidelong glance on him again, and knowing the colonel would mistake his tears of rage for grief, Peter slammed his fist again, this time against the car door.

"Doesn't that take the fucking cake?" Peter said. "Avram! I should've known. A fabulist, that's what he said he was. Well, where I come from, we have a different name for it."

He wiped aside his tears with the fingertips of both hands. They were tears of rage, but he couldn't force the words "lying S.O.B." from his mouth.

The colonel let Peter out at the checkpoint after telling him that all he had to do as a detainee was drop by the orderly room once a day and tell the duty sergeant where he'd been during the past twenty-four hours.

"One more thing," the colonel said as Peter opened the passenger door. "You knew him at least as well as anybody here. If you have any insight into why he did what he did, leading up to and during our visit from Victor Charlie, pick a time when you can explain it to me. You can do that behind closed doors if you want. I just want to know."

"Colonel, all I know about what he did was he got himself killed," Peter said. "And I just learned that today."

"I see," the colonel said. He looked at the floorboard and drummed his fingernails on the steering wheel. "Well, I think the other men in your villa can fill you in on all he did before that. Just based on the bare facts, it seems crazy as hell. But there has to be more to it. Maybe a lot more. A scrap or two of information has come to my hand. I don't know what to make of it, but it might help you find out just how much more there is. And among all of us here, you're the only one who could do that. That seems pretty clear. But we can delve into all that when you stop by the command shack. I'll leave word at the front desk to bring you in unless I'm tied up. Be careful you don't trip on the pavement, now. It's a little chewed up. A gunship strafed it after Charlie got in here from both this end and the beach end. Oh, and here. I took the liberty of retrieving these for you from the mail room." He handed Peter a letter from his parents, one from Stephie and an envelope from the alumni office at Peter's university. "Fundraising, no doubt," Jesperson said. "I'd mail them one dollar in military scrip."

Two seasoned-looking Arvin soldiers had replaced the little teenagers who had long seemed to be permanently detailed to the checkpoint. After Peter got out, the guards moved aside the barrier with its coiled wire, and the colonel pulled past them toward the academy. The checkpoint had been altered to include, on one side of the street, a little bunker enclosed by sandbags. It was shielded from the sun by a canvas roof and equipped with a swivel-mounted machine gun on a tripod. Behind the machine gun stood a third guard, barely visible in the roof's deep shadow. Behind the bunker was the cemetery wall, with two V-shaped holes blasted through it.

Peter turned to take a long look down his street. It was a Sunday, and Jesperson had told him everyone was still confined to quarters. Peter could see chunks of concrete lying in the street outside the grillwork gate to the CIA villa. Otherwise, at first glance the street seemed unchanged, except for the absence of people, but when he let his eyes scan more slowly, it appeared stippled, like a pointillist painting. As he walked down the street, the stippling resolved itself into bullet holes, shredded foliage, little glittering shards of the bottle glass that routinely topped walls, and what he assumed were flecks of sun-dried blood. From the checkpoint, foliage had blocked his view of the CIA villa's wall, but as he drew closer he saw in it the same sort of V-shaped hole he'd seen in the cemetery wall, except that masons had already half-sealed this one with concrete blocks. Across the street's far end, where you could step off the pavement onto beach sand, he saw a new, wire-wrapped wooden barrier manned by two more Arvin soldiers. Normally on any Sunday in the dry season, there'd be clusters of fruit sellers and whores squatting in the shade of a pair of palm trees near the edge of the beach, but today there was no one on the entire stretch of beach from the palms to the waterline. Quiet, so quiet, he thought. It's like all the life's been sucked out of it.

When he turned off the street to reach his villa, he spotted the concertina wire. A swirl of it ran from the edge of the officers' villa down one side of the patio between that villa and the one where Peter lived. As he drew closer, he saw the gleaming barbs that marked it as razor wire. The swirls of wire were anchored to hedgehogs—sturdy little structures, each consisting of three lengths of lumber, crisscrossed, bolted and braced. He couldn't have explained how he knew it, but he knew instantly the wire barrier had to be Rabby's idea.

"Who'd he con into building that?" he breathed. "Rabby wouldn't know which end of a hammer to pick up."

When he approached near enough to have a full view of the patio and screened porch, he saw Sergeant Winfrey, the villa's NCO, sitting on the porch steps, wearing fatigue pants and flip-flops but nothing from the waist up. The sergeant clasped and unclasped his fingers and looked distractedly toward the far end of the patio, which was sealed off by a second, identical barrier of razor wire and hedgehogs. Peter saw no movement within the doorway leading to the sergeant's two rooms. The first of those rooms was a little kitchen. Peter was used to seeing Huê's shadowed form darting about there, often preparing a cup of the instant coffee that Winfrey, in what seemed to Peter an awkward gesture of affection for the child, called for about twice an hour every evening. Dan came out of the room he shared with Peter and down the steps past Winfrey. Approaching the wire, Dan rolled his shoulders, turned his head aside and spat between his teeth. Peter couldn't recall ever having seen Dan spit. He took it as a sign Dan was moved or distressed and could find no better way to cope with it.

Winfrey waved a hand at Peter and managed a half-smile. "Good to see you back, troop," he said. "Be careful of that wire, now." Then he went back to interlacing his fingers and casting pained glances toward the far end of the patio, as if allowing for the possibility that something longed-for might appear there.

Dan stared at Peter at close range through the swirls of razor wire. Then he nodded toward the ladder leading to the rooftop.

"Know about that part yet?" Dan said.

"No," Peter said. "All I know is Rabby got killed."

"Yeah, They shot him up there on the roof. They killed Pham up there too."

"What in hell was Pham doing here?"

"Good question," Dan said. "He just showed up here, outside the wire. Rabby rigged up these wooden braces , whatever you call them, right after the soccer game. He bolted them together and then he stretched out the wire and tacked it on. He'd scrounged razor wire somewhere, stored it in his room."

"They call them hedgehogs," Peter said. "Somebody must have helped him. Rabby wouldn't know diddly about working with barbed wire."

"Nope, he did it all himself," Dan said. "It was almost dark when he started. The rest of us were cleaning our weapons and trying to figure out what would come next. I mean, after the CIA guys snatched Pham off the soccer field. Somebody asked what Rabby was doing out on the patio, and Doucet ducked out and told us. Emmet and I volunteered to help, but Rabby waved us off. Made it pretty clear he didn't want help. He must have had the two-by-fours and bracing blocks all pre-cut. After that, all he had to do was bolt together those—what you call them?"

"Hedgehogs."

"Yeah. He had to build those and then stretch the wire and hammer in staples. Dicey, though, working with razor wire. He had heavy-duty gloves, but still his arms and legs had caked blood all over them next morning from where those barbs nicked him. The whole thing was Rabby's idea, nobody's but his."

"So that was what—two weeks ago? Had he gotten some order to seal off the villa that way?"

"An order?" Dan said. "He said nothing about that. Never said much of anything about why he did it. We thought it was nuts at first, but then we felt kind of glad for the extra protection."

"So he strings wire and leaves it to the rest of you to have weapons fit to return fire," Peter said. "I guess he viewed that as a fair division of labor."

"Oh no, he cleaned his M-16. Turned out Rabby and a captain across the way were the only ones of us who did return fire. Day after the soccer match, Rabby stayed home, and he cleaned up his rifle then. He had Winfrey look it over, and Winfrey said it was in good field condition."

"So Rabby was banged up bad enough he had to stay home a day?"

"It wasn't that. The spooks across the street wanted to debrief him."

"About what? Just what happened in the match?"

"Don't know. He said he couldn't talk about it."

"What about Huê? That was his other big hang-up."

"Yeah, he got all mother hen-ish about making sure Huê was inside the wire whenever she wasn't at school. Remember that tutorial he used to give her? Once he'd strung the wire, all he had to do was show her a quick toss-and-catch pantomime and she'd scoot back in here."

"She was in here when the attack hit, wasn't she?"

"Oh yeah. We all were. Status was yellow alert. Not quite confined to quarters, but ordered to stay together and keep our weapons by."

"God, I wish I'd been here," Peter said. He drew back a hand, preparatory to the kind of despair-fueled blow he'd given a window on the plane and Jesperson's car door. He dropped the hand when he realized he was about to impale it on razor wire.

"I tried to get back before the VC hit you, Dan," he said. "I really did."

"Don't know you could've made any difference. Nobody could've guessed the part about Pham, so there was no way to prepare for it."

"But, Jesus, there's got to be some reason."

"Yeah, well I'd better let someone else fill you in on that. All I can tell you is, when the VC got loose on our street, Pham shows up out of nowhere with a bunch of them on his tail. He's carrying a rifle with a banana clip. From our windows, we can see he wants to come in. Rabby goes out to talk to him through the wire, like you and I are talking now, except that Pham keeps glancing over his shoulder toward the street, and he gets really agitated. Finally he points his rifle at Rabby's chest, and it looks like he's saying let him in or else, and then Rabby must have told him something like, 'fine, shoot me and you'll draw fire from all four windows on this side of the villa.' And it looks like Pham backs off a little, and Rabby negotiates with him. Rabby could have just said something like, 'good luck and *di di mau*,' you know? But he doesn't do that. I couldn't hear, but I figure he tells Pham the people chasing him might not look for him on the rooftop, but if they do, they'd have to come up after him one at a time, so he'd be in a good defensive position. And then Rabby clinches the deal by telling Pham that if he picks the rooftop, he'll come up there with him to help defend it. And Pham buys it. Trouble is, after all this back-and-forth, the people chasing Pham have spotted him. Rabby pulls aside that hedgehog down there by the wall and slips out. Then Pham hops on the ladder and Rabby hops on behind him, and one of those VC chasing Pham is close enough that he hops on the ladder right behind both of them."

"Did you give Rabby any cover?" Peter said.

"Couldn't. We were all hunkered down by our windows. We'd locked and loaded, but our orders were to fire only if fired on. From our angle we couldn't see the ladder, but we could hear it clang from all the feet climbing up it. And a few seconds later, here comes a body falling down, whump. It's the VC troop, and he groans and rolls around a little, and then he gets up and beats it out of here. Then a little dude in black pajamas scoots out from behind the near corner of the officers' villa over there. We can see he's got wire cutters. Another one pokes his rifle around that same corner, and we can see he's trying to give cover while the first one snips through the wire."

"Oh, Jesus," Peter said. "Why would they try to get in here, if all they wanted was Pham?"

"Maybe they thought there was another way up to the roof. It didn't work out well for them, though. One of the officers over there was able to lean out his window and blow the brains out of the one who was trying to give cover. When that happened, any of us over here could've had a clear shot at the one with the wire cutters, but Rabby beat us to it. I poked my head up in time to see that one edge up to the concertina wire, but next second he was spread-eagled up against the wire like a swatted fly. Rabby had got him in the back. That captain had a clear view of it. He said as soon as Rabby fired, two or three bullets hit him and he fell down out of sight below that low wall around the roof edge. In a little bit, another VC tried to climb the ladder, and the captain shot him too. He can tell you all that he saw. He says it was Rabby who clubbed down that VC who'd followed him up the ladder. So Rabby did some real damage—unlike the rest of us in here. That captain can tell you how the VC finally got Pham, too. I think he's the same officer that hauled you off the soccer field before the MPs showed up."

"Captain Tomczak?" Peter said.

"Yeah, Tomczak. That's him. Tall guy, wide forehead, big dark eyes."

"And Huê?" Peter said. "What about Huê and her mom?"

"They're fine," Dan said. "I mean, they didn't get hurt or anything." He glanced over his shoulder at Sergeant Winfrey, then lowered his voice. "After this whole thing was over, Hien said she was taking Huê to live with the kid's grandmother near Vung Tau, where she thinks it's safer. Rabby's getting killed, and then the gunship strafing the street and killing a bunch of VC out there—that was it for Hien. I don't know whether she's coming back, but if she does, she won't bring Huê. Sergeant Winfrey's really busted up about it. About Rabby too, of course, but Hien and Huê were his family."

Peter asked if the men in the villa intended to take down the concertina wire. Dan said that didn't seem right, since Rabby had strung it to protect them all, and now he was dead. Besides, Dan said, they could come and go through the door on the other side of the villa.

"No wire on that side?" Peter said.

"We just had the one door to defend back there. Plus Rabby said stringing wire on both sides would seal us in as surely as it'd seal VC out."

Peter moved down the wire to the hedgehog nearest the villa wall, and Dan pulled it aside. Peter squeezed through the gap between wire and wall.

"But why?" Peter said. "Once he'd created a good-enough line of defense, he left it to help Pham put up a last-ditch defense on the roof, where God and everybody could see them. And this was a man Rabby hated, for good enough reasons. Why would he do that?"

Dan turned his head aside. Breathing hard, he shot Peter an exasperated look.

"How in hell would I know why?" Dan said. "There aren't but two people who could answer that question. Rabby was one of them, and he's dead. We go through this attack and Rabby gets killed while you're off getting meals brought to your hospital bed on a tray. And then you just sashay in here and casually ask why? Jeee-sus."

"Okay, okay," Peter said. "Tell me then—"

"Your Captain Tomczak tried to save him, did you know that?" Dan said. "He was the only one able to see him get shot. And then he thought maybe he could save him, so he climbed up there when there were still VC active in the area, but Rabby was already dead. We didn't know Rabby was dead or that Tomczak had gone up there until the all-clear finally sounded. And then Emmet and I felt so bad, because we'd done nothing. We felt so bad."

Dan looked down and shifted his weight from foot to foot. "Hey, I'm sorry, Pete," he said. "It's not like you wanted any of this to happen, or like it was your choice to be away when it did."

"No, I deserve it," Peter said. "For reasons that go way back before anything you could know about. But trust me, I deserve it."

"Well, Emmet and I talked about going up there and trying to get Rabby down by ourselves. I don't know whether that would've worked, though. Rabby's a big guy, Emmet not so much. Besides, Hien and the kid were already freaked out, and seeing Rabby lying dead on the porch would've just made that worse. So we didn't go up. That was a good thing for another reason, too. They sent out a truck from the air base and threw the VC bodies in the truck bed, but they sent some kind of civilian investigator—CIA is my guess—up on the roof with a sketch pad to try to piece together exactly what happened to Rabby and Pham. Then some Army guys went up there and put the bodies in bags and lowered them with a pulley hitched to a stretcher. We made sure Hien and Huê were inside so they wouldn't see that. Turned out there were three bodies, because one of the VC had made it up there and Pham shot him."

"Who else might be able to explain it, then?" Peter said. "You said there were two people who might know why Rabby would take his chances on the rooftop with Pham. Who's the other one?"

Dan cocked his head, and his eyes narrowed in a puzzled squint.

"Why, the other one is you, Pete," he said. "You knew him better than anybody here. If you can't figure it out, nobody can."

Twenty-seven

"If I'd fired when I had the chance, he might have come out okay," Captain Tomczak said. "Pham took up the best position he could, and they still picked him off. But they weren't after Rabby. I don't think they would ever have targeted him if he hadn't tried to brain that little cadre who was chasing Pham up the ladder, then fired on the one who was going to cut the wire."

It was evening, and they were standing on the rooftop, trying to make sense of what had happened there. A few radios in nearby villas chipped away at the silence.

Earlier, Peter and Emmet Doucet and Dan Beauchamp had pooled their K-rations. They had fried and sliced the canned meat and dumped the meat, bouillon cubes and two cans of vegetable soup into a pot and heated the concoction over Sterno. Doucet kept shaking pepper sauce into the pot until Peter wrested the bottle from his hand.

Once they'd eaten they climbed to the roof, together with Tomczak and Captain Earnhart, the smaller of the two officers who had gone up there to Spooky-watch on the night Rabby spun out his fable. Earlier in the day, Tomczak had broached the idea of all of them going up there around sunset.

"If that sounds ghoulish to you, you can opt out," Tomczak had said. "Nobody has tried yet to scour off the blood stains up there, right? So you're going to see where Rabby and Pham bled to death."

Tomczak climbed the ladder first. He pointed out to the others the stain left by Rabby's blood, and they all carefully stepped around it. Then he led them to the far side of the cistern, where Pham had made his stand until he was shot from the rooftop of another villa. He pointed out more stains on the roof where Pham had shot a pursuer who reached the roof from a concrete awning over the villa's back door. Peter idly picked up one of the aluminum lawn chairs that were propped against the cistern's wall. One of the crosshatched plastic strips in its seat had been shredded by a bullet.

"That cadre who chased them up the ladder?" Tomczak said. "I could have shot him in the back, but he and Rabinowitz were moving up it so fast, and that little cadre's head and chest nearly overlapped Rabby's legs, so I didn't risk it. I was waiting until Rabby cleared the top of the ladder and the cadre was on it by himself. Just a second would've been time enough for me to squeeze off a clean shot. But as soon as Rabby's feet touched the roof, he wheeled and grabbed his rifle barrel and swatted the guy in the head with the gunstock. The guy pitched sideways off the ladder, and that made Rabby the perfect target. Then I heard a scratching sound below my window and leaned out and shot the cadre who was taking aim at your windows. At the same time, Rabby blasted the one who was trying to snip the wire. Got him in the back with a short burst. Then Rabby looked straight at me. Odd thing was, he looked totally calm. His eyes made a sort of slow-motion blink, like he'd just finished up a big job and was taking a breather. Then there was a volley of fire from cadres who were well enough concealed that I couldn't spot them. As best I could tell from my window, several bullets hit Rabby, judging from the shreds of clothing that flew off him and the way he twisted when he fell. He dropped below the edge of the parapet there, and his rifle fell and hit the ground butt-first. He had it switched to automatic, and it fired another short burst when it hit. I saw his hand come up onto the parapet, and it looked like he was trying to lift himself up on it. A couple of those cadres fired again and got a bullet through his hand. After that he pawed at the parapet a couple more times with that bloodied hand, and then I didn't see any more movement.

"Down below, one of the others made a move toward the ladder. I opened up on him, but I don't think I killed him. Another cadre hauled him around the corner of your villa, where I couldn't see him anymore. The one Rabinowitz poleaxed was lying further out in the open. I could see he had a thick white scar running up his throat from his collarbone almost to an ear. He must have come around on his own, because next time I thought to check on him he was gone."

"That makes five, then," Peter said. "I mean, you're saying that three of those people chasing Pham tried to get at him by climbing the roof, counting the one Rabby knocked off the ladder, the one you shot and the one Pham killed. Then there was that two-man team that thought snipping the wire would open one more route to get at Pham. And only after all five of them got neutralized did another one shoot Pham from a different rooftop."

"Apparently so," Tomczak said. "That forensics investigator who came up here could probably tell us which villa the shot that killed Pham was fired from. Not that CIA would share that information with us, of course."

"So they made multiple stabs at getting at close quarters with Pham up here, and only then did they blow him away," Peter said. "What does that tell us?"

"It's pretty obvious, isn't it?" Earnhart said. "They wanted him alive if they could get him that way. If that didn't work out, killing him was their fallback."

Doucet was furiously twisting a corner of his mustache. The way his eyes glimmered in the near-darkness made it look like he was on the verge of either tears or laughter.

"What are you thinking, Emmet?" Peter said.

"If we're going to hash out what happened to Rabby, how 'bout we go down under the blow in somebody's room to do it?" he said. "Dark's coming on. Call me a superstitious coonass, but we're speaking in the presence of the dead up here. After dark, the dead get to be all ears."

"Let's go down, then, Tomczak said. "I'm going to treat you guys as need-to-know, so I'll spell some things out for you. But understand you could get in trouble if you blab them elsewhere. And listen." He pointed at the Rorschach blot near the roof's edge where Rabby's blood had pooled. "You guys should scrub out those bloodstains. Shouldn't be all that hard. Water, dish soap, hydrogen peroxide, stiff-bristled brush."

"*Allons, allons,*" Doucet said.

Again they stepped carefully around Rabby's bloodstain. Then each of them had to take a step backward to catch the ladder's top rung, with only the low concrete parapet as a handhold. When Peter tried that, his left knee wobbled painfully as he swung the right foot around and caught the rung. He shut his eyes and muttered, "Goddamn you, Rabby." Before his eyes dropped below the edge of the parapet, he glanced again at the bloodstain. No, it's not getting bigger, he thought. It's just the near-darkness blurring its edges.

They went into Peter's and Dan's room. Peter switched on the ceiling fan and lay on his bed and propped his left foot on its bottom rail, hoping the knee wouldn't swell. The others sat on Dan's bed and the room's two chairs. For a little while they all just listened to the rhythmic clanking of the off-balance fan.

"All right," Captain Tomczak said. "I think we left off with a logical next question: Why did those cadres chasing Pham want to take him alive?"

"Let's take a step back from that one," Peter said. "Why did they want him at all? But no, two steps back. Where did Pham come from when he showed up outside the wire here?"

"That part's easy," Earnhart said in his flat, hill-country twang. "The CIA boys had him over there in their villa. We can assume they did their best to pry out of him anything that could shed light on what he'd done as a double agent. Polygraph, sleep deprivation, stress positions, truth serum—they'd have used all those, plus maybe some off-the-books methods involving electricity or water or both. Remember that little fellow that Special Forces delivered to them all trussed up like the Thanksgiving turkey? The CIA would want to pin down whatever working relationship Pham had with him. Beyond that, they'd have welcomed anything Pham could tell them about connections between his work passing misinformation to the other side and Charlie's plans to dig up those arms in the cemetery and swarm over the wall like Mississippi fire ants."

"Wait, wait," Peter said. "Pham handed over misinformation? How? To whom?"

"Okay, three steps back," Tomczak said. "The spiky-haired dude you saw getting muscled through the CIA gate? His name was Trang Chu, and he was a Special Forces operative, based at an outpost on the border with Laos. Most days, Pham would leave the academy around noon, head to the Special Forces communications shop downtown and send Trang a fresh batch of poison-pill information concocted jointly by Special Forces and CIA. Transmission was via a secure radio teletypewriter link. Pham did the translation, typing and transmitting himself, using a Vietnamese keyboard. Trang was then supposed to feed this flimflam to commanders of communist units headed down the Ho Chi Minh Trail. Trang's cover story with the communists was that he worked for the Americans, helping translate day-to-day operational and order-of-battle information into Vietnamese so we could keep our South Vietnamese allies apprised. Apparently all went as scripted until Special Forces noticed some of their best intelligence agents in Laos had started to disappear. A double agent seemed the likely cause, so they put South Vietnamese who had access to that information under a microscope. At first they found a few who'd sold weapons and medical supplies to the communists, but nothing worse than that. Then one of their reconnaissance teams came across documents in a communist base camp where they knew Trang had spent time, supposedly handing over phony intelligence. Problem was, the documents they found there were the real ops plans, not fakes, and it seemed obvious Trang had stolen them, translated them and handed them over. That didn't necessarily mean he'd also fingered those other intelligence assets whose lights had winked out, but that seemed likely too. So Special Forces tied him up and brought him to Nha Cat. The Army field manual doesn't allow for the persuasive methods that might prove necessary, so they delivered Trang to the CIA, who brought him across the street for a come-to-Jesus.

"Now, sometime between the discovery of those operations plans over in Laos and the day they muscled Trang through the CIA gate, somebody raised hard questions about how and where Trang might have stolen those plans. See, a document that comprehensive wouldn't routinely be sent to a little Special Forces outpost. But Army Special Forces types come and go between Nha Cat and the field all the time, since their whole Vietnam operation is based here. So one of their officers could have picked up a copy of that document here and taken it to his outpost in the boonies. He might've belatedly realized the sensitivity of what he had and dropped it in the to-shred basket, and Trang could've seen it there and swiped it. Nobody who'd come and gone between those two points fessed up to that sort of negligence, but the people who were trying to fit together the puzzle pieces knew from experience how unremarkably common it would have been. So that was the scenario the CIA interrogators tried to get Trang to confirm: that instead of handing over the phony ops and deployment report he'd received through the secure electronic channel from Pham, he'd found the genuine article lying around. Knowing or guessing what it was, he'd delivered it to the enemy at that base camp in Laos. The CIA guys also hoped he'd confess to blowing the cover on those other sets of eyes and ears in Laos who had been delivering intelligence to Special Forces by whatever means they could, which was usually just word of mouth, since most of them were illiterate. What, if anything, either Trang or Pham confessed to, we don't know. Everything we're telling you now, Colonel Jesperson told us in dribs and drabs over the past few weeks, because that's how he was getting briefed on it. He wasn't given specific clearance to brief his own officers, but he told us he figured we had as much need to know it as he did."

Earnhart hitched his chair forward and spread his big-knuckled hands on his knees.

"Now, up to this point, Pham's totally in the clear, right?" Earnhart said. "Better than that, actually. Once he saw that everybody felt the evidence pointed to Trang and nobody else, Pham became our man Friday. He told his Special Forces handlers he was shocked, shocked that Trang could do such a thing. He sent Trang a string of phony reassurances—sweet nothings you might call them—over that secure radio line until Special Forces could get a helicopter to that outpost and arrest him. And Pham took pains to witness Trang's delivery to the CIA through that gate across the street. He was doing all he could, see, to make it appear this unmasking of a traitor was his handiwork. And it seemed to work, right up until a bent letter on a typebar scrambled the picture, and scrambled it in a way that this supposed traitor, Trang, might have helped clarify. Trouble was, Trang was dead by then. Remember that scuttlebutt I mentioned during our session on the rooftop a few weeks ago? About what the motor pool guy had said? Well, he was right. The full version is, when the CIA decided they'd gotten all they were likely to get from Trang, they handed him back to Special Forces, who drugged him, took him by boat out to sea, shot him twice in the head, wrapped enough chain around his ankles that he wouldn't float up, and dumped him in. Once that bent letter entered the picture, the decision to kill him looked sadly premature. Not to mention a clear violation of military law."

"It looked downright FUBAR," Tomczak said. "At some point, it crossed somebody's mind to really scrutinize that document the recon team had brought in from the communist base camp. To look for any clues to its origin, or to how it got all the way from Nha Cat to the jungle in Laos. And—what should have been obvious all along—right there on its face was evidence of where that copy of a weekly ops plan got printed out."

Earnhart pinched together a thumb and forefinger to indicate something very small. "A single typed letter," he said. "Every time the lower-case 'e' appeared, it tilted a little to the right, like it was fixing to head-butt the next letter over."

"Sweet Jesus," Peter said. "And they killed somebody before they thought to check that out?"

"Oh, they checked, but in the wrong place," Tomczak said. "Once they noticed that single out-of-kilter letter, they did what they figured was proper and sufficient. They checked the Vietnamese language keyboards and printers at Special Forces HQ here in Nha Cat for one that produced an off-line 'e.' But that letter typed out straight and true on every one of them. So they thought, 'well, since that ops plan was a couple of months old, maybe the device with the defective typebar got repaired or replaced.' Anyhow, the point didn't seem crucial, since Special Forces HQ was the only place that ops plan could have originated."

"Now, where else didn't they check?" Earnhart said. "Think, think, think!" He struck his knee with the heel of his hand, and his teeth glinted with what looked like malicious glee. "Where else?" he said.

"Finally somebody did think where else," Tomczak said. "Trang was dead by then, of course. They checked out the teletypewriter at the Special Forces outpost. That was the one that printed the Vietnamese language documents Trang was supposed to use to snooker the communists. And they found it had a lower-case 'e' that matched perfectly the tilted-over letters in the copy that turned up at that base camp in Laos. The only documents being printed on that device at the outpost were the ones being transmitted by secure radio from Nha Cat. And who was sending documents to Trang by that means?"

"Why, slap me in the head with a trace chain!" Earnhart deadpanned. "It was our good buddy Pham!"

"And just because our recon team found only one bona fide operations plan in that base camp, do we know for sure that other bona fide plans didn't end up in communist hands by the same means?" Tomczak said.

"Why, slap me up the other side of the head!" Earnhart said. "No we don't!"

"At a minimum," Tomczak said, "what that little tilted-over letter 'e' does is raise the possibility that Trang was doing exactly what he was supposed to do. That is, he was handing over the versions of weekly operations and force deployment plans he'd received by that secure channel from Nha Cat. And when he got one that was the real McCoy, he had no way of knowing it wasn't just another of the phony ones. And if Trang could be fooled that way once, he could be fooled the same way a dozen times. In which case the whole high-risk enterprise, which was intended to keep accurate information on our deployment and targeting and battle plans out of enemy hands, would be having exactly the opposite effect. Now how might the CIA try to find out whether that document retrieved from the jungle was a one-off or part of a pattern?"

"You design a list of questions to sift out the truth," Earnhart said. "Then you use it to interrogate Trang and Pham separately, and see how their answers match up."

"But Trang's dead, so that approach is out," Tomczak said. "So they do the best they can. They grab Pham off the soccer field after you decked him. They use the same methods of gentle suasion on him they'd used on Trang. If he cracks, then what might he fess up to? Well, a likely scenario is he's at the table while his American handlers go through the ops plan and compose their poison pill, and all the while he's taking crib notes in Vietnamese. Which seems just fine to his handlers, since they don't know he's taking notes on the real plan, not the fake. When he heads off to the secure transmission desk with the poison pill in hand, he instead types in the eagle's-eye view of exactly where our troops and aircraft will be deployed over the next week and which targets they'll try to take out. If he'd confess to doing that, everything would add up. But Pham's a tough little nut, and he doesn't crack. He says all he sent from Special Forces HQ here in Nha Cat were the fake reports. He's burned his crib notes, so there's no documentary record that can prove him wrong, and there's at least a faint possibility that some third party could have generated a printout on that teletype machine over on the Laotian border. So what to do now with this guy who'd done yeoman service for us back when we had a different prime suspect and we needed Pham's help to reel him in?"

"Then, suddenly, it must have looked like God answered that question," Earnhart said. "And I wouldn't rule out the possibility He did."

"Charlie used his wristwatches well," Tomczak said. "At almost the same moment, Charlie blew holes in the cemetery wall, ran that stolen boat up on the beach and hit the Korean infantry battalion hard enough to pin them in their camp for nearly an hour. At the time, the beach end of this street was completely unguarded. The guard contingent at the checkpoint at the other end had been beefed up. All the Arvin troops there were combat-qualified, but the VC killed two of them and drove the rest back up the road toward the air base. That gave Charlie the run of our whole street, and the way he converged on the CIA compound from both ends made it clear that was his main target.

"It must have flashed across the CIA boys' minds then that Charlie probably knew where to look for Pham. In the same hard adrenaline rush, it must have hit them that Charlie probably also knew which side Pham had been playing on in his role as translator and transmitter of supposedly phony documents. It followed, then, that the communists would have an interest in getting Pham out of the Americans' hands, for one of two reasons: either to liberate one of their own skillful and intrepid agents, or to kill a man who'd done their cause a great deal of harm. And then, based on that hurry-up bit of mindreading, the CIA guys took what looked to them like the obvious next step. They escorted Pham to the gate, unlocked it, handed him a loaded AK-47 and an extra banana clip, wished him all the best, and shoved him out."

Earnhart leaned in again. He looked decidedly un-Christian: wolfish, his teeth half-bared, a gold crown on an upper tooth glinting in the light from a standing lamp.

"The hope, see, was that parking Pham in the open would enable the VC to either welcome him or kill him," Earnhart said. "It would also leave the VC with one less incentive to try to overrun the compound. But then Pham did something that made the CIA look extra smart. Once that gate clanged shut, Pham must have glanced toward one end of the street and then the other end. He must have heard those little guys' sandals slap-slapping on the pavement and seen they were trotting straight at him from both directions. And then he ran for it. That meant, if the VC wanted Pham, some of them would have to peel off to chase him down among all these villas where folks like us had our rifles sticking out the window and hankered for an excuse to use them."

"That diversion might have spelled the difference for the CIA," Tomczak said. "Though it's unlikely Charlie could have overrun them even if he'd brought his full force to bear. Charlie did punch through their compound's wall with a tube-launched rocket, and he got some people in through the hole. But Special Forces had a fifty-caliber machine gun set up in some bushes inside the wall, and they wiped out those cadres in short order. When the body collection crew came through, they hauled eight bodies out from behind that wall and threw them on their truck bed. Even if Charlie could have neutralized that machine gun, there were enough other Special Forces types on the villa rooftop to counter any risk he'd get in the building."

Earnhart cut in, seemingly on cue: "Now I think that brings us back to your top-of-mind question," he said. "Why, out of the half-dozen villas where the troops crouching at the windows would have recognized him and likely let him in, would Pham pick this one? And I think the answer is simply the razor wire that Private Rabinowitz tacked up. We all thought of Pham as just an enforcer with a deep-dyed nasty streak, because that was all we saw of him, but Colonel Jesperson told us Pham spent several years in the NVA before he defected South—if defected is the right word. It could be, see, that he was all along a one-man sleeper cell. In any case, he was a seasoned enough soldier to know a good defensive position when he saw one. And when he saw the way Rabby had secured your patio with concertina wire, he decided that was the best position available. Trouble was, Rabby wouldn't let him in, and by the time he was done bickering with Rabby, the VC were so close on his tail he had no choice but to accept Rabby's offer to help him make a stand on the rooftop."

"And given the way things played out up there," Tomczak said, "who's to say Charlie knew him better than we did? I mean, knew whether it was Pham or Trang who'd doubled on them? The only way they could know for sure was to take Pham alive and pry it out of him—maybe using leverage we didn't have, like threats to family members up North. It was only after they'd lost the chance to take him alive that they signaled the cadre who was standing by on one of the other rooftops to go ahead and shoot him."

"So they might have killed the guy who played it straight for them," Earnhart said. "Just like we might have killed the guy who played it straight for us."

Propped on his elbows, his twisted knee still throbbing, Peter felt his shoulders tremble as weariness pressed him down. He let his head drop to his pillow and shut his eyes. When the two officers paused in their relentless logic-chopping, his mind came to rest on a vision of Rabby's bloodstain spreading slowly on the rooftop above his room.

"Tell you what," Peter said, sitting up too suddenly, then dropping back to his elbows and blinking as his blood found its way back to his head.

Both officers stared at him. "Yes?" Tomczak said after a while. "Tell us—what?"

"Just bury us in the idiots' row."

They listened to the clanking of the ceiling fan. Then Tomczak said: "Bury us with or without separation by rank?"

"No, I started us off with the wrong question. I mean, when I asked why Pham did what he did. You answered that about as well as possible, I guess. We haven't even gotten around to whatever role Thanh played in this whole affair. And I know that's important too. Sure it is. It's all part of what people like you need to know so you can pick your next move in the chess-game side of this war.

"But look: It doesn't shed any light on why Rabby did what he did, does it? Because whatever was driving him had nothing to do with what was driving the Viet Cong or driving us. It might have had nothing to do with anything that goes on here. And to get anywhere close to it, we might have to go farther back in Rabby's life than any of us can go. So I guess, after all, I did raise the only question worth raising, because it was the only one any of us had any way of answering. If I'd raised the other one, about what was driving Rabby, all we could do is look embarrassed and shrug. And maybe then we'd do what you said we ought to do. The only thing we can do, really. We'd go topside and scour his blood off the roof."

Twenty-eight

Next morning before daylight, Peter heard tapping on the shutter by his bed. Still half-asleep, he thought for a joyous instant it was Huê come to taunt him. It was Emmet, who held a brown plastic bottle in one hand and the handle of a metal bucket with the other. A bristle brush floated in soapy water in the bucket.

"Let's get it done," Emmet said in that oddly tense tone that wavered like a compass needle between amusement and distress. "The mamasans'll be here in an hour. They'll want their bucket back."

"Hydrogen peroxide?" Peter said. "How'd you conjure that?"

"We always kept some on the boat," Emmet said. "Slosh it on nicks from the tackle."

"It's still dark," Peter said. "Aren't you scared of haints?"

Emmet's glimmering eyes grew fixed. "You see something funny here?" he said.

"No. I'm sorry," Peter said.

"Then stop talking coo-yon. Winfrey says confine to quarters got lifted. In an hour we go teach."

They climbed the ladder. Emmet dropped to his knees and started scrubbing Rabby's blood, first on the rooftop, then on the parapet where Rabby had reached up with his hand. When Emmet finished a first pass with the brush, Peter pulled aside the wire mesh atop the cistern and dipped out a pailful of water and splashed it on the stain. Emmet had a squeeze bottle of dish soap in a pocket of his fatigue pants, and they kept scouring and rinsing.

"Like me to spell you?" Peter said.

Emmet didn't answer or look up. The sky brightened as they worked. Finally Emmet rocked backward and dropped the brush in the bucket, and they both stared at the stains' dim outlines.

"I'm not seeing any more change," Peter said. "But your call."

Emmet squirted hydrogen peroxide on the bloodstains and scrubbed it in with the brush. He scrubbed faster and faster, and Peter watched the peroxide seethe on the wet concrete. Then Emmet stood abruptly, picked up the bucket and started down the ladder.

Peter took care this time to keep his left knee stable while his right foot found the top rung. He glanced once more at what had been the pool of Rabby's blood. It had flipped from black to foamy white like a photographic negative.

"Maybe we can come up tonight, huh?" Peter said. "Just to make sure we got it all out?"

"We're done," Emmet said. He was already headed down the patio to return the bucket to the mamasans' cache of cleaning supplies. "*Tout est fini*. The next part's got to be all yours, looks like."

"Next part?" Peter said. By the time he squeezed between the razor wire and the villa wall, Emmet was already back in his room, and Peter followed him there. "What next part?" Peter said.

"Catch up with the colonel," Emmet said. "He's got the pieces."

"Pieces of what?" Peter called. "Pieces from where?"

"Pieces of the next thing. Which I don't know what that is. You're the only one who can maybe figure it out. And he got the pieces from me."

That morning Peter was told to babysit about a dozen newly minted Veenaf officers until they could be sorted into ability levels. He found none of them knew much English but several spoke French. To kill time, he tried leading a group sing-along of *"Frère Jacques"* and *"Sur le Pont d'Avignon,"* but some of the new lieutenants shook their heads. One managed to say, "no, teacher. Cannot." Peter saw that the somber mood left by the attack had infected them all.

When Peter reported to Colonel Jesperson's office at noon, the orderly sergeant said the colonel wanted to talk to him right away.

The colonel glanced up at Peter. With a single loose-jointed gesture of his arm, he dropped an oblong glass paperweight on some papers on his desk, invited Peter to take a seat and dismissed any need for military formality.

"Guys in your villa give you the full picture?" the colonel said.

"They told me what happened," Peter said. "I was hoping you could help with the full picture part."

"Could be. I did tell you, didn't I, that some more information had come my way?"

"Doucet told me that too. He said he'd given you pieces of the next thing."

Jesperson sighed and reached to turn off a rotating fan on a metal pole beside his desk. Then he opened a drawer and took out a brown envelope that looked repurposed. The all-caps word SECRET, stamped in red across the envelope, had been crossed out with a black marker. The colonel had his wrist cocked to toss the envelope across the desk when he paused, looked up at Peter and instead dropped it next to the paperweight.

"Why'd he do it?" the colonel said. "Your best guess, based on all you know." He gave another dismissive wave of the hand. "And you're not betraying anybody's confidence. Captain Tomczak probably filled you in. I intended he would."

"All I can give you is my best guess," Peter said. "I doubt what Rabby did had much to do with anything here. It had to do with parts of his life that go way back before he showed up here."

"About what I'd figured," Jesperson said. He picked up the envelope and tapped its edge against the desktop. "That has to be why he left these. He wanted to open a window just enough for you, or somebody, to lift it the rest of the way." He tipped open the envelope and a smaller, white envelope and what appeared to be two photographs spilled out of it. The colonel aligned the photos and looked down at them with his head cocked.

"Why the razor wire?" he said.

"Rabby had a thing about barbed wire," Peter said. "You knew, didn't you, about the time Pham tied lengths of barbed wire on recruits from the crawl line, and Rabby and an Arvin major made Pham lose face?"

"Sure I knew."

"Well, that major was just doing what he figured was a good officer's duty to stop needless abuse. With Rabby it was something else. The whole time it looked like he was sleepwalking. When it was over, he wanted me to bury the strands of wire that had blood on them. Practically ordered me to do it."

"And you did that?"

"Good and deep, like he wanted."

"I see." For a while Jesperson drummed his fingernails on the desktop, first in one direction, then the other, then in a bebop rhythm. "Well, that might help explain why he wanted you to have this." He picked up one of the photos and handed it across to Peter. It was about three inches square. Framed in it Peter saw a woman with a smiling, sun-bronzed face standing next to a barbed wire fence. Her hair was a mass of curls the color of dark honey. She wore a blouse and cap that mirrored his own jungle fatigues, and she held wire cutters with blades poised to cut a strand of the barbed wire.

"Read the back," Jesperson said.

Peter flipped the photo over and read: "Don't fence me in! Wouldn't this drive Aunt Miriam crazy? Love, Nina. Kibbutz Joachim. September, 1965."

Peter started to hand the photo back but Jesperson shook his head. "It's yours," he said. "So's this."

He handed over the other photograph. In sepia-tinged black and white, three children gazed out from behind barbed wire fencing fastened to rough-hewn wooden poles. Two of the children sat on a plank resting on concrete blocks, while behind them stood an older boy, wearing a striped shirt with sleeves that dangled to his knees. The back of the photo was stamped "U.S. Army Signal Corps," and below that was a handwritten note: "Secret radio saved them too. Third Army played the part of A."

"See anything that rings a bell?" the colonel said.

Peter set the two photos side by side and peered from one to the other.

"This one must be his Aunt Nina," he said, tapping the color photo with a finger. "He called her a kibbutznik. He also called her half-Catholic, whatever that meant. But this other one—" He slowly shook his head. "It must have been taken in one of the concentration camps liberated by the Americans. But why Rabby would have that with him—maybe just because of the barbed wire. These must be the pictures he showed the little girl who lived with us."

Peter described to the colonel the toss-and-catch that Rabinowitz pantomimed for Huê and Rabby's effort to get her to see some connection between that performance and a pair of photographs.

"Maybe I can help a little with that second picture," the colonel said. "The Third Army got to Buchenwald before the Germans could ship out or kill off all the people they'd penned up there. I remember reading about that in the *Stars and Stripes*."

The colonel tossed the smaller envelope across the desk. Written in pencil across its front was "Give to Peter." Jesperson said Doucet had found the photos and envelope when mortuary affairs asked that someone at the villa gather up Rabby's personal effects.

"Private Doucet decided on his own you ought to have these items," Jesperson said. "He said the envelope was an easy call, but he thought you should have the photos too, since they jibed with something Rabinowitz had said or done. But he did the proper thing. He left it to me to decide who gets them."

"Maybe you're right," Peter said, staring at the photograph. "I mean about opening a window just enough to give a fingerhold. But I can't open it any further. I'd have to know things I have no way to learn right now."

"I think I can help you with that too," the colonel said. "But one more thing. There might be nothing important to it, but it sticks with me because of the strange turn of phrase. A private who lives a villa or two over from yours must have had a good view of that chase up the ladder to the rooftop. This fellow was one of your fellow assailants on the soccer field that day, by the way. He said that, when Rabinowitz wheeled around and grabbed his rifle barrel, he didn't just swat that VC cadre. It was more like he was trying to chop down through him, shoulder to beltline. The phrase he used was it was like a peanut farmer killing a copperhead with a hoe."

"Your source would be Carlton Beshears," Peter said.

"I think that's right," Jesperson said. "Private Beshears. He said after Rabinowitz did that, he kept standing there exposed, taking his sweet time before he shot the one with the wire cutters."

"Like he was chopping a snake," Peter said. "Rabby might have likened it to a Polish noblewoman making good use of a cavalry saber. It'd take me a while to explain."

They looked at each other across the desk. Then Jesperson said, "I'm set to retire in two years. If you've got a clearer picture by then of why Private Rabinowitz did what he did, come out to the ranch and tell me what you've learned. I mean that. What else can I answer for you right now?"

"What about Lieutenant Thanh? I liked him. I never quite got past liking him, even after I figured out he was playing me. What happened to Thanh?"

"Thanh made a clean getaway, but the whole mousetrap plan was premised on the likelihood he would. He had to stay free, see, until he could give Charlie the start signal, and then all he had to do was disappear. It was easy to justify letting Thanh slip away if we could stop the loss of our own operations and order-of-battle plans, and collar or kill the people who were serving up that intelligence to the enemy. Of course, that calculation also assumed we could stage-manage Victor Charlie's attack through the cemetery. And that part didn't work out so well. Witness what might stand as the first amphibious assault in Viet Cong history."

"What I don't get," Peter said, "is why Thanh seemed so eager to cast suspicion on Pham, when they were supposed to play complementary roles."

Jesperson's bleached-blue eyes had started to wander again, but instantly they switched to a tight focus on Peter's face.

"There you touch on both the strength and the weakness of the communist cell system," he said. "Pham and Thanh each functioned as the head of a separate cell, see? They had no contact with each other, so neither one knew all the other knew. From the communist perspective, that was a strength. Pham couldn't tell Special Forces or the CIA about the cemetery plot because he wasn't in on it. Same with Thanh, but in reverse. His job was to put pieces in place for the attack on the CIA villa, then give the go signal. But if the CIA had nabbed and grilled him beforehand, he couldn't tell them diddly about the way Pham was shoveling bona fide intelligence across the border to Laos, instead of horseshit like he was supposed to. But, flip side, neither Pham nor Thanh knew how much the other didn't know, either. And for Victor Charlie, that was a weakness, since it caused Thanh to assume, or at least fear, that Pham would blow the cover on plans to attack through the cemetery.

"The setup for that attack was entirely in Thanh's hands. Funeral processions leave from the hospital. So, step one, Thanh wangled the job of turning bodies over to relatives. Step two, he worked black market contacts to buy weapons, boxed them up in whatever came to hand— medical equipment crates, crates swiped from our ordnance depot—and entrusted them to subordinates in his cell. Those young bucks then tagged along in funeral processions and buried the weapons once the grieving relatives left the graveside.

"And then Thanh heard rumors that Pham was coming under scrutiny as a suspected double-agent. The cell system held firm, so he didn't learn particulars, but he had reason to fear that Pham knew enough to pose a threat. And then all Thanh could think of to do was cast as much doubt about Pham's credibility in the minds of as many Americans as he could. He had to hope that would buy enough time to bring off the cemetery attack as a complete surprise. But once Special Forces swooped in and grabbed Pham off the soccer field, Thanh had to assume any extra time he'd bought by raising that cloud of doubt was running out. It looked to him like the only way to salvage a modicum of success for this plan he'd carefully pieced together was to give the start signal before every last piece was in place. Exactly what we'd hoped he'd do, in other words. But then—testimony, maybe, to Thanh's resourcefulness—the preemptive attack on the Korean camp and the beach landing got added on. What we'd game-planned as a total smackdown of Victor Charlie ends up looking more like a near disaster and an object lesson in hubris."

The colonel's eyes left Peter's face, and a moody abstraction crept back into them.

"Thanks for filling me in on that," Peter said.

Jesperson gave another dismissive hand-wave. "Oh, thanks aren't in order," he said.

Peter stood up. "I'll report back tomorrow, sir," he said. "I've taken a big chunk of your time."

"No, sit down, sit down. I've got time. Tomorrows are in short supply, so let's get through our checklist if we can. First item. And nothing that I or the U.S. Army can do officially will accord with what I'm telling you right now. Understand that. But you probably ought to get a medal for your actions out there on the soccer field. Why? Well, you brought appropriate force to bear when you thought a fellow soldier was at risk of serious injury. While engaged in that effort, you went down with a pretty nasty injury yourself. Then, impeded by that injury, you tried to break up a bunch of lamebrains who were abusing an officer of our military ally. Never mind that the officer getting kicked around in the dust was a sadist and a suspected spy whose voice box you'd just crushed with your rifle butt. I wouldn't overload a medal citation with details like that. Besides, the part about his being a spy was never proved. Now that he's been killed resisting enemy action, there'll be no record of his being anything other than a loyal Veenaf officer. One who was victimized by American enlisted men during what was supposed to be a friendly athletic contest. You triggered that part. Without it, we could justify letting CIA seize Pham, based on all both we and the Vietnamese high command knew about him. But back to my main point: if I were free to do it, based on all I know, I'd put you up for a medal. It doesn't rise to the level of a Bronze Medal. For that you need engagement with the enemy. Private Rabinowitz cleared that bar. But you deserve an Army Commendation Medal, for sure."

For a while it was so silent that Peter could hear a droplet of his own sweat hit the collar of his fatigue blouse.

"Sir, I know I ought to thank you," he said. "But the best I can do is call that a first-rate job of gilding stupidity."

"Well, since when did a medal citation do much else?" the colonel said. "Damn, it's hot in here."

Jesperson swung around in his swivel chair and reached toward the fan. He glanced back at Peter before he flipped its switch.

"You got the photos and envelope secured?" he said. Peter patted a breast pocket.

Jesperson switched on the fan. "It's sealed, you know," he said.

"Sealed?"

"The envelope. Now understand that what I'm about to ask is strictly up to you. Understand second that, far from what I just said I'd like to do, I've got to slap you with an Article Fifteen. That means you'll serve out your two years. But understand third that whatever's in that envelope could influence where we go from here, with regard to where you spend your remaining time and what I might hope you'd do there. All clear?"

"What's clear is you want me to open the envelope and show you what's in it."

"No. What I'm asking is that you open that envelope, look at whatever's in there, take time to think about it, and then tell me whether it might help you pry open that window we've been talking about. You don't need to tell me the content. Just your opinion of whether it might help."

"Why should you trust me on that?"

"Because that's what I choose to do instead of recommending you for that medal you deserve but won't get."

"Why should you care about the reason, if there was one, that Rabby got himself killed in the way he did?"

"Because I'm an officer in the U.S. Air Force. I thought I was going to make it through a twenty-six year career without a single man under my command getting killed by hostile action. It didn't happen. That's reason enough. I don't want to spend any mornings back of my little place outside Durango, Colorado, draped over the fence rail, wondering why."

Peter took the envelope and photos from his pocket. On the front of the envelope was a map of Vietnam. He had used the same kind of envelope and matching stationery to send letters postage-free to his parents and Stephie and Teddy and a few other friends. He plucked a letter knife from a coffee mug on the colonel's desk and sliced open the envelope and pulled out a single sheet of the familiar stationery. He unfolded it and stared at it, flipped over the photo and studied what was written on its back, then looked again at the letter paper.

"That doesn't add up," Peter said.

"Take it with you," the colonel said. "Think about it."

"No, no. Read the name. And the address." He tossed the opened sheet of stationery back across the desk.

Jesperson gave him a look of crinkle-eyed inquiry. "All right," he said and picked up the sheet. "'Ilana Rabinowitz,'" he read. "'Kibbutz

Joachim, Judean Hills, Israel.' Then what looks like a phone number and the international code you'd need to dial it from the States."

"Ilana," Peter repeated. "But the photo says Nina."

"So? Different individuals."

"Can't be. He used to go on about his Aunt Nina. He called her a crazy half-Catholic kibbutznik. And both Rabby and Nina were supposed to be named for somebody really important in their family history. Somebody so important that both of them wore a distinctly non-Jewish name and felt pressure to live up to it. But that was all a fiction in his case, and in hers too if her name is really Ilana, so—"

Jesperson lifted a hand and shook his head. "That's more than we need to get into," he said. "All I need to know is whether you see here some line of inquiry, even a zigzag line, that might explain why he stage-managed his own death. Why he plotted it out in a way that made no sense to anyone else. Now, what about this last bit?" He tilted the letter paper and read aloud two lines Rabinowitz had printed at the bottom: "'In life, as in the Torah, it is assumed that everything has deeper and secondary meanings, which must be probed.'"

"It's something I heard him say a time or two, when he was trying to foist off some fable on us," Peter said. "He must have been quoting from something, but I don't know what it was."

"I see. Well, it hardly seems I should have to ask, but since I've offered you a sort of contract, I guess I'd better: You do intend to act on the hints and nudges that he's…but, hell, they're more than that. He's pleading with you, it looks like to me. You do intend to carry out what he wants you to do, don't you, when you have time and resources to do that?"

"Sir, whatever offer you have in mind to get me to do what you want, what Rabby wanted—that isn't necessary," Peter said. "I don't have any choice. Rabby's seen to that."

"Well then," the colonel said, slapping the arm of his swivel chair. "Here's the deal, and fortunately I can order you to take it. You've got better than a half-year left on your enlistment, right? Question is, where would you be best situated to follow up on what this man has left you. How do you feel about Turkey?"

"Turkey?" Peter said. "Not to sound stupid, but you mean the country, right?"

"Yes, the country. In forty-five I flew missions out of Okinawa with a guy who now commands the air mobility squadron at Incirlik. He'd take you on if I asked. I'll bet he could come up with some excuse to send you TDY to Israel, too. That'd get you a free round-trip to Tel Aviv."

"But I'd bet this Aunt Nina, or Ilana, will level with me as willingly by letter or phone as she would if I showed up on her doorstep in the kibbutz," Peter said. "Besides, she's just one source. In Turkey I'd be as cut off from the rest of his people as I am here."

"Point taken," Jesperson said. He rested his elbows on his chair arms and propped his chin on his steepled fingers. "Where would you like to go, then?"

"But surely you can't just send me anywhere."

"Oh, in this case my powers are vast. I'm a commander in a war zone. A man who reports to me has caused severe friction with our ally. To set things right, I need him gone. I could send you pretty much anywhere and assign you casual status, which means folks on the receiving end have to figure out what to do with you. Plus, since I have joint command here, I can switch-hit. I could ship you to either an Air Force base or an Army post. Rabby's home address was in New Jersey, right? Tell me you want to go there and I could have orders cut for you by tomorrow to ship for either McGuire or Fort Dix."

"But if I promise I'll try to find out why he stage-managed his death, as you put it, you're willing to send me anywhere? And how about I throw in another promise? I'll try to find out why he came here at all. Which as a member of a silk-stocking reserve unit he certainly didn't have to do."

"Unless he did have to do it," the colonel said. His eyes had wandered toward a little window. Peter could see nothing through the window except some palm-like fronds coated with pink dust. "Unless he just got borne along by the river," the colonel said.

"So if that sounds okay as my side of the bargain," Peter said, "then …" He blinked. "What river?"

"When I do go out and hang over that fence rail, I can just make out the river rippling along beyond a stand of blue spruce I planted a few years ago," the colonel said. "And I wonder why the Spaniards came up with that name for it. *Rio de Las Animas Perdidas*. Now, the Animas is a perfectly fine-looking little river. Prone to flash flooding, but what river in that part of the country isn't? But whoever named it might have been a pretty deep thinker. Maybe he was saying the river of lost souls must look a lot like any other river. You can't always pick out lost souls as they stream past. You can't predict which souls are likely to end up lost, either. Coming up in a family where you have to drag a picking sack between cotton rows by age six—that won't condemn you to that river. Nor will a silk-stocking pedigree keep you out of it."

The colonel's eyes shifted back to Peter's face, and his sharpened glance told Peter they were done.

"In your place, I think I'd argue that what you've just promised to do should be good enough to get sent close to home," Jesperson said. "I'll buy that. I'll have your orders cut for casual status at Fort Bragg. You'll get the lowest-level Article Fifteen. I'll have that attached to your reassignment orders. The only penalty is you lose two weeks off what would normally be thirty days' home leave. That's the minimum I have to hit you with. The air transport office will let us know when you'll ship out. Be packed and ready by the end of this week."

PART II

A SOLDIER, ABOVE ALL ELSE

Twenty-nine

Through cottony wisps of cloud beneath the aircraft he could make out the early-fall mix of yellow and orange and red and still-green foliage and the glittering farm ponds and the dingy little game-board pieces that were tobacco barns. This is my place on earth, he told himself. Yet there stole over him a hollowed-out, slightly nauseous feeling that he was about to touch down in an alien landscape.

When his mother seized and held him with wordless ferocity, he felt little except embarrassment. She had not known until two days earlier that he was coming home. For the month before that, his parents had heard nothing from him. During his three weeks in the hospital in Khoang Trong, he had felt unable to unravel for them what had happened and might yet happen. He had finessed that problem by not writing them at all. Finally, during a layover in Honolulu, he had called from an airport USO and told his father he was headed home.

"I'm getting the boot, sort of," he said. "Not demoted. Really nothing bad except I have to serve out my two years."

"You could have let us know," his father said.

"Look, we got hit by the VC, and a man I knew got killed. I wasn't there when it happened, but it all relates to that."

"I see. Well, just say you're sorry."

"What? Like I'm in third grade?"

"Just say it, so that I can tell her you said it. You can go into the rest of it with me later on if you want to."

So he had said it. When he reached home and his mother clung to him and pounded her fists into his back and sobbed into his chest, he kissed the top of her head, but something cold and aloof in him wondered: Why this show of distress? She doesn't even know Rabinowitz is dead.

Later, his mother told him she had tracked down Stephie through the medical college in New Hampshire.

Peter hid his annoyance. "How'd she sound?" he said.

His mother gave him a red-eyed, hostile look. "Pissed off," she said.

"At me for not writing or at you for calling?"

"Hard to tell," she said, turning away toward the stove. "Why don't you ask her that?"

His father ducked into the kitchen from the hallway, holding his faded baseball cap by the bill and tilting it back and forth on his head. He watched his wife as she pulled a pan of shriveled-looking sweet potatoes from the oven and clanked it down on the cast iron grate atop the burners. Then he pointed a little finger at Peter.

"Come take a look at the new calf," he said.

In the granary, Peter's father scooped sorghum and corn silage into a pail.

"Any luck persuading Grandma?" Peter said.

His father pursed his lips. "My sister stands a better chance," he said. "No way will Mama sell the house and land. Polly could drive her there every week or two to check on it. Which Mama would pester her to do, unfortunately."

"Shame she won't let you move her here."

"I offered. She knows I meant it. But I never expected she'd come. That farm came down in her family, just like this one did in your mother's. Good luck ever getting your mom to leave here."

At the barn, the calf, a red Angus, eyed them from a bed of fresh straw. Peter's father lifted the pail through an opening in the logs and poured the feed into a wooden trough. The calf trotted over, bleating. They leaned against the lower log, watching the calf.

"Be careful how much you tell her," his father said. "You might think if you spell it all out for her, that'll smooth things over. Not likely to happen. You could just make it worse, because then she'll know you've got all this stuff you're carrying around and she can't even make sense of it."

"Did that happen to you?"

The calf drank from its metal water trough, then lifted its wet muzzle, coated with grains of silage, and rubbed it against Peter's hand. He jerked the hand away from the log.

"It's still trying to nurse," his father said. "Just be careful who you pick to talk to. I can tell you the exact moment I understood that. It was Thanksgiving dinner after I got home from Europe. I'd tried to tell my folks. I told them how close I'd come to killing those wounded Germans in Normandy. I told them about that Polish woman and her three kids huddled up against the cold in a bombed-out building, and how she'd sliced that mess-tent bread like it was cake and insisted I eat a slice of it. And I told them how good I felt about the work I'd done building a camp for people like her. I told them about what I saw after I drove our colonel through the gate at Buchenwald. I told them how they'd fertilized the fields with ashes from the crematorium. I told them about driving the jeep through the Alps. The snow piled up on the windshield so bad I had to fold it forward to see to drive. Then we heard the Germans had strung piano wire high enough to slice the heads off drivers who'd done that. So it was either run that risk or risk driving off a mountainside because I couldn't see.

"And then, after I'd told them all that, when my mother gave the prayer at Thanksgiving dinner, she said, 'Thank you, Lord, for bringing Albert home safe from over there, just like you brought his Uncle Clarence and his Uncle Wingate back safe from over there.' Clarence and Wingate had been doughboys in the First War, see. And when she said 'over there,' I honest to God felt like standing up and throwing something at her. Not to hurt her, understand. Just to get her attention. A big gob of turkey dressing, maybe. Because Thionville and Buchenwald weren't 'over there' for me. They changed what my life was about. And here my own mother was stuffing this big, changed part of me into a lock box labeled 'over there' so she could bring it out to pray over it once or twice a year, and then lock it up again and forget about it."

"Mom's really smart, though," Peter said.

"Has nothing to do with it," his father said, shaking his head. "You press the matter and you'll see. I advise you don't press it. And don't ever bring up your Article Fifteen with her. If she asks why you have to serve out your two years, tell her the rules have changed. She'll be fine with that."

Peter called Stephanie that evening. First he had to find a way to make his voice work when Stephie picked up the receiver and said simply, "Doctor Ames."

"I guess I'd better get used to hearing you answer the phone that way," he said finally. "I can do that. No problem."

"Peter, Peter, Peter," she said, embedding his name in a long, weary-sounding exhalation. "I have to answer the phone that way. I'm doing this pulverize-the-intern thing, you know? Eighteen hours on, six off."

"And I'm just making things harder for you. I mean, just turning up this way, with no word since—whenever the last time it was that I wrote. My mother said you were pissed."

"I'm over it. That said, you've got some explaining to do."

He started warily, keeping his father's warning in mind. But, finding that Stephie's questions led inexorably to the heart of the matter that consumed him, he told her he needed to call a woman in a kibbutz. Then, compressing the facts as best he could, he told her why.

"Probably you should call that number right away," she said. "If this aunt was close enough family, she'd want to come to sit shiva. You might be able to meet her before she goes back to Israel."

He told his father he was going to run up the phone bill with an international call. But when he dialed the number Rabby had written down, there was no answer. He figured out the time difference and dialed the number when he knew it was evening in Israel. Again the phone rang unanswered.

He called Stephie and said he'd wait until he reported to Fort Bragg before trying the number in Israel again. For the first time, she sounded annoyed.

"No, Peter. That must mean she's come to the States to sit shiva. And it just strengthens the case for finding her while she's here."

"But how's his family going to feel if I barge in on them when they're grieving?"

"Can't say. But this isn't about how they feel. It's about what you have to do. Losing your friend this way, when you weren't there to do whatever you could to prevent it…Look, you let yourself get drafted so you could get some kind of war wound, right? Well, this is as close to a wound as you're going to get. Do you know what wounds do if they're left untended? They fester or they scar, or both. Now tell me: what did your friend count as his home?"

All Peter could think of was Rabby's comment about asking for a tickertape parade through downtown Hackensack.

"Good," Stephie said. "Let me work with that."

When he awoke next morning he saw the day was going to be dry and warm enough for the calf to graze, so he staked it out next to the barn in a grassy patch that would catch the sun until late afternoon. The calf stood watching him as he walked away, then threw back its head and bleated.

"It's called grass," he said. "You're supposed to eat it. You'll figure it out."

When he reentered the kitchen, his mother wagged the phone receiver at him, then picked up her books and folders and headed out to her car.

"South Jersey," Stephie told him. "Avram Rabinowitz, age twenty-six. Killed in action during a Viet Cong attack on his duty station near Nha Cat. He was rescued from the Holocaust and grew up in the household of Isaac and Miriam Kleinfield in Arborville, New Jersey. Only known family members are two cousins, Meir Rabinowitz of Hackensack and Ilana Rabinowitz of Kibbutz Joachim, Israel. Avram was a graduate of Princeton University and Rutgers Law School, and he belonged to an Army Reserve unit in Trenton."

"But that has to be wrong," Peter said. "Rabby was ready to enter his second year of law school. He never mentioned any school but Princeton, so he must've gone to law school there. And his reserve unit was in Manhattan."

"Can't answer about the reserve unit, but Princeton has no law school. How much leave time do you have left?"

"I have to report to Fort Bragg in ten days."

"That's plenty of time. I found an Isaac Kleinfield listed in Arborville. Tell them you were his friend and that you'll answer any questions they have. They'll say yes."

"But New Jersey? All we've got now are the car and the truck, and my parents need them both. How am I supposed to get there?"

"Same way I got from New Hampshire to North Carolina for four years. Riding the dog. I already checked. You take a Greyhound express to Philadelphia, then a local to Arborville."

She read him the phone number. After he hung up, Peter stood with his hand still on the receiver, watching dust motes swirl in a shaft of sunlight. He heard the sloshing of the washing machine in the narrow hallway leading to his parents' bedroom. He thought, I could be five, twelve, any age standing here on a fall morning, and it would always be exactly like this.

Then the motor in the refrigerator across the kitchen switched on, and he heard the wavering hum of a faulty compressor. That's where they put him, he thought. Into that mortuary fridge where the compressor wheezed and rattled. Surely to God they've replaced it by now. He shut his eyes and saw the black bunkers stretching on and on against the glittering white sand. *No, nothing can be the same again. Not now. Not ever.*

He dialed the number Stephie had given him. After the third ring, a man answered. Peter told him he was just back from Vietnam, and that Avram Rabinowitz had been his friend, and that Avram had asked him to get in touch with Ilana Rabinowitz. "And I wondered if she came over from Israel for the funeral," he said.

Peter heard the sound, a double clunk, of the receiver being placed on a table. Then he heard the man's voice again, this time from a distance. And then, directly into his ear, another voice spoke in a raspy near-whisper that was both commanding and strangely intimate. Not until later that day, when he had raked together brittle leaves and burned them, could Peter attach a name to the quality of her voice: It was like leaf smoke.

"Oh, you are Peter! You are the one he wrote to me about! And you must come, do you hear? I will find a place where you can stay, and you must come. And you must do it now."

Thirty

Early in his 13-hour bus ride to Philadelphia, he dredged his memory for all that Rabinowitz had told him about the woman he called his Aunt Nina. Bearer of the heroine's actual name, Rabby had said—except that, as Peter now knew, she wasn't. So inspired by that heroine's sacrifice that she enrolled at a Catholic college and drew close to the enticing flame of conversion. Then she'd veered off toward another beacon of true belief, life on a kibbutz, toting with her some pacifist Catholic baggage. She taught young children in the kibbutz school, Rabby had said. During the run-up to the Six-Day War, she had followed a kibbutz-wide order to carry a weapon, but declined to clean it. She had parked the Uzi by the chalkboard in her classroom, and several weeks' worth of chalk dust had drifted into its barrel by the time the war broke out. The sound of approaching gunfire gave her enough advance warning to herd the children into an adjoining room, lock the door and position herself, arms folded, in front of it by the time an Arab fighter burst into her classroom. She had left her rifle propped by the chalkboard. The Arab barely glanced at her before he seized the weapon and left. She heard later that a couple of Israeli soldiers had killed an Arab outside the kibbutz after he tried to ambush them with a chalk-clogged Uzi that misfired.

Rabby said his aunt received a citation for bravery for protecting the children. She was exempted, as a conscientious objector, from bringing a weapon to class. For several months after the war, her classroom, alone among all schoolrooms in the kibbutz, had an armed guard posted outside its door. And, a year and a half later, her nephew had followed her example by declining to clean the weapon he carried daily to his classroom in Nha Cat.

All this was per Rabby's telling, of course, and Peter knew now that the name and relation were false. He had no way of judging whether any of the rest of it was true.

By the time the bus left Richmond, he had lost the ability to distinguish between sleep and wakefulness, and dim, vaguely threatful figures drifted through them both. On the local bus from Philadelphia to Arborville, he kept his eyes fixed out the window, feeling flickers of gratitude toward the driver for keeping his voice low when announcing stops—Woodbury, Glassboro, Franklinville, Malaga, Newfield. Several times, Peter tapped a pocket of his shirt for reassurance the notepad with Isaac Kleinfield's phone number in it was there.

When the driver pulled over in Arborville, she was standing with her back against a maroon-colored wall near the little terminal's far end. He knew it had to be her, though he wouldn't have recognized her from the photograph Doucet swiped from Rabby's room. Her skirt was dark blue, and over her hair she wore a scarf that appeared cut from the same thick blue cloth as the skirt. She wore a white cardigan and her arms were crossed. There was something nun-like in her appearance as she stared intently at the bus.

He climbed down with the faded duffel from his father's war slung from his shoulder. He had started to crane his neck to look toward the wine-colored wall, when suddenly she stepped around the opened door of the bus and smiled at him. She had green eyes with amber rays that flared like spokes from the pupils. Wisps of curly, bronze-colored hair trailed from beneath her scarf.

"Peter, you're here!" she said. "I studied the bus schedules, you see, and I was betting you'd catch this one. Oh, you must be still suffering from jet lag, and here I've piled this awful bus trip on top of that!"

Along with the light, smoky rasp in her voice he heard the effort she was making to set him at ease.

"Ilana?" he said.

She gave a small, forced-sounding laugh. "Yes, I'm Ilana. I'm surprised you know me by that name. Avram decided long ago that I was going to be his Aunt Nina. But that's a piece of all we need to talk about, you and I, when we have time. But right now you're exhausted, aren't you?"

She grasped his elbow, guided him beneath a sign that read "Board here for 408 to Millville" and led him out a side door of the station.

"I don't know Jewish customs," he said. "I hope I'm not interrupting—you call it shiva, right?"

"No, no, you're not interrupting. Yes, it's called sitting shiva, but that's all done." She patted his arm with her free hand, and again he sensed how much she was straining to sound casual.

"And Rabby—that's what we all called him—has he already been, you know—?"

"Buried? Oh yes, he's buried. That's one thing you might find different about the way we do it. I mean death and funerals. We don't dither about burying the dead. We're pretty emphatic about it, really. Each of us might throw in a few shovelsful of earth, if we feel up to it. It's like we're saying, 'There now, you're dead! So stay put while we get back to the business of, you know, living.'"

Still guiding him, she turned down a side street lined with shops and office buildings. Peter was so lightheaded with fatigue he felt he might topple without her support.

"Of course, there was all that time we had to wait for the military to bring him back," she said. "But once they did—and the funny thing is, it would have been so easy to bring him home then, if they had let us. Because the men killed in Vietnam, you know, they bring them in right over there."

She pointed, it seemed to Peter, back toward the bus station. Without thinking, he turned his head to look.

This time her laughter seemed unfeigned. "No, I mean across the bay from here," she said. "They bring them to the air base at Dover. Meir kept pestering them, and finally they told him that next day they'd fly Avram in. And we thought, since it was so close, why not go over? So we did, Meir and I. Isaac and Miriam said it would be too hard for them, and we understood. So it was just Meir and I who went. We saw the honor guard carry the casket out of the cargo hold. I believe Avram would have wanted us to see that. And I was hoping we could just rent a trailer in Dover and bring him back on the ferry. But the military said no, their mortuary people had to take a whack at him first, even if we said we didn't want that. Then they'd deliver him to us, they said, by way of the bridge at New Castle. Everything by the book, you know? In Israel, the family could make a case, and the military might bend. Not here."

"Meir. That's his cousin, right?"

"Meir is my older brother, and of course that makes Meir and me Avram's cousins. I know how confusing this must be for you. It upends the elaborate kinship system in Avram's imagined past, doesn't it? Here someone like me comes along and replaces all his fictitious characters with real people who bear some of the same names but play very different roles. Less glittering roles than in Avram's—I've never been sure exactly what to call it. Tall tale? Fable? I've listened to version after version of it over the years, as he's adapted and shaded it so that even he could almost believe it. But however the roles in it might shift, they never touched on our actual adventures, which were much more down-to-earth. Like vaccinating five hundred chickens by poking a two-pronged thing-y through their wings. Or cutting through barbed wire to liberate a goat. Nothing like that in the story you heard, was there? Avram could spin out endless versions of it, but each one ended, always, with his family's hair's-breadth escape from Odessa. Odessa, of all places, for a Polish family! Well, while you're here, you'll see where he got that strand of it. But not today. Today, after coming all the way up here so willingly and so soon, you get to rest. But one thing you must do first, because he says he has to leave. Something about a grand jury and a witness who got cold feet. You must meet Meir, right? And now here we are."

Tightening her grip on his arm above the elbow, Ilana turned him toward a narrow doorway at the edge of a building that housed a mattress store. She paused long enough to stare through the store window at two pajama-clad dummies that lay facing each other on a king-sized mattress. Ilana shook her head and shrugged. "Fifth Avenue it's not," she said. "Up we go."

A brass plate beside the door read, "Nathan Grutsky, Attorney at Law." As they climbed the single flight of stairs, Peter heard a man speaking in a level, patient tone: "Tell her she doesn't need to worry about that. Look, just tell her to come back in the morning. I'll talk to her then. Okay?"

The door at the top of the stairs had a jagged crack in one of its four panes of bubble glass. Ilana opened the door without knocking. Through the doorway Peter saw a burly, gray-haired man replace a phone receiver in its cradle, glance briefly at Ilana, then turn toward a smaller man who sat behind a wooden desk.

"Nathan, more days than not for my whole professional life, I've told people they don't need to be afraid to testify," the big man said. "The problem is, about a third of the time, that turns out to be a lie. I just wish I knew in advance which third it was."

The smaller man rummaged through the drawers of his desk. His shirt collar was so oversized it barely moved as he craned his wrinkled neck to peer into the drawers. One of his brown shoes, the toe so scuffed it looked colorless, stuck out beyond the edge of the desk. "Damn it, I know I had it here somewhere," he said.

"Meir, Peter's here!" Ilana said. "I guessed right about which bus he'd be on."

The big man seemed to shrink a little. He turned toward the door with his eyes lowered. He had thick, jutting eyebrows, and he wore a ratty-looking sweater and faded brown corduroy pants worn smooth at the knees. Peter could tell the man wasn't struggling to welcome him, exactly. Rather, he seemed to be thinking: So it's really come to this, has it? Now I have to find a way to get through this too. As the man moved toward them, Peter was reminded of a high school classmate who had shuffled, bearlike, through the hallways between classes but moved with power and grace on the football field.

"Meir Rabinowitz," the big man said, extending his hand. The corners of his mouth twitched, and Peter knew he was searching for a quick, sure U-turn away from awkward sentiment. "You were Avram's close friend, and your coming here is a great act of friendship."

Abruptly, Meir Rabinowitz gave a rumbling laugh. "There, I've said the most hackneyed thing one could say under the circumstances," he said. "But under these particular circumstances, what else could one say?"

"Tomorrow morning, you were saying on the phone," Ilana told her brother. "If you can put it off that long, why not tomorrow afternoon?"

"Because I can't. The grand jury convenes at ten. She's either prepped and ready then or we have to pull the case."

"But we need to talk, and first Peter needs to rest."

Her grip above Peter's elbow tightened again, and he fought down his annoyance. Weary as he was, he knew this woman's sense of urgency was an extension of Stephie's, and he knew he should trust them both.

"No I don't need that," he said. "I mean, sure I'm tired, but this is the very thing he wanted most. That we should try to figure out—"

Peter caught himself in time to avoid saying, stupidly, that together they could figure out the unknowable.

"What he wanted most was just that we talk," he said. "At least the three of us. And this other couple who were his foster parents, maybe talk with them too, if they're willing. But at least us. And if right now is the only time we can do that face-to-face, then let's do it now."

The man at the desk propelled his wheeled office chair sideways, stood and held aloft a booklet of coupons, waving it so that the coupons fluttered. "Ha!" he said. "Five cents a gallon off at the M and H! You know where that is, right?"

"Sure," Meir said. "I'll fill up on the way out of town. Nathan, this is Peter, Peter—"

"Dandridge," Peter said.

"Peter was Avram's buddy in Vietnam. Peter, this is Nathan Grutsky. He was a law school classmate of mine at Rutgers. Sometimes when I'm down this way and have work back home to tend to, Nathan lets me use his office."

"I let him use it *gratis*," Grutsky said. "That way I know I'll never have to pay a traffic ticket in Bergen County. And hey," he said, patting Peter's shoulder, "it's good of you to come. Avram was—well, you know what a gifted mind he had. He used to come in here and help me think through cases, even before he started law school."

"Nathan's people were part of the original settlement group at Covenant," Meir said. "So were the Kleinfields. You know about the Covenant Colony? Well, Ilana and I can fill you in about that later. And for the record, I have no contact of any kind with traffic court. Now, if Nathan ever gets indicted for stealing enough Bergen County chickens to constitute a felony, I can offer him a plea deal."

Meir took a gas coupon from Grutsky. As Peter, still carrying his duffel, descended the dim stairwell behind Meir and Ilana, he glanced back at the cracked pane of bubble glass in Grutsky's office door. So this is where Rabby cut his eyeteeth as a lawyer, he thought. An ambulance chaser's shabby, windowless office in Nowheresville, New Jersey. One hell of a long way from the Harlowe & Rabinowitz suite, where even the brass wastebaskets looked spit-shined.

When he reached the street door, Peter braced himself with one hand against its frame. He still felt wobbly but decided it was as much from hunger as fatigue.

"Could we maybe stop in someplace where I could buy a sandwich or something?" he said. "I haven't eaten since yesterday afternoon."

They walked a half block, then Meir stopped at the driver's door of a dark green Austin-Healey Sprite. The little convertible's collapsible hood was up, and without a word, Ilana clambered into the narrow space where the hood would rest when folded down. She wedged herself in horizontally with one shoulder against the driver's seat.

"Jeez, Ilana, I could ride back there," Peter said.

"Nope," she said. "That would break with patriarchal tradition."

"Straight on to Isaac and Miriam's?" Meir said. "They'll have plenty to eat in the fridge."

"I think not yet," Ilana said. "We'll be freer to talk if there's just the three of us."

"Ho-Jo's it is, then," Meir said.

He drove several blocks to a Howard Johnson's restaurant, humming a tune that Peter recognized as "Froggy Went A-Courting." Ilana insisted that Meir and Peter go in first so she could extricate herself from the car unobserved.

As Peter wolfed down a grilled chicken sandwich with extra fries, he told Meir and Ilana about the Viet Cong's intertwined spy and attack plans, and about Rabby's role in detecting them and then in complicating the way things played out. He explained that he hadn't witnessed Rabby's death or events immediately before or after it because he'd been in a military hospital. When he spoke of the pantomime Rabby would sometimes perform for the little girl who lived in their villa—in which he seemed to toss something over a barrier and catch it on the far side— Ilana's eyes grew fixed and she clutched at her brother's hand on the table. That happened again when he told them Rabby had built a barbed wire barrier around the villa's veranda. When he told them how Captain Tomczak had described the chase to the villa rooftop and the way Rabby had swatted the cadre off the ladder, he added that another witness had likened the blow to an effort to chop down through the man, shoulder to beltline. When Peter mentioned that detail, Ilana shut her eyes and uttered a soft cry. Through all of this, Meir looked stolidly at Peter, just nodding a little here and there.

Finally, Peter raced through Rabby's outlandish story of his family's rescue by a beautiful, aging courtesan named Antonina Tarnowski. Ilana and Meir just blinked and nodded at most of it, as if signaling him to hurry along. He knew instantly when Rabby had inserted some new twist in the version he told on the villa rooftop. Rabby must have done that when he located his Army Reserve unit next-door to the Metropolitan Opera House and adduced the Little Ice Age to explain the risk an infant might freeze beneath her father's cloak in southern Ukraine. When elements like these cropped up, Meir or Ilana or both of them would lean forward bug-eyed and laughing and exclaim, "What? He said what?"

"So I guess, like you said, you've heard most of the made-up parts time after time," Peter said when he had finished the tale.

"The made-up parts?" Ilana said. "What part wasn't made up?" She untied her scarf and draped it across her shoulders. Coils of hair spilled across the blue cloth, glowing like beaten bronze in the sunlight that fell through a window.

"Some of those made-up parts contained so much truth, though," she said. "Like giving himself the name Antonin."

"You mean he'd done that before?" Peter said.

"Oh, yes. He did it only with me, but yes. For a long time. Dating back to the goat, really."

"To the goat? He never said anything to me about a goat."

Her laugh sounded both tender and rueful. "No, of course he wouldn't. That would have given away the game, to tell you that."

From then on Peter mostly listened. As the three of them lingered in their cubicle, ordering coffee often enough to stave off delivery of the bill, he began to understand that the Rabby he had known—the man of wealth and privilege and refined sensibility who had evoked in him a bewildering mix of resentment and envy and admiration—had never existed. Or rather, that man had been a creation that arose from roiling currents of pain and guilt, like a bird of brilliant plumage arising from the River of Lost Souls.

"You know, I'd thought he grew up in really high-toned surroundings," Peter said. "Not that there's anything wrong with growing up here, but—this is where all of you are from, right?"

Ilana and Meir looked at each other, as they would do often over the next hour, seeming to agree silently on what to say next and which of them should say it.

"No, we have no connection to Arborville," Meir said. "Well, none except for Avram, and of course Isaac and Miriam, who all these years have treated Avram as their own child."

In a tone so low and calm that Peter, in his fogged state, had to strain to focus on his words, Meir spelled out a history that flatly contradicted the tale Rabby had spun out on the villa rooftop. But even as Meir demolished Rabby's story point by point, Ilana would now and again interject some fierce claim of its overarching truth.

Meir's and Ilana's father had come to New Jersey in 1905, from Poland. Both he and his older brother had trained as rabbis. Their native town, near the city of Lodz, was too small to provide a living for more than one rabbi, and the older brother, also named Meir, got that job. At the time, the Russians were provoking a wave of pogroms against Jews throughout the Pale of Settlement, which included Poland.

"Our father, Yosef, wasn't married yet, and he had nothing else to tie him down, so he figured: Why put up with this crap every time the Russians want to blame an assassination or food shortage on the Jews?"

One of Yosef's classmates from the Warsaw Rabbinical School had emigrated and started a Torah Academy in New Jersey. Yosef took him up on an offer to go teach there. Meir, his brother, was married and had the only job he ever wanted, and he had no way to foresee the future. So Meir hunkered down and worked to keep people safe until the Angel of Death, in the form of the Tsar's secret police, passed them by. That worked out well for a lot of Polish Jews then, so it became a template, one that thousands of Jewish families relied on thirty-odd years later, when what looked like a new round of pogroms came at them.

"But when that happened, it came from a different direction, and the perps spoke a different language."

Meir, as the most looked-up-to figure in his town, decided that again they should sit tight and act deferential and yield up whatever requisitions of labor and potatoes and made-to-order clothing were demanded of them, and wait until the Dark Angel had passed. Only this time it didn't pass. In the fall of 1939, one of the traveling squads of killers called Einsatzgruppen arrived in town. Their orders were to kill Polish leaders and intellectuals, so they rounded up the town's mayor and priest and the faculty from the Catholic school and shot them all in the town square. They left the Jews alone on that first pass through town, but their commander told Meir they'd be back.

As soon as they were gone, more than half the town's Jews fled to Lodz, believing if they melted into a city that was one-third Jewish, it would give them some semblance of safety. Most of the older people chose to stay in their village, and Meir stayed with them, but he told his son, Asher, to go with the rest to Lodz. Asher had completed his rabbinical training, and he was considered the town's rabbi-in-waiting, which made him a fit leader for that departing group. Asher had a wife, Dalia, and a newborn baby named Esther.

"Probably Meir didn't think twice about telling this young family to go, knowing that was their one chance of survival. But Meir and his wife were old. They were ready to greet death on their doorstep."

"Your father, who'd come over those many years earlier—he was still alive then, wasn't he?" Peter said.

"Very much so," the burly man sitting across the Formica-topped table said, nodding somberly. "He was alive, and very much aware."

"Well, look. I guess this is a stupid question, but couldn't he do something?"

Slowly Ilana leaned forward. She was tall enough to draw almost nose-to-nose with Peter across the table. The amber spokes that radiated through her green irises seemed to pulsate with anger.

"Yes, that is a stupid question, Peter," she said in a hoarse whisper.

As she paused, seemingly to gather steam, Meir slowly and silently mouthed the words: "Your question is entirely reasonable." He stretched his lips comically to ensure Peter could read them. Then he winked at Peter as Ilana went on:

"Do you have any idea how people like our father labored and pleaded and pounded on the doors of the men who make our laws, all to save a life here, a life there, lives bound to ours by blood and affection and memory, only to be told this country already had plenty of our kind and no need, no room and, above all, no taste for more of them? You are a nice young man, and may God reward you for coming all this way to help us come to terms with Avram's death. Still, you ought to be ashamed to ask something so horrendously stupid."

Meir covered the fingers of his sister's nearest hand with his own massive hand. "Our father did what he could," he told Peter evenly. "But, as Ilana says, his was just one voice among thousands. And even if those voices hadn't been ignored, there was so little time to act that the end result would have been the same. A few months after that first Einsatzgruppe wiped out the gentile leadership, another one came, specifically to kill the Jews. The town's name meant 'Little River,' and you would pronounce it 'Zechka,' though you wouldn't know that from the Polish spelling. But the town's not there anymore. After the war, see, there was no one left to come back to it. So that's how my uncle, the man I was named for, met his end."

"And did your father know?"

"Oh, no. Nobody knew at the time. Nobody outside occupied Poland, that is. I found out after the war. I even learned the names of some of the men who did the killing, though that wasn't one of the cases I was assigned to. The Nuremberg Tribunal sentenced the chief of that Einsatzgruppe to death, by the way, but his sentence got commuted to fifteen years."

"So that was a place where Rabby—Avram, I mean—took a piece of truth and reworked it?" Peter said. "About your work for the Nuremberg court?"

"Oh, I wish," Meir said, chuckling with what sounded like a long-nursed note of regret. "I'd have volunteered in a heartbeat to work for the tribunal, even if that meant extending my Army hitch. But the Army ran its piece of the tribunal as a closed shop, and junior legal officers like me weren't invited. No, my chance to delve into what the Nazis did in places like my uncle's little town came thanks to a private effort called A Sword from the Ashes. Some donors, Jewish of course, from back in the States set up a headquarters for it in Vienna.

"I hadn't known Isaac Kleinfield before or during the war, but after VE Day, he and I were both in Bavaria, and we both saw the same posting in our orderly rooms. It was a call for men with legal training or who spoke certain languages to help investigate Nazi war crimes. That sounded to both of us like a venture we'd like to be part of, at least for a while. So we both took our Army discharges there in Germany and signed on with A Sword from the Ashes, and that's how we became pals. It was thanks to that friendship that Avram ended up in a home here, with a foster family that became the only real family he'd ever have."

"So both of you—so Isaac was a lawyer too?" Peter said.

"Oh, no. As we described ourselves to each other, we were one each aspiring shyster and chicken farmer. During the war, I'd done legal work, all of it behind the lines, all run-of-the-mill. Low-grade courts-martial, compassionate discharges, fielding civilian complaints. Isaac, though, was an infantryman in the Third Army. Rose to sergeant. Isaac's division liberated Buchenwald. He got an up-close look at what had gone on there, the piles of corpses, the photos from the medical labs."

Meir said A Sword from the Ashes got only a trickle of volunteers, for a couple of reasons. There'd be no pay beyond a skimpy per diem. And without government backing, the group couldn't compel testimony. As a result, most volunteers fit the same profile: men with the needed language skills and, more important, an intimate sense of outrage.

"Isaac grew up in the old Covenant Colony, just outside town here, and those settlers, his parents included, spoke Russian or Yiddish at home. I could find my way around in Polish. And this was personal for men like

Isaac and me. We hoped to bring evidence to light that would lead to prosecutions, if not at Nuremberg then in some court somewhere with power to hang or imprison. And the people we wanted to place in the dock hadn't just done things we found offensive on humanitarian grounds. They'd murdered men and women we knew as grandfather, grandmother, aunt, uncle, cousin. Sometimes the people they'd murdered amounted to every living soul our parents or grandparents had known in whatever shtetl or urban warren they'd come from. So for some of us, the chance to help call those killers to account was too special to pass up."

As soon as Meir's Army discharge came through, the fledgling volunteer group assigned him a Russian translator.

"That's how I got paired with Isaac. No need and no time now to go into the cases we worked, though I can tell you Avram did a creditable job of adapting the facts to fit the contours of his tale. With one big exception: the Russians wouldn't let us into eastern Germany or Poland or Ukraine or Romania or anywhere else under Soviet control at war's end."

"And it's no wonder that Avram should work into his tale the search for a cross hidden among weeds in a Jewish cemetery," Ilana said. "What he'd done there, you see, was take Meir's search for a Jewish child, hidden among the thousands of children, Jewish and gentile, left parentless in refugee camps at the end of the war, and transmute it into something rich and strange."

"Well, that's getting a little ahead, but I can clear that up," Meir said.

Once Meir and Isaac found they couldn't travel east to work cases they'd been assigned, the best they could do was interview people in displaced persons camps inside Austria who'd been at Auschwitz and Treblinka and Sobibor. They helped build case files against several Nazi guards and medical staff and a couple of low-lifes in the Einsatzgruppen. They encountered long stretches of idleness, but Meir found in them an upside, since they gave him time to scan newspapers from Munich and Vienna. The papers routinely published photographs of children who'd turned up in displaced persons camps unaccompanied by any relative.

"I'd always give those photos a close look, though at that point I wasn't searching for Avram, since I didn't know of his existence. I was hoping to find Esther, the little girl born to Asher and Dalia before the Nazis invaded Poland in 1939. I was searching for her parents, too, of course, if they'd happened to survive. But that seemed unlikely, since they would have contacted my father as soon as they could after the war ended. Dad's brother had written him about Esther's birth, but it wasn't until 1942 that Avram was born. By then, Asher and Dalia had been penned up inside the Lodz ghetto for going on three years, with no way to let my family know they were still alive, let alone that they'd had another child."

Again Ilana leaned far enough across the table to draw nearly nose-to-nose with Peter. Her voice fell to a soft rasp.

"And no one in our family could ever have known," she said, "but for Antonina."

"Antonina had not only saved Avram," Meir said. "She'd gotten his name, and his sister's and his parents' names, and she knew at least roughly when the children were born. And she made sure that information got passed on."

Peter shut his eyes and tried to reconcile what he was hearing with what he thought he knew.

"But Antonina was a fiction," he said. "You've said so yourselves. I mean, both of you. Haven't you?"

Ilana and her brother exchanged wan smiles.

"The Antonina of the story that Avram told you—the woman born in the 1830s who grew up to become the protector of the Rabinowitz family in, for God's sake, Odessa—that Antonina is a fiction," Ilana said. "But she's also the product of Avram's penchant for leaving key truths intact, no matter how drastically he'd changed the surrounding circumstances."

"Antonina was brave enough, or some might say foolish enough, to attempt a rescue that common sense should have told her was impossible," Meir said. "Brave enough, strong enough too, to charge an armed Nazi guard from behind and cold-cock him, clobber him with the barrel of an ersatz Sten gun."

"Oh my God," Peter said, more to himself than to the pair across the table. "In the neck. She whacked him in the neck, didn't she?"

Ilana's half-smile was almost a smirk. "Now you see, don't you?" she said. "Now you see why he felt you had to come talk to me? You, who tormented him with your disbelief. Not just your disbelief in his story, but in him. Oh yes, he wrote to me about that. But now you see, don't you?"

"It was almost like Antonina found me, rather than the other way around," Meir said.

By the time Meir met her, everything had worked out the way Antonina had set it up to work. Avram had turned up at the Rothschild Hospital in Vienna, which had become a funnel's end for the torrent of people pouring out of Poland and Hungary and Romania. Most were survivors of the camps, or of years in the attics and cellars of gentiles who'd risked their lives to hide Jews. But for an unaccompanied three-year-old, just turning up at a place like the Rothschild Hospital wasn't enough to enable relatives to find him. There had to be some accompanying information, at least a name, or better yet the parents' names and some account of where they came from and what happened to them.

"Well, in October 1945, a photograph ran in the Wiener Zeitung that showed a curly-haired little boy holding what looked like a foot-square chalkboard with 'Rabinowitz' in all capital letters across the top, and below it the name 'Avram.' Of course the family name caught my attention, but the name's fairly common in Poland. I might not have made any inquiry if I hadn't noticed that the photo was submitted by the Rothschild Hospital. It was about eight blocks from where I was sitting in the erstwhile office of a Nazi Party local group leader, so I walked down there. Doubtless the most consequential twenty-minute walk I ever took."

The hospital was run by and for Jews, so the Nazis had closed it during the war. Meir found the grounds lined with wooden shipping pallets, with the narrowest possible space to walk between them. Hanging from a nail inside the gate he found a clipboard that contained as much information as had been provided about each unaccompanied child. There he learned that the parents of Avram Rabinowitz were named Asher and Dalia, that

Avram had a sister named Esther, and that his parents and sister had been killed the same night he was rescued from the Lodz ghetto. At the bottom of that sheet of paper was a handwritten bed number.

"I walked up and down those rows of pallets until I found that number scrawled on one of them. The kid was asleep there, right on the slats. Somebody had folded up a coat and wedged it under his head. I didn't know who left him the coat, but it was pretty ratty-looking, so it wasn't much of a sacrifice."

"So Rabby didn't even make it to the States until he was three," Peter said.

"Wrong," Ilana said. "He was nearly six. He was stuck in DP camps in Austria and Germany for another three years."

"Even in 1948 it was touch-and-go getting him a DP visa," Meir said. "Despite the clear evidence he had close relatives in the U.S. What turned the trick was Isaac and Miriam's agreement to foster him. I was still unmarried, see, so I couldn't offer a suitable home. My dad would gladly have taken him in, but Dad was past sixty and a widower, so his home wasn't a fit placement either. Plus we kept getting the hint-hint, nudge-nudge from the immigration folks that the proper thing to do with a Jewish orphan was recruit a family in Palestine to take him in."

"I was twelve when the war ended," Ilana said. "My mom had died. I wanted my big brother to come home, and it really ticked me off that he wouldn't do it. And then, in the summer of forty-six, he did come home. And that left Avram marooned in DP camps for another two years."

"And if Ilana felt ticked," Meir said, "imagine the pressure Miriam put on Isaac to cut short his role as an amateur, unaccredited war crimes investigator. Which, in honesty, turned out to be a mostly futile endeavor for all involved. She wanted him back in south Jersey chop-chop, so they could start a family."

After working for about six months as Meir's translator, Isaac headed home in time for New Year's 1946. Meir stayed on until the following July, working strictly on Polish cases, including the murders of Jews in his grandparents' village. With help from contacts in the Army Judge

Advocate General Corps, he was able to get a copy of the Nazis' field report on that act of butchery.

"The prosecutors in Nuremberg already had that and much more, of course," he said. "But they were only going after the biggest fish."

Meir tracked down home addresses for an officer and two noncoms mentioned in the field report, intending to provide that information to German prosecutors. He had to wait until 1950, when West Germany finally set up a public prosecution office.

"I don't know to this day if they ever took action. So that was what I did for pay those extra six months. Except we weren't getting paid, and the per diem we got would cover about one schnitzel and one stein of beer—which is what I usually spent it on."

But over those extra six months he had a hand in something else that paid off handsomely. He gave chief credit to a young American nurse. Meir paid her out of his dwindling military savings to teach Avram as much English as she could impart to a three-year-old in an hour or two a day. Her name was Magdala Finkelstein, and she'd been hired to work with displaced persons at the Schlachtensee Camp in Berlin. Avram got shipped there in early 1946, along with other orphaned DPs from the Rothschild Hospital. Magdala worked with him until he could take English classes in the school the DPs set up for themselves at Schlachtensee. Avram stayed at Schlachtensee until the Soviets blockaded Berlin in July 1948, when the whole camp population had to be airlifted to Frankfurt.

"But by then, we had him cleared for placement with Isaac and Miriam," Meir said with a sigh of remembered satisfaction. "So the stop in Frankfurt was just a steppingstone."

Ilana was looking at her brother with a puzzled squint. "Well, I guess that makes sense," she said.

"What does?" Meir said.

"You skipped right past Antonina. But maybe you're just trying to build suspense."

Meir lowered his eyes. "Or maybe I'm just yielding to the tendency to leave the hardest part for last," he said.

Thirty-one

"Suppose you start with where you first saw her name," Ilana said.

"It was right there on Avram's sheet on the clipboard at the Rothschild."

Appended to what seemed at the time more consequential details—names of the child's parents and sister, where and when he'd been rescued and the fact the others were killed—was a line saying all that information came from Antonina Tarnowski of the Polish Home Army. With a little reflection, Meir realized he had the name of someone who must know all anybody could ever tell him about a branch of his family.

"I had a good stretch of time ahead of me to try to find her. Finding her even fit my job description, sort of, since it looked like she'd devoted herself to saving Jews. Which meant we were in the same business, except she was better at it than I was. She'd proved that much by saving one infant Jew from certain death."

"And how exactly did she prove that?" Ilana said.

Peter, listening through mists of fatigue that now and again yielded to moments of stark clarity, realized Ilana was playing the prompt role in a call-and-response with her brother.

"By the date she rescued him," Meir said. "September 1942."

Assuming Avram was newborn then, Meir said, he would have been conceived just as the Germans were starting to deport people from the Lodz ghetto. They'd even set up a new death camp at Chelmno, just outside the city, to cut transport costs. So by conceiving a child, Asher and Dalia were flinging a desperate seed of hope into the future.

"From where they stood, the future must have looked like it was paved with endless rows of corpses," he said. "Their own among them."

"Wasn't that date important in another way too?" Ilana said.

"Very. Because, thanks to Antonina, they got him out of there just before children in the ghetto were rounded up to be murdered in the gas vans at Chelmno."

Once the Germans gave the roundup order, their hand puppet in the Jewish hierarchy inside the camp, Chaim Rumkowski, enforced it. No ghetto in Poland was more completely sealed off from its surroundings than the one in Lodz, so there was little hope of spiriting any of the kids there to safety. Some families committed collective suicide rather than see their children shipped off to be killed.

"But you say this one family found another option?" Ilana said.

"Created one," Meir said. "I had to do a little guesswork, but not much."

Rumkowski preened himself on the productivity of workshops he set up inside the camp to produce goods for the Germans. One workshop turned out electrical equipment, items like replacement parts for field radios. After the Germans ordered all children to be shipped to Chelmno, a shot-in-the-dark plea to rescue a child went out from the ghetto by shortwave transmission. It was picked up by a Home Army radio monitor who kept tabs on German radio traffic.

"After Antonina told me that, I took the train to Nuremberg to look at the Lodz Jewish Council's lists of work assignments. Sure enough, Asher Rabinowitz was assigned to the electrical components workshop. Using bits of metal and wire and the knowledge he'd acquired working there, Asher must have built a crude radio that could transmit beyond the ghetto walls, plus a little generator to power it. There might have been a Morse code handbook in his workshop, or maybe a fellow worker there knew the code and wrote it out for him."

Peter fished from his shirt pocket the photograph of the children behind barbed wire that Emmet had found in Rabby's room. He flipped it to read what was written on the back: "Secret radio saved them too. Third Army played part of A." He said nothing as Meir went on.

"Asher sent the message in a seat-of-the-pants encryption so well chosen that for a while it had even the partisans stumped," Meir said. "Fortunately, one of them was a Jew. For the most part, Jewish partisans fought in their own units, but there were a few sprinkled around in outfits like Antonina's. She said this fellow grasped right away the key to Asher's encryption."

The message contained the Hebrew name of a Bible verse, Shemot 3—the verse in Exodus where Moses's mother makes a basket from papyrus and hides her baby in it along the Nile's bank. Aside from that, the message just identified a time and day of the month and an alley by the ghetto's fence. But the indicated date in September had already passed, so it didn't make obvious sense to the partisans until their Jewish comrade said they should read it as a date in the Jewish calendar. And that date in the Jewish month of Tishrei would fall a couple of days in the future. So Antonina's outfit understood the message to mean that, if they took a concealed position by the alley on that day at the indicated time, they might somehow save a child, despite the ten vertical feet of razor wire that ran along the alley's edge.

"Why that particular spot?" Ilana said.

"It must have been the weakest bit of the ghetto perimeter," Meir said. "Maybe outside the line of sight from any elevated guard post."

"But didn't this message say there'd be a guard there in the alley?"

"More than that. It said there'd be guards inside and outside the fence."

"What was any rescue team supposed to do about that?" Ilana said.

"The message didn't say."

"And how could Asher know the Germans wouldn't intercept this shot-in-the-dark message?"

"He couldn't," Meir said. "Nor could Antonina's Home Army commander know the message itself wasn't a lure thrown by the Germans. Antonina told me that when her commander asked if anyone wanted to attempt what it asked, he looked at her for quite a while after she volunteered. Then he said, 'Go ahead, but you're on your own.'"

"So what was up with her?" Ilana said. "Recklessness? Addiction to danger? Selfless devotion to good works, or to children in particular?"

"I think—" Meir said. For the first time in a while, Meir seemed to be searching for the truth, rather than just reciting facts. "Maybe some tincture of all those things. But I think Antonina, by this point in her life, had become above all else a soldier. She was ready for any action, large or small, that would weaken the enemy. If it involved proving the enemy wrong when he assumed something was impossible—such as a newborn child's being pitched over a barrier intended to seal off 20,000 children so they'd die with a minimum of fuss—then so much the better."

"But she didn't run that risk alone, did she?" Ilana said.

"No. She was soldier enough to know she'd have to remain as hands-free as possible. Which meant if a child landed in her hands, she must pass it swiftly to other hands, so she could tend to other matters with her knockoff Sten gun."

"Landed in her hands?" Peter said, remembering the pantomime of tossing and catching that Rabby had performed for Huê at the far end of their villa's patio. "Do you mean—across that barrier of razor wire?"

As the back-and-forth among the three of them narrowed to Avram's rescue from behind a razor wire barrier, Ilana's expression soured and her shoulders hunched inward, as if she were preparing to fend off a blow. Meir glanced at his sister, touched the sleeve of her cardigan and told her softly, "I'll let you know."

Then, to Peter, Meir said, "First a little background about what fueled Antonina's hatred for the Nazis."

He said Antonina's father was both a soldier and an engineer. Casimir Tarnowski had fought the Russians for Polish independence in 1905. After they caught him and sentenced him to death, his mother, who was from a highborn German family, used her connections to get his sentence commuted to exile. Casimir used his time in exile to earn a degree in electrical engineering in Belgium and collaborate with a French scientist on the concept of a train that levitates within a magnetic field.

Casimir and his wife settled in Grodno, a city in eastern Poland, and he founded a business that manufactured light fixtures and electrical components used in timing devices. The family had five children, including Antonina, who was born in 1922. When Casimir came home from work, he'd spend hours in his study, working on his inventions. He hoped to get them developed once he retired. His target date for retirement was 1939.

But 1939 was the year Hitler and Stalin carved up Poland. In September, the Russians invaded from the east and the Nazis from the west. In Grodno, the Russians overwhelmed the Poles' ragtag defense. Casimir evacuated his family to Warsaw, where his wife and children moved in with relatives. He headed further west, hoping to take up his old commission in the Polish regular army and fight the Germans. Apparently he interrupted that journey to pray. Antonina said he was in a church when German troops broke in, rounded up the congregation, packed them into vans and shipped them to Germany to do forced labor. Still, Antonina said, her father had a way out. Since he was half-German, he could have claimed all the rights of a native-born German citizen. Plus, as a skilled engineer, he could probably have gotten a job designing machinery for the Nazi war effort.

"All he had to do to get on that gravy train was swear allegiance to Hitler," Meir said. "But he wouldn't make that pledge, so for the next six years he did slave labor."

Casimir worked as a tool-and-die maker at a plant that made tanks and heavy artillery until Allied bombers shut it down. Starting in the fall of 1944, he worked at a place called the Mittelwerk in the Harz mountains, first building an underground rocket factory, then on the factory's assembly line for V-2 rockets. At the war's end, he was working at the front, digging ditches.

"But for years, all Antonina knew was that the Nazis had seized her father and shipped him off to Germany," Meir said.

Antonina was a first-year university student in Warsaw, studying mathematics, when she learned that. She joined the resistance, but for a while she attended enough classes to hold onto papers that identified her as a student. That made her useful for intelligence gathering. With that student ID in her pocket, she could walk around openly and take notes on the haunts and habits of Nazi officials and SS men who struck her as targets for assassination.

One hit she arranged was on a German lieutenant who'd terrorized a little town she passed through. As she walked into that town, just to catch a train there, she saw a squad of soldiers shoot a woman in the town square. She learned it was one of a daily series of executions of people accused of aiding Jews. Just selling a Jew a loaf of bread or helping a Jew hunt in the snow for a lost glove could cost you your life. The lieutenant was spacing out the executions, for maximum traumatizing effect. Day after day, he'd have all the residents herded into the main square. That day's victim would be shackled by one wrist to a lamppost, then shot and left hanging by the wrist from the lamppost until time for the next day's execution.

"Antonina ended up spending a couple of nights in woods outside that town, waiting to see the hit delivered on that bastard," Meir said. "By the time she left town, his bloodstained uniform hat was dangling from the top of the lamppost. She hadn't carried out the hit herself, but she did shoot the corpse through the mouth, to give the hat that special touch."

This period when she could walk around openly ended when she got tipped off that her student papers would no longer serve as cover. After that, she had to merge in as a regular soldier. She quickly lost count of the railway bridges she helped blow up. She was issued a knockoff of the British Sten gun. She had that weapon with her when she rescued Avram.

"So should we say that Antonina had a deep commitment to protecting Jewish life?" Ilana asked her brother. "And to avenging its loss when that seemed called for?"

"I asked Antonina why she'd helped Jews at the risk of her own life," Meir said. "She said, 'It was entirely natural for me to help anyone the Germans intended to kill.'"

"That's not quite the same thing, is it?"

"Not quite. But it's a soldier's answer. And she lived up to it."

"You said she took something else important with her that night to the alley at the edge of the Lodz ghetto," Ilana said. "Besides her weapon, you said, she took an extra pair of hands."

"She got a nun to go with her," Meir said.

The nun belonged to Zegota, a network that helped Jews survive by whatever means fit the case. That often meant moving them quickly from one hiding place to another. Antonina cajoled the nun into coming along on the off chance they could get a child out. If they did, they'd have to get the kid moving at speed along a chain of safe houses. The Germans were sure to deploy search teams if they knew a Jew had made it out of what they'd touted as an escape-proof ghetto.

"Well, that seems borderline suicidal," Peter said. "You're saying the two of them, Antonina and this nun, risked their lives on the strength of a message that might have been a decoy? A message that, even if legit, posed the inconvenience of ten feet of razor wire with guards on either side? And the odds of success were what?"

"Vanishingly small," Meir said. "But here's the thing. The Nazis were demanding twenty thousand children for shipment, and every parent knew that meant certain death for their child. How many families came up with some desperate ploy, even if not one as well thought-out as Asher's and Dalia's? Hundreds? Surely dozens, at least. Not one of those attempts, considered alone, stood a snowball's chance of success. But the Nazi guards must have been stretched thin countering them all. Just the sheer number of attempts would have increased the odds that one would succeed. So far as I could ever determine, Avram's case was that one."

Meir placed a massive hand over his sister's fine-boned fingers. "Ten minutes," he said. This, too, Peter realized, meant something understood by the two of them. Meir slid from the booth to let her out, then kept his eyes on her as she walked toward the counter and signaled to the cashier that she'd be back. She stepped outside and stood beneath the big orange canopy over the diner's entryway with her arms folded and her dark blue scarf drawn across her shoulders. She gripped her elbows, and her bleak gaze was fixed straight ahead.

"This part's still too hard for her," Meir said.

"Okay, look. Antonina and the nun eased up on the alley, across from where the concertina wire was tacked to the walls of a building on the alley's far side. Antonina said the moonlight made the alley's cobblestones almost luminescent. She couldn't see the German guard at first, but she could hear the hollow sound of his boot heels hitting the cobblestones. She and the nun took position behind the corner of a building where she could peep around. She spotted the German guard and a little later the one across the wire, and she realized that one was a Jewish policeman. Rumkowski figured maximum compliance gave his people their best chance at survival, so he recruited a corps of bully-boys. Unarmed, of course, except for wooden clubs. He'd reward them with extra rations when they cracked the heads of other Jews to enforce German orders. The German guard had to patrol the whole alley, checking on the spaces where the wire stretched between buildings. Asher must have timed this patrol routine earlier, because when the German reached the far end of the alley, Asher darted out from behind a building and swatted the Jewish policeman from behind with what looked to Antonina like a piece of firewood. A shiv would have been a better means of ensuring silence, but even at the risk of death for all of them, Asher probably couldn't bring himself to kill a fellow Jew. So the guy he clobbered moaned or cursed loudly enough that the German guard came back down the fence just as Dalia came trotting toward it, wild-eyed and with her bundled-up infant in one arm and dragging along the three-year-old with her other hand. Antonina could see what was shaping up, and she knew that as soon as the German caught sight of Dalia he'd shoot her. She knew, too, that at the sound of gunfire the Germans would cordon off the whole area, and she and the nun would likely be trapped. And she'd learned by then that violence in combat goes incredibly fast, and it leaves no time for second thoughts.

"As the German ran past the building where Antonina was crouching, he spotted Dalia and stopped and raised his weapon. That gave Antonina enough time to dash out and bring her rifle barrel down on that guard's neck. She heard a satisfactory crack that persuaded her she'd broken either neck or collarbone. She flung the guard's weapon what she figured would be far enough away to keep it out of his reach. When she looked up, she saw Dalia standing at the fence, weeping and calling, 'Come! Come here! Come now!' The baby was bawling in Dalia's arms, and the other child was sitting on the pavement, bawling too. So she beckoned to the nun to follow her, and they both dashed up to the wire. And finally it was clear to Antonina what Dalia had in mind, because Dalia jerked tight and knotted the ends of the piece of blanket that she'd wrapped around the baby from all four directions. And then she gripped those knotted ends planted her feet and bent her knees. Antonina said Dalia shut her eyes, and her lips moved. And then Dalia heaved that bundle up and over. Antonina said it just cleared the swirl of wire at the top, but it snagged a little on a barb of razor wire on the way down the other side. That razor edge sliced through the cloth and pierced the baby's thigh, and it caused the bundle to tumble off-line. Antonina had to dive to catch it before it hit the pavement. She could feel the squirming inside the knotted blanket and see the blood from that gouge in his thigh start to seep through, and now the baby was crying louder, but she didn't take time to untie the bundle before she handed it off to the nun. As she did that, she saw that the German guard she'd clubbed down had crawled most of the way toward his rifle. At that same moment, she saw the nun staring open-mouthed toward the concertina wire. When she looked that way too, she saw that Dalia was trying to climb the wire with both feet and one hand while with her other arm she tried to hold Esther clear of the wire. Dalia was trying to climb high enough to save her daughter, too, by lifting the child over the top and dropping her. But that wasn't going to work. Dalia's hand and arm and feet were already streaming blood from razor wire cuts, and both her own clothing and her child's quickly got so snagged she couldn't either keep climbing up or climb back down. Antonina knew if she shot the guard, more Germans would show up, and then the woman and her daughter would die there, dangling from the wire. But she knew, too, that if she didn't shoot him, she and the nun and the infant bound up like a trussed-up joint of meat would die as well. So she shot the German twice, the second time point-blank to make sure he was dead. Then she hurried with the nun back along the route they'd taken to reach the alley. She glanced back once and saw that Asher had tried to pull his wife and daughter down from the wire, but instead he'd gotten ensnared as well. So all three of them were just hanging there, with one of Asher's hands gripping his wife's clothing and the other hand clutching his daughter's ragged little coat.

"Antonina said that by the time she and the nun had run a couple of blocks, they heard several bursts of gunfire from the direction of the alley, and then she heard orders shouted in German. She told the nun to run ahead to her convent with the child in the blanket while she stayed behind to delay pursuit. Zegota's success, see, depended in part on quick transfers. An extra ten minutes could be enough to get a rescued child through the convent and on to the next pair of hands, and for the convent to return to the appearance of quiet contemplation of the divine. Antonina said she found a sheltered spot with a clear field of fire and waited about a quarter hour for a German pursuit party that never came. She figured the Germans must have concluded their only loss was one dead guard, and that wasn't reason enough to cast some dragnet in hopes of catching the assassin. Based on appearances, see, this was just an escape attempt that had failed pathetically. The only visible evidence, aside from the dead guard and a woozy Jewish policeman, was three dead Jews, two adults and a child, dangling from the razor wire. The Nazi eye would see no more significance in those three corpses than we'd see in bugs splattered on a windshield. The Germans had no immediate way, and maybe no way at all, of detecting that the headcount of Jews inside that ghetto had just been reduced by one. Now, remember I told you that Antonina struck me as, above all else, a soldier? When I finally got to talk to her about that rescue, she told me that while she was hunkered down, waiting for the German pursuit, at the moment she realized it wasn't coming, what she felt was disappointment. Rescuing one Jewish child against incredible odds—sure, she was glad she'd done that. But what she wanted most was what a soldier would want. She wanted the Germans to know she'd beaten them."

"And she told you all this?" Peter said. "She told you face-to-face?"

Meir pursed his lips and looked reflective. Then he said simply: "She did."

"But didn't you say the Russians weren't letting Americans into countries like Poland that they controlled when the war ended?"

"Indeed they didn't," Meir said. "But remember when I said it was almost like Antonina found me, rather than the other way round? Well in June of 1946, a couple of months before I gave up being a bush league war crimes investigator and caught a troop ship home, I found Antonina the same way I'd found Avram."

Meir spotted her picture and her name in the *Allgemeine Zeitung*, published in Hanover. For months, the dwindling number of ex-servicemen, nearly all of them Jewish, who had stayed on with A Sword from the Ashes had each day passed around the sections of German and Austrian newspapers that ran the photos and names of displaced persons. Over time, fewer of the DPs so identified were orphans, and a growing number were searching for people they knew, hoping they too had survived. Some of Meir's colleagues clung to the hope of finding people who had been in a particular camp when particular events there took place. Meir's driving interest was more personal.

"Antonina's newspaper posting said she was from Grodno and was a veteran of the Polish Home Army. I figured the odds were good she was the same Antonina Tarnowski who'd put her name to that crumpled piece of paper listing vital facts about Avram. But she was pretty far from Vienna, where I was. She was up in northern Germany, in the British zone, at a DP camp near a little town called Augustdorf. Most Jewish DPs seemed to end up in camps in the American zone, and most gentile DPs in the British zone. There was some mix of self-selection and discriminatory placement going on there. In her case, though, I think Augustdorf was just where her feet took her."

As Meir learned when he finally got to talk to her, Antonina was captured by the Gestapo in May 1944. She was imprisoned, beaten and herded with dozens of other prisoners onto a cattle car for shipment to the Ravensbruck concentration camp. She tore loose a floorboard, waited until the train was going slow enough, let herself down onto the tracks and lay there until the last car rolled past. Then she made her way back to her old Home Army unit. When the war ended, she saw quickly that the Soviets meant to crush the Home Army. Those among her old comrades who resisted were all either shot or shipped to the gulag. She didn't intend to follow suit. She'd fought the only war she'd committed to fight, the one against the Germans. She took on a new mission, which was to find her father, or at least discover what had happened to him. She made her way across the Soviet-occupied zone of Germany, trekking through forests, sleeping in haystacks. She swam across the Elbe near Luneburg and found her way to the DP camp outside Augustdorf. Meir went there to talk to her in July 1946.

"And did she find her father?" Peter said.

"She did. She learned where he was, thanks to diligent tracing by the camp staff at Augustdorf. And she wrote to him."

When the war ended, Casimir Tarnowski was in a forced-labor camp in Ulm that quickly got converted to a DP camp. The inmates were mostly Poles and Ukrainians, including some Jews who were moved there from death camps after the war. They thought highly enough of Casimir to petition that he be named camp director. When he answered his daughter's letter, Casimir enclosed a photo of himself lying on one of the bare-board shelves, like catacombs for the living, that served as beds in Nazi labor camps. The photo must have been taken after the camp's liberation, since Casimir was smiling in it.

"She said when she first saw it, she cried because of what he'd suffered, and for all he'd done in his life, and for the man she knew him to be. But she wasn't crying when she told me that. What I saw in her face then was cold anger."

"When did Antonina get to see him?" Peter said.

"It took at least a couple of years. The DPs were confined to their camps for the first few years. Plus those two camps were far apart. Casimir's was down south in the American zone. Finally he got clearance to travel north to see her, probably because he'd earned enough respect from the Americans by then. I never got to meet Casimir Tarnowski, and I regret that."

"And did you meet Antonina just that once?"

"Twice, actually."

"Well, I guess it shouldn't matter," Peter said. "But Rabby made a big point of it: was she tall and regal-looking? And did she wear a necklace with a big, ornate cross hanging from it?"

"No," Meir said. "If she wore a cross, I didn't see it. I'd say she was on the small side—certainly not tall. And regal? Would you call a wolf regal? For me, the word regal implies an air of serenity. And there was nothing serene about Antonina Tarnowski."

Meir stood and slowly waved a hand until Ilana, still standing under the restaurant's orange canopy, saw him and came inside and slid into the booth. Before he sat down, Meir checked his watch and gave a small snort of impatience. Whether imagined or real, Peter thought, Antonina—this woman out of Rabby's past—took more time to explain than most people could easily spare.

"We covered all the toughest part, Lani," Meir murmured to his sister. "We've got him outside the wire, and on to the convent."

After it became clear to Antonina, crouched behind the rubble of a demolished wall, that there'd be no German pursuit, she hurried on to the convent too. By that time, the nuns had passed the baby on to some other safe house. The nun who'd aided in the rescue told her that, when she untied the blanket, she saw the gouge in the baby's thigh wasn't deep, and she cleaned and bandaged it. One of the other nuns had a heated bottle of goat's milk ready for him, but the child was so near starvation he didn't show much interest in it at first. The nun said his eyes looked several sizes too big for such a scrawny body, and he just kept his eyes fixed on her and teethed the improvised cloth nipple they'd attached to the bottle. But she said that by the time they bundled him up for transfer to the safe house, he'd figured out the goat's milk was a good idea, so they left the bottle in there with him.

"So goats figured large in his life from the first," Ilana said.

"Maybe there was a courtyard in the convent and they kept goats to trim the grass," Meir said.

"And the list?" Ilana said.

"Oh, yeah, they found that in the blanket with him. His mother must have put it there."

It was a crumpled piece of paper with his name and the names of his parents and his sister, and a date that must have been his date of birth. Antonina asked the nuns to make a clean copy. Then she added to it a few words saying he'd been rescued from the Lodz ghetto but the rest of his family had been killed, and she signed her own name. The nuns promised they'd do all they could to make sure that information got passed on from one hiding place to the next, along with the child. It was still with him when he turned up three years later at the Rothschild Hospital.

Meir's tone suddenly switched from measured and confidential to offhand but hurried. "We need to move chop-chop now, folks, if we're going to see Isaac and Miriam today," he said. "I've got to drive north tonight and prep for a grand jury presentation, and I've got this balky witness to deal with in the morning."

Meir paid at the counter and handed the car key to Ilana. "Hop in if you're ready, Lani," he said. He prodded Peter gently with an elbow. "Peter and I need to go take a leak."

The men's room was empty except for the two of them.

"One more piece I'm going to tell you," Meir said as they stood by the sinks. "Everything I told you while Lani was outside—she knows all that, but she doesn't need ever to listen to it again. But this part she's never heard, because I've never told anyone except my father. But I think you ought to know it.

"When Antonina told me the full story of what happened that night, after I caught up with her at that DP camp outside Augustdorf, I told her she shouldn't feel bad about having to leave the rest of the family back there to die at the wire. She'd done all she could, I said, and it was better that they died all together. And her lips wrinkled in a scornful sort of way. She said she didn't feel bad about that at all. She said she'd signed on to save one child, not two. She said the woman who climbed the wire had no one but herself to blame that she and her husband and daughter all died there. Maybe your time in Vietnam will help you understand how she could say that. Because that's what a soldier might say, see? A soldier who's seen and done way too much."

Thirty-two

Ilana had already wedged herself into the narrow space behind the seats. As Meir and Peter approached the little car, Ilana's amber-flecked eyes gazed at them through a plastic side window. The sight of her that way, craning her neck to look at them, merged with somber images that had flowed through Peter's mind during his miserable overnight bus ride. It's like one of the photos from the liberation of the camps, he thought. She could be one of those starving prisoners, gazing out from a bare wooden bunk, looking strangely indifferent to the prospect that she might, after all, survive.

Then his eyes were drawn to the car's headlights. They jutted above the hood as if they'd been stuck on as an afterthought.

"The headlights," he said. "They look like—"

"Frog's eyes?" Meir said. He smiled and hummed the "Froggy Went A-Courting" tune as he climbed in and revved the engine. "No surprise, is it," he said, "that the Brits call this model Frogeye?"

"This is his third Austin-Healey in the past ten years," Ilana said wearily. "You may understand my fear that I will someday get a phone call at my kibbutz school from the Bergen County prosecutor. He'll tell me his chief deputy has been charged with deviant behavior for copulating with a large green machine."

They crossed a narrow stream at the edge of town. "This is Baumanville, where the Covenant colonists settled," Meir said.

He said the first group, mostly Russians, arrived in the 1880s. European philanthropists sponsored the colony, and the rules they laid down for it reflected a curious dichotomy in the treatment of Jews in Odessa. Jews there were targeted in attacks that culminated in the 1905 pogrom—the same one where the heroine of Rabby's tale rescued a Jewish family with a single slash of her father's saber, then died in a hail of bullets. Yet, apart from these violent outbursts, Jews in the Odessa region faced little day-to-day discrimination. They could farm and trade in agricultural goods and even attend Russian universities.

"That degree of freedom gave rise to the notion that Jews could gain acceptance in America by supplying gentiles with goods that can be planted and harvested, or bred and slaughtered, or squeezed from udders, or coaxed from a chicken," Meir said. "Picture a Jewish 'American Gothic' couple, okay? Even if you know they're Jewish, the sidelocks on Pa look less alienating if he's wearing coveralls and carrying a milk pail. And you're not put off by Ma's Semitic nose and dark eyes if she's toting a wire basket filled with fresh eggs."

That strain of agrarian thinking, he said, became a template for other Jewish settlements in southern New Jersey. Covenant had an edge on the others, though, since it straddled a rail line running to markets in Philadelphia and New York.

"There's not much trace left, though, of the first colonists here, except for the old synagogue and cemetery. Most of their descendants rose in the world and moved away, or at least gave up farming. There was a second wave of Jewish farming here after World War Two. Some descendants of the old Covenant families, including Isaac and Miriam, took part in that one, along with refugees who'd survived the Holocaust. Those were boom years for chicken farming here. Sales at good prices at the soup factory in Arborville and in the kosher markets in Philly and New

York. In the early fifties, I'd have given you even odds that, if you ordered matzo ball soup at a deli in Manhattan, the chicken in it came from right around here."

Down a narrow lane, Peter spotted what appeared to be a row of abandoned, unpainted dwellings under a single roof. "What the heck is that?" he said. "It looks like a bunch of jammed-together sharecropper shacks."

Peter heard a note of wry satisfaction in Ilana's raspy laugh.

"Chicken coops, Peter!" she said. "Fifteen years ago, you'd have seen about two hundred white Leghorns pecking in the dirt over there. Haven't you shed your delusions yet about Avram as some kind of bred-in-the-Hamptons Jewish princeling? You know what else you'd have seen fifteen years ago, not here but at Isaac and Miriam's place? You'd have seen Avram in coveralls, heading out to the chicken houses to flush and scour the algae and chicken poop out of the waterers. Did Avram ever treat you to his sneer of profound distaste? Well, he perfected it performing that chore."

Peter stared back at the row of tumbledown coops. He tried to peel away in his mind Rabby's languorous mannerisms and lacerating snubs. He tried to picture the man he had known as, instead, a child standing there alone—utterly alone, lacking any firm mooring to family, class, position in the world. And he couldn't do it. Freeze-frame syndrome, he thought. Captain Cottingham was right. Even knowing I've got it, I can't work free of it.

"When the door finally opened for DP immigration in 1948, the law put orphans first in line," Meir said. "Jewish families all over the country would've bought lottery tickets, if they'd had to, for a chance to adopt this kid who'd been saved from the Lodz ghetto. But neither my dad nor I wanted him adopted outside the family."

Ilana swatted the back of her brother's head.

"Right," he said. "Lani was almost thirteen then, and she wanted that even less than we did. At least, she was more vocal about wanting us to find some way to take him in. Now, between my coming home from

Europe in the summer of forty-six and the start of DP immigration two years later, I'd walked right up to the verge of what would have been a train wreck of a marriage. The closer we got to the wedding, the more wreckage I could see piling up down the tracks. But in those days I still clung to this prim notion that a promise was a promise. Vestige of military honor, I'd have called it then."

"And now?" his sister said.

"Arrogance. Callousness, too, because that marriage would have promptly gone to smash, and my fiancée would have borne the wounds of that. She really did come from that cut of Jewish society that Avram pretended to belong to. She started to balk in advance at the constricted life she'd lead as wife of a deputy county prosecutor. Then when Truman signed the Displaced Persons Act, giving orphans first priority under the law, I told her I wanted us to adopt a kid who'd been plucked from the Lodz ghetto. At that point, she pretty much turned around and left. It was like watching a show horse canter away from a rickety barn door."

"By then, Miriam knew she could never have a kid the usual way," Ilana said. "With the bust-up of Meir's engagement, Miriam's sterility looked like our good fortune."

"Remember what I told you about Isaac and Miriam agreeing, after Avram turned up at the hospital in Vienna, to take him in as a foster child, if we needed that as a stopgap?" Meir said. "Well, when we could finally bring Avram over, we did need that. I'd expected to be married and able to adopt, and now I couldn't. Their offer to foster him held as firm as ever, though what they really wanted was a kid they could adopt."

"But think of what did happen for them—for Miriam, especially," Ilana said. "Avram was six years old when she first saw him. For her, it must have been as if the child she'd despaired of ever having had materialized in front of her, dressed in the third-hand jeans and polo shirt that were all he had to wear on the troop ship that brought him over from Bremen."

I've heard this before, or something very much like it, Peter thought. It wasn't in a voice like this woman's, smoky-sounding and resonant with her own share in the fear and disappointment and joy she is talking about. What I heard was spoken in a voice a little clipped but not cold, a voice unburdened by the anguish it described but fixed on the problem of healing it. It was Stephie's voice, when she figured out why my mom threatened to bury me in the idiots' row.

"And you were, what, twelve or thirteen when he came over?" Peter asked Ilana. "And, from the first, did he think of you as what he ended up calling you, his aunt?"

"God, no," Ilana scoffed. "For those first years, we were the big sister and little brother that neither of us would ever have had otherwise. Until I finished high school, I practically moved in down here every summer. Isaac and Miriam were fine with that. Plus by staying here, I helped free up time for them to take summer courses at Glassboro. They were both able to finish teaching degrees before I started college. By the time I was sixteen, I'd mastered the chore routine, and I had Avram drilled in the parts he could do. Between us, we could get through a whole day unaided, from early-morning feeding to cleaning and candling the eggs to sorting them for size. Do you know all the things you have to do to make eggs market-ready?"

"Indeed I do," Peter said. "Smaller scale. But yeah."

"Well, that was our days. And every evening, unless it stormed, Avram and I would grab inner tubes from the tool shed and hike to the river. When Miriam was home and had time, she'd go tubing with us too. And on the days when they didn't need Avram and me for chores, Isaac would drive us into town and drop us off at his sister's house. Then we'd spend the whole day with a roving pack of Jewish kids. There'd be about a dozen of us. We always minded our manners, understand, but we could pick even a well-stocked kitchen clean. Some of those kids were local, but those tended to peel off and go home at some point during the day. It was the out-of-towners, kids from as far as Mississippi, who formed the hard core of that pack. They'd come to Arborville to spend time with grandparents, see. I think they found their grandparents' households so dull that only exhaustion and hunger could drive them back there at night. By the end of the day, I'd call Isaac to tell him where to pick us up."

"So no summers at a toney camp in the Berkshires?" Peter said.

"God, no," she said. "Is that what he told you? Well, I guess he had to, to sell you on that whole made-up version of himself, with never a speck of chicken shit on his shoes. It was during those summers, roaming with that pack of kids from one Jewish household to the next, that he discovered his gift for that. I mean, not just for making up stories, but for elaborating and refining them until even smart, skeptical people would buy into them. The first one I heard him tell was to a couple of city kids who visited us out here. Avram told them that snakes from the river sometimes got in the house, and that when Miriam found one hanging from a coat hanger in her bedroom closet, she told Isaac to get a goat. Why? Because goats can hypnotize snakes and then trample them with their hooves. One of the kids asked for proof, and Avram told him the pupils in snakes' eyes run vertically. Then Avram coaxed those kids close enough to Isaac's goat to see that the pupils in the goat's eyes ran horizontally. And that's all it takes, he told those kids. When a goat locks eyes with a snake, it's all over for the snake. Of course, there never had been snakes in the house, and Isaac kept the goat to control weeds and to rent out for breeding. But Avram sold those kids on that wacky tale."

Listening to Ilana, Peter slowly shook his head, thinking, *This isn't it. None of what we're saying gets at whatever Rabby wanted to happen once I'd tracked this woman down. There has to be something else.*

Meir turned down what had once been a gravel road, as Peter could tell from the popcorn-like clacks beneath the floorboard. Meir turned in at a white clapboard house roofed with green tiles that had begun to mildew and curl. He parked next to a rickety, carousel-like clothesline apparatus. A man's blue work shirt and several women's undergarments hung from its lone unbroken strand of clothesline.

"Well, I'd planned to leave you here," Meir said. "But the car's gone. That could mean they're both out."

"Doesn't matter," Ilana said. "I've got the house key, and Isaac's truck key will be on the hook in the stairwell."

"All right, then," Meir said. "I'll stop back through town at the M and H and use Nathan's coupon to gas up and then head north. You sure there's nothing else you need? How about you, Peter?"

"I'm fine," Peter said. He patted the worn duffel bag balanced across his lap. "Everything I need right here," he said.

"There is one thing you could do for me, dear brother," Ilana said.

Meir hitched himself upward to smile down at her over the seat back. "Anything at all," he said.

"You can get your substantial hindquarters out of the car. You too, Peter. And both of you can slide your seats as far forward as they'll go. And don't you dare look at me as I extricate myself from my brother's latest sex toy."

Peter climbed out and pulled his seat forward. Across the top of the car he saw Meir's eye-roll of annoyance.

"I perform all you ask cheerfully, my dear," he said. "In return, I ask that you stop implying I have sex with a machine."

"Well, all I know is you've test-driven three women, only one of whom deigned, briefly, to become your wife," Ilana said, wheezing with effort as she backed out of Peter's side of the car. "And since you apparently gave up on marriage, you've had three toy-sized cars. Pardon me if I suspect some continuity there."

Meir broke into the same kind of open, generous laugh that had now and again broken through Rabby's pose of aloof disdain. Meir came around the car, still laughing, and embraced his sister.

"You've met Julia, my dear," he said. "And you know perfectly well that's no test drive. Now, when is it you fly out?"

"Wednesday. I've told you twice. Write it on your cuff or something."

"And you'll stop by and see me, won't you, before you head out to Kennedy?"

"Unless the public decency patrol has caught up with you by then."

Meir looked at Peter, squinting a little.

"You have a little time left before you report to Fort Bragg, right?" he said. "Call me before you head down there, okay? There's something more you ought to know, I think. You might want to follow up on it. So call me. Please." He reached beneath his sweater to fish a business card from a shirt pocket.

Peter and Ilana watched the pallid dust cloud raised by the little green car until they could no longer hear the trip-hammer sound of its engine.

"He hides it well, doesn't he?" Ilana said. "And all the time he's got to be thinking, 'If I'd just done this or that differently,' you know?"

She led the way to a side entrance to the house, where she pulled a folded sheet of notepaper from behind the wooden frame of a screen door.

"Oh, they're making an egg run, and then going to the cemetery," she said. "Well, we could just wait here until they come back. Or we could go up to the cemetery. They were probably hoping we'd do that, if we got here in time. It's close enough to walk, but we can take the truck. That's where Avram's buried, see. But I should let you choose. Maybe what you want, what you need, is just to go inside and sleep."

Peter brought his dwindling mental energy to a rapid focus.

"What I need right now, Ilana, is for you to tell me whatever it was that Rabby thought was so important I had to track you down, all the way to your kibbutz if necessary, so the two of us could somehow deal with it. All that history of how he got rescued as an infant by a real woman named Antonina—maybe that's a big part of what he wanted me to know. But if that was all of it, he could have just left directions for me to call Meir. But Rabby's note didn't mention Meir. It said I had to contact you. So whatever he thought it was urgent for me to know had to be very particular to you and him. Now, before I sleep or go see his grave or anything else, I need you to tell me what that is."

The afternoon had grown warm. Peter shucked off the windbreaker he'd worn on the bus and stuffed it in the duffel bag. Ilana tilted her head and gave him a long look that seemed more amused than critical. Finally she snorted and said, "Yes, he would do that, wouldn't he?"

"Who?" Peter said.

"Who do you think we're talking about? Here, give me that," she said, pointing at the duffel bag. She took it from him and stripped the scarf off her shoulders and draped it across the duffel. "Wait here," she said. "We'll walk to the cemetery, then ride back with Isaac and Miriam. I need to change first."

When she came out of the door, she wore sneakers, jeans, a long-sleeved yellow flannel shirt and a long-billed, tight-fitting khaki cap.

"We can cut through the woods," she said. "The bridge is a little over a mile. The cemetery is on a rise beyond the bridge."

She led him past a set of four chicken coops beneath a common roof. Each coop had a big rectangular screen in front and a small flap door at the bottom for the chickens to get in and out. About thirty white Leghorns pecked haphazardly in pea gravel inside a fenced-off space in front of one coop. The chickens squawked and skittered as Peter and Ilana squeezed between the fence and a shed.

"This is the only coop they use anymore," she said. "They hand-deliver eggs to about a dozen customers in town. Nowadays they do it more for the chance to socialize than for the money."

Ilana led the way through a patch of tall grass. Then, suddenly, they were walking soundlessly on a bed of brown pine needles beneath tall, widely spaced trees. A few shafts of sunlight reached the forest floor.

"If you told me right now I was hiking in the Carolina Sandhills, I'd buy it,' Peter said.

"I thought you might like this," Ilana said. "We're at the southernmost tip of the Barrens."

She was a fast walker. Peter had a rolled Ace bandage in the duffel bag, and he wished he'd wrapped his knee before they set out. While he was berating himself about this, he stumbled over a tree root and fell forward, twisting a little so his good knee and right elbow took the impact.

Ilana turned and gave him an openmouthed, mortified stare. Her cap made her curls stick out like bronze springs, and he couldn't stifle a double bark of laughter.

"You look like Medusa of the Pine Barrens," he said, standing up slowly to make sure his knee was still stable.

"Oh, are you hurt?" she said, hurrying back and holding his elbow while he found his balance.

"No, I'm fine," he said. "I just need to slow down a bit. I was in the hospital with a screwed-up knee before I shipped for the States. The knee's still a little wobbly."

"Oh, we should have driven!" she said. "We'll go back and get the truck."

"No, no, I'd rather walk," he said. "It's just—can you walk a little slower? Then I can keep up, no problem. Hey, it's kind of like a cathedral in here, isn't it? I mean, the way the light angles in through the trees."

She walked on for a while with her head down. She glanced back a couple of times to make sure he was keeping pace, but she said nothing.

"Of course, you must know a lot more than I do about cathedrals," Peter said. "I mean, assuming Rabby told the truth about you getting enamored with Catholicism, and choosing a Catholic college, and coming close to converting. I've never even set foot in a Catholic church."

She turned, and her expression had switched from solicitude to anger. She stopped him with a hand against his chest, then leaned close and spoke in a measured, even tone.

"Peter, I will tell you what you're asking for when I'm ready," she said. "I'll do that as soon as we get to the river. Please stop trying to draw me out now with mindless chatter."

At the edge of the woods they crossed a fallow field littered with last year's cornstalks. Then they stepped onto a paved trail that ran atop old railroad tracks. Bits of track showed through the asphalt.

"Used to be, this was part of the railroad that connected farmers here to markets in Philadelphia and New York," Ilana said. "Now it's just a hiking and bike trail."

Peter followed her along the trail and out onto what had once been a railroad bridge. For such a short bridge over a small river, its rusting iron superstructure seemed overly grandiose. A wire barricade blocked access to the tracks, but a walkway of pierced steel planking ran along one side of the bridge, above the level of the tracks.

Ilana stopped in the middle of the bridge and put her hands atop the outer rail and gazed out over the river. The reddish-brown water reminded Peter of a freshly steeped pot of strong tea.

"Whatever that stain is, it's not mud," he said.

Ilana looked back at him and smiled. "The water always looks dark like that," she said. "We call it 'cedar water.' That color comes from tannins in the scrub oaks and cedars along the banks. See that beach over there?"

She pointed to a strip of sand along the bank. Peter thought that only in the soft haze cast by a childhood memory could that be called a beach.

"That's where Avram and Miriam and I would go tubing on summer afternoons," she said. "Sometimes Miriam's younger sister Sonia would bring her two kids out from town, and we'd all pile into an enormous inner tube that Isaac had picked up somewhere. It must have been a tube for a long-haul truck. At the kibbutz, I have a photo on my nightstand of all six of us out on the water in that inner tube. I don't remember who took the picture—probably Isaac. That little photo has the power of a religious icon for me. It must have been taken the first year Avram was here, when he was just six. He's got one arm slung around my neck, but the other arm is outside the tube with his fingers trailing in the water, and he's smiling down at that hand. And for all the years since then, whenever I heard the word 'rescued' and thought about why it's such a powerful word for me, that image would pop into my head. But now when I go back home and look at that photo on my nightstand, what will it say to me? Will it say something like, 'reprieved, but only until fate sharpened its axe'?"

"*Rio de las Animas Perdidas*," Peter said. "We're all afloat on that one."

Ilana squinted at him, and her mouth wrinkled in what looked like tentative amusement. "Well, I'll have to guess that's from a Spanish translation of Dante," she said.

"No, it's a real river, out in Colorado," he said. "The Spaniards named it that: river of lost souls. No one knows why. My commander in Vietnam owns a little ranch that overlooks the Animas. He says he leans on a fence rail sometimes and just looks out at the river, the way we're doing now."

"And did you like your commander?" she said.

"Very much. He did slap me with something called an Article Fifteen, which is a low-level form of military punishment. But he had to do that. Plus if he hadn't done it, I couldn't be here now. He took Rabby's death really hard, and he asked me to find out all I could about why Rabby seemed almost to orchestrate it."

"I see," Ilana said softly. She turned back toward the river and removed her cap and shook out her curls. Then she loosened the sizing strap and pulled the cap back on her head. "Well, orchestrate might be a fair enough word," she said. "If it is, I'm not sure Avram was the maestro of it, though he took a star turn as soloist at the end. Trace it back and you might say the German commander in Lodz drew up that composition, if we want to call it that. He had the ghetto's children shipped off to Chelmno and gassed, just so their parents could keep turning out uniforms and parts for field radios a little longer. Who else, then, had a hand in orchestrating Avram's death? Antonina, certainly. She rescued him in the only way possible, and who could fault her for that? But she also made sure the details of that rescue were recorded and passed on, and those details became a theme that ran all through Avram's life. Others? Well, my brother, of course. No one more than Meir. At every point well-intentioned, at every point blameless, at every point moving the music onward. Once he heard the finale building, he was powerless to stop it. But one other set of hands meddled in that composition. Their meddling took the bare facts of Avram's rescue and the lawyer's brief for Antonina's heroism and force-fed them into Avram's mind and heart."

Still gripping the walkway's top rail with both hands, she tilted her face toward Peter. Her smile had a light challenge in it, as if she meant merely to pose an amusing puzzle.

"And who do you think did this?" she said. "Whose hands could have given such a drastic turn to a life that was proceeding quite well before this intruder mucked it up? They were my hands, Peter. That's why Avram asked you to seek me out. He wanted you to know it."

When Meir returned from Europe in 1946, Ilana said, she was just ten. Her brother had told her the short, sanitized version of the story. He said a woman named Antonina Tarnowski, a fighter with the Polish resistance, had rescued an infant who was the grandson of their father's brother. With a nun's help, Antonina had somehow gotten the child, named Avram, through the barbed wire fence surrounding the Lodz ghetto. Then Avram had survived three years in hiding, cared for by Polish Catholic families. Now he was in a refugee camp in Germany, and her brother and father would do all they could to bring him to America.

That was all Meir had told her. In her imagination, Ilana had cast the unnamed nun in the lead role in the rescue of little Avram. She pictured in this role a young nun on whom she had, at the time, a terrible crush. The nun was her social studies teacher, Ilana's mother having decided a Catholic girls' school was superior to the available Jewish school for girls.

When Avram arrived, Ilana recruited him to play the part of the female soldier in the rescue, there being no male roles, other than the child himself, in the bare-bones rescue story that her brother had told her. One of her dolls filled the need for an infant wrapped in a small, ragged blanket. Ilana, of course, was the brave Polish nun. At the farm, they sometimes played that game day after day, always passing the doll through a barbed wire fence. After a couple of years, Ilana had aged out of her taste for the rescue game. Only later did she realize how deep an imprint it had left on Avram's imagination to play, at age six and seven, the role of the woman who had rescued him from certain death.

"Then, during the summer when Avram turned nine, he decided we should revive that game just long enough to accomplish a real rescue," she said. "Miriam had badgered Isaac to get rid of the goat, and Isaac promised he'd take it to the slaughterhouse in Arborville. The goat liked to butt Miriam when she was hanging out laundry. She was sick of having to constantly look over her shoulder while she held up a sheet or a pair of pants to the clothesline with clothespins in her mouth, just to make sure the goat hadn't zeroed in on her backside. Isaac usually had the goat out on a long chain during the day, so it could graze, but he kept it in a pen next to the chicken coops at night. After he promised Miriam he'd have it slaughtered, he kept it penned all the time. Avram knew where Isaac kept his wire cutters, and he woke me up late one night and said now was the time. He told me he was Antonin Tarnowski of the Polish resistance, and he would guarantee my safety as we did our best to save an innocent life. I asked if he meant Antonina, and he said no, Antonin was a man's name, and his commander had chosen to send a man for this job. We went out to the pen, and he handed me the wire cutters, and he said, 'set him free, sister. And may the Lord forever bless you.' And I snipped through four strands of barbed wire, and we shooed the goat out. Isaac was furious, of course—it took him most of a day to track down the goat. But Avram confessed it was all his idea, and Miriam could never stay angry at Avram more than two seconds. So the goat survived. Isaac just put him on a shorter chain during the day and in a larger pen at night."

Over time, Ilana said, without any formal decision being made, everyone accepted that Avram would stay with Isaac and Miriam, and he became their child in every sense except the purely legal.

"The original plan was for Avram to live in Arborville with the Kleinfields only until Meir and his wife-to-be were ready to adopt him," she said. "Well, his first wife-to-be turned out to be a wife that never was. The next one did marry him, but it took her less than four years to opt out, or up, by leaving him and hooking up with an investment banker. Why? One reason, maybe, philandering on Meir's part. I wouldn't put that past him. But I think the greater problem was that he kept choosing women who wanted more glitz and social standing than he could give them. As far as I could tell, Meir never even put the idea of adopting Avram on the table with Rona, the one he did marry. For which I blame my brother not at all. He read correctly the odds against his household ever becoming a stable home for Avram, and he judged the best thing was to leave him where he was. I feel sure Isaac and Miriam would rather have adopted Avram, but they weren't going to rub Meir's nose into his inability to offer the kid something better. Julia, the woman he mentioned before he drove off, is the one he should have married in the first place, even if she is Presbyterian or something. She was a public defender when they got together. I think initially they felt marriage would complicate their professional lives. Now she does legal work for state social services in Hackensack, but they've never tied the knot. Julia's been right for Meir, but whether they married was beside the point where Avram was concerned. Avram was already in high school when Meir and Julia hooked up. So Avram has all along remained a foster child, and his name remained Rabinowitz, and his home remained here with Isaac and Miriam."

"How did Avram feel about that?" Peter said.

"Probably he felt a variety of things about it," Ilana said. "Ranging from pain that his only blood relatives seemed to want to keep him at a distance to outright thank-God gratitude that he was instead living with people who loved him as deeply as any parents could love a child."

"What about his claim later on to have a father who was managing partner of a big Manhattan law firm?" Peter said. "Is that what he wished were true?"

"I think that part's pretty straightforward," Ilana said. "Beginning back when he was in the DP camp in Germany, he understood his fate was in the hands of a man who was some sort of lawyer, and that this man was the nearest thing he had to a father. In later years, he just dressed out that early image of Meir in ways people like you might find convincing."

"And I bought that part completely," Peter said, shaking his head. "I mean, the whole upper crust image."

"Well, he enjoyed testing the limits of what his listeners might find credible," Ilana said. "But the rich-boy pose—that's just icing. The more densely layered part of how he felt about his life lies, I think, in that tale about his family's rescue from the mob in Odessa. The parents in that part, you know, are named Isaac and Miriam. Unscramble that tale and it might tell us how he felt about growing up where he did, and with whom."

"A little kid named Avram figures in toward the end of that part, right?" Peter said. "When Rabby told us the story, he called Avram a little shit."

Ilana uttered a small gasp. Then she shut her eyes and groaned. "Yes, yes, I can't be surprised," she said. "So the harm I caused tormented him until the end."

She seemed to tighten her grip on the rail, and she took several slow, deep breaths, like a high diver nerving herself for the plunge.

"In 1955, our father died," she said. "Meir and I had been with him at a Seder dinner at the school where he'd been principal. Dad said he'd walk home with some friends. Our house wasn't far from the school, and he never wanted to drive on any holy day. On the way home, he had a heart attack, and he died on the roadside. That was in early April, and Meir wasn't sure whether Dad had already filed his taxes. Dad always did that himself, so there was no accountant we could ask. I was in my second year then at the College of Saint Elizabeth, and it was Easter break, so I was home. Meir was busy at work, and he asked me to look in Dad's study for his tax files. He said if Dad had mailed his return, there'd be a copy in the file, together with a post office receipt.

"I found the tax folder, and sure enough Dad had filed. In fact, he'd filed in early March, as he always had in the past, because until that year the filing date was in March. But his tax records were in a bottom drawer of his desk, and before I looked there I opened a top drawer, and I spotted a folder labeled 'Avram.' And I thought just for a moment about whether I should open it, but it seemed silly even to wonder, since everything in that desk was our father's papers, and at some point Meir and I would have to go through them all.

"It was just a brown manila file folder with a single typed document inside. I could tell right away what it was, because I'd heard Meir mention that he'd nominated the Polish woman who'd rescued Avram to an honor roll of people who'd risked their lives to save Jews. It's called 'The Righteous Among the Nations.' The Holocaust memorial in Jerusalem, Yad Vashem, set it up in the early fifties, and as soon as Meir heard about it he sent in a letter nominating Antonina Tarnowski. When he told me that, I of course berated him for not nominating the nun. And he said he couldn't because he didn't know her name. When I asked him what he'd written about this Tarnowski woman in his nomination letter, he said it was what I already knew: that she and a nun had rescued a baby by somehow whisking him through a barbed wire fence. Well, what I found in Dad's desk drawer was a copy of that letter, but the description of Avram's rescue in it wasn't the sanitized version that Meir had fobbed off on me. What he'd written spelled out the nightmarish details, just like Meir did for you today back at the diner.

"Now you'd think, wouldn't you, that it might dawn on me why he'd fed me that grade-school version back when I was ten, and why he stuck with it when I asked him about it again five years later? Out of brotherly concern for my tender sensibilities, do you think? Well, maybe some of that. But how much more likely was it that Meir knew Avram would eventually want exact answers? He'd want to know why he alone had survived and now lived a life of safety and comfort, even if it was just on a New Jersey chicken farm. He'd ask how, exactly, he'd ended up on that wooden pallet where Meir almost tripped over him, when his parents and sister and everyone else who could have meant much to him had perished. Wouldn't you think it would dawn on me why Meir would try to limit the number of people who could give those detailed answers to a thirteen-year-old boy?"

"Before that, had Avram ever asked you for those sorts of answers?" Peter said.

"A few times, yes. But not often, because it was obvious I didn't know any more than he did. I remember he asked me a time or two how he'd come by that little scar on his thigh, and I said he must have gotten it in the DP camp or back in Poland when he was too young to remember."

"I think I know where you're headed, Ilana," Peter said. "But I think you're wrong to believe—"

She cut him off. "Oh, how I burned with indignation on Avram's behalf when I read that letter," she said with a laugh. "Indignation stoked by a paper I'd written at school on laws that deny adoptees information about their birth parents. Had Meir been there then, I'd have mounted my righteous pedestal. 'This is a story as heroic as it is awful!' I'd have told him. 'And it's Avram's birthright! How dare you withhold it from him?'"

"So you told him yourself," Peter said. "Told Avram, I mean."

"Oh, no-o, Peter." She shook her head with mock solemnity. "No-o. That would have cheated poor Avram of a primary source of the pride he deserved to feel for the part he played in his own rescue. A minor part, but essential."

"I see," Peter said. "So you gave him that copy."

"That's right." Gripping the rail, staring out at the dark-hued water, she almost spat the words. "That's right. Because my little cousin deserved the immense satisfaction of knowing his name would be preserved as a footnote in the archives of Yad Vashem. The pain and turmoil that the contents of that letter might set swirling through the mind of a thirteen-year-old child seem a small price to pay for such a source of lasting pride, wouldn't you say? So I drove down here and gave it to him at the end of Easter break, before I headed back to school at Morristown. And you know? I didn't even stick around to see what his face showed when he read it. I just said something like, 'here's something that'll really interest you,' and I hopped in the car and drove off. Mustn't be late for curfew at a woman's college, you know."

Peter heard a clattering sound from the end of the walkway where he and Ilana had entered. Two boys who looked about 12 years old were rolling their bikes toward them on the steel planking. The basket on the handlebars of each bike contained books and a baseball glove.

"Hi," the boy in front said shyly.

"School day over?" Peter said.

"Ye-aah," both boys answered in an oddly drawn-out tone, as if it were something to be lamented.

"You gonna play ball while daylight lasts?" Peter said.

"Yeah," the one in front said. "Probably can't find enough guys to make up teams, though."

"What's the least you'd need?" Peter said. "Five on a side?"

"We almost never get that many out where we live, except sometimes on Saturdays," the other boy said.

The boy in front squinted up at Peter. "You in the Army?" he said.

"How'd you guess?" Peter said.

The boy pointed at Peter's chest. Peter saw that his dog tags had flipped out between two buttons when he fell in the forest, and hung outside his shirt.

"You been in the war?" the first boy said.

"I've been at the war," Peter said. "It'd be a stretch to say I was in it."

Both boys leaned their bikes against the railing and came closer to look at Peter's dog tags.

"My dad says it looks like that war will never end until they kill every gook over there," the first boy said. "Did you kill any gooks?"

"I didn't," Peter said. "I clobbered a Vietnamese officer during a soccer game, because I didn't like the way he was playing. That was a mistake, because at the time he was officially on our side—in the war, I mean. Later on, it turned out he was probably on the other side, but there was no way to make certain. Turns out the Viet Cong were as confused about that as we were, because they killed both that Vietnamese officer and an American soldier from right around here who was trying to protect him."

The first boy frowned and lowered his eyes and started to gently kick the front tire of his bike. "That doesn't even make any sense," he said softly.

"You're right, it doesn't," Peter said. "I'm sure there's a lot about that war that does make sense, but the part I saw close-up didn't."

"You want to play ball with us?" the second boy said. He was smaller and darker than the other boy, and Peter wondered if he was Jewish.

Peter leaned close to the smaller boy and dropped his voice. "Tell you the truth, I do," he said. "I don't think she'll let me, though."

"She your sister or something?" the first boy asked.

Ilana laughed. "Or something," she said. "Where do you boys play ball?"

"You know where the old synagogue is?" the first boy said. "Up the hill over there? We've laid out some base paths in a field next to that."

"It's got wheat stubble on it," the second one said. "We trimmed down the base paths with a weed cutter. You don't want to slide on it, though."

"We'll be up that way in a few minutes," Ilana said. "I don't know if we'll have time for him to play ball, though."

The boys rolled their bikes on across the bridge and pedaled up the path on the far side.

"Avram was just a little older than those two," Ilana said softly, "when he read that his parents and sister had been shot to death trying to climb the razor wire surrounding a ghetto, right after his mother had pitched him over that wire. And he learned he'd cleared it safely, except for that little nick on his thigh. All highly appropriate information to unload on a child, don't you think?"

"And you were, what, just nineteen?" Peter said. "And, hell, a case could be made for letting the kid know all that stuff, even the worst parts. You felt then that it was his birthright, correct? Well, I can't say you were wrong."

Ilana shook her head steadily as he was speaking. "No, no, look," she said. "I could see the change in him right away, the next time I came down here. I could see how deep inside him this had sunk. And only then did I realize why Meir took such care to guard it not only from Avram but from me, because he couldn't trust me. Meir must have shown that letter to Isaac and Miriam, or at least told them what it contained. If anyone had the right to decide when Avram was ready to absorb the truth as that letter spelled it out, it was those two, who'd loved and cared for him more than anyone. And they'd chosen not to do it."

"Well, what did Avram say?" Peter said. "I mean, in later years? Did he ever accuse you of fracturing his tender psyche?"

"Oh, no, he never accused me. Avram was never one to traffic much in resentment or hate."

"I'm not so sure about that," Peter said. "I've seen him work up a pretty good head of hate against a Vietnamese lieutenant."

"No hate, no hate," she said, shaking her head. "The first change I saw in him, after he read that letter, was just that he grew so quiet. And he'd walk past people, me included, like we weren't there. That worried me enough that I spent as much time as I could down here that summer, even though I was interning four days a week at social services in Hackensack. That summer, a girl who was about five years older than Avram—someone none of us knew, though she was from Arborville—hanged herself right here on this bridge. She threw the rope over that upper beam and climbed over this rail. Well, Avram's bedroom was next to mine, on the same side of the house as the chicken coops. One night not long after we read about the suicide, I heard what sounded like footsteps. I waited a while and heard nothing else, and I'd nearly gone to sleep, but then I thought to check Avram's bedroom. Sure enough, he was gone. So I pulled on my jeans and sneakers and ran all the way down here. And he was out here like we are now, just leaning on the rail and looking out at the water. He seemed perfectly calm. He even smiled at me, I remember. But it was like his face and the smile on it were a facade and the real Avram was perched up somewhere behind his face like a prisoner in an isolation cell."

Starting that same summer, Ilana said, Avram came up with an embryonic version of the tale that would ultimately stretch from Warsaw to Odessa. A figure named Antonina played a leading role in it. Ilana could easily trace this Antonina back to the role Avram had assigned himself a few years earlier, when they'd rescued Cyrus the goat from his barbed wire pen. She could also see that Avram embraced this Antonina figure more as a desperate necessity than as a mask worn in a game.

"And what's wrong with that?" Peter said. "He called himself a fabulist, right? So it's not like he didn't recognize that yarn was a creation. Look, maybe you fed him the whole, awful story of his real history a year or two earlier than Meir would have, but regardless, he would've gotten it. And let's say it caused him deeper pain than he could put into words right away, which it would have done whenever he learned it. And then what does he do? He says to the pain: 'Fuck you, you think I can't find words?' And he does find them, and he keeps finding better and better words, until an audience can find beauty in it and never recognize that it's just brutal pain transmuted by an act of will. How's that different from what any real artist does?"

Ilana kept gazing out over the water and shaking her head, but she smiled faintly. "He did do a craftsmanlike job of shaping that story," she said. "He might have sampled from Isaac's and Miriam's family tales, and maybe from things he'd heard from other families around here, the Covenant families. But always looming large in his telling of it was this mythical Antonina, guardian angel of the Rabinowitz clan. He tested out the story on me for a while, but he quickly gave that up, probably because he could see how much it distressed me to hear it when I knew I'd implanted in him the need to tell it. Once I started work full-time at social services I wasn't down here nearly as much, so I don't know whether he tried to foist that story off as fact on any of his high school friends. If he did, I suspect he might have gotten away with it, since most of them assumed Isaac and Miriam were his real parents, and stories of hairsbreadth escapes during pogroms were pretty common among Jewish families around here. But of course, with people who knew him, he couldn't use the piece that perhaps he valued most, since it bound him so closely to the rest of the story. He couldn't lay claim to the name Antonin."

"He really did go to Princeton, right?" Peter said. "Did he wheel out that story there? Perhaps to inspire wonder in, say, women he'd like to seduce?"

"Oh, I hope so!" Ilana said, laughing. "Except, you see, women weren't admitted to Princeton when Avram was there. So he'd have had to deploy his fable-selling powers on townies. They might have been easier to con than women who were his intellectual peers. With fellow male students, I'll bet he dined out well and often on that story. As a graduation gift, I sent him airfare to come to the kibbutz, and when I took him out to dinner in Haifa with some of the other teachers, I asked if he remembered the Antonina story. I wasn't trying to tear open an old wound, understand. I was frankly just curious. After finishing college, I'd worked three years for state social services, and then I'd emigrated. So I didn't know whether he'd shelved that story since the last time I'd heard him tell it, which would've been when he was fourteen or fifteen."

"And was he rusty?" Peter said.

"Rusty? God, Peter, he'd refined that tale to the point that, if I'd heard it cold, without knowing the tormented history behind it, I'd have believed it. I chalked that up as a legacy of an Ivy League schooling, where your fellow students will zero in on the weak spots in any argument or on fiction dressed out as fact. Still, he never used that story cynically. The closer he could come to convincing others it was true, the more he believed it himself. Not that he was ever delusional, understand. He knew very well that his story of Antonina was, at bottom, his own creation. But he also knew his life, or at least his mental health, depended on it."

"But even then, he couldn't present himself under the name Antonin, could he?" Peter said. "I mean, the way he'd done when he was first trying out the story on you, back in the goat caper?"

"No," Ilana said. "In Arborville, Princeton, Haifa too, he still had to be just Avram Rabinowitz—one beneficiary, but only one, of this Polish woman's bravery. He couldn't yet assign himself a role in the story as her namesake. To do that, he had to exile himself to a place where the people around him had no prior knowledge of his real name. In a setting like that, he could buckle on Antonina's name like a breastplate with '*in hoc signo*' inscribed on it. He could make them believe, and make himself believe, that he was on some kind of quest to prove his right to wear it."

"So that's what took him to Vietnam?" Peter said.

Something caught Ilana's attention. She shaded her eyes, looking toward high ground on the west side of the river, where Peter could make out a pair of brick pillars connected by an ornate grillwork arc.

"I think I saw their car," she said. "I think they just got to the cemetery. We should go up."

"All right," Peter said. "But tell me first: You're saying he went to Vietnam so he could turn himself into a living, breathing character in a tale he'd already perfected in every other respect. And once he'd stepped into that tale, he figured he could sort of pick up the saber that fell from Antonina's hand. Have I got that right?"

"You judge for yourself," she said. "And it sounds like you already have. Look. He went to Princeton on full scholarship, and he graduated at the top of his law school class. He could have had his pick of jobs in Trenton or North Jersey. Meir would have brought him on as an assistant prosecutor. Meir knew the commander of an Army Reserve unit in Trenton, who signed him up to insulate him from the draft. And once Avram is mustered in, what does he do next? He volunteers for Vietnam."

"And all that's somehow your fault?"

"'Somehow' my fault?" she said. "Yes, I think that's the perfect word. 'Somehow,' what happened to Avram, up to and including his lying dead in the cemetery up there, is my fault."

"So that's it!" Peter said, pounding his hand hard against the top rail. "That's why he wanted me to come find you!"

"And I already told you that," Ilana said. Her voice wavered a little. "He wanted you to know it was me. Maybe he was worried you'd feel guilt—I don't know."

"Christ, Ilana. Rabby wouldn't want anything of the kind. First off, I'm pretty sure that when he wrote that note, he didn't plan on dying. He wrote it so that, on the off chance he did die, I could come and try to carp some sense into you. If we're listing everybody who 'somehow' contributed to his death, then include me, for sure. Listen, you heard me tell those kids I'd made a whacked-out charge onto a soccer field and assaulted a Vietnamese officer? Well, what I did that day touched off a chain of events that ended with Rabby getting shot on our rooftop. How bad do I feel about that? Bad enough, but there was no way I could foresee it, and the only penance I'll ever do for it is to serve out my full two years as a draftee. If we're looking for what a keen legal mind like Rabby's would call the proximate agent of his death, then there's no contest: title goes to Lieutenant Pham, that officer I clobbered with my rifle butt. If we want the broad field of candidates, surely we can't omit Antonina for saving Avram's life in a way certain to traumatize him once he found out about it. And let's not absolve his mother. She should've known it would heighten his future mental anguish if she pitched him over a razor wire fence at midnight, and then got herself and his sister and father killed by trying to climb it. Looks like a lot of people who touched his life contributed to his death 'somehow.' What you did hardly ranks."

She had turned her amber-flecked eyes on him with a look of disdain.

"'Carp,'" she said. "I had never heard that word used in just that way. It does fit, though, Peter, for the thing you seem to do best."

"Well, just to cement your opinion on that score, what's with the nun thing?"

She frowned, then snorted with exasperation. "I made that clear," she said. "I was very fond of a teacher who was a—"

"No, I mean now," he said. "When I first saw you through the bus window this morning, wearing that skirt and dark blue scarf, I thought for a moment you were a nun. Rabby always referred to his Aunt Nina as a crazy half-Catholic. I know you went to Catholic schools up through college, so maybe it's just that. But tell me: Have you ever been married, or anything close to it? You gave Meir hell about his spotty performance on the marital front. What about yours?"

She turned her eyes back out over the river. "That's none of your business, Peter," she said. "We should go up to the cemetery now."

"No, no, listen," he said. "First let's get to the bottom of why Rabby wanted me to track you down."

"I thought you'd just done that," she snapped, "by ridiculing the regret I've felt for dropping the cruel truth on Avram like a stone from the sky. And as to why you're here, you've completed your mission, as far as Meir and I are concerned. And done it well. But please use discretion in what you say to Isaac and Miriam. Oh, *what?*"

He was shaking his head and making apply-the-brakes motions with both hands. "You mean I've done all you wanted me to do," he said, "which was just to fill in your blank spots about what happened to him in Vietnam. But I didn't sign on for one miserable overnight bus ride up here and another one back just to give polite answers till teacher says I'm dismissed. I did it because it's what he wanted. And a couple of things keep ringing in my ears. One is something he'd toss off when he wanted to sound oracular. He'd say life was like Torah, in that everything has deeper and secondary meanings that have to be probed. And the other thing I keep hearing, Ilana, is something the woman I hope to marry, who's a medical student—only no, now she's a doctor, and I'd better get used to that—something Stephanie told me once. She said that often the first steps in good doctoring are figuring out who's the patient and what, exactly, the patient needs fixed. For sure the patient here isn't me. All I need is a little sleep and some time alone with a woman I haven't seen in ten months. That means the patient has to be you. You're a beautiful, intelligent, warmhearted woman. Why the half-habit of a nun? Why no ring, no mention of some honeybunch back on the kibbutz? Does that trace back to the guilt you feel about Rabby? Have you vowed to steer clear of marriage and motherhood for fear you'd do something to botch it? Is that what Rabby wanted me to try and help you fix?"

Ilana glared at him with a mix of incredulity and rage. Then, seemingly despite herself, she began to laugh.

"I felt prepared for you, Peter, based on what Avram had told me in his letters," she said. "But the true you is so much worse. You're rude and intrusive."

"Well, thanks," he said. "At least that makes me top-flight at something. That's better than I get from Stephanie. She just tells me I'm about as smart as the guy who mucks out the stalls on her dad's dairy farm."

Ilana's laughter subsided into a sad smile.

"You're not stupid, Peter. That's the best I can say for you. Still, I understand why Avram chose you as his friend. Now we really should go up to the cemetery. I'm sure Isaac and Miriam are there now, and we don't want them to leave before we get there."

They went on across the bridge and along the paved-over railroad tracks on the other side. Ilana hurried now and made no allowance for his knee. To keep up, he took long, ungainly strides with his good leg and gingerly steps with his bad one. Soon he was out of breath, but sensing this might be his last chance to talk to her alone, he unleashed a disjointed argument that Rabby's death was worth admiring, maybe even deserving of envy, and was in no way her, Ilana's, doing.

"Look, I told you and Meir how he felt about that little girl, Huê, right? Well, remember this is a war, Ilana. You can't conjure up deadly situations in a war. They just happen. Rabby didn't cook up either the ground attack or the risk Huê would get hurt in it. They just happened. And that barbed wire barrier he strung around our villa? Maybe it harked back to the ghetto fence in Lodz, but the one he built around the villa served a good purpose too. The other guys there said they were glad he did it. And if he hadn't come out from behind the wire and climbed up on the roof, Pham would've forced his way into the villa, see? And the VC would've come in to get him, and that would've endangered Huê and everybody else in there. And listen, listen. What I'm saying is Rabby was dealing with a real threat. He wasn't just throwing his life away in some screwball apotheosis. And okay: Maybe he died just when he'd closed the gap between defeating that threat and living out the myth he'd worked on all those years. But so what? Who of us is likely to find a better way to die than that?"

Ilana gave him a couple of annoyed glances as she hurried on. She veered off the paved trail and along a weed-filled corridor that had been cut through a stand of trees to accommodate poles for a power line.

Across a grassy field ahead of them Peter could see the brick pillars and grillwork he had first glimpsed from the bridge, and he could make out the lettering on the arc: "Covenant Cemetery." Inside this gate were a parked car and a truck. When they stepped from the tall grass and weeds onto the closely mowed field, Ilana wheeled and stopped him with the heel of her hand against his breastbone.

"Who are you trying to convince, and of what, Peter?" she said. "You think I have illusions about life in a war zone? I'm a citizen of Israel! In the war two years ago my kibbutz was almost overrun. You have nothing to teach me about surviving a war and coming out the other side and then living with what you'd done in it. Yes, I take Avram's death hard, and how could I not? But I don't think what you're doing now is aimed just at me. You're trying to reshape the details of his death so they absolve you too. Well, good luck with that, Peter, but I've had my fill of that exercise, at least for today."

As they approached the gate, Peter saw that one of the parked vehicles was a battered-looking green Nash Rambler with a spare tire mounted above the back bumper. The other was a truck with the name and logo of a landscaping company printed on its door. The truck's driver was standing with one elbow hooked over an edge of the truck bed. He was smoking a cigarette and watching a man and a woman who stood side by side a few rows deep among the tombstones, looking down at a fresh grave.

"He's brought sod," Peter said. "He wants to plant it on that grave before the end of the work day."

"He can wait," Ilana said. "Or he can come back tomorrow. Isaac and Miriam will be gone then, but the grave will still be there, so that should be ideal for him."

The woman was much shorter than the man. She wore a flower-print dress and her dark hair looked freshly permed. She repeatedly half-turned toward the man and made swift motions with her hands, talking, while he stood there inert, his big hands dangling from the cuffs of a faded blue work shirt. Peter thought she might be describing some long-past moment spent with the dead that served to briefly distract her from the raw, sandy-looking mound at her feet. Here and there along the row of graves where the couple stood, Peter saw handkerchief-size American flags hanging from tiny flagstaffs stuck in the soil next to the tombstones.

"Ilana, is that row that Rabby's in…see the flags?"

"They reserve that row for war veterans," she said. "It's up to the family, of course, if they go in there."

"Good God, they've put him in the idiots' row!" Peter murmured.

"That's one way of putting it," Ilana said. "I wouldn't repeat that to Miriam or Isaac, though."

Peter kept hearing a series of cries that at first he mistook for the cawing of crows. Through a sparse row of trees, he saw a tall, white clapboard building with vertically extended windows. Past this building he could make out several small figures darting about in a field.

"That's the old synagogue over there, isn't it?" he said. "And I think I see those kids playing baseball."

Ilana didn't answer. Turning, he saw she had covered her mouth with one hand and was looking toward Rabby's grave with her eyes flared wide.

The woman had fallen to her knees on the mounded earth. Her head tilted sharply to one side, and she stroked the soil as if she were smoothing a blanket on a sleeping child. The man leaned toward her and reached out a hand, but the hand stopped short of her shoulder.

Watching her, Peter thought, Mom wouldn't do that. She'd look for a long time at the earth covering me—our red clay, not this sandy stuff. And then she'd turn away, trembling but rigid and tearless. But then, these people are different.

"Is that a Jewish custom?" Peter said. "What she's doing now? I mean, I've heard about casting stones on a grave, but not—that."

Slowly Ilana turned to face him, and her gaze hardened with what looked to him like disgust.

"I said a while ago that you weren't stupid, didn't I?" she said softly. "Well, I take it back. What Miriam's doing, that's not some ancient Jewish ritual, Peter. That's just what mothers do when they grieve."

Thirty-three

They had oyster stew and saltines for dinner. Then Peter slept eleven hours in the bed where Avram Rabinowitz had slept as a child. Before he turned out the little bedroom's overhead bulb by yanking on its dangling string, he noticed a framed certificate propped atop a scarred wooden dresser. The certificate bore the image of a Bronze Star suspended from a purple ribbon. So he got it, Peter thought. But why put it there? But no: This is exactly right. Now, whoever climbs into this bed will see it, and will feel its radiance as he falls asleep.

When he awoke, he tried to burrow back into his interrupted dream. In it, he had buried the blood-tainted strands of barbed wire as Rabby instructed. Then Rabby walked nearby, and the lengths of wire wriggled from the ground and coiled around his ankles and lower legs. The wire piled up layer upon layer, a metallic elephantiasis creeping toward his knees that would surely drag him beneath the soil. Rabby, though, kept plodding at the same pace, merely glancing down in mild annoyance. In his dream, Peter at first despaired, since it seemed just a matter of time before the wire would have its way. Then he began to feel giddily happy, because Rabby kept plodding ahead, and it looked like he'd outlast the wire's efforts to erase him from the world.

Grief had made ciphers of Isaac and Miriam. Peter had seen this happen before, to the parents of the twin boys who were his childhood best friends. The twins' parents, whose farming ventures ranged from small-scale dairying to breeding Shetland ponies, had seemed perpetually happy. Then, during Peter's third year of college, the family's youngest child, a six-year-old boy, was killed by a car that failed to stop for his school bus. When Peter was home for Christmas, he had visited the family and found that the Ed and Viola Shelton he had known for most of his life were absent. Grief had inhabited their bodies and left just enough of the people they had been to answer the door and pour him a cup of coffee and ask in flat voices how he and his parents were doing. When Peter gently probed for the rest of Ed and Viola, he found it gone. When he said awkwardly that little Ed's death was the worst thing that had ever happened to any family he or his parents knew, the father winced and craned his neck to look away, out the window, toward a fenced pasture.

Peter saw now that Isaac and Miriam Kleinfield were as absent from their bodies as Ed and Viola Shelton had been, and it was no use to probe for them. What remained of them seemed to manifest itself chiefly in their hands. When, at dinner, Peter gave them a brief, heavily redacted description of his friendship with Rabby, Isaac silently grasped one of Peter's hands with both of his own, tightened his grip almost painfully, then patted the hand before letting it go—all without meeting Peter's eyes. When Miriam circled the table next morning to ladle out chicken scrapple from a platter, she brushed her fingers lightly over Peter's hair in a way that seemed practiced to the point of absentmindedness, and she sighed as she passed on.

Ilana borrowed the Rambler to drive Peter to the bus station that afternoon.

"When is it you fly out?" Peter said.

"Day after tomorrow," she said. "One more day here I think I can take."

"Will Isaac drive you up?"

"No, Sonia's going to take me. I don't think goodbyes at airports are good mental hygiene for people who've suffered what Isaac and Miriam have gone through."

"Do you think you'll stop in to see Meir?"

"It depends. If he's not too busy and Sonia has time, then yes, probably."

"I owe you a lot for letting me come up here. I probably said some things that were out of line."

"Peter, I've listened to so much that was in line over the past nine days here that I'm sick of it. Meir was my sole escape from it. You, as I'd hoped, proved even better."

"At carping and insulting, you mean?"

Her raspy laugh sounded heartfelt, but she cut it short.

"Yes, well, you did wander off into ill-chosen terrain yesterday," she said. "Maybe we both did. But you were exhausted, and I'd been riding around sideways, packed like a sardine in my brother's absurd little car. So there you have excuses for us both."

The bus door opened with a pneumatic hiss, and he looped his duffel's strap over his shoulder. For a moment, he thought he would tell her he would miss seeing her coppery ringlets spilling in all directions from beneath the too-tight band of a baseball hat, but all he said was:

"Well, *shalom*, Ilana."

"*Shalom*, Peter. And thank you. You didn't have to do this. You could have ignored that note from Avram, torn it up and tried to forget him. But you didn't. And once I get over being pissed off by some of the things you said yesterday, I'll be forever grateful."

She grasped his arm as he started to turn away.

"Now, listen," she said. "Call Meir. If not right away when you get home, then soon."

"Sure, I will. Does he want me to do something?"

"Just call him. I'm done forever with getting out ahead of Meir on matters he wants to handle his own way."

When Peter got home he still had another nine days of leave. He called Stephanie and said he wanted to see her.

"Tell me what happened in New Jersey," she said.

"It's too much to tell over the phone, Stephie."

"Try. Compress."

So he told her about Meir and Ilana and about how Rabby had been rescued from a ghetto and had spent his early years in hiding and then in displaced persons camps, and that he had then grown up on a chicken farm with foster parents who loved him. He told her how Rabby had learned the truth about his rescue and how it had metamorphosed into the Antonina fable, and how Rabby had taken that fable to the other side of the world and created a role for himself in it that led him, finally, to the rooftop where he died.

"What about Antonina?" Stephie said when he was done. "Where is she now?"

"Where is she? She must have just—died, I guess."

"Why would you think that? She was a young woman during the war. After the war ended, she was strong enough to make it to West Germany, and your friend's cousin, the legal officer, saw her there. Did he say nothing about what happened to her after that?"

"No. Why would he?"

"Look, you need to call him. You need to ask him what else he knows about Antonina."

"Sure, I'll call him. Before he drove off the other day, he gave me his card, and he asked me to call."

"And you said he's what? A prosecutor in New Jersey?"

"Yeah. Bergen County deputy DA. He said he wanted me to know one thing more."

"Ka-ching, ka-ching!" Stephie said. "Call him. Calling him now would be good."

"I'll call him. But what I want right now is for you to tell me when I can see you."

"How do you propose we make that happen?"

"How? Well, we both arrange to be in the same place at the same time. Soon."

"That wouldn't work for me right now. But let's think on it."

"Jesus Christ, Stephie! You move me around like a pawn on a chessboard! First off to New Jersey, and now it sounds like you want me to go chase a ghost in Poland or somewhere. Avram Rabinowitz is buried outside Arborville, New Jersey. I've seen his grave. I've even slept in the bed he slept in as a kid. I know all I need to know about him. Why isn't that enough for you?"

She was silent for so long that Peter thought the phone connection had gone dead. "Stephie, you there?" he said.

"What I care about," she said, "is seeing you complete the one thing that might make your time in the Army worthwhile. Your mother was right, I believe, about the idiots' row. I mean, in saying your dead Confederate ancestors deserved to have their graves called that. When you allowed the draft to snatch you up, I didn't hear much more in your reasoning for it than what those two young men could have offered so long ago. You believed going off to the war would deepen your life, or perhaps just darken it in ways that amounted to solidarity with other men whose lives were also darkened by war. I encouraged you to go, since there was no shaking you out of that belief. But I didn't hope for much, except that you'd get through your two years safely and without great cause for regret. Against the odds, though, this war has given you a chance … No, strike that. It's given you the obligation to explore this story of your friend's life and death. And at the deepest point of that story you've run into this Antonina, who was both a real Polish resistance fighter in the 1940s and an imagined protector of your friend's ancestors decades before that. The real one gave him a chance at life when she caught him after his mother pitched him over a ghetto fence. The imagined one drew him deeper into her myth and off to the other side of the world and, finally, up to a rooftop where the two of them apparently, for an instant, merged. And then he died."

"We have the whole picture, then, right?" Peter said. "What more do we need to know?"

"His cousin thinks there's something. I could guess at it, but why guess when you can just call him and he'll tell you?"

"All right. And if he tells me what you think he's going to tell me, what should I do about it?"

"I think you should pursue it the way a good soldier carries out a direct order."

"Yeah? How's that?"

"To the last full measure of devotion."

Thirty-four

He left a message at Meir's office. Peter was alone in the house, and he paced the living room, swearing at his dead friend, until Meir called back.

"Ilana was here when you called earlier," Meir said. "She and Sonia are off to the airport now. By way, I think, of a shoe store in the West Village."

"Ilana seemed to know what you wanted to talk to me about. She wouldn't say what it was, though."

"Before we plunge in, let's get a couple of things clear," Meir said in what sounded to Peter like his courtroom voice. "Will anyone else need to use your phone line soon?"

"My parents are teachers. They won't be home for at least a couple of hours."

"Here's my second point: Give me your home address, and I'll mail a twenty-dollar check, payable to you, to reimburse your parents for the phone bill we'll run up. Don't waste our time by pretending to object."

Peter fought down his impulse to call out Meir for so crudely seizing the upper hand. He gave him the address.

"Ilana knew in a general way that I wanted you to act as a sort of emissary," Meir said. "Your friendship with Avram, I felt, fits you for that role. I want you, acting on my behalf, to make an offer. Also, once you've had face-to-face contact with the person I hope to benefit, maybe you could advise me on whether her best interests could be best served in some other way, such as through a court's appointment of a guardian."

"Please cut the lawyer-speak, Meir," Peter said. "Who's this about?"

"Antonina Tarnowski."

"So she's alive?"

"Oh, yes. In good health too, at least physically, so far as I know."

"And if she's healthy, why would she need a guardian?"

"A court would have to find she was mentally unfit to look after herself."

Peter took a moment to absorb that and another moment to decide to flee from it.

"Look, Meir, you and Ilana have both been really good to me," he said. "If you need someone to track Antonina down, I wish I could give it a try. But until next July twenty-third, I'm just a PFC at Fort Bragg. Based on what I know of stateside duty, the main thing I'll be tracking down till then will be shit stains on toilet bowls."

"Oh, you won't have a problem finding Antonina," Meir said.

"In Poland? Germany? I'm supposed to get there and back on a weekend pass?"

"Absolutely not. How much time before you report to Bragg?"

"Nine days, counting today. But, Meir, look. No way am I going to hop on a plane and spend the rest of my home leave—"

"You won't need to. You're not that far from Birmingham, Alabama, are you? A day's drive? I'll pay for your car rental and pay you a per diem for meals and lodging. It'll take you four days, tops. One day down, one back. A day or two in between to get the best read you can on Antonina's intentions and state of mind, and try to bring her around to what I've asked her to do."

Peter started to laugh.

Ave Antonina   Michael Jennings

"So what's funny?" Meir said.

"You want me to bargain with somebody I know only as a character in a fairy tale, like Cinderella or Rapunzel."

"Well, try to shed that notion. Remember what I told you in the diner? Antonina was a soldier. Nothing meant as much to her as engaging the enemy and beating him. For her, the enemy meant the Germans. And that hasn't changed."

"But in Birmingham? Has she ferreted out some Klansman named Schicklgruber?"

"No, no. She's got a prime set of bona fide Nazis quite close by. Men she can harass and threaten, if that's her plan. Have you heard of the Marshall Space Flight Center in Huntsville?"

"That's where NASA built the moon rocket, right?"

"Right. But, more to our point, and to Antonina's, we're talking about the men whose missiles hit London and Antwerp in forty-four, forty-five, killing thousands of people."

"You mean von Braun's rocket team?"

"That's right. Hang on."

Meir put his hand over the mouthpiece. Peter could hear a woman's voice from a distance, then Meir's muffled voice saying: "Oh good. And did you tell her *nesiah tovah*? Yes? You're a sweetheart. Oh, and please keep the door closed for a while. If anyone calls, tell them I'm tied up."

The door shut. "My secretary," Meir told Peter. "Lani had called to tell me she was about to board. Somehow all the women in my life suffer temporary hearing loss when I tell them no interruptions."

"If you're going to tell me Antonina might assassinate German rocket scientists, Meir, then I'll be seeing you. It's been grand."

"No, no. I'm all but certain, no. Listen. Remember I told you I saw Antonina twice? Well, the second time was eight years after I first met her in Augustdorf. In between, she'd married and had two children, both boys. She and her husband had earned advanced degrees in, of all places, Antwerp. While they lived there, they must have gotten visual reminders of how well von Braun's gang had calculated matters like thrust and trajectory and payload capacity. Her husband, also Polish, was a pharmaceutical researcher. He'd been brought to the States to work on antibiotics development at a lab in Connecticut. She was coming in not as a displaced person, but on her husband's coattails, and I could tell it riled her. Starting as soon as the DP law passed in 1948, she'd hounded me with requests to get her on the list. She asked me to vouch she'd borne arms against the enemy during the war. Of course I did that, and I put in some of the details I've told you about. Combatants like her were supposed to get priority status under the DP law, but she never got it, probably because she was a woman. Her letters got more frequent and urgent, asking me to pull strings. As if I had any to pull. Then, after about three years, her letters stopped."

Peter stretched out the coils of the phone cord and began pacing the length of the kitchen table. He let the fingertips of one hand glide along the table's Formica top, aware that he craved that much contact with the familiar while he was being sucked into something utterly alien.

"Twenty bucks buys you a lot of phone time, Meir," he said. "Remember all I have to do is listen."

"Got it. So a few years after she'd stopped writing me, her husband got sponsored by the drug company, and Antonina cabled me their arrival time. I met them at the dock in New York. As soon as I saw them, the husband carrying the youngest kid and Antonina leading the other one by the hand, I thought: how did this come about, and how long can it last? He looked like a decent fellow. A man whose guiding lights are trust and reason, a man bred for peace. Competent, I'm sure, in the search for the best stopgap for the day the penicillin ran out or didn't work. And there was Antonina, looking the way she must have looked when she climbed out of the Elbe after trekking across half of Poland and half of Germany: wary, watchful, ready to react as quickly and violently as any threat might require. Most women flesh out a bit once they've had children, but if anything, she'd lost flesh since I'd seen her in the DP camp. The older boy, the one she held by the hand, looked like he'd caught the drift of his family's story and knew it couldn't end well, so better that it ended soon."

"Rabby was already in Arborville then, right?" Peter said.

"He'd been there more than six years," Meir said. "I told her that. I told her he was well taken care of."

"Did she want to see him?"

"When I told her the child she'd saved from the Lodz ghetto was a couple of hours' drive away, it was like she didn't even hear me. She gave me this stone-cold look and said, 'he died, you know? My father. He died in Boston, and I couldn't be there to help him.' I'd known nothing about that. When I pieced things together later, I learned her father had come in under the DP law in 1950 and died less than two years later. If she'd let me know her father was coming over back when he got approved for entry, I could have made a case for her. The DP law said displaced persons who were blood relatives of alien residents of the U.S. could come over too. I never found out whether Antonina just didn't know about that piece of the law or whether she was so fixated on getting admitted as a Nazi killer that she wouldn't budge.

"Since she'd let me know when they'd arrive, I figured she thought I could be useful to her. But she'd lost any trust in me as a confidant. That day I met her on the dock, it looked like the capacity for cold, patient, focused anger that the war had honed in her had come to include me, and potentially anyone close to me. So I never again brought up with her the subject of Avram's whereabouts or welfare or prospects in life."

For a while, Peter had been hearing his mother's dog—half beagle, half something bred to track and tree raccoons—tap her claws sporadically against the storm door on the back porch and make shrill pleas to be let in. Finally the little dog lost patience, clattered against the Plexiglass with both front paws and bayed like a full-sized hound.

"Hang on," Peter said. "I need to tend to a pint-sized jackass."

He opened the porch door, and the spotted dog followed him to the phone, licking from his pants legs grains of the silage he'd fed the calf.

Whipsaw, Peter thought. I'm being whipsawed again between the alien and the utterly familiar. Difference is, I know now which one I'd choose, if the choice were mine to make.

"But you didn't break contact with Antonina entirely, did you?" he said when he picked up the phone.

"I did break off direct contact, but I kept tabs on her. Just from what I saw and heard on the dock that day, I could imagine some oddsmaker taking bets on how long a woman with her history would last in Peyton Place America before her pent-up anger exploded. It took a couple of years. Her husband worked at a lab in Branford, just outside New Haven. I checked occasionally with a county prosecutor up there, a man I knew from a training we'd both attended. I asked him to let me know if Antonina's married name cropped up in the news or court proceedings. In late 1957, he called to tell me her husband had accused her of battery, then quickly withdrawn his complaint. A few months later, my contact called again to tell me Antonina had been questioned after one of her husband's co-researchers accused her of smashing equipment in his lab. It seemed to be common knowledge at the lab that her accuser had experimented on prisoners at a Nazi concentration camp. I called an old Army pal who's with the Justice Department and asked him to check her accuser's last name, Herschorn, against immigration records on Nazi scientists. Sure enough, Herschorn took part in immunization experiments on prisoners at Sachsenhausen, but the screeners found he'd done nothing clearly contrary to law."

"Except experiment on prisoners who had no say in the matter," Peter said.

"Well, yeah. But no inmate at a Nazi camp ever had a say in what happened to them. Anyway, Antonina was asked whether she'd smashed Herschorn's flasks and Petri dishes, and all she said was, 'prove it if you can.' She could have used her husband's keys to enter the building after working hours, but so could any family member of anyone else who worked there. The only other evidence was that she'd twice called Herschorn, to his face, a Nazi *schweinhund*. The lab building had a night watchman, but of course Antonina was a past master at eluding guards."

"Or poleaxing them," Peter said. "Rabby never learned any of this?"

"I've told no one," Meir said. "Not my dad or Ilana or Isaac, and certainly not Avram. By the time I learned of Antonina's problems in Branford, I'd long since nominated her to Yad Vashem. She's one of several thousand Poles listed there, and God knows she deserves it. I've kept my inquiries into her further history strictly private for a lot of years now. Until right now, in fact."

Peter had sat again at the phone table. The dog rested her chin on his knee, with her eyes rolled up toward his face. He stood and shooed her away, thinking, That's one too many demands on me.

"Well, why break secrecy now?" he said into the phone. "And why break it to me?"

"One reason is Avram's death. There's no risk to him anymore. The other reason is that Antonina's life is on a knife edge. I'm afraid she'll botch her chance to live it out in freedom. And you might be better suited than I to talk her off that edge."

"You're saying she graduated from vandalizing a pharmaceutical lab to—what, exactly?" Peter said. "Meir, I'm an Army private. I've already got one black mark on my service record. I'm not going to risk putting my fingerprints on some nutball effort to sabotage the national space program."

For a while he just heard Meir breathing into the receiver. The sound reminded him of what everyone in his high school would hear whenever their principal came on the speaker system: the effort to draw breath through the tortuous channel in an old football player's nose.

"Well, you get to choose, but hear me out," Meir said. "Antonina made no effort to fit into a housewifely mold in Branford. No surprise there. She'd force-marched herself to an advanced degree in electrical engineering at Antwerp. That was good enough to get her hired as an instructor at Yale. Non-tenurable, but still: Yale. That German researcher, Herschorn, left for a Defense Department job at the Walter Reed Institute in Maryland. Antonina's husband made no more complaints about domestic abuse, but my friend at the prosecutor's office in New Haven said he'd caught wind of two police summonses to the house. Those calls weren't from the husband but from a neighbor who complained of late-night shouting next-door, with the female voice dominant. The morning after the neighbor had called in the first of those complaints, she called again to report that Antonina had just stepped onto her own back porch carrying a handgun and a box of shells, looked coolly at her across the fence, loaded the gun's magazine and fitted it into the pistol. Then Antonina had glanced across the fence again, this time with a smile, and stepped back inside."

"Let me guess," Peter said. "Protection order? End of the Yale job?"

"No, no. Nothing at all, except an entry in the police logbook, which noted that Antonina had permit. If you're a permitted gun-owner, you're free to load your pistol on your own porch and smile at your neighbor while you do it. After I learned about that complaint, I prodded my contact to check divorce records for Antonina's married name, Zielinski. Eventually he got a hit. The divorce record showed the father retained sole custody of both children. Antonina got ample visitation rights, but no financial support. That didn't surprise me. She was cut free, and I suspect that's what she preferred."

"So she really wasn't good for much except blowing up trains, decorating dead Nazis' hats with their own blood, slapping around her mousy husband and teaching electron theory to sons of the East Coast elite," Peter said.

"Also for rescuing an infant from a sealed-off ghetto, just before thousands of other kids there were shipped off and gassed," Meir said. "Don't forget that."

"Noted. But you said earlier that rescue was an ego trip."

"No, I didn't. I said she was a soldier, and she rescued Avram for the reason soldiers do dangerous things: to defeat the enemy."

Peter resumed his patrol of the kitchen table, his fingernails gliding along its glassy surface. The coils of the phone cord expanded, then contracted as the cord seemed to reel him in. The dog lay curled by a heating vent, and her eyes tracked him.

"So once she'd ditched the husband and children, it was off to Alabama, to ferret out the enemy there?" Peter said.

"No, though probably it was just a matter of time. She stayed on in New Haven until last year. She was even married again, briefly, to an Air Force major who taught ROTC at Yale. He'd been a bombardier on missions over Dresden in forty-five. He and Antonina had no kids. He got reassigned in a couple of years, and they filed for an uncontested divorce. Around the time she cut that bond, she also gave up visitation rights for her sons. Zielinski had remarried too by then, so I guess Antonina saw no further reason to muddle the mommy role for her two kids."

"So one more thing she wasn't much good for," Peter said. "Undying love for her own flesh and blood."

"Oh, I don't know about that," Meir said. "Sometimes the best way to deliver on your love for your kids is to give them up forever, even if that means pitching them over ten feet of razor wire. I grant you, she'd figured out it was time to narrow her life down to her driving passion, the one seared into her by the war years. That required cutting free of everything that smacked of bake-sale mommyhood. Starting about the time her first marriage ended, Antonina found a new way to channel her passion to kill Nazis, now that she could no longer actually kill them. She wanted to torpedo the reputations of von Braun and as much of the rest of the rocket team as she could get the goods on. They'd been brought over en masse after the war. Prayers were going up all across the heartland that they'd put American footprints on the moon before the Russians did. And here Antonina was trying to dredge up these guys' wartime past. It made sense to me that she'd do that, given that her father had worked in a factory that made V-2s and she'd spent years in Antwerp, a city those rockets had terrorized. But I didn't fully grasp what drove her until my boss here, Tim Hargrave, who's a Yale Law grad, told me Yale had turned down a faculty member's offer to donate what sounded like a document of real scholarly value. It was a memoir written by a concentration camp prisoner who'd worked at a Nazi rocket factory. My guess is that, after Antonina's father died without anyone local to claim his personal effects, somebody at the Boston PD recognized the importance of that memoir and saw to its safe storage. Then when Antonina showed up a few years later and could prove her relationship, the police turned the memoir over to her, along with whatever else her father left behind.

"When she offered it to Yale, some tight-assed lawyer in the university legal office recommended the worst thing possible, which was to turn the memoir over to the government. It ended up at the Defense Department, and DOD lawyers classified it secret, subject to further review. I asked Tim to work his contacts at Yale Law to find if there was more to that story. They told him DOD just got a typed copy, while the original remained with the engineering instructor who'd offered to donate it. Which I took to mean Antonina had foreseen the government might try to seize and suppress her father's memoir, so she'd kept the original in a lock box."

"Couldn't the feds seize it anyway?" Peter said.

"They could try. But she'd fight them and draw publicity, and they knew it. Already she was writing letters to newspapers and popping up at candidate forums, claiming the von Braun team was responsible for hundreds of deaths at the rocket factory and asking Congress to investigate. But seventh-graders all across America were being taught that von Braun, in particular, ranked as an American hero and their parents would have agreed. For the most part, Antonina was written off as a kook. As long as that was the case, DOD felt content to leave her alone."

Remembering the bebop rhythm Colonel Jesperson would drum with his fingers as an aid to thought, Peter tried to recapture it on the tabletop.

"Couple of questions," he said. "You're a full-time Bergen County prosecutor, right? Yet you seem to track Antonina's life like a heart doctor monitoring bleeps on a cardiac machine. How do you find time for that?"

For a while Peter just heard the air moving both ways through the obstacle course in Meir's nose.

"You probably think that, in a few months, you can just file what you did and saw and heard in Vietnam under the heading 'the past is past' and move on with your life," Meir said. "Not so, if you're the man I take you for. What happened to you there will loom larger over time. You'll try to amend parts of it, even if only inside your head. Antonina turned out to be a piece of my war that I could track in real time and, if opportunity arose, try to amend in some real and helpful way. I didn't expect that, but it's what I've been offered, and I feel obliged to accept it."

"And now you want me to serve as a sort of extendable wrench you can use to torque Antonina's life to a degree you find proper?" Peter said.

"I think you and I have a mutual interest in doing that," Meir said. "My interest is rooted in my war, yours in your war. Both also rooted in our regret for things we did and didn't do that affected Avram, and in our desire now to make amends."

Peter sighed. "Okay," he said. "Spell it out. But count me curious, not committed."

"Starting a couple of years ago, Antonina quit publicly branding members of the rocket team as repurposed Nazi criminals. She might be obsessive, but she's also smart enough to see that effort was getting no traction. I'm guessing that around the same time she gave it up, she started looking for ways to relocate to Alabama."

"What would moving there get her?"

"My concern? Moth to the flame. It would get her closer to a set of men she'd like to ruin."

"Or see dead?"

"I think she'd rather see them ruined. From the time she was seventeen, Antonina's ruling passion was to deal the Nazis an outright defeat, then leave them knowing she'd beaten them. That passion might have gone dormant after the war, but what she read in her father's memoir surely revived it. Can I foresee some tabloid scenario? Such as Antonina mounting to a rooftop in Huntsville with a high-powered rifle and picking off rocket scientists? I think only if she'd tipped over into delusion, and I think she's too tough-minded for that."

"Why move to Alabama, then?" Peter said. "What does close range get her, if all she wants is to ruin their reputations? And how would she support herself?"

"The support part's simple. The engineering dean at Yale said Antonina got a tenurable job at a new state university in Birmingham."

"There's another new state school in Huntsville," Peter said. "My dad's from north Alabama, and he told me. So why not there?"

"Maybe the school in Birmingham had an opening and the Huntsville one didn't. Or maybe she wanted to keep a little distance from a town where she knew she'd stir up bad blood. Practically the whole rocket team has lived in Huntsville for two decades. I'm sure some of those men are town councilmen, school board members, church deacons. Pillars of the community. They'll have lots of friends and defenders, even among people who'd have gladly sprung the trap door to hang a Goebbels or Himmler. So probably what she had in mind was logging road miles to Huntsville and dredging up these guys' past in public forums, same as she did in Connecticut, and then driving back to a place where she's just a woman with a funny accent and eyes that look like a pair of carving knives."

"She thinks she can stay low-profile while she bad-mouths men who just put Americans on the moon?" Peter said. "Good luck with that."

"Exactly. I'm sure she knows that now. I'm not sure if she knows something else, though. In a place like Alabama, if she's flinging claims of war crimes in the faces of the men she's accusing, what might count as free speech elsewhere could get her prosecuted. So what's her game plan? And will she buy into mine? That's what I want you to find out."

Still searching for a good bebop rhythm, Peter realized his own curiosity had all but fully reeled him in.

"And you can do what, exactly? Whistle off Alabama's bloodhounds?"

"I contacted a guy I went to school with at my dad's Torah academy," Meir said. "He's principal partner at a New York publishing house. Not a major publisher, but well-respected. Based on my description of what her father's memoir must contain, and on Yale's kowtow to the DOD, this guy promises to have it translated and then publish at least a limited edition. If the document's as explosive as I made it sound, his house could go full-bore, with thousands of copies, plus promotion. He's sent a letter to her university address that makes that pledge, plus a contract for her to sign."

"So all she needs to do is sign it and ship him a copy of the memoir, like the one she offered Yale?"

"Here's the thing," Meir said. "Before he can publish, he's got to have the original. Authentication is key, and he's lined up a faculty member at Yeshiva University to oversee that. Dating of paper and ink, the works. You can imagine the backlash if a publishing house puts out something that slimes the space program and it turns out to be a fake."

"But Meir, look," Peter said. "You think she's going to mail you or this publisher the one thing she values most in the world, all on the strength of what I tell her, when I can't even satisfy myself that it's true?"

"Oh, no," Meir said. "No no no. Not mail. Not shipment by any means. The DOD knows she still has the original. A little hand-in-glove work with the FBI, a secret order from a federal court? Voila! All outgoing mail and parcels from either her home or her university address get screened. I feel pretty sure an order like that's already in place, since the FBI clearly intercepted and read my friend's letter to Antonina, then resealed it and sent it on to her."

Peter had uttered the word "bull" before he caught himself. The annoyance that burbled up in him like heartburn, he knew, was the same sort that had rendered him unable to hear the deeper layers of the story Rabby told on the villa rooftop.

"How could you possibly know all that?" he said.

"Simple. My publisher friend, Bernie Nussbaum, got a notice from the U.S. attorney for the Southern District of New York, directing him to surrender any material his house receives for publication from Antonina, as identified by any of her several last names. The only way a U.S. attorney could know she might send something to L'Chaim Publishing would be if they'd first intercepted and read Bernie's letter to her, offering to publish. Now the FBI must have a couple of choke points where they might intercept that memoir, plus a backup plan. There's the one choke point in Birmingham and another one at the sorting station in Manhattan that handles mail deliveries to L'Chaim Publishing. And then, as a backup, that bluff, the notice to L'Chaim from the U.S. attorney. But there they outfoxed themselves."

"How is it a bluff?" Peter said.

"Because it's a blatant attempt at prior restraint. Here's some bedrock First Amendment law: You can't censor anything somebody might say or publish before they've said or published it. Once speech or publication has taken place, you can censor it only if it poses a clear and present danger. Now, no court open to public scrutiny is going to rule, twenty-plus years after Hitler blew his brains out in a Berlin bunker, that publishing a bona fide memoir by a slave laborer on a Nazi production line presents a clear and present danger."

"So, say your publisher pal calls the FBI's bluff, and he wins. Why wasn't it smart for the FBI to at least roll the dice on it?

"Because when Bernie got that letter from the U.S. attorney and told me about it, that tipped us off to the all but certain existence of those choke points in the mail, in Birmingham and Manhattan. So now we know the only safe means of delivery is by hand. And for our purposes, that means first your hand, then mine. You hand-carry that memoir as far as some agreed-on rendezvous point. I meet you there and hand-carry it to Bernie at L'Chaim Publishing in Manhattan."

"So I appear out of the blue and describe that series of handoffs and Antonina just tosses me the memoir and says, 'here you go'? Why in hell do you think she'd—"

"Because desperate times require desperate measures," Meir said. "She's got to know it's just a matter of time before the feds get tired of waiting and simply seize her father's memoir, especially if she pushes ahead with publicly branding German rocket engineers as war criminals. And remember. Once in the past she initiated a series of handoffs that had no greater apparent likelihood of success. It turned out I was on the receiving end that time, too. So dropping my name with her this time might help."

Meir gave Peter her university and home addresses and her office phone. "I'd need a subpoena to get her home phone," he said. "But I got her home address from driver's license records. Those are public. But be careful if you show up where she lives, since she's tried to keep that address secret."

"What, exactly, did she tell you after she got this offer to publish the memoir?" Peter said.

"Nothing. I haven't heard back from her. If you head down there, I'll try calling her office again while you're en route."

"Then she might tell me to kiss off. Or worse."

For a half-minute, all Peter heard was respiration so slow and laborious it would be a fit anthem for smash-mouth football.

"I can't predict how she'll react," Meir said finally. "But I feel it's essential to act now. Like I said, desperate times, desperate measures."

As soon as he hung up, Peter's first thought was of his father's pistol. It was a .45 caliber revolver made of blued metal, with a plain, worn-looking wooden handgrip. His father kept it on his side of the bed in a drawer fastened with a hasp and padlock. Peter had never seen his father fire it, but he had once seen him wield it in earnest. That was on one of the driving trips Albert Dandridge made twice a year with his wife and son to the farm where he grew up in Alabama. They had stopped at a roadside gas station to buy fuel and soft drinks. When they stepped from the building with their Cokes in their hands, they heard shouting and then a prolonged scream from a house next door. A man stumbled down an outside stairway from the second floor of the house with blood streaming from a cut that had laid bare his cheekbone. A second, red-faced man carrying a hatchet stumbled down the stairs after him.

"Get in the car," Peter's father said softly to his wife and son. Then he stepped quickly to the trunk of his car, unlocked it and took his pistol from his duffel bag. Already at age 10, Peter knew his father kept the pistol unloaded on road trips. By the time the drunk with the hatchet reached the bottom of the steps, Elmer Dandridge stood there blocking it. Peter couldn't hear through the rolled-up car windows, but he knew from the genial nodding motions of his father's head that he was speaking softly and politely, as he always did, while he pointed the unloaded pistol at the man's heart. He kept that up until the drunk man put the hatchet down on a step behind him.

"Dad didn't have to do that, any more than I have to do what I'm about to do," Peter said aloud. "I bet he'll let me borrow it. I bet he'll let me take his pistol to Alabama. As long as I carry it unloaded."

~ * ~

The woman who answered the phone at the university's engineering department said she was sorry, but there was no one on faculty named Tarnowski.

"Her first name's Antonina," Peter said. "Can you check for that?"

"O-oh, honey, no need to check. That's Professor Farnsworth. She's not in again till Monday, though."

"Can you give me her home number? It's kind of important, and it needs to be confidential."

"You're not the one that has the code word she wants, are you?"

Peter said he knew nothing about a code word.

"Then I can't give you her home number, hon, but I can tell you she don't answer her home phone a lot. Probably best thing is you trust me with that message. I can tape a note to her mailbox that says 'urgent message for you at desk,' and I won't tell anyone but her what it says."

Thirty-five

She awoke at the sound of something clanking and rolling on the concrete of the tiny balcony outside her apartment. Her eyes flicked toward the little Beretta pistol lying atop her nightstand, but she willed her hand to make no move toward it. Then she smiled faintly, as the rolling sound came again, and she knew it was just an empty flowerpot the wind had tipped over. Good, she thought. No wasted motion. No clutching of the checked handgrip, no flick of her little finger against the little metal spur at the bottom of the magazine. No wasted hammering of the heart.

She flipped aside her blanket and took a flat, black nylon holster from a shelf of the nightstand and put the pistol into it. With the holster in her hand, she crossed the bedroom and drew aside a curtain, then the sliding glass door to the balcony. The brick flowerpot still rocked slightly on the concrete, nudged by the wind. She looked at it with a dismissive lip-curl that bared tips of her upper teeth. Then she glanced at Vulcan's buttocks. They were on eye level with her balcony and about fifty yards distant. The sun was up, but the statue was still in deep shadow from the waist down. Rita, the department secretary, had told her the sculptor left Vulcan nude front and back, but the statue had been retrofitted with the semblance of a leather apron on the side facing the city, which stretched away from the base of Red Mountain beneath a shroud of soot and smoke. Vulcan's backside remained bare, though. Antonina kissed her fingertips and blew on them toward his cast-iron butt cheeks. Then she set the flowerpot on its top, shut the sliding door and crossed to a closet, where she slipped the pistol in its holster into a handbag. She pulled on a white cotton blouse with puffed sleeves and a sleeveless blue jumper, and she gave her short, dark hair ten strokes without bothering to look in a mirror. She slung the bag from her shoulder and, with her hand on the pistol grip inside the bag, she cracked open her front door and peered outside. Then she unlatched the inside door chain, stepped out, locked the door and went down three flights of stairs.

It was a Thursday and she had no class to teach. She went into the tenants' parking lot and unlocked her Corolla. She paused, standing by the open door. Then she looked toward the entrances to the parking lot on each of the two adjoining streets. Through one of them she saw a young man with blond, crewcut hair leaning against a light post in a pose of studious inattention. Watching him light a cigarette with his head turned aside and his eyes fixed on nothing, she thought: stupid, clumsy little cat's paw. In the war, the ones who did it no better than you would be dead by sundown. She locked the car door and walked quickly out the other entrance to the parking lot, then to a bus stop on an intersecting street. She caught a bus and got off at the building that housed the offices of Birmingham's morning and afternoon newspapers. She stood on the sidewalk until a police car passed, and she stared fixedly at the policeman until she was sure she had caught his eye. Good, she thought. I've been seen here, but not followed. Then she passed through the building's revolving glass door.

A bearded, long-limbed reporter for the afternoon paper waved at her through a transparent plastic barrier as she passed down a corridor toward his newsroom on the second floor.

"Professor Farnsworth?" he said, pulling up a wheeled chair for her to sit in. Looking at her face, he wondered if he could get away with putting the term "gimlet-eyed" in a news story. He laughed, hoping to put her at ease. Antonina did not laugh.

"I didn't know Farnsworth was a Polish name," he said.

"It's my married name," she said. "I didn't know it was funny."

"Oh, if any name's funny, it's mine," he said. "Jacoby! Now, that's a name to laugh at!" The reporter chuckled. Antonina looked at him, her expression flat. He tapped his pencil point several times on his desk.

"So, did you bring that memoir?" he said. "Your letter was all about that."

"Your paper didn't print the letter, and you didn't ask me to bring anything. You said you'd like to talk with me about what my father knew about the Mittelwerk."

"Yeah. But see, the claims you make here are pretty serious."

"The paper in Huntsville published the letter," she said.

"Yeah, but we have different standards here. If we can attribute the claims you make in that letter to a document written by a prisoner in the rocket factory, then maybe we can write a news story. That'll have more impact than a letter to the editor. People know a letter's just somebody's opinion."

"Can you read Polish?" she said.

"No."

"If you want to see the memoir, perhaps I can show you. I keep it in a safe place, but I can bring it to my apartment for you to look at. I can translate for you any parts you want."

"But, see, my editor says we have to take a close look at the original. Maybe pass it around, call in some experts."

She had already stood. "Then we are wasting each other's time," she said, turning away.

"Well, think it over," he said. "I work tomorrow. You could call me then."

After he heard the elevator door close, the reporter tapped his pencil point on his desk some more and stared abstractedly at his typewriter. His editor strolled over.

"Didn't you say she might be our ticket to a Pulitzer?" the editor said. "Just curious, but how did you piss her off so fast?"

"I didn't," the reporter said. "She didn't sound mad at all. It was just like she'd set herself a fixed quota of time and effort, and she'd used it up."

The bus route back to her apartment ran past the university's engineering school. She got off there and found the message taped to her faculty mailbox. The department secretary told her someone named Peter Dandridge had called and said he would arrive in Birmingham Friday and hoped to meet with her about getting her father's memoir published. Dandridge had said he was acting for Mayor Rabinowitz, the secretary said.

"He didn't say what town this Rabinowitz was mayor of," she said. "I should've asked him."

"When he comes here, ask him first to show you his driver's license," Antonina said. "If the picture looks like him and the state is the one he says he came from, then have him give you a phone number where I can reach him. Tell him I'll call him there."

"But what if you're here in the building, in class or your office? I think this fellow's okay, Professor. He sounded young, and like he could be from right around here. And he knew you'd recognize this mayor he talked about."

"Listen, Rita," Antonina said. She braced her hands against the secretary's wraparound desk, leaned forward and looked fixedly into the woman's eyes. "Very important. Do you remember the two men who came a few days ago wanting to know how to find me?"

"Sure I do. But I knew right away something was off about those two. One of them didn't even sound like he was, you know, American."

"Like I sound not American?"

"Oh, no, he sounded worse."

"And you knew then to send them away, and to call me and tell me they had asked for me, and you suspected they meant me no good?"

"Yes, and you told me I did the right thing."

"And you did, Rita. Now suppose you were the one who sent those two men to find me. Suppose you had figured out why they couldn't fool the smart, careful person at the engineering department desk. What sort of person would you send next time? Would he sound like a harmless young man who might come from right around here? Would he also mention a name he knew was familiar to me?"

"I see," the woman said. She was a half-foot taller than Antonina and much wider in the shoulders. Her whole upper body nodded in grave agreement with the little woman across the desk.

"The man I told you about hasn't called yet, has he?" Antonina said. "The one who can give you that code word?"

"No, ma'am. Nobody else has called for you."

"One more thing, Rita," Antonina said. "If anyone else calls asking for me today, please tell them you know that today I went to the newspaper office. It's true that I went there, Rita. I'm not asking you to lie."

At her apartment, Antonina locked and chained her door, and dialed a number on the phone on her nightstand. She heard a click when someone picked up the receiver, but she did not wait for a voice.

"Simulacrum?" she said.

"*Kompletny*," said a man's voice.

"*Dobra. Do jutra*," Antonina said, and she hung up the phone.

She changed into jeans and a checked shirt so oversized it reached her knees. She ran a belt through the trouser loops, fastened the holster to it and left the shirt hanging loose to hide the holstered pistol. Then she pulled on a fatigue cap she had bought at an Army surplus store, and took a metal strongbox from one of the built-in shelves along one wall. The key in the box's lock had a lanyard attached. Antonina removed the key from the lock and looped the lanyard around her neck.

A woman who lived in the apartment building smiled at Antonina in the parking lot, thinking she might be a child dressed in a parent's work clothes. The woman quit smiling when she glimpsed the face beneath the cap's bill. Antonina put the strongbox in the Corolla's trunk, beside the kind of folding spade that infantrymen use as an entrenching tool. Then she drove north out of town.

When Antonina returned four hours later, the knees of her jeans were blackened, and she no longer had the strongbox. She checked her body for ticks, found two and incinerated them in an ashtray with a match. Then she showered and dressed in the same clothing she'd worn in the morning. She drove downtown to a seafood eatery she liked both for its fare and for the subcurrent of urgency she sensed there. Hospital workers, many of them wearing surgical scrubs, crowded the restaurant during all its open hours. Usually they would either take their food orders with them or eat hurriedly at tiny side tables.

This time, Antonina ordered grilled shrimp with chickpeas and spinach. When unseen hands scooted a tray with her order on it down a stainless steel chute, she took the tray outside and sat alone at a wrought iron table. When the weather was warm, as it often was in October, she liked to sit outside and gaze toward the crest of Red Mountain, where the Vulcan statue symbolizing the city's iron industry held aloft what looked like an electrified snow cone. It was supposed to resemble a lighted torch. Its light glowed green unless someone had died in a traffic accident in the city in the past twenty-four hours. Antonina had long ago given up crossing herself, but when Vulcan's torch glowed red, she would put down her fork, close her eyes and touch the spot on her clothing that concealed the little crucifix she had worn on a necklace since she was a child. But on this night the torch glowed green, and Antonina merely blew a kiss toward the cast-iron equipage concealed beneath Vulcan's apron.

~ * ~

Next morning, in her "Engineering Applications of Calculus" class, Antonina invited three students to the blackboard to calculate the thrust over time produced by a multi-stage rocket.

"Congratulations," she said when they had finished. "You have now launched Apollo Eleven on a correct heading toward the moon. *Sturmbannfürher* von Braun, the Nazi Party's gift to the American space program, would be proud of you."

The class laughed, and she laughed too, baring only the tips of her teeth.

After her class, Antonina made two phone calls from her office. The first took a long time. Throughout, her voice sounded harsh and guarded, and briefly it rose in anger. The second call took less than a minute, and she spoke in Polish. Her voice was warm and she laughed a little. Then she drove over Red Mountain. through Mountain Brook's stone gate, past expensive homes in plantation, chalet and Tudor style. She parked near a toylike cluster of shops and a footbridge that led across a creek to a little gristmill, also toylike. Antonina went into a shop with a sign over the door reading "Klemens Filipowski, Repair and Restoration of Artwork and Documents." Inside, she twice tapped a bell on a countertop. A big, round-shouldered man with wavy white hair peered at her from the rear of the shop, where paintings and books and big plastic envelopes containing documents were arrayed on shelves and a few large paintings were propped against the walls. The man wore thick glasses and he didn't appear to recognize her until he had shuffled closer. Then he motioned her toward a half-door on one side of the counter. As soon as she passed through it, they embraced and murmured a few words in Polish. They went to the rear of the shop, and the man unlocked a metal chamber the size of a refrigerator. It had knobs on the door that controlled temperature and humidity. He took from the chamber two small items covered in plain brown paper and unwrapped them to expose two apparently identical, battered-looking composition books. He set them both on a scarred wooden worktable that spanned the width of the shop. Every other horizontal surface in the workshop was covered with jars of chemicals and containers crammed with brushes and tools, some as small as those used by jewelers or locksmiths. He switched on a gooseneck lamp suspended from the ceiling, taking care to adjust the flexible shaft to prevent the bulb's heat from reaching the paper. He had set up his worktable so he could work on documents and paintings at his own chest height. Antonina's chin barely cleared the table's varnished plyboard top, so he brought her a footstool. He gave her a pair of latex gloves and she pulled them on. Then he handed her a magnifying glass, and for nearly two hours she studied the two composition books. She started with the covers, then turned one page at a time in each book. She would peer through the glass, switching back and forth from one book to the other, and then move on to the next set of matching pages. While she worked, the man laid out a vintage prewar color print on another part of his worktable. It was an advertisement, printed in German, for tickets from Antwerp to New York on the Red Star Line. It depicted a stylishly dressed mother and her daughter, both with red hair, standing on a quay watching a ship steam into the harbor. Mildew stains of the sort art preservationists call foxing marred the print. The man spread towels on his worktable, laid out the print on the towels, mixed a solution in a beaker and, using cotton swabs, dabbed it on the foxing. Once in a while Antonina would murmur in Polish. Twice she put down the handheld magnifying glass and wiped her eyes with the backs of both hands. Finally she closed both books and she and the man spoke again in Polish. He pointed to one of the composition books and seemed to explain what distinguished that one from the other. Antonina rewrapped the one he had pointed at and wrote out an address on the wrapping paper. The man put that book back in the climate-controlled cabinet, and Antonina rewrapped the other book and put it in her purse. They embraced again, and then the man grasped Antonina by the elbows and spoke to her urgently, shaking her a little with hands that encircled her arms. When he released her, she set her purse on the worktable and withdrew her pistol in its holster from her purse and wordlessly held it out to him, not threateningly but as if it were an artwork she was asking him to evaluate. He nodded and she put the pistol and holster back in her purse and left the shop.

Antonina also taught a late afternoon class on Fridays. When she approached her apartment parking lot after class, she noticed a man sitting in a car parked on the curb outside the tenants' lot. He seemed to be studying her building. She pulled to the curb several parking spaces behind him and watched him until he got out of the car, opened the trunk and rummaged through a duffel bag. He removed from the bag a pistol that even from a distance she recognized as a clunky .45 caliber revolver, a weapon she had never expected to see outside a museum's or gun collector's display case. He held the pistol for a few seconds, as if debating what to do with it. Then he shoved it muzzle-first inside the rim of a spare tire braced against a wall of the trunk. He shut the trunk and flipped open a little spiral-bound notebook and seemed to check what was written there against the number on the wall of her building. Then he walked through the parking lot and into the building.

Antonina waited a couple of minutes, then parked in the tenants' lot. With her hand on the grip of the Beretta in her purse and the composition book in its brown wrapper wedged beneath one arm, she climbed the three flights of stairs to her floor.

Thirty-six

He stood, his clenched hand lifted, at the door bearing the number Meir had given him. The gray-carpeted hallway had just two overhead lights, one above the stairwell at either end, and the door was midway between the lights. He began to count down from ten to the moment when he would begin to knock, but the image of what might emerge from behind that door brought forth a torrent of other images, and he quit counting. He could see now how those images had evoked in him yearnings that had shaded, finally, into bitterness and denial. The soft glow of the Bronze Star from the cubicle in the writing desk where his father had hidden it. The shift and flow on the football field that could appear so subtle, almost delicate, until the instant of violent impact. The flashing bayonets on the rifles spun by drill team cadets when he would pass by, head down, ears burning, at his college. And finally, the image his dead friend had created out of his own pain and need: the tall, gray-eyed figure whose claim to be called noblewoman rested not on lineage or title but simply on what she was. And now, judging from all Meir had told him, he'd have that image demolished by whatever would emerge from behind that door.

He saw the small, fiftyish woman in a saddle-brown dress and burnt orange cardigan moving swiftly toward him with one hand in her handbag. She gave no sign she'd even noticed him. He made a distracted effort to smile at her as she passed him. Then, with his hand still poised to knock, he felt the pistol muzzle wedged, pointing upward, between the tendons at the back of his neck.

"Don't bother to knock," she said. "I'm right here."

She dropped her handbag and a parcel wrapped in brown paper onto the floor beside his foot. The cold muzzle against his neck wobbled slightly as she reached around him with one hand and turned her key in the door lock.

"Put your hands down," she said. "This isn't a cowboy film. Open the door."

She prodded his neck with the pistol and he stepped inside. She flicked on the light. It was a midsized efficiency apartment—a long single room with a kitchenette at one end, a bathroom and closet door at the other, a sliding glass door that opened onto a little balcony. Peter saw no clue that this space was inhabited by anyone with tastes or needs or affections, let alone a woman. The bed was the kind he could expect at Fort Bragg, just a mattress and metal frame. By the head of the bed was a rickety-looking table with an alarm clock, and against one wall a cluster of used office furniture—desk, chair, metal file cabinet, lamp—with a litter of papers and an ashtray. There was no couch, just a padded bench seat with a back of wooden slats. In the kitchenette there was a single wooden barstool, a teapot on the two-burner gas stove, a miniature refrigerator on the counter.

The muzzle left his neck, and he heard a snap and guessed she had secured the pistol in a holster.

"Can I turn around?" he said.

"No-oo," she said, drawing out the word sarcastically. "You must face away from me at one hundred-eighty degrees at all times. Else I blow out your brains. Don't be ridiculous. Of course you can turn around."

He turned and had to adjust his line of sight downward. Her dark brown hair was evenly cropped over her shoulders and face. Beneath her bangs her eyes were close-set, dark and wary, like a weasel's. Her eyes stayed fixed on him as she tucked the holstered pistol in her handbag and set the handbag and parcel on her bed.

"I can tell you who I am," he said.

"I see three possibilities," she said. "One, you're another Baptist come to invite me to go to church with you on Sunday. If you were that, I would have shot you and told police you had come to rob and rape. But I ruled that out when I saw the pistol in your trunk. Two, you are one of the people sent to steal from me something that is sacred, but no serious thief would carry a pistol that old. So, three, you are the one who called my office and said you were coming because Meir Rabinowitz sent you."

"That's it," Peter said. "Meir sent me. And then you—you have to be—"

"What I have to be is a Farnsworth," she sighed. "The name sounds like something that fell off a hay wagon, no? But who I am is Antonina Tarnowski. Perhaps you know me by that name."

"Yes, yes I do," he whispered. "You are, you are—Antonina."

She cocked her head a little, peering at him.

"Your name had better match the one given to the woman at our department office, or I will shoot you yet."

"Peter Dandridge," he said. "I was in the Army, in Vietnam, with Avram Rabinowitz. And I'm sorry, but he was killed there about a month ago. The Viet Cong got onto our street, and Rabby—Avram—was on the roof of our building. Nobody knows exactly why he went up there, but that's where he got shot."

While he was talking, she went into the kitchenette, switched on the gas beneath the teapot and reached into a cabinet for a cup and a teabag. "Would you like tea?" she said. "Instant coffee?"

"No, but thanks. And—look, I thought I should try to find you as soon as I got to town. But I ought to check in at my motel. It's in Homewood. That's close to here, right? I can come back here then, if you'd like me to do that. I can tell you anything you want to know about Avram. And—and Meir said you have something important to send him. He hopes you'll let me take it with me, and then I'll hand it off to him."

As soon as he mentioned going to a motel, Antonina switched off the gas under the teapot, went around the counter to her bed and put the paper parcel back in her purse.

"Listen carefully," she said in a low voice, turning toward him with the purse strap over her shoulder and her hand inside the bag. "You will stay here, not in your hotel. You have arrived here at an awkward time. Now I have to make sure you don't ruin everything. Perhaps there's a way you could even help, and I will try to think of what that might be. But at a minimum, I cannot let you out of my sight before tomorrow night."

"Stay here?" he said. "But that's…I don't understand how—"

"There's a Sears a mile from here. We'll get you an air mattress there. You need to eat, don't you? Good, we'll get the mattress, then we'll go to a place where the food is very good. And listen. The mission you want to perform? The only way it will happen is for you to do exactly as I tell you. And do you remember what I have here?" She patted her bag. "Do you think I would hesitate to use it? Good, then let's go."

In the tenants' parking lot, she told him to wait beside her car. She walked to each entrance and peered outside.

"Good, we go in my car," she said when she returned. "If they spot us, better they have no knowledge of yours."

He bought an air mattress and a cheap bicycle pump to inflate it, and Antonina bought a small padlock. Then they went to the restaurant at the foot of Red Mountain where everyone's order came sliding on a tray down a metal chute. Peter ordered shrimp and grits with sweet tea and Antonina ordered a bowl of gumbo and a salad. They sat outside at a wrought iron table, where Antonina finished her food quickly. Then she smoked, watching him closely. She kept the purse on top of the table and kept one arm through its strap.

"Green again tonight," she said.

"Pardon?"

"The light on the Vulcan," she said, flicking one hand dismissively toward Red Mountain. "It means no one killed in traffic today. Shooting or knifing or rat poison, maybe, but no one in a car smashup. So hurray."

"You've seen people killed in a lot of ways, I guess."

She shrugged.

"Still, it must be kind of tough for you to hear about Avram. I mean, after all this time, and after what you did."

"People get killed in wars," she said. "If it were hard for me to see it or hear about it, I would be dead myself many times over by now."

"But, the way you saved him. That had to be kind of special."

"What we did, that nun and I?" She tapped her glowing cigarette on the edge of an ashtray, and the corners of her mouth turned down, as if she were considering the question. "Yes, that was special, but no one else saw it, so no history book will say a partisan and a nun saved one Jew from that ghetto. But is the child special to me? I never saw the child. He was wrapped in a filthy blanket, I gave him to the nun, I wrote down what I knew of him. Away he went, and I never thought about him much after that. Now, was his uncle, cousin—whatever he is—special to me? He said he tried to be, but whatever he tried to do for me, it didn't work. So Meir Rabinowitz turned out to be special to me only on a scale of disappointment."

"But he's trying to do something special now. He's trying to make up for what he couldn't do all those years ago. He's got an agreement with a publisher to—"

Instantly she shed her mask of indifference. She leaned forward across the table, her eyes blazing.

"You do not talk about that where anyone can hear," she whispered. "Has Meir really sent me someone with so little brains? Come, finish your dinner. Then we go."

It was nearly dark when they drove back to her apartment. While Peter pumped up his air mattress with the bike pump, Antonina slipped the circular tab on her door's chain into its slot. Then she doubled the chain to draw it taut. She fitted the padlock's arm through two links of the doubled chain, snapped the lock shut and attached the padlock key to her keychain. Then she turned on the gas burner under the teapot.

"I have a plan," she said. "And now we will have a tutorial. Would you like tea? Coffee?"

"Coffee, sure. But why the padlock? All it does is lock us in."

Her gaze was so cold his shoulders shivered a little. "So this is the best Meir Rabinowitz could send me," she said. "You brought your toilet bag up, yes? Tomorrow when we are ready to go to Huntsville, I will unlock the chain, and then you can go out. Not before."

When she'd made the tea and coffee, she pulled the bench seat next to her desk and told Peter to sit on it. She switched on the little lamp on her desktop and put the brown paper parcel in the cone of light from the bulb.

"You know something about my father's memoir, yes?" she said.

"Meir said your father was forced to work at a rocket factory in the Harz Mountains, and after the war he wrote down his memories of life in the factory."

Antonina's lips crinkled with scorn. "'Memories of life in the factory,'" she mimicked. "Happy days on the old production line, yes?" She pulled aside the brown wrapping paper, opened the composition book's creased and stained cover and riffled through several of its pages. Peter could see they were filled with closely spaced writing, interspersed with detailed pen-and-ink sketches.

"You can look in it if you like," she said. "The writing's all in Polish."

He opened the book to one of the sketches. It seemed to depict a man looking backward over his shoulder while his hands were hidden inside a concave shape that Peter took to be a section of a rocket's fuselage. The drawing was so small and crammed with detail, though, that Peter would have needed a magnifying glass to be certain.

"What my father tried to do was bear witness to crimes," Antonina said. "And he did better. He provided evidence. He includes names and dates and stages of production and ways that prisoners could sabotage the rockets. He wrote down the numbers of people the SS hanged or shot for doing any of those things. If you failed to tighten a set of screws properly, you could end up in a line of people with ropes on their necks. They'd all be lifted up slowly by a big crane and left there to strangle, and all around them the work of assembling rockets went on as usual. And executions were the least of it. The SS worked thousands of people to death in those tunnels. The demands for more rockets grew, and the food for prisoners became less, and more and more of them died."

"So the SS ran the show?" Peter said.

"Oh, you should be a lawyer for the defense! I will advise them to hire you, because that is the argument they must make, if they are ever brought to trial. You must tell the court the SS ran the show, and von Braun and his men could not have known about their atrocities because they were so absorbed in the science of getting a guided bomb to go up, up, up, and then down, down, down on the heads of innocent people. Besides, those experts, those engineers and technicians, had been based for years at Peenemunde on the North Sea, very far from where workers at the rocket factory were being starved and beaten and hanged. As a lawyer for the defense, you must try to confuse the judges about a simple fact: By the time the rocket factory opened, Allied bombing had shut down Peenemunde. The research and testing scattered around to places the Allies were less likely to bomb, but everything centered on the tunnels of the factory, the Mittelwerk. Still, von Braun's men will claim they were ignorant that workers there were being starved and murdered. But here my father's testimony proves they lie. Because he saw rocket engineers who came to make inspections at the Mittelwerk while prisoners were falling down from hunger and exhaustion and being carted off to die. More than that, he knew some of those men who strolled past him down the assembly line. My father had trained as an electrical engineer, you see, and he ran an electrical business in Poland between the wars. He had some clients in Germany then, and he knew Franz Lichter from business trips in Hamburg. In January 1945, my father overheard a conversation between Lichter and an SS security officer at the Mittelwerk. Lichter said von

Braun's team had identified sabotage at the factory as the main reason so many V-2s were blowing up in flight, and they wanted the SS to clamp down on it. Lichter told the SS officer that Dieter Vogelsang would send evidence that might show where in the production process the sabotage took place. Vogelsang was another of these so very innocent, head-in-the-clouds rocket scientists. My father says von Braun himself came to the Mittelwerk, and he must have known about the hangings and the starving of prisoners there. Of course, all three of those men, von Braun, Lichter and Vogelsang, today live in Huntsville. I'm sure they sleep well at night and drink their wine from fine crystal."

"Didn't the American military know about these guys' backgrounds before they waved them in?" Peter said.

"Of co-ourse," she said. She had tilted back in her office chair, and her face had fallen into shadow. He could hear in her voice the sneer. "Of co-ourse they knew. They just kept it secret. They have kept it secret until this day. But if my father's memoir gets published, it won't be secret anymore. That is why I have come to live here. That is why I must carry a pistol. That is why I protect my father's memoir with my life."

"He brought it to America himself, didn't he?' Peter said. "Didn't he try to get it published?"

"I don't know," she said. "I couldn't be with him to help, not with that, not with anything. Perhaps he had a plan to publish. Death cut short whatever plans my father had."

She tilted forward and rewrapped the workbook in the brown paper. Then she opened a drawer of the file cabinet beside the desk, took out some oversized Manila folders and plopped them on the desk.

"You know already some things about my father, don't you?" she said. "You heard them from Meir Rabinowitz, yes? My father was many things: an engineer, a soldier, a businessman, always a patriot. But what he dreamed of most was to invent something good for the world. He was half-German, you know? He could have gotten a nice job with the Nazis. But what path did he choose instead? Slave labor, almost starving to death. He chose that, because he saw what the Nazis were about and he would not be part of it. Then after the war, director of a refugee camp, and finally a chance to come to America. But by then he was old, and who wants to hire an old man who struggles to speak English? The only job he can find is washing dishes. That is what killed him. He did meaningless work for eight hours a day. But look, when he came back at night to the room where he lived by himself, he was doing this."

She flipped open one of the manila folders and pulled out a sheaf of papers. They were drawings of engines, with descriptions written in the margins in Polish and French.

"Magnetic levitation," she said. "A train engine that hovers in the air and flies. It rises and it flies down the tracks. He was trying to patent these designs when he died in Boston. Would this machine work? I don't know. But I understand the principles involved, and I can tell you a well-designed engine based on those principles will work. He saw the future, and he left behind these pictures of it. He was a visionary. And do you know the occupation listed on my father's death certificate? Kitchen worker. Kitchen worker."

She leaned back again in her chair. "Now, from what I have just told you, I have an ethical case, but nothing more," she said. "These Nazis were brought here to chase their vision of the future. When they achieve it, they are placed on a pedestal, while my father was left hardly being able to exist. From an ethical perspective, all we can say is that's just too bad. Tut-tut, you know? But we can't say that's just too bad if those men worked hand-in-glove with the SS, and the SS was killing and beating some and letting thousands of others starve, and von Braun's people knew it. That's what makes the memoir so important. It turns things that are just too bad into crimes."

She closed the folder and dropped the stack of folders back in the file drawer. Then she patted with one hand around on her desk until she realized she had dropped her cigarette pack and lighter on her bed. With one practiced thrust of her feet, she propelled her chair on its rollers backward to her bedside, where she shook a cigarette from the pack. To Peter, his vision altered by the light of the desk lamp, she appeared as a silhouette against the otherworldly green glow cast through the balcony's glass door by the torch in Vulcan's lifted hand.

"Antonina, I'll tell you now, you've answered one question Meir wanted me to help him with," Peter said. "He wanted to know whether I thought you'd tipped over the brink mentally and needed someone to take over your affairs."

In the brief flare from her lighter, her features looked impassive and her eyes coal black. She laughed softly.

"Someone much like himself, I'm sure," she said. "For my own good, of course."

"Well, I'll tell him you're not nuts. And that you're focused on the same thing he is, getting that memoir published."

"So Meir Rabinowitz sent you here as his tool, and you are just trying to be a good tool. Why you would agree to do that is not my business. But from now at least through tomorrow, I intend to use you as my tool. I hope you will show the same willingness to work for me. But understand that to me you are a tool, nothing more. If you get in the way of what I am trying to achieve, I will treat you as I would a broken chisel."

"Well, thanks at least for likening me to a tool with a sharp edge," he said.

"Here is your tutorial then, little chisel. Tomorrow morning I will make a telephone call to a reporter at the newspaper office here. I have talked to him already. I know he has an appetite for a story about my father's memoir. I will tell him I am taking the memoir to Huntsville, to a public meeting with a member of Congress. They call it a town hall. I will tell this reporter that I will quote some of the things my father wrote about these rocket scientists."

"That's it?" Peter said. "Isn't that just cycling back to a ploy that didn't work for you in Connecticut?"

"Ah, so Meir Rabinowitz was having me surveilled even then," she said. "It seems he'll go to great lengths to look after my best interests. No, I'm not just cycling back. Three differences. One, Huntsville is where those old Nazis live now. Some of them might even be in the room with us tomorrow. Two, their rocket has just put Americans on the moon. Since July, their star has been in the ascendant, yes? And here I come trying to shoot it down. But, most important, I will have a document filled with details of their criminality in my hand. Until now, I never carried the memoir in public, because I knew government agents would seize it if they could. But this time I have a plan to secure it."

Peter leaned forward, placed his forehead in his hands and muttered "no, no, no."

"And even a fourth difference, one I hadn't planned on, but now it has come as a gift. This time I have someone to help me. Someone equally devoted to preserving an eyewitness account of war crimes."

"No, Antonina!" he said, looking up from his hands. "You say I'm Meir's tool, and now I'm yours? I'll tell you whose tool I am. For the next eight months, I'm a tool of the U.S. Army. So as to you getting me crossways with the FBI or whoever's after that memoir? No."

She put the lighted cigarette down on the ashtray on her bedside stand. He sensed the coiled-spring rigidity of her body.

"Poor little chisel," she said in a coddling tone. "Long ago I grew accustomed to working with forged steel tools. Now I must work with a different kind. Did you think I expect you to draw your pitiful six-shooter on the FBI? These men don't know I am going to Huntsville tomorrow, so they are not likely to come either, unless it is on a guess. Even if they come, they will think I am not foolish enough to bring the memoir, since I have never done that in public. So they will not have a warrant ready that would enable them to seize it. But whether they are there or not, they will learn quickly that I was there, had the memoir with me and said publicly it would soon be published, together with a preface by an expert who says it is genuine."

"Which you don't yet have," Peter said.

"Which the head of L'Chaim Publishing House says in his letter to me that he can get and will include in the book. So once the people from FBI, NASA, Defense Department, wherever, hear of this, they will act quickly to seize the memoir. I expect they will have a warrant by the time we drive back to Birmingham. So before we come back, we must return the memoir to the secure place I have made for it."

"But what if they stop you at a roadblock on the way back into town?"

"Exactly right, little chisel," she said. "Your edge is not quite as dull as I thought."

She lifted the cigarette from the ashtray and took a long drag. He saw its glowing tip reflected in her eyes. He remembered something Rabby had said about the mythic Antonina before she slashed a pogromist's neck with her father's saber: Her eyes didn't look anything except intent.

"I had planned to take care of everything myself. Your presence complicates things, of course. But I think if you do just as I say, it may even prove an advantage. Do you know something of the history of coal and iron mining in this region?"

"Yeah, a little. There were rich seams of both, so the mining companies could use local coal to smelt local iron ore into pig iron, then refine it into steel."

"And who mined the coal and the ore?"

"Well, miners, right? Like anyplace else where stuff gets dug out of the ground."

"No-ooo, little chisel, not like anyplace else. For a long time, it was prisoners who worked the mines here. Convicts who ate rancid food and lived in filth, who died of hunger and exhaustion and disease and were whipped when they tried to escape. Slave laborers in tunnels underground. The mining companies rented them from the state. Of course, nearly all the prisoners in the mines here were black. Apart from that, they were a lot like the ones at the Mittelwerk. Many of those mines are worked out now and abandoned, but if you walk back in the woods away from the roads north of here, you can find the tunnels, the falling-apart buildings where the prisoners slept crammed into bunks just like in the Nazi camps. So when I was trying to think of a hiding place for a precious document, the answer came to me: where better?"

"Wait, wait, wait," Peter said. "That memoir, you're saying, could change what we know, or think we know, about a slice of history. And when you're not doing something else high-risk with it, you're storing it in a mine shaft?"

She took another puff from her cigarette, and he glimpsed a corner of her smile.

"I have buried a strongbox at the fifteenth crosstie of a mineshaft railway, beside the left rail," she said. "To find the mine, you pull off the highway at the Tyree exit and climb the embankment on the west side of the road. The mineshaft is a quarter-mile back in the woods. You must memorize those directions."

"This is nuts," he said.

"How nuts?"

"Your risk is off the charts. Mine timbers collapse. Mines flood. Kids poke around in mines."

"Where do you suggest, then? A bank box? The trunk of my car? Maybe trunk of your car, beside your antique pistol?"

"How about somebody you trust at the university?"

"And what is this friend at the university going to do when a federal agent comes with a warrant and cites the penalty for lying or failing to comply? No, I prefer my metal strongbox in a hole in a mineshaft. In the war, where did we hide things? Always in the ground, in the forest. Because nowhere else was safe. A building is never safe. Someone can see you hide things there and betray you, or maybe the building is simply blown up. But when you hide things of value in the ground and you secure them properly and you take careful note of where you buried them, then they are safe.

"Good thinking, I suppose, in occupied Poland, in 1942," Peter said. "In 1969, in Alabama? It's nuts."

"All the better then," she said. "I wouldn't want to disappoint Meir Rabinowitz and whoever else thinks I'm nuts. Sometimes, little chisel, the best means of evasion is simply to play true to expectations."

"So you want me to go find this mine shaft? When? And what am I supposed to do when I get there?"

She stubbed out her cigarette and waved the smoke away from her face. Some of the smoke drifted toward the glass sliding door, where it became tinged with the greenish hue that illuminated Vulcan's buttocks.

"Tomorrow morning at ten o'clock we will be at the town hall with this congressman, Milton Pettigrew," she said. "It is at an elementary school. I will have the memoir, wrapped as it is now. When it is my turn to speak, I will unwrap it and explain what it is and why it is important. I will announce the contract to publish. The FBI already knows of that, and if it becomes public knowledge they might be more guarded in their efforts to seize it. If the *Birmingham News* reporter is there, I will answer his questions. If a news photographer wants to take pictures of me with the memoir, we pose. Publicity we like. If any of the Germans are there and want to talk, or if anyone else speaks in their defense, we do not contradict. We say what we have to say, answer questions, and then we go."

"When you say 'we,' Antonina, it needs to mean just you."

"But you will stand close by, understood?" she said. "If for any reason I need hands free for a moment, yours must be the only other hands that touch the memoir."

"So then we drive back here?"

"We drive as far as the Tyree exit and pull off the road. Before you appeared uninvited at my door today, I had planned to take the memoir up to the mine myself and secure it in the lockbox. Now I think it best that I entrust that part to you, while I remain at the car as a lookout."

"Lookout? And if the FBI or cops show up, you do what? Shoot holes in their warrant?"

"What I do will depend on the circumstances. A better tool than you would make fewer arguments."

"Oh, I'm barely started," he said. "Say we succeed. Say we squirrel away this manuscript in your mineshaft. Say we just grin and shrug when the FBI hands us its warrant. What then? They tail us twenty-four hours a day until one of us leads them to the hidey-hole? Maybe you've got time for a game like that, but I don't. Two more days, tops, and I head home. If I have to leave without that memoir, too bad. I've done what I could."

Her figure in the chair by the bed was in complete darkness, save for a faint green aureole around her hair. She looked perfectly still, yet he sensed her mental change of tack.

"Tell me, do you know fly fishing?" she said. She had purged her voice of its rasp and given it a girlish lilt.

"What? Yeah, I've fly fished. Never with great success, though."

"And what makes a good fly, one the fish will bite?"

"You'll hear different schools of thought on that. Some say the fly needs to flash and spin like a go-go dancer. Traditionalists say a good fly should match something from the natural world that a fish would count as prime dining."

"Which do you believe?"

"I guess I'm old school," he said. "It just makes sense to me. If something looks like a midge larva and wriggles like one, then fish are likely to bite it."

"Yes. I think you should hold to that old-school belief."

"So your point is what?"

"I fly fished a little in Connecticut," she said. "I am just making small talk. Now it is time for you to sleep."

She stood and went to her closet and stood on tiptoe to reach an upper shelf. Then she turned and threw a blanket onto the floor by his air mattress.

"Use the bathroom now," she said. "Tomorrow will be a long day for you. Maybe longer than you expect."

After she had drawn the curtain over the glass door to the balcony, he heard the little clunk her pistol made as she set it on the bedside table. Then she climbed into her Spartan little bed.

"Funny thing is, you shaped his whole life," Peter said into the darkness. "Avram's, I mean. First you saved it. And when he finally learned how that had happened, you shaped it even more."

He heard her sigh. "Stop your babbling," she said.

"No, damn it. You need to hear this. At least, I need to tell you. His idea of you was the grain of sand inside his shell. Over time it encrusted into this weird pearl. A high-value pearl, at least to the eye. He even had a phobia of barbed wire, for Christ's sake. Everything he aspired to centered on this heroine named Antonina, who was this impossible mix of nobility and self-sacrifice. Of course she wasn't you. It was that impossible Antonina he was following when he volunteered for Vietnam. It was that Antonina who beckoned him up to her rooftop, to draw the VC away from a little eight-year-old Vietnamese girl who lived in our villa. And you? You, the real Antonina? You don't remember him at all, except as something bundled in a filthy blanket and tossed over a ten-foot fence. To you, he was just a token in a game. A game you're still playing, this time with a token that matters to you a lot more than Avram ever did."

For a while he thought she was asleep. Then, in the darkness, he could tell she had propped herself on an elbow.

"Now I will tell you a little story of my own, and then we sleep," she said. "In the last winter of fighting, the Nazis caught me when I was trying to deliver a message in a town beside the Oder River. I was a little careless, and I was caught. They took me to a jail and they called the SS. The SS came and they beat me, I do not talk, they beat me some more, I still do not talk, and the SS went away and I am alone in my cell. The jailkeepers were Sudeten Germans. Regular German Army, not SS. They were not bad guys. Then one day they brought in a little Jewish girl and put her in the cell next to mine, all by herself. Her name was Joanna. I think these Sudeten men thought they could keep her safe there and no one would notice. She cried and cried, and I began to talk to her. I would hold her hand through the bars. After a while the jailers sometimes let her come from her cell into mine, and I would take her on my lap and sing to her and tell her stories. My father had a wonderful voice. When I was a child, I loved to hear him sing. My voice was not so good, but I would sing her the songs my father sang to me. Sometimes she would go to sleep on my lap. And then one day the SS came again, but this time they did nothing to me. They took Joanna from her cell, and they took her outside my window into a little courtyard, and they shot her. And a few days after that I was put on a train to Ravensbruck. So no, little chisel, I do not think about your friend, the child I was able to save. But I think every day of Joanna, the child for whom I could do nothing but sing badly."

Thirty-seven

She prodded him awake with her foot. When he opened his eyes she was already at her desk, spinning the phone's dial. The clock beside the pistol on her bedside stand read 6:30. As soon as she finished dialing she fixed her eyes on Peter.

"Is your reporter Reginald Jacoby there?" she said. "Can you please take a message for him?"

She said into the receiver that she would be at Congressman Pettigrew's town hall in Huntsville at ten o'clock, and she would bring her father's memoir. She said the newspaper was welcome to send a photographer to take pictures of it.

By the time Peter came out of the bathroom she was wearing dark blue denim culottes and a maroon turtleneck sweater and low-heeled shoes with snakeskin uppers.

"Do you have shoes better for climbing?" she said, pointing at the worn brown loafers he had worn on the drive to Birmingham.

"I've got sneakers in the car," he said.

"Good. Put them on before we leave."

"Shouldn't we drive up in my car?" he said. "They'll have ID on your car, but not mine."

"We take my car. If they want to follow us, then they follow us. I want them to know exactly where to look until they find the thing they want."

"You mean…until they can't find it. Right?"

"Of course. Until they can't find it."

She unlocked her file cabinet and took the memoir, still wrapped in brown paper, from the top drawer and handed it to him. "Put it inside your shirt," she said. "I want you to carry it that way until you hand it to Meir Rabinowitz, so get used to it."

He put it under his shirt, propped up by his belt. "I'm afraid I'll squish its pages," he said. "Why's this necessary?"

"Because multiple times on your way home you will leave the car, if only to pee. You must never be out of contact with the memoir, and no one else must see it. Crinkled pages we can live with."

He got the sneakers from his car and put them on and they climbed into her Toyota. She pulled in at a fast food window and bought an egg-and-sausage biscuit for him and coffee for them both. She drove unblinking into the sunrise as they descended Red Mountain, while Peter shielded his eyes with an arm, then flipped down his visor.

A half hour out of Birmingham, Antonina flicked her head to the left as they approached an exit. "The mine is that way," she said. "When we return, we take a different road that runs nearer to it." She gave him precise directions from the roadway to the mineshaft and asked him to repeat them twice. She said the ascent included a section of loose rock spread on the slope to halt erosion, and he told her about his unstable knee.

"Then you must climb the rocks slowly and carefully," she said. "Unless we are being pursued. And then the hell with your knee, you must climb as fast as you can."

"One more thing I still don't get," he said. "Getting this memoir to the publisher—that's the key to everything you want, right? Well, how does it move things in that direction to bury it inside a metal box in an abandoned mine?"

"Think of fly fishing, little chisel," she said. "Imagine you are a beautiful little dry fly. Picture how you skip, skip, skip over the surface of the water. Every time the fish thinks, 'oh, now I've got this tasty bug,' you give another skip, and that just makes the fish chase harder and harder."

"But even if you wear the fish out, you want him to catch the artificial fly in the end, right?" Peter said.

"Hmmm, yes, that's true," Antonina sighed and nodded gravely. "We certainly don't want them to seize the actual document, even if we wear them out chasing it. Yes, I see the problem."

They reached Huntsville more than an hour early. She drove up a little mountain at the edge of town and pulled over near a house that had cedar walls atop a stone foundation, split cedar shingles on its gables and a slate roof.

"Haarmacher lives here," she said. "He was von Braun's grand wizard of missile guidance systems. Someone I know in Germany sent me a clipping of an interview Haarmacher gave to a newspaper in Munich. He said he was proud of his work on a plan to send submarines into New York harbor, where they would launch V-2 rockets. They even had street maps marked with spots to blow up, like Times Square, Radio City. The purpose, he said, would be the same as in London and Antwerp: less material damage than to weaken morale. But the war ended too soon, alas. Now, here he is, honored American citizen, living on a lovely mountain in Huntsville, in his own little Berghof."

As their car was stopped at a downtown stoplight, a man and woman and two little girls crossed the street. All four of them wore Saturday-morning, going-out-for-pancakes smiles. The children held their mother's hands, and the smaller girl skipped a little. Peter felt a sudden yearning to merge with this tableau of normalcy, thinking: How did I let this happen? How did I let myself get trapped in this warp in reality and time? Why have I come to this quiet, normal place as sidekick to a figure who's both a fairytale heroine and a real, capable, dangerous avenger of wrongs that took place before I was born? Who is all those things, and maybe a borderline psychopath to boot?

The steeply pitched roof over the elementary school's entrance and the bands of inlaid tile in its supporting pillars made Peter wonder if it was modeled on a Swiss chalet, though he had no clear idea of what a Swiss chalet looked like. Antonina parked the car and swiftly removed the holstered pistol from her purse and thrust it into the glove compartment. She told him to take the memoir out of his shirt, carry it inside and hand it to her when instructed.

She had opened her car door and already placed one foot on the pavement when she switched her eyes toward him so quickly and with such ferocity that his hand froze on the door handle.

"What is it?" he said. "What's wrong?"

"What is it you call yourself?" she said contemptuously.

"I could call myself a lot of things," he said. "One of them is ready to get on with whatever we came here to do."

"You call yourself a soldier, don't you? A true veteran, just back from the front?"

"I'm enough of a soldier to know military culture thrives on petty harassment," he said. "I wonder why you think now's the time for it."

"Do you know what a real soldier needs more than anything?"

"Raw guts? Enough smokes to last the night in a foxhole?"

The corners of her mouth drew downward in mock disappointment. She shook her head.

"No, little chisel," she said. "But today I think you will learn."

The cafeteria door was held open by a wooden wedge at the bottom. Peter had expected to hear chatter and laughter, perhaps even the raised voices of people eager to pepper their congressman with demands and grievances. Instead, he heard only the light, rapid tapping of Antonina's heels on the hallway's tiles.

When he followed her through the doorway, he saw about two dozen heads, most of them gray- or white-haired, clustered near a far wall, where a row of windows, each with its hand crank, ran the length of the cafeteria.

Between the people in their plastic chairs and the windows was a table with a coffee urn, Styrofoam cups, a bowl of green grapes and a boxlike half-podium. As Antonina and Peter drew closer, several of the seated people turned, one after another, and gazed at them through the outsize lenses of their eyeglasses as silently and noncommittally as a conclave of owls. A stocky woman seated behind the table greeted them with a curt wave.

"Coffee's just perking," she said. "Grapes are from Tuesday lunch. Might be a little past prime."

"You must be with the newspaper," a woman sitting in the back row said. She had freshly permed gray hair, a broad, unfocused smile and a neck bowed by collapsing vertebrae.

"No, ma'am," Antonina said. An attempt at a smooth, polite tone was draped awry over her grating voice. "We drove up from Birmingham. We have an issue we'd like to bring to the congressman's attention."

"Oh, good!" the woman said. "I was hoping somebody would bring some issues. A lot of us just come to these politician things because there's nothing good on at the theater."

A couple of seats away from the woman, a man who wore a striped, red and white golf shirt half-turned and snorted scornfully. He lifted one keratosis-splotched arm and whispered behind his hand to Antonina.

"Throw Milton a good hard issue, and watch him whiff," he said. "This time of year, he figures he can just fly down from Washington, tell a few people he can't help them with garbage pickup on their street or with some dumbass bill in the state legislature, and then spend the weekend dove hunting."

Beyond the cafeteria windows, a black sedan with heavily tinted windows pulled into the school parking lot, followed by an orange Ford Falcon with a deep dent in the front bumper and scratches along the passenger side doors that bore witness to a sideswipe. The driver of the black sedan got out and hurried around to open a rear door. The congressman planted his gleaming shoes on the pavement, gripped the doorframe with one hand and swung himself out and into motion toward the school, flicking dust from his lapels with his fingertips as the aide hurried to keep up. Pettigrew had waves of graying hair and his cheeks looked lightly rouged.

"That's our boy," said the man in the striped golf shirt. "That's Milton. If you brought your stay-awake pills, pop 'em now."

The congressman was already halfway to the lobby door when a tall young man with a brown beard and a young black woman with a camera slung from her neck leapt from the battered Falcon.

"Very good," Antonina said quietly. "A photograph will help."

The young man pulled a jacket off the back of the driver's seat, flipped it on, hurriedly patted its pockets and jogged after the congressman, apparently hoping to get in a quick question. He tucked his notepad under his arm and, as he tried to straighten his tie, the notepad fell and skidded across the pavement. He leaned to pick it up and two pens and a candy bar fell from the breast pocket of his jacket. By the time he retrieved everything, the congressman and his aide had entered the building.

The congressman's aide took position inside the cafeteria door like a one-man honor guard. The congressman hurried forward, beaming and holding both hands aloft as if he'd been greeted with an ovation instead of near-silence. Close behind him, a burly woman with a television camera balanced on one shoulder waddled through the doorway. Her blonde ponytail was yanked back so severely it resembled a taut mooring line. Her massive torso stayed perfectly vertical as she swung left of the cluster of occupied chairs and took position at an angle from the podium.

The man in the golf shirt leaned back toward Antonina and Peter and again whispered confidentially. "That's Francine Needham, WHUV," he said. "Francine's a legend hereabouts. Does all her own camera work. Catches politicians off-guard with questions they aren't ready for, then films their mouths working with no sound coming out."

The bumbling newspaper reporter and the photographer saw where Francine had set up and took up a similar position on the other side of the little crowd. The congressman's aide was still looking back through the doorway. His smile had turned brittle.

"A-ah, now they show themselves," Antonina said, though no one else had yet appeared in the doorway. "So it's seamless. Police, army, FBI, even the postal."

Peter didn't immediately grasp the reason for his own unease with the undersized man in a baggy windbreaker who stepped through the doorway, took something from his pocket, unfolded it and showed it to the aide. There was something off about him. Not until the man turned face-on toward the windows could Peter see clearly that his gray-flecked beard ran a couple of inches too high on both cheeks. It arced downward from his temples to the bridge of his nose.

"An acquaintance of mine," Antonina said. "FBI. In Connecticut, I took care to say nothing to him about his resemblance to a werewolf."

The extra stretch of beard had been clipped evenly with the rest, accentuating the beard's likeness to a mask. The man's eyes, though, were a different matter. They had the kind of crinkled, slightly chastened look that Peter had learned to recognize in the eyes of men like his father and Colonel Jesperson. Men who had learned to prize avoidance of harm as much as accomplished good.

A taller, younger man with fair, crewcut hair stepped through the doorway, and made an odd little bow to the congressman's aide.

Antonina spoke softly into Peter's ear. "Polish," she said. "Translator for FBI. Defector, I think."

"Defect how?" Peter said. "From where?"

"My guess, just from his looks, is Polish Army choir. The choir is very popular in New York, Philadelphia, Chicago."

"But surely somebody like that couldn't authenticate the memoir," Peter said.

"Of course not. But if they could seize it, he could tell them it's not just *Uncle Wiggily's Story Book* translated into Polish."

"Can this guy seize it here, today? If you knew that was a risk, why did you bring it?"

"That's where you come in, little chisel." Her tone hovered between soothing and mocking. "I depend on you to defend it to the death. I depend on him, too, that he won't push matters that far."

"So the 'to the death' part—that's hyperbole, right?" Peter said.

"I said I depend on him," she said. "I didn't say you could depend on me. To him, this is just handwriting in a language he doesn't understand. To me it's a sacred trust."

The FBI agent folded his hands beneath the edge of his baggy windbreaker and fixed his eyes on Antonina, who stared back at him with what might have passed for a smile. It seemed to Peter there was something twin-like about them. After a long, unflinching stare at the agent, she turned toward the table with its box-sized podium. The congressman was thanking the little crowd for putting citizenship ahead of yard chores, grocery shopping, grandchildren and the opportunity to drive to Birmingham and tailgate at Legion Field ahead of the Alabama-Tennessee football game on this beautiful October day.

As he spoke in the comforting tone of a preacher's invitation to the altar, Pettigrew's hands reached out as if he yearned to embrace his listeners.

"I've been in Congress right at thirteen years now," he said. "But lots of times up there, I still feel like I fell off the turnip truck and didn't bounce. There's a lot about our wonderful federal government I still don't understand. Now, I don't hold with giving voters half-answers, especially if the half I leave out is the half they need. So if I can't give you a good, complete answer, I won't flounder around up here. My aide here, Quin Cheatham, will write down your question, and my staff will research it and call you with the full, complete answer that you deserve."

"Translation is, you can ask him any question you want," the man in the golf shirt said behind his hand, "and it'll be like dropping a rock in a dry well. The splash never comes."

Cheatham, clearly used to the drill, sat by the congressman with his ballpoint poised above a legal pad. People asked about hours at the local post office, plans to raise the price of stamps, the Tennessee Valley

Authority's electricity rates, TVA plans to build a nuclear power plant and the possibility of federal support to expand the cardiac wing at the local hospital. Cheatham would scribble furiously. The congressman would listen to each question with a show of intense concentration. The flesh beneath his eyes would contract and expand, wrinkling and smoothing like pale blue crepe cloth. He would smile and say, "We'll get back to you with the best possible answer." He would remind the questioner to give his aide a name and address, and Cheatham would raise his ballpoint pen and wave it as if doubts might have arisen about where he was and what he was there for.

After a long pause, the congressman, with an air of finality, raised his hands in a benedictory pose. "Anyone else?" he said.

"Watch closely now," the man in the striped golf shirt said behind his hand to Peter and Antonina. Then he stood and asked the congressman for a status report on the boll weevil eradication tests the Department of Agriculture was supposed to be running.

Pettigrew nodded gravely.

"That's an excellent question," he said. "Now, if you'll just give your name and contact information to Mister Cheatham here ..."

"But you're on the ag committee, right?" the man said. "And you sit on the subcommittee that deals with horticulture and research, right? So why can't you bring cotton growers up to date on a matter this important?"

Peter noticed that Francine Needham had switched on her camera and was slowly panning from Pettigrew to his questioner and back again.

"Sure, sure. We've talked over the need to finally put a complete stop to this terrible pest. I think ... As I remember, the scientists say chemical means alone won't do it. They're looking for, you know, other tools."

"Isn't the Agriculture Department testing possible ways to reduce the weevil's food supply?" the man in the golf shirt said. "How's that going?"

Francine swung her camera toward the congressman, who had the presence of mind to beam at his questioner.

"We-ell, in Congress, you know, the press of business on so many vital matters leaves no time to master fine details," Pettigrew said. "But my staff will get you every scrap of information you could want. Seems you're pretty well up on the matter. I guess you're in the cotton business?"

"No, I sell and install swimming pools," the man said. "But everybody who lives around here has a stake in weevil eradication. I just figured you might catch us up on how it's going."

He sat down and tilted his chair back toward Peter and Antonina. "See what I mean?" he said.

The young black photographer from Birmingham had snapped several photos, but the reporter showed no interest in this revelation that Pettigrew had brought his constituents nothing of value beyond his mellifluous voice and waves of hair that flowed as smoothly as a placid sea. The reporter merely tapped his pen against the spiral rings of his notebook and glanced nervously at Antonina.

"Well, I reckon that's all, then?" Pettigrew said, extending his arms again in a pose of pastoral benediction. "Again, I certainly want to compliment all of you on answering the call of citizenship on this glorious fall—"

"I have something very important to bring to your attention," Antonina said, snatching the wrapped memoir from Peter's hand as she stood. She shucked off the brown paper and dropped it to the floor for Peter to gather up. "I hope you will bring it to the attention of Congress," she said, drawing a sheet of paper from a side pocket of her purse and unfolding it with a flick of her wrist.

"Living among the citizens of Huntsville are men who should be charged with war crimes, perhaps even complicity in murder," she read from her script. "They are some of the same men who designed the Redstone missile and the Saturn Five that put Americans on the moon. They have done many things for this country, but their crimes should not be forgotten or swept under the rug in the name of national security."

She held aloft the memoir and waggled it a little. The workbook flapped like a broken wing, proof that its paper and binding were cheap, flimsy and old.

"I have here written testimony from a witness to some of these crimes. It is a memoir written by my father, who was a prisoner of the Nazis. He was forced to work in the factory that built rockets the Germans used to spread terror. The rockets killed thousands of people in England and Belgium, but far more people died building the rockets in an underground factory and in the camps where those prisoners lived. They were starved and beaten and often worked to death. If they were suspected of sabotage, they were hanged. My father's memoir tells of all these things. A copy of the memoir that I translated into English has been seized by the FBI, which claims it could harm national security, but I have the original, handwritten by my father. It identifies members of the rocket team whose actions would be criminal if proved. I believe you should request a copy of the memoir from the FBI, so that the appropriate people in Congress can examine it, even if they must do so in secret. As the congressman whose district includes the Marshall Space Flight Center, surely you have standing to ask that."

As Antonina spoke, Francine and the young newspaper photographer raced across the room from opposite directions. Francine elbowed Peter aside with the power and finesse of a lead blocker on a halfback sweep. She held her camera uncannily steady about two feet from Antonina's ear, then panned slowly from her face to the memoir in her hands and back again. Somehow, while still filming, she managed to free one hand and wave it angrily at her two competitors to clear them from the frame of her camera's lens. The reporter, scribbling furiously, edged aside, but the young black photographer coolly ignored her.

Pettigrew listened with what looked to Peter like dawning dread until Antonina said the FBI had seized a copy of the memoir. Then the congressman took a deep breath, rolled his eyes skyward and began repeating the word "purview" like a mantra.

"Not within my purview, ma'am," he said, almost jovially. "I understand why you feel so strongly about this, but it's outside the purview of Congress. National security? Strictly the purview of the executive branch. You'll have to take it up with them."

"But can't you convey her request to the appropriate party, to the FBI or whomever?" a man's voice said. "What this woman is saying concerns me deeply. She is right that the government should not hide a document like this, particularly if it was confiscated from a private party."

Peter could not at first see who was speaking. Pettigrew's aide pointed his ballpoint pen at the man with peremptory abruptness. "Name and contact information," he said.

The man stood. His clothing—suit, tie, handkerchief in breast pocket—seemed oddly formal for a small civic event on a Saturday morning. He had widely spaced, earnest eyes and a wide mouth. His hair, rather than thinning, had made an orderly retreat to the center of his skull.

"My name is Konrad Oberholzer," he said. "I work in the test division at Marshall. You can contact me there. During the war, I designed facilities at Peenemunde, and I helped test V-2 components, both in wind tunnels and from launch pads. We tested engines and all parts of the rocket body—the cone, the frame, the fins. If our tests showed a need for design improvement, we would draw up new specifications. Then we would wait for the improved part to come in from the factory. Until it arrived, we thought no more about it. Certainly I did not."

The woman with the swayback neck looked rapturously from the scrimmage around Antonina to the front of the little crowd, where the tall man in the dark suit was making his calm appeal and where dismay was dawning in Pettigrew's face as he realized he was not going to be able to simply raise his arms in another benedictory gesture and make a clean getaway.

"He said Peenemunde up there, didn't he?" the woman said. "Isn't that where they fired those rockets from?"

443

"He was more than just there," the swimming pool contractor said. "He helped build it. That's Oberholzer. He's a key guy out at Marshall. It's due largely to him that the moon shot went off without a hitch."

The woman clasped her hands joyfully. "Oh, I'm so glad I came," she said. "And to think, if there'd been anything good on at the movies, I'd have passed this up."

"Perhaps we should have raised questions," Oberholzer said. "Perhaps we should simply have known conditions at the factory had to be beyond abusive. But we chose not even to wonder, let alone ask. Out of sight, out of mind, *nicht wahr?*"

Turning his frank blue gaze backward over the heads of the people sitting in the molded plastic chairs, Oberholzer said, "I wonder if the lady would be so kind as to …" But Antonina was already moving briskly around the edge of the little crowd, memoir in hand, with the reporter and the news photographer and the burly woman balancing the camera on her shoulder all sidestepping frantically to keep pace. When Antonina turned the corner at the first row, without a word she handed the memoir to Oberholzer, who towered over her. Then she glanced back past everyone in the chairs, past Peter as well, with a taunting little lift of her chin. And when Peter looked over his shoulder, he saw that the little bearded man with his hands in the pockets of his black windbreaker was smiling back at her. He looked like an athlete who'd been bested on one play reminding his opponent there were more plays still to come.

As Oberholzer flipped a pair of reading glasses onto his nose, the TV reporter served as a one-woman flying wedge, clearing enough space within the audience for her to capture in the same frame the German rocket engineer and Antonina and, just beyond the table, the congressman. When he realized her intent, Pettigrew scuttled aside so nimbly that Peter was reminded of the toe-dancing hippo in Disney's *Fantasia*, but it was too late.

"Gotcha', Milton," Francine said, glancing up from her viewfinder and grinning wickedly. "You looked kind of panicked in that shot, though.

Why don't you edge back in and give us your big old country-boy smile instead? That might wear better with constituents."

Pettigrew flashed Francine an aggrieved look, but the instant she returned her eye to the viewfinder, he beamed like the sun breaking through.

Oberholzer leafed through several pages of the memoir, peering at the writing. Then he closed it and looked a little sadly at Antonina.

"I'm sure this is exactly what you say," he said. "Your father's painful memories of a terrible time. I just wish that I could…" He lifted the workbook in one hand, as if trying to estimate its weight. "The language, you see."

Peter wondered if anyone other than himself and the intended targets could have noticed the quick, saberlike thrust Antonina's eyes made toward the FBI man and the blond young Pole at his side.

"That's right, it's all in Polish," she said. "My native language, and I could translate, of course. I could even translate into German if you preferred. But why should you trust someone so deeply biased? Luckily, you don't have to. See that young man in the rear there? No, not the one in the black jacket. That one is FBI. He came here hoping to seize this memoir from me. That tall young man beside him, that's his translator. If you'd like to hear a sampling of what my father wrote, that young man could translate it for you, in English. He would bring no bias to his reading. His only function here, you see, is to give the FBI a clear notion of what the memoir actually says, so they can argue it would somehow harm national security, and therefore it must be hidden. But now I see they are leaving. They must have been called away."

When Peter turned, the two of them had nearly reached the door. The agent gripped the young Pole's elbow, hurrying him along then yanking his arm hard enough to propel him through the doorway. Before he stepped through it himself, the agent glanced back at the little crowd of voters. This time, the smile amid the clipped black bristles looked more forced than appreciative.

"Sorry we can't oblige you, but we do have a fairly urgent appointment down the road," he said mildly. "Mrs. Farnsworth, we'll be in touch with you soon."

"I'm reassured," Antonina said.

What had started as a politician's orderly, soporific town hall then simply fell apart. Part of the little crowd wandered off, and the rest broke up into excited or quarrelsome gaggles. As Peter wove through the emptied chairs, he heard the reporter pepper Pettigrew with questions about executive power to suppress information.

"Let's say Anne Frank had a line in her diary about missile testing," the reporter said. "What then? Could the president just impound the diary?"

"Entirely outside my purview," the congressman said. "That'd be one for the courts to sort out."

Antonina was explaining to Oberholzer that a publisher would bring the memoir out in hardback if she could get it past the several nets the FBI had deployed to snare it. Oberholzer said that if she wanted him to store it in his office safe, he'd guarantee its security for as long as she needed to keep it there. As he spoke, Antonina's eyes hardened.

Oberholzer glanced uneasily at Peter. "I shouldn't have mentioned that option so openly, should I?" he told Antonina.

She laughed. "Him?" she said. "He doesn't worry me. He is my tool, my little chisel. What surprises me is that you think I would place my father's memoir in the hands of a Nazi."

Now it was Oberholzer's pale blue eyes that suddenly looked glazed. "I was never a Nazi," he said. "I was then what I have always been, an engineer, and only that."

"Did you wear the uniform?" she said. "Yes? Then it does not matter."

"Of course it matters."

"I see," Antonina said. She had shifted into her mode of lip-lifting scorn. "You were an engineer with much to offer, not just to the Nazis but to the world. And your family, your career, your future were at stake. All correct? My father was an engineer too, also with much to offer. He was half-German. He could have been a Nazi officer, like you. He might even have joined the rocket team—imagine that. But you will say, won't you, that you could have advanced still further if you had joined the Nazi party, and therefore no one should call you a Nazi? I will tell you my theory about that. I am an engineer too. In my field of electrical engineering, no principle is more fundamental than Newton's Second Law, force equals mass times acceleration. With Nazis, I make a simple application of this law. Hitler needed true believers, yes? So I think of their belief in his insane doctrine as his accelerant. But he needed mass, too, to achieve his full effects—Europe a ruin, perhaps twenty million dead. You did not join the party? Then I grant you were not part of the accelerant, that crazed belief system. But Herr Oberholzer, you were certainly part of the mass. And by Newton's Second Law, Nazism required mass just as much as it did acceleration. So I say that you and every other member of the von Braun team was a Nazi then. And by another principle, the legal one that there is no time limit on prosecution for murder, I call you a Nazi to this day."

Oberholzer seemed to absorb Antonina's attack on him so calmly that Peter thought it must simply repackage accusations he'd heard often. The German walked silently beside her and Peter to the parking lot, where he asked if he could tell her something that seemed to him an odd parallel.

"At the end of the war, we too faced a dilemma about preserving documents of immense value," he said. "Hitler had by then descended into total delusion. He expected the country to self-immolate, to serve as his funeral pyre. We were ordered to destroy all documents and blueprints related to rocket technology, whether for military or other uses. We had tons of such material, some of it dating back more than ten years. Von Braun told me to find a good hiding place for it. That was a dangerous undertaking. If we had been caught disobeying the Führer's orders, it could have cost us our lives, even at that late date. Those documents had originated at points all the way from Peenemunde to testing grounds in the

Alps. By the end of the war, though, they were pretty well consolidated at the Mittelwerk, due chiefly to our desire to keep them out of the Soviets' hands.

"So what was the best hiding place? We didn't know, and the urgency left us no time to explore. We backed up trucks to our offices in Nordhausen and loaded those tons of material into them and set off through the mountains to the north. By the end of the day, someone in a village called Dornten told us about an abandoned iron mine nearby. We found it had a little railway and some rail cars and even a locomotive that one of our truck drivers was able to tinker with and get running. And so we transported all those documents deep in the mine. We found a little chamber where they would stay dry, and nobody was likely to get at them unless they knew they were there. The American soldiers got to Nordhausen soon after, and we told them what we'd done. They recovered the documents, which was exactly what we'd hoped."

Oberholzer looked off toward the hills south of town. Peter could read no subtext in his pale eyes and nothing in Antonina's eyes but impatience to be gone.

"There must be dozens of worked-out mines around Birmingham," Oberholzer said. "Perhaps our history as Europeans inclines us to view caverns and mines as hiding places. The myths about trolls and their hoards of underground treasure—they all come from places like Germany and Poland, don't they? It's such a motif, really, that others might suspect us of it."

~ * ~

Antonina got into the driver's seat of her car, handed Peter the memoir and told him to rewrap it in the brown packaging paper and secure it with string from a roll in the glove compartment. When he opened the glove compartment door, she quickly reached into it, took out her pistol in its holster and slid it into her purse.

"I thought you weren't going to get into it with anyone who spoke out in the von Braun team's defense," Peter said as she drove out of town.

"That's asking a lot," she said. "Even if I'm the one who asked it. And especially if one of them claims to my face that he, in particular, counts as simon-pure."

"What was he trying to tell us there at the end?"

"Several things. One, that somehow history qualifies him as our ally, which I would laugh at if I could get past my impulse to spit on him for it. Two, he assumes I've kept the memoir hidden in an abandoned mine and might return it there. Three, the FBI has figured that out and might by now even know which mine I'm using."

"What do we need to do about that?" Peter said.

"Nothing" she said. "I've already taken all of it into account."

She took a different road this time, a two-lane highway. She'd driven south about half an hour when they passed a county sheriff's car parked on the shoulder. Peter saw a moonlike face tracking their passage from the driver's window.

"So FBI has enlisted the local gendarmerie," Antonina said with a gratified-sounding downward curl in her voice. "And how does that advantage them, little chisel?"

"It means that deputy can pull us over for anything from a broken taillight to tossing a candy wrapper out the window," he said. "He can detain us long enough for your special agent friend to show up and hand you his warrant for the memoir."

She nodded, eyes narrowed. "Very good," she said. "But suppose we give the deputy no pretext—no speeding, all lights functional, no littering. What then?"

"Then the deputy trails us all the way to the mine and radios your FBI pal from there. Assuming we're foolish enough to go to the mine, which we won't be."

"Very good again. Except for the last part."

"You mean we drive to the mine regardless?"

"You never engage the enemy 'regardless,' little chisel. You do it with close regard for changing circumstances, and you expect they will keep changing, and you will have to adapt."

"And my part in this is supposed to resemble a dry fly?"

"Oh yes, that too. Skip, skip, skip across the surface, so fast they can't see you've tricked them."

Without warning she swerved to the right and braked, setting off a controlled skid that left them in the opposite lane heading back toward Huntsville. By the time Antonina's car passed the sheriff's vehicle headed in the other direction, her speedometer clocked 85 miles per hour. In another minute she made another U-turn, and this time the low-slung little Toyota went into a fishtail skid on the graveled shoulder of the southbound lane. Beneath the shoulder was a wooded ravine. Gazing down into it, Peter wondered if Stephie would regard his death among the young pines as fulfilling the deal he'd struck when he turned his back on a draft exemption, but Antonina calmly steered out of the skid and headed south. Then she turned off onto a narrower two-lane marked "Tyree" and slowed to legal speed.

"You think you lost him?" he said.

"He'll read the skid marks," she said. "We've gained a little time, that's all."

She had cranked her window down a little. Her eyes looked as hard and fixed as inlaid black stones beneath her short, wind-whipped hair.

She pulled over next to a mining company's no-trespassing sign and fished the parcel containing the memoir from under her seat, where it had ended up after the two U-turns.

"You remember the route?" she said. Her voice sounded almost casual, but when he started to open his door she grasped his forearm and said in a near-whisper, "Look at me."

She took the holstered pistol from the glove compartment and held it in front of his face. "You may hear me fire this," she said. "If so, I will have a reason."

"Jesus, Antonina. You're not going to shoot Barney Fife, are you?"

"I will not shoot anyone," she said. "It will just be diversionary. But don't let it divert you. Remember, the strongbox is buried outside the left rail, at the fifteenth crosstie from the mine entrance, one foot below the surface. The soil and the coal dust are loose enough you can get to it using only your hands."

Her grip on his forearm tightened. Her eyes bore into his like drill bits.

"Now, suppose something changes and you cannot get to the mine shaft," she said. "What then? Listen: do with the memoir whatever seems best to prevent them finding it. Maybe stuff it under a rock. Even throw it into a deep ditch. Does the package split open then? Are pages torn? Even so, if that is the best way to delay their finding it, that is what you do."

"But then, I have to remember exactly where I tossed it, right? Since we have to come back and find it before they do."

She seemed to waver a little. "Yes, try to remember where it is," she said. "But now you must go. Go!"

Peter took the package and headed up a shallow ravine that narrowed to a lumpy layer of bare limestone—the legacy, he guessed, of decades of flash flooding. A little higher up the ravine he ran into boulders, and he stopped and frowned. He'd never seen stones that big above ground in country like this. Then he understood. Miners must have blasted these out of the ground, then just rolled them down the nearest slope, and they ended up here.

He needed both hands to thread through the boulders, so he wedged the flimsy package into the back of his waistband. As he tightened his belt to secure the package, he began hearing the deputy's siren. Now she'll have to adapt, he thought. But what am I supposed to do, except speed up?

As he clambered on all fours over the boulders, he traced in his mind the steps that had led him to a moment so bizarre and perilous that surely it could never have been the outcome of his own choices. Whom, then, could he blame? Death had removed Rabinowitz as his go-to option in moments like this. So as his left foot slipped between two boulders and he felt the familiar warning twinge in his knee, he muttered through clenched teeth: "Damn you, Stephanie Ames. Damn your snippy little New England soul."

He was nearing the point where the ravine petered out when he glimpsed, through foliage to his right, the stretch of gravel that Antonina had instructed him to follow to the mineshaft. He scrambled out of the ravine and was clearing a path through underbrush, sweeping it aside with a swimmer's breaststroke, when he heard the first gunshot and several diminishing echoes. The shot sounded too close for her to be firing from where she'd parked the car. As he jogged toward the layer of gravel, he could tell it matched his father's description of a good erosion barrier. The stones were crushed granite, with angular edges that would interlock to impede water flow. On the far side of the granite he saw a low barbed wire fence, then nothing but open space between the fence and a far hillside. He paused long enough to catch his breath and remove the flimsy and sweat-stained paper parcel from beneath his belt. Then he sighed with relief when he saw how close he'd come to the mine. Less than 50 yards up the slope, below flat, boulder-sized stones jumbled like the playthings of gargantuan toddlers, the mine's trapezoidal, timber-edged mouth opened into darkness. A set of narrow-gauge rails ran out from it a little way, then disappeared beneath the layer of stones.

He heard another gunshot, and he flinched and cursed. A spurt of dirt kicked up a few paces to his left. He realized that, whatever Antonina's purpose, her method was to govern his movements, using shots from her Beretta like puppet strings.

"As if I needed one more manipulative bitch in my life," he said as he stepped out onto the layer of gravek. Even as he said the words, he realized that, as unjust as they were to Stephanie, it was absurd and dangerous to think they applied to a woman who had seen and suffered as much as Antonina, and had long ago learned to kill without compunction. He quickened his pace toward the mine's mouth as he recalled Meir's story of Antonina shooting the German officer's corpse through the mouth. He was picturing what the officer's hat had looked like, hanging on a pole in the town square next morning, when he heard the next shot and the zing and whine of the bullet as it ricocheted from a stone a few feet to his left.

He lurched to his right, stumbled and dropped the packet with the memoir. As he bent to retrieve it, he saw her standing clear of the tree line, below the sheet of crushed granite. Her head was cocked, birdlike, her feet wide apart. She held the pistol with both hands, the barrel pointing upward near her ear. She drew one finger to her lips, then brought the pistol forward and flicked it toward her right, once, twice, then again more urgently, and he saw she meant he should alter course. Like any other woman, he thought, wanting him to move at her direction like a chess piece. Except this woman wouldn't complain or scowl if he disappointed her. She'd just shoot him.

He started up the slope again, this time moving diagonally to the right, which would leave him wide of the mine's mouth if he didn't run into the barbed wire first. But again she fired to his left, missing him by no more than an arm's length, and he shifted to a still harder diagonal, stumbling but managing not to fall. He searched in his mind for some witticism to quell his growing panic. If his mother just knew his dilemma, he thought, she might get a good epitaph out of it: Here lies an idiot, shot in the back by a figment of a Jewish orphan's imagination.

Once more Antonina fired the pistol. His left eardrum popped as the bullet passed close enough to the ear to lower air pressure there. He lurched to his right, feeling the sudden pain that meant his knee had twisted in its socket. He knew the bone had immediately popped back into place, since he was still stumbling toward the fence. Bent double and raising both hands to avoid plunging head-first into the barbed wire, he caught sight of Antonina making sweeping motions with one hand while with the other hand she tracked him with the pistol barrel.

Christ, she wants me to throw it, Peter thought. He stumbled again and fell to his knees as his left arm plunged between strands of the wire and his right wrist came down hard on barbs in the top strand. He looked upward, struggling to retain his grip on the memoir in its brown wrapper as blood began to trickle from his wrist. Then Antonina blasted the memoir from his fingers with a bullet through its center. Peter watched it bounce down the wall of the ravine, shedding first the wrapper, then the workbook backing, then torn bits of handwritten text, until the remnant came to rest on the stones of a dry streambed. Peter could see the bullet hole clean through it as he hung by both arms from the fence.

There has to be some way this makes sense, he thought. Perhaps in a moment I'll think of it. Either that, or Meir was right in fearing she'd gone unhinged. But no, she's stone-cold sane. Maybe even sane enough to shoot me now that I've served her purpose.

He heard a pebble land nearby. He saw she was beckoning him to come where she was standing, beneath the granite erosion barrier. He rose high enough on his knees to pull his right hand free of the barbs in the top strand of wire. Two streaks of blood ran up his forearm and onto his shirtsleeve. When he stood he could tell, based on his long, painful experience with the knee, that it would likely swell but not balloon the way it did when wrenched badly enough to cause internal bleeding. Limping down the layer of jagged stones, he remembered that simple swelling had the upside of stabilizing the joint enough to lessen the likelihood of further injury. But as Antonina beckoned him with a growing show of impatience, Peter, suddenly furious, mulishly planted his feet and glowered at her.

"I've had it with you, lady," he said, loud enough for her to hear. "If you plan to deliver some *coup de grace*, you'll have to do it from there."

"Play your part!" Antonina hissed at him. Then she whirled around, pointing her Beretta at the red-faced deputy as he floundered through a patch of underbrush and into the open while struggling to get his pistol out of its holster. Past the deputy, Peter saw the gangling newspaper reporter and the young black photographer picking their way up the wooded hillside.

The deputy had the glassy-eyed look and the open, spasmodically gasping mouth of a freshly landed fish. He stood with his pistol's barrel half out of the holster, and he looked at Antonina long enough to fully appreciate how steadily she held her aim at his chest with a two-handed grip. Then he slid the pistol back into its holster and unclipped a pair of handcuffs from his belt. As soon as the deputy took his hand off his pistol, Antonina lowered her own.

"You up there?" the deputy said, panting and nodding toward Peter. "You willing to swear you witnessed this woman threaten an officer of the law with a loaded gun?"

"I'm sure he will swear to exactly what he saw," she said with that vocal curl of mockery. "I encourage him to do so."

The bearded reporter and photographer had made it past the tree line. The photographer edged carefully to one side, peering through her viewfinder to frame the confrontation between the deputy and Antonina. Without pausing to flip to an unused page of his notepad, the reporter scribbled furiously on its cover.

The deputy, now that he had caught his breath, spoke in a milder tone. "You know, ma'am, we have a countywide ordinance against discharge of a firearm," he said.

"With exceptions," Antonina said. "One is lawful defense of person or property. I saw a rattlesnake crossing those rocks as this man was climbing down."

"You'd not likely hit a rattler with that weapon, ma'am, at that distance," he said.

"Does the law say something about that?" she said.

"Well," the deputy said. He grimaced in a way that to Peter looked more amused than annoyed. "You seem to have an answer for everything."

"Not everything," she said. "For one: Why would you approach a lone woman from behind with a weapon and handcuffs without announcing yourself? I don't have an answer for that. Here's another question I can't answer: Why go through this charade of enforcing local law when your only reason to follow me is you are the stalking horse for FBI, and then to wait until they show up?"

The deputy looked down at the handcuffs, jangled them a little, then clipped them back to his belt. "All right," he said. "Put your weapon away, and we'll wait. Otherwise, I'll have to cuff you and take you to the magistrate and file charges, and we'll do the rest of our waiting there."

"Just one moment," Antonina said. She glanced at Peter over her shoulder and beckoned with one hand and said, almost gently, "Come, come."

Peter hobbled closer. He saw in her eyes that she was calculating something. He realized too late it was distance, because by then she had already lashed out with the reversed pistol, and the little spur in the bottom of its magazine had opened a cut in his cheek.

"That's for dawdling inside the mine," she said. "I told you exactly where to put it, and how quickly you must do it. And now look where you have gotten us." She angled her head a little to remove her lips from the deputy's line of sight. Then she mouthed silently at Peter, "play your part, play your part."

"I did exactly what you wanted me to do," he said, wiping a palm over his cheek and staring at the blood, then back at her. "And you know what? I'm done doing stuff for you."

"So the memoir is somewhere inside the mine now?" the reporter asked excitedly. "Is it buried? Did you put it in, like, a crevice in the wall? Or maybe hide it in some sort of old mining equipment?" He held his pen poised above his notebook and impatiently tapped the point against the page.

"Sure," Peter said. "All of those places. A chapter or two in each."

The reporter excitedly wrote down what Peter had said.

"You interested in bringing an assault charge?" the deputy said. "I'll be your witness."

"No," Peter said. "She's got her reasons, though right now I'm damned if I could tell you what they are."

"Suit yourself," the deputy said. "I reckon we just wait, then."

"Anybody mind if I sit?" Peter said. "I've got a bum knee, and just now it's more bum than usual."

He searched out a patch of moss near the tree line and lowered himself onto it, keeping his leg with the wrenched knee extended. He ran a palm over his cheek again and wiped the blood on the moss. The deputy crossed his arms and tilted his head and gazed, squinting, into the middle distance, his jaw working slowly from side to side. As a picture of country-bred repose he lacked, if anything, only the occasional sidelong jet of tobacco juice. Peter felt himself warming toward this man about his own age who so much resembled men and boys he'd known all his life. Then he looked at Antonina. He knew he could never feel anything toward this strange, cold woman but disbelief that she could really exist. Yet here she was. Even standing still, she resembled a feral animal ready to spring.

"So we're waiting for something?" the reporter said. "What are we waiting for?"

"Preacher said the Rapture's due before first frost," Peter said. "It's prob'ly that."

The black photographer giggled and snapped a photo of him with blood trickling down his cheek and his hands cradling his swollen, throbbing knee.

Thirty-eight

It was nearly midnight and Peter—with the intact memoir in its envelope pressed so tight to his breast by his buttoned shirt that he could hear the paper crinkle when he turned the steering wheel—was halfway to Atlanta before he could make his eyes and ears quit straining for whirling blue lights and a police siren. Two days ago in Weston-Carmel, he had chosen, on a whim, a rental car with automatic transmission. Now he realized a car with a clutch pedal could have ruined the plan Antonina had worked out. With this car, he could slide back the driver's seat and prop his left heel on a stack of outdated Birmingham phone books that the master forger, the man she called Klimek, had fetched from a corner of his workshop and bound together with masking tape. That way, Peter could keep his leg nearly horizontal. Still, with his throbbing knee and the stinging, freshly stitched wound in his cheek and the fatigue he was trying to beat down with slugs from the Thermos of black coffee Antonina had given him, the drive to the rendezvous with Meir, and then home, seemed hardly doable. But he was starting to feel he could make it.

Twelve hours earlier he could have foreseen none of this. It had been early afternoon then, and he'd been sitting on a cushiony patch of moss, inhaling the dry, throat-stinging scent of leaves fresh-fallen from red oaks and poplars and silver maples. He had watched Antonina and the FBI agent with the masklike beard and tried to guess what sort of agreement they were working out. The two of them stood far enough uphill toward the mouth of the abandoned mine to be out of earshot from Peter, the deputy, the Polish translator and the reporter and photographer from the Birmingham paper. Antonina and the agent were nearly the same height, and each wore a shrewd squint and skeptical smile. They appeared no more hostile than neighbors haggling over the price for a piece of used furniture. When they finished, the agent beckoned to the young Pole, and he and the agent started climbing uphill toward the mine. Antonina stood watching them.

"You should look carefully where you step on those stones," she called. "I was shooting at a rattlesnake before you came. Perhaps it is hurt but still alive." Then she turned and headed downhill, barely glancing at Peter as she passed him.

"Come," she said. "We go now."

The agent paused with one hand on a knee, as if to catch his breath. He glanced back and caught Peter's eye long enough to signal, with that crinkling about his eyes, that he didn't buy whatever Antonina had told him about the whereabouts of the memoir, but also that she had purchased time, and that he held no brief against whatever good use she might make of it.

The gangling reporter helped Peter to his feet. "Mind telling me your name and where you're from?" the reporter said, whipping his notepad from a back pocket of his pants.

"Mah name?" Peter said with an exaggerated drawl. "Mah name's Joe Bob Petree. I live up Petree Holler in Shacktown."

For a few seconds the reporter scribbled on his notepad. Then he stopped with his pen poised above the page.

"Shacktown, huh?" he said. "Is that on the map?"

"Prob'ly not," Peter said. "It's on up in back of Turwilliger. You can prob'ly find Turwilliger on the map. Depending on the map."

"So you're not going to tell me who you are?" the reporter said, flipping the pad shut and returning it to his pocket.

"You can write this," Peter said. "I'm a friend of a friend of hers. A friend she barely knew she had."

Antonina already had the car engine running. When he climbed in the passenger seat, she reached her fingers toward his wounded cheek. He swung his elbow to knock her hand away.

"Poor little chisel," she said in a gravelly tone that for once sounded more heartfelt than mocking. "I meant to hit you only with the Beretta's handle, not with that little hooked piece of the magazine. I did not want to tear your skin like this."

"So you only meant to knock out teeth or break my jaw," he said. "I guess that makes it all right then."

"It was necessary," she said, her tone no longer soothing. "And you played your part perfectly. Now even your cut has proved useful."

"Funny, I was just thinking the same thing. Because if you hadn't gotten enough blood out of me this way, you'd probably have to go ahead and blow off my ear, like you tried to do earlier."

Before he'd finished his complaint, she flashed at him a look of disgust and steered her car onto the blacktop.

"Remember when I asked you what does a soldier need more than anything else?" she said. "I will give you this hint: it's not whining over a flesh wound."

She drove back out the Tyree Road and turned south on the two-lane toward Birmingham.

"When I say your cut was useful, I mean I used it to persuade Basior that he should let us leave," she said. "I told him he could question you later, after we get you medical attention."

"So that's his name? Basior?"

"That is only my name for him. I do not call him that to his face. Basior is Polish for wolf, a he-wolf."

"How did you explain why I was there at all?"

"I told him you were my new young lover, and you would do anything I asked."

"And he bought that line?"

"The part about stitching your cut is not a line. I am taking you to someone who can do that."

"And the other part?"

"You would not be the first. Basior is aware of that. You would not even be the youngest. I do not require an intelligence test."

"The woman I want to marry does, apparently."

"Then you might have trouble."

"But with you, it would never happen. Right?"

"Did I think of it? Yes. But I knew that if I slept with you last night and then had to shoot you today, you would find that confusing. Also, I did not want to do anything that might dull the edge of my little chisel."

There flashed across his mind a vision of himself grappling beneath a blanket with a dark creature like an outsize spider with little barbs on each of its many legs.

"So wolf-man believed everything you told him?" he said.

"What matters is that Basior takes note of the arguments I make. Then when he includes them in his report, his bosses will find them to be good enough reasons for him to act as he did. Whether Basior believes them is beside the point."

"Translation?"

Her eyes narrowed. She seemed to rummage in memory.

"I do not know Basior's past," she said. "I suspect it is much like mine. Perhaps his was in wartime, perhaps not. Basior will do all he can to seize the memoir, based on what he knows of its whereabouts. But he will also accept limits on what he seeks to know. I understand that. In the war, at first I pretended I was still a student. Several times I was able to report where certain Nazi officers would be sleeping. Then our people would find them at night and kill them. If today was still wartime and I could learn where Franz Lichter and Dieter Vogelsang sleep tonight, then tomorrow they might be dead. But Konrad Oberholzer? I would not ask where he sleeps. I think it is similar with Basior."

"So when do we head back up there?" Peter said. "We need to go get it while it's still daylight, don't we?"

She made a little backward toss of her head and smiled. "Skip, skip, you skipped so well," she said. "Like the perfect dry fly, though you required a little help from my Beretta. We do not go back at all, little chisel. We go now as fast as we can to where my friend holds the memoir in safekeeping."

"Safekeeping?" Peter said. "What's that you blasted out of my hand, then? What's that on the rocks down below that fence?"

"That's a copy of the memoir. A copy so good in every way that if my father could see it, he would say it was his own."

"A forgery? You chased me across those rocks with that pistol like I was a duck in a shooting gallery, all to protect a forgery?"

She smiled faintly. "I like that: duck in a shooting gallery," she said. "A nice image."

"Jesus. Why didn't you just tell me it was a fake? I could have handled that, you know."

"No, I needed you to believe. I needed that look on your face when you came limping down the rocks. That look said we were beaten. The deputy saw it. The reporter saw it. Every time you thought about losing the memoir, that look came back, so Basior saw it too."

"How's that better than letting me bury it in the strongbox in the mine?"

"That was not possible. The sheriff's car was too close behind us. It was maybe three minutes after you started to climb that I saw his light flashing. For all I knew, Basior might be right behind him. There was not enough time for you to dig up the strongbox and put the memoir in it and cover it and smooth out the coal dust. They would have caught you before you finished. Even if they did not, Basior would find it there eventually. I knew all along he would—eventually. And after that he would learn it was a forgery, even though Klimek did such a masterpiece that it would take chemical testing of the paper and ink to prove it. But then, when you intruded last night, I began to have another idea. If we made it appear the memoir had gone into the mine, but you threw it over the fence instead, we could gain more time. And I think it worked. The deputy saw me hit you with the pistol, and he heard you complain that you'd done all I asked, and he told Basior what he saw and heard. So unless Basior has a great power to penetrate my mind, tomorrow morning he will have agents from the FBI Birmingham office on their knees scratching through the coal dust inside the mine. Eventually they will find the strongbox, and it will be empty. Then maybe they will look around outside the mine and find what they are looking for in the ditch below the fence. And that Polish Army choirboy tells them it looks genuine, and maybe they take it to a laboratory for testing of the paper. But none of that matters, because by then the publisher has my father's memoir. Maybe it is already found to be authentic and sent to the printer. And to seize a book as it is being published is a step the government will not take."

She told him then that at sunrise next day, Meir Rabinowitz would be parked beside a roadside peach stand outside Gaffney, South Carolina. Peter could recognize the stand by its waist-high walls decorated with peaches painted red, which made them look more like strawberries, and by its circular, pointed roof that resembled a circus tent. She knew of the peach stand for the same reason she knew of the mineshaft near Tyree and a dozen other potential hiding places or rendezvous points. She had to take note of such places during the war, and she had never lost the habit.

Since peach season had ended, there should be no one near the peach stand to witness the handoff. She had called Meir and arranged for him to be at the stand Sunday morning. At the time she called him, she had expected to deliver the memoir herself.

"So you and Meir had set this up before he recruited me to come down here," Peter said.

"About you, I set up nothing," she said. "I called him yesterday to tell him I would bring the memoir to him, but he must come to the place I am telling you about, to pick it up. Then he told me he had sent a young man to persuade me. I told him that thanks to his meddling, I would have to either lock you up or shoot you."

"So you did a little of both," Peter said.

"No, no-o. Instead I fashioned you into a perfect little dry fly. Skip, skip, skip across the water until they bite."

As she drove past the hospital and medical college and on toward Red Mountain, Peter asked whether she had forgotten about getting treatment for the gash in his cheek. In his own voice he heard what sounded distressingly like a whine.

She smiled with narrowed eyes. "In Poland when I was young, a young man does not complain about a cut like yours," she said. "He looks forward to the day when he has a nice scar there and can claim it is a saber cut."

"Goddamn it! Let me out right here, then. I can walk back to the emergency room. And I'll find my way to my car. And then, lady, I'm out of your life. And you, thank God, are out of mine."

Her smile remained unchanged while he shouted at her. "Until I am ready, I do not let you out of my sight," she said evenly. "You will get what you want for your little cut. You will get it from Klimek, and you should value it as a privilege. One you share with those of us who ambushed Nazis in the forests of Poland, and who felt very lucky if they received such small wounds."

Hours later, driving on toward Atlanta's skyglow, sipping coffee from the Thermos, Peter winced at the tug of the stitches in his cheek. He remembered the glare from the gooseneck lamp, the sallow, sagging jowls, the eyes like moonlit ponds behind bottle-glass lenses, the sausage-sized fingers that drew the nylon fishing line taut with a little curved needle. The lidocaine gel had helped some, but the near-hypnotic focus of those huge, pale blue eyes had helped more.

"In a week, you must see someone to take them out," Klimek had told him after spraying the freshly stitched cut with antiseptic and handing him the little spray bottle. The man's voice resembled the muted rumble of heat lightning. "No more fistfights with Nina until then," he said.

"If he fails to deliver the memoir at the proper time, it will go much worse for him than a fistfight," she said.

The man had pursed his lips and given Peter a quick wink. "I could tell you how much worse," he said. "I could tell you what she might do to your hat. Better you don't have to think about that, though."

Before they arrived at the little shop on the brick-paved square near the footbridge, she had told Peter that Klimek was the reason she had come to Birmingham. She had said it was Klimek who forged the papers that enabled her and dozens of other partisans to slip time and again through the Nazis' grasp. When she learned Klimek had emigrated and opened a business in Alabama, she had applied to teach at the nearest university. At first, she had thought only of restoring a personal bond from wartime. Not until later, after the government confiscated the typed copy of the memoir she'd made in Connecticut, had it crossed her mind that Klimek's talents as a forger might help her protect the original, handwritten document.

When the suturing was done and Klemens Filipowski had switched off the overhead lamp and helped Peter down from the worktable, Antonina had spoken to her friend in Polish. She spoke rapidly at first, then more haltingly, seeming to watch closely for his reaction. He had listened calmly, removing his glasses and rubbing his eyes. The earpieces had worn deep grooves in the shaggy gray hair at the man's temples. Peter felt a small visceral shock, as at a magician's trick, when he saw how small, weak and watery Klimek's eyes actually were. Without the lenses' hocus-pocus, it was the vast gray thicket of the all-but-conjoined eyebrows, not the eyes, that dominated the face. The man had nodded reassuringly as Antonina spoke, and when she was done he had smiled and shrugged and said something in that quiet rumble. From his tone and demeanor, Peter understood it to mean, "that's the way things go sometimes."

As Antonina drove Peter back to her apartment with the genuine memoir in a manila envelope between them on the seat, she told him that

Klemens Filipowski had worked nights and weekends since midsummer to create the forgery.

"I told him what had happened to it today," she said. "I also told him it has served its purpose even better than I'd hoped—unless something unforeseen happens. Such as a blunder on your part that would require me to track you down."

At her apartment building, she parked and told him to wait in the car. She returned in a few minutes and told him to follow her upstairs and bring the memoir in its envelope. When they were inside her apartment, she locked and padlocked the door. She explained that, when she left him in the car, it was to check the street and her building's entry and stairwell to make sure no trap had been set for them.

"Now rest," she told him, pointing to the air mattress on the floor. "Two hours you must rest. Then we will eat, and then you must go."

"So I just take it to that peach stand, but Meir has to drive all the way from Hackensack, then back north," he said. "Sounds tough for him."

"He can take an airplane if he wants," she said. "He would have to come just as far if I took it to him, as I planned to do."

"Halfway's not an option?"

"It might have been for you, but not for me. If I am away from here for more than overnight, Basior becomes suspicious. Why do I not fly, then, in the morning to Newark and back at night? Because Basior would not overlook a risk so simple. He must get daily passenger lists for flights from Birmingham. If he sees my name, then when I get off the plane, an FBI agent is waiting to say, 'welcome to Newark, Mrs. Farnsworth.' So the best plan was to drive it as far as I could go in one night and return early the next day, and to hand it over in a location no one could suspect. Meir Rabinowitz knows that. And now the plan improves, thanks to my little chisel. Now I do not have to leave at all. Basior does not know who you are or where you came from. He does not know what car you drive. It is a rental car, no? So there is no simple way for him to put together your face and the car and what you will carry hidden beneath your shirt. Now rest."

He lay on his back on the air mattress and watched her as she switched on her desk lamp and began marking handwritten papers covered with scientific and mathematical symbols. He wondered how she could grade student work so soon after almost blowing his ear off and then assaulting him with the pistol butt. Then, as he drifted toward sleep, he wondered why his desire to be rid of her seemed so closely paired with a growing trust in her. Then he noticed his air mattress was floating on gentle billows but not going anywhere, so he tried to steer it with his hands but it seemed moored in place. Then he felt something prod his arm and he opened his eyes and saw the thing was covered with black scales.

Driving on toward the faint, distant gleam he figured must be the gilded dome of the Georgia capitol, Peter winced, remembering he had swatted at the scaled thing until he realized Antonina was prodding him with a snakeskin-shod foot.

"Quit flapping like a seal and get up," she had said. "It is time to eat, and then you must leave."

"Chattahoochee," he said aloud as he drove over that river. He had acquired the habit from his father, who liked to measure progress on road trips by the names of rivers crossed. It was a legacy of country breeding. Peter remembered how, on their summer trips to Holden Beach, his father would ignore his wife's requests for the time or distance remaining, and with what delight his father would finally announce, "Waccamaw River bridge! That means we're almost there."

He lost sight of Atlanta's skyglow, then realized he was within it. How good it was, he thought, to drive onward toward people he understood deeply, and put behind him that deadly little woman whom he understood not at all.

After she had prodded him awake with her foot, she had driven him to the seafood restaurant. When their trays slid down the stainless-steel chute, they had taken them to an outdoor table. This time, the electrified snow cone in Vulcan's upraised hand glowed red. Antonina sat facing the statue, and almost too swiftly for him to notice, she shut her eyes and touched her turtleneck sweater above her breast.

467

"Why do you wear it that way, like it was a soldier's dog tags?" he said. He had glimpsed the little silver crucifix back in her apartment. "I mean, I'm not Catholic, but don't people usually wear it where people can see it?"

She flashed her little lip-wrinkle of derision at him. "There is nothing Catholic about shoving it in people's faces." she said. "Especially if you think it is sacred. That is a stupid thing Americans do. Whatever is important to them, they flaunt. Their Jesus license plates. Their desks crammed with pictures of ugly children. A hat with the name of the battleship where you shit your pants out of fright. Where I come from, we learn better than to show the things that matter to us where everyone can see. Else they might pick one of those things and order you to sew it to your sleeve and then kill you for wearing it. Now shut your mouth. Or use it to eat only."

That was the moment, he thought—murmuring "Ocmulgee River" as the sign's lettering glittered briefly in his headlights—the moment when he had tried to stifle the impulse to bite back. He had tried to instead make some generous valedictory gesture toward a woman who had, improbably, come to mean so much in his life. As his car passed over the bridge and he sensed the dark unseen space between the pavement and the water, he took sour comfort in knowing he had at least tried. As usual, though, his carping demon had gotten its licks in first.

When she ordered him to shut up and eat, his hands had trembled with anger as he tried to use his knife to nudge yellow rice onto his fork behind a piece of grilled snapper. Then, breathing hard, he had let the knife and fork clatter onto his plate.

"I guess that's why you don't have any pictures of your children in your apartment," he said. "You think that would be stupid. Or maybe you think your two sons are ugly."

He recognized the look she fastened on him as the same one he had seen that afternoon before she swung the pistol at his face. He rested his fists on the table, ready to parry the blow, but all that came was her barely audible voice.

"You think I need you so much now that I will not kill you," she said. "If you say anything more about my children, you will find out."

"Okay," he said. "Here it is, then. That kid you saved from the Lodz ghetto? Once he grew up and came to Vietnam, I think he somehow got it right about you and your sons. See, the main character in the tale he spun out for us was a woman named Antonina. Unlike you, she was tall and beautiful. But like you, she had to give up a lot of things a woman would want, and that most women could expect to have. Like you, she felt her father had laid a duty on her that pretty much ruled out everything else. She couldn't, for example, keep her two sons, so she turned them over to the men who fathered them. She knew those men had clout and would use it to give the kids opportunities. So she gave up the right to even see her sons again. Sound familiar?"

She had eaten only a salad, and while he spoke she lit a cigarette.

"I suppose you think of this as payback for your little bit of suffering," she said, eyeing him warily through the smoke.

"No I don't," he said. "I do think it's something you're due, though. And I think you're sort of the mother of that other Antonina, too. Because if you hadn't done what you did, there would have been no one alive who could have made the other one up."

"Now you simply make no sense," she sneered. "Finish quickly, and we go."

He had been about to go on, then. He was prepared to say something like: *I'm done being jerked around like I was your dry fly. I know it made sense for you to give up your kids, by the rules you've always played by, but those rules inflict a lot of collateral damage. You're deceitful when it serves your purpose, and you're about as personable as a cornered wolverine. Still, though, on the measure that counts most, you're up there with the Antonina who was beautiful and tragic.*

But looking into her dark, wary, close-set eyes through the smoke that curled from her nostrils, with Vulcan's torch glowing red in the evening haze above and behind her, he knew he would not tell her any of that. She was a cunning, viperous little woman, shaped by history into a perfect instrument of retribution and willing to sacrifice anyone and anything to accomplish it. Willing to sacrifice her children or others if it suited her purpose. Willing to sacrifice her own life, if necessary. But, purely for the sake of efficacy, that sacrifice would come last.

"Finish quickly, and we go," she had said, stubbing out her cigarette in the table's black plastic ashtray. And without another word, he had gulped the last of his iced tea.

Oconee. Broad. He spoke each river's name as he crossed it and felt relief swell in him each time, as if from some atavistic instinct that crossing a barrier as formidable as a river increased his margin of safety from a wily and tenacious predator. After he crossed the Tugaloo River into South Carolina, he stopped at the welcome station and slid his seat back as far as it would go and lifted his left leg through the car door. The knee remained stiff and swollen, but it hadn't bloated the way it did when blood pooled inside the joint and made the leg unusable. Could be worse, he thought as he limped inside to pee.

From here on, he knew, each river's flow tilted incrementally farther north, like the ribs of an opened fan. Perhaps too, his flagging brain told him, the rivers acted as filters that clarified his thought.

There had been no farewell. Antonina had driven him back to her apartment, and after she'd surveilled the street and parking lot, she had led him to her room and handed him the packet in its brown paper wrapper. She had watched him button his shirt over it and reminded him to keep it there until he could hand it to Meir Rabinowitz. Then she had followed him to his car and ordered him to leave his ancient pistol in the trunk and handed him the Thermos of coffee. She had stood at the parking lot entrance and peered in each direction, then signaled to him to drive out. Once he reached the street, he had glanced in his rearview mirror, but she was already gone. He knew he would never see her again, and he had breathed, "Thank God."

Saluda. Reedy. Enoree. In the thinning darkness, he could read the rivers' names before his headlights' beams reached them. What Rabby could have known of her was just enough. He could see that now. The same way that a fabulist of genius could know just enough to transform a Bronze Age thug into Achilles, Rabby had known just enough about Antonina to transform her into the beautiful and selfless and tragic woman who could sacrifice her good Catholic life to save a family of Jews. But then Rabby had made the mistake of a fabulist possessed by his own creation. He had volunteered for a pointless war so he could find the one place on earth where he could try to become her—become Antonin to her Antonina—and if possible die the way she did, as an act of willed sacrifice. Still, though, a death chosen with the mark of genius.

Tyger River. Back there at the restaurant, once she had snarled at him and he had realized that what he was on the verge of telling her was stupid and false, he had known there was something else he should say instead, but he could not find the words for it. And now, as he flipped the passenger seat's visor outward as a preemptive defense against the first spearlike shafts of dawn, the thing he had not pinned down in time to tell her finally came to him. It was a pair of questions: What, exactly, did it take to rescue from that ghetto a single life from among the doomed thousands? And could anyone have done it without her precise mix of cunning, ruthlessness and desire to deal a blow that would not just defeat the enemy but shame him? But even if he had thought of those questions in time to pose them, they would have meant little to her, he knew. She had not even counted her rescue of the infant at Lodz as much of a victory, since she'd had no chance to rub the enemy's face in it.

Then, out of the four years of poorly taught Latin he had taken in high school, there came to him the words due any soldier with so potent a blend of devotion and ferocity: *Ave atque vale*, Antonina. Hail and farewell.

He slugged back the last of his coffee from the Thermos. Amid the scattershot winking on of houselights, Spartanburg's city lights suddenly switched off en masse. "North Pacolet River" he muttered as he drove onto the bridge. He could see the mouth of a creek where it entered the slate-gray water, and beside the creek a strip of red Piedmont clay that might have been washed there by a flash flood. When he passed the

Cowpens exit, he slowed a bit, then turned off onto a state road as she'd instructed. Blinking in the unwelcome morning light, he peered ahead along the roadside, searching for a little building with a round, pointed roof that had a slight concave swoop to it, like the roof of a circus tent.

He saw the peach stand and Meir Rabinowitz at the same moment. The stand had a graveled parking area. Meir was leaning against the door of what Peter knew must be a rental car, since it had a Pennsylvania license plate. Meir wore a snap-top cap and the same ratty gray sweater he'd worn in Arborville. Through the zippered opening at the sweater's neck, Peter could see he also wore a tie. There was a thin coating of frost on the window of Meir's car, and he had his arms folded with his fingers tucked beneath his armpits. The peach stand was just as she'd described it, down to the painted peaches that looked more like strawberries. Peter swung through the parking area and stopped so that both cars faced back toward the interstate. Meir leaned down by his window. His cap resembled a collapsed parachute of woolen tweed, afloat on his gray curls. Peter could see Meir's breath, and when he lowered his window he could see his own.

"You must have been here a while," Peter said.

"About an hour," Meir said. "Wanted to make sure we saw each other straightaway."

"Straightaway?" Peter said. "Bet you picked that up during the war."

"Spot on. Have you got it?"

Peter undid enough of his shirt buttons to extract the memoir in its envelope. Meir opened his car door and took out a battered-looking brown satchel with a brass clasp lock on its flap. Peter guessed from the satchel's dog-eared corners that it had been thrown often and hurriedly onto the floorboards of jeeps.

"Also from the war?" Peter said.

"Seems fitting, don't you think?"

Meir opened the flap and slipped the memoir into it.

"Is that secure enough?" Peter said. "I mean, she said I had to keep flesh-to-paper contact."

Meir smiled and pulled a set of handcuffs from the satchel. He snapped one cuff to the satchel's handle. Then he pulled a keychain from his pocket, flipped through it to a small brass key and locked the satchel's clasp.

"Soon as I turn in the rental car, I clip the other cuff to my wrist," he said. "Cuffs don't come off until I make the handover to my publisher friend in Manhattan tonight. Nearly as secure as shirt buttons, wouldn't you say?"

"Tonight?"

"I fly out of Charlotte to Newark this afternoon. By midnight, this memoir is under lock and key at L'Chaim Publishing."

Meir tossed the satchel onto the passenger seat of his car, shut the door and again tucked his fingers beneath his armpits.

"Well," Peter said. He breathed deeply, and as he exhaled he allowed the weariness he had fought since he left Birmingham to sink into his bones. "We're done, then. She said the less time spent on the handoff, the better."

The rumbling laugh. "That's our girl," Meir said. "Lucky for us she's not here."

Meir squinted a little and leaned closer. "Turn your head this way a little," he said.

Peter rolled his eyes and turned his head enough for Meir to see Klemens Filipowski's handiwork on his slashed cheek. He listened for a moment to the air threading the zigzag passage in Meir's nose.

"Oh, my," Meir said softly. "Honorable wound, is it?"

"Friendly fire. Sort of."

"Well. She's a soldier, above all else. I think I told you that."

"You did. And, all due respect, but I doubt you know the half of it."

"Sane though?"

"Sane? You might as well question a chainsaw's sanity if it cuts your thumb off."

Meir tossed the satchel back into his car and shut the door.

"So she not only hit you, she intended to," Meir said. "No Purple Heart for you, then. But you do rate a Victory Medal."

Peter snorted. "Medal?" he said. "I'm just hoping I don't get another Article Fifteen, or worse, if the Army gets word of what I did in Alabama. What victory, anyway?"

Meir gazed aside with a distant smile. He cupped his hands and blew into them, then rubbed them together.

"Victory in Europe. May eighth, 1945."

"I could only wish," Peter said. "But that was before I was born."

"No obstacle," Meir said, sounding almost cheery. "Wars worth fighting never really end. They keep getting fought in all sorts of odd places. Casualties keep rising. There aren't many wars like that. Yours, I'm sorry to say, isn't one of them, but mine certainly was. And you've been privileged to share a little piece of my war. One that ends, for you, outside a roadside peach stand in October 1969. A happier ending, I'd venture, for your piece of it than Avram found for his."

Peter shut his eyes and leaned back against his headrest. He tried to think of something to say that rose to the level Meir had set, but all his weary brain offered him was yet one more cynical needle to poke what seemed to him a moralistic balloon. Something like: Sure, Meir. Well, good luck getting the Army to dig Rabby up to pin that Victory Medal on his chest.

Finally, he merely said, "Good luck, Meir. I'd better head on now. I've got a few more rivers to cross."

Meir stepped backward, stumbling a little on the gravel. His smile looked a little sly.

"Take your time with those rivers," Meir said. "I think they're expecting you at home, by the way. Once you walk in the door, you might receive a little expert attention to that cheek."

Thirty-nine

She shaded her eyes, gazing at a red-tailed hawk perched in a pine tree that appeared to grow out of the rockface halfway up the mountain's quartzite dome. The light, chill breeze ruffled the coppery feathers at the hawk's neck as it edged along the limb, lifting first one taloned foot, then the other. The bird's head moved constantly, in swift segments of a circle, scanning the earth for prey.

"I'd hate to be the mouse that catches that bird's eye," she said. "On the other hand, it would all be over in a second or two, wouldn't it?"

"I can tell you, from recent experience, what it's like from the mouse's perspective," Peter said. "Except for the part where it's all over quickly."

Stephie turned toward him and smiled. He was the taller by several inches, but looking into her steady blue gaze above those cheekbones always felt to him like staring up a sloping rampart.

"Maybe I should feel guilty for saying you had to go," she said. "But I still think you had to."

"Maybe you call me to higher things than I'm fit for. Maybe I'm like the field mouse that ventured too far and caught the hawk's eye."

"If you're a field mouse, you're one with leopard tendencies," she said. "Tendencies worth encouraging."

"Leopard?"

"Hemingway's story, adapted to fit the case. Nobody has explained what the field mouse was seeking at that altitude."

"Once or twice, Rabinowitz reminded me of a leopard," Peter said. "I'd see him sort of prowling along in the heat, his shirt all splotched with chalk dust and sweat."

He could tell from a slight lift of her eyebrows that she felt this image of his dead friend should stand in silence.

"Tend to that cut so you don't get a raised scar," she said. "You'll remember to have the stitches taken out, right?"

"I'll remember. One thing I don't remember, though. When did I tell you how to get in touch with Meir?"

"You said the cousin, the one who wanted you to track down Antonina in Birmingham, was a deputy prosecutor in Bergen County. I called the DA's office there. By the time Meir called back, he'd already been summoned south to make the pickup. He said you'd make the first leg of the delivery run. I told him you'd come home after you made the handoff. Then he asked me about my work schedule at the hospital. An hour later he called again and said he'd booked a round-trip flight for me out of Boston, so I could spend a little time with you. I tried to talk him out of it—but frankly, knowing you'd carried out a pretty perilous mission on his behalf, I didn't try all that hard."

He followed her along the rocky trail that hugged the dome. Her frayed-looking blonde hair was bundled into a careless ponytail, and she wore a red-and-black checked shirt and denim coveralls with brass buttons. The shiny green foliage of the laurel bushes beside the trail appeared sharply etched against the burnt orange of leaves fallen from chestnut oaks.

"You're not sorry we came up here, are you?" he said.

She paused, standing on a little rock ledge, and cocked her head at him.

"How could I be sorry?" she said. "But I wasn't sure about your knee."

"It's fine. The wrap helps. It might swell some tonight, but it's worth it, to come up here again."

"You sure you don't want me to set up a quick consult at the med school? Any orthopedist who looks at that knee would say you aren't fit for duty yet."

"If that worked, could you stay longer?"

"No. If you're in my business, skiing season in New Hampshire means all hands on deck. Besides, my return flight's booked and paid for."

"Then there's no point. I'm fit enough for anything the Army might ask me to do. If I want to see my parents, all I need's a weekend pass."

"And next fall?"

"Soon as I have time, I'll find out if my admission to the master's program at State's still good. With the GI Bill plus in-state tuition, I shouldn't have to wheel bricklayers' mud along catwalks anymore."

They went on to a point where the trail ran flush against the sheer rock face. She stopped and pressed the sharply angled fingers of one hand against it, as she'd done that spring day when he first brought her to Pilot Mountain. Again it seemed she was taking the mountain's pulse. Then she flattened her hand against the stone, and smiled as if she found it pleasing to the touch.

"Where does that leave us, then?" she said.

"Short term, about a thousand miles apart. Long term? There must be places where both a bone doc and an architect can find honest work."

"What if the memoir changes things for you?"

"It won't. I didn't leave my name with anybody down there but her, and she has every reason to stay mum about that."

"What if the memoir really draws attention?"

"Why would that make a difference?"

"She might ask you to go with her on a book tour. So you could help her, you know, explain."

"Explain what?"

"How you worked together to change the historical narrative about the German rocket team."

"Tell me that in twenty years and I might think it's funny."

She shot him an impish glance. Then she took a step away from the stone and beckoned him with a nod of her head. "Now you," she said.

He moved closer to the stone and pressed one hand flat against it as she had done. It felt cold, but less cold than he'd expected. He wondered if the cold within it ever changed much, and whether the center of the immense stone column was exactly as cold as its surface.

"Keep your hand there," she said. "Now close your eyes and tell me if some image comes to your mind. Don't tell me what it is you see, though."

"Stephie, are you testing your psychiatry chops on me again?"

"I am indeed. I'm subbing in this geological freak for a Rorschach blot. Now be quiet. Open your mind to whatever might come."

He closed his eyes and waited. He heard a hawk screech twice in the distance. The rock's mild chill had penetrated his hand and crept up his forearm. Suddenly he was looking down into the hole Rabby had ordered him to dig, and in its depths he glimpsed the blood-flecked strands of barbed wire. Then he was gazing at a row of dark bunkers that stretched on and on in sand so glaring white it hurt his eyes. The cold from the stone crept above his elbow, and he saw his lovely little street in Nha Cat stretching away toward the beach, but as he walked along it he saw the pavement was stippled with bullet holes. Then he felt the cold had made his arm and shoulder one with the stone, and he saw, at the edge of the villa's rooftop, the stain of Rabby's blood spreading in the near-darkness.

"Keep your eyes closed," she said. "Tell me now whether you've seen anything."

"Yes. Several things. All sort of connected."

"Where were they from? What part of your life?"

"From the war."

"Do you want to tell me about them?"

"No. They wouldn't make any sense to you."

"Do they frighten you?"

"No. They just belong to me, that's all."

"You went to the war because you wanted to draw close to the death in it. Was there death in the things you saw just now?"

"Yes."

"Do you think you'll remember those things? Do you wish you could forget them?"

He listened for a moment to the faint whistling of the wind through crevices in the rock high above him.

"It doesn't make much sense to talk about remembering or forgetting," he said. "They're all just part of me."

"Do you feel the cold of the stone?"

"For a while I did. I could feel it moving up my arm. Now I don't know where it stopped, or if it did."

"Does that frighten you?"

"No. I guess as long as I keep my hand here, the cold belongs to me too."

"So you've felt the cold, and you felt the presence of death in it, and neither of them frightens you now. Good. But I think there's one other thing you need to feel."

"What's that?"

"Keep your eyes closed."

She wedged herself between his body and the stone, and the cold that had suffused his body was swept away by a torrent of warmth from her thighs and hips and breasts and arms.

"The cold belongs to you, does it?" she said. "That's good."

"And this," he said, still with his eyes closed. "This…here…now. This belongs to me too. That's what you mean, isn't it?"

He opened his eyes into a blue gaze aslant with tender mockery.

"We'll see about that," she said. "Won't we?"

Acknowledgments

Special thanks to Ruth Weinstein, who shone a light on the path this story needed to take; to C. Ray Hall, who tried to show me how to tell it right and to my editor Jeanne Smith, whose patience and generosity proved limitless.

Meet Michael Jennings

Michael Jennings is a North Carolina native and a former newspaper reporter and editor. He served in the Air Force in Vietnam in 1969-70. He holds an undergraduate degree from the University of North Carolina and a master's degree from the University of Virginia. In 1993, he won a first prize in non-deadline writing from the American Society of Newspaper Editors.

Visit Our Website

For The Full Inventory
Of Quality Books:

Wings ePress, Inc. = *https://wingsepress.com/*

*Quality trade paperbacks and downloads
in multiple formats,
in genres ranging from light romantic comedy to general fiction and
horror.
Wings has something for every reader's taste.
Visit the website, then bookmark it.*
We add new titles each month!

*Wings ePress Inc.
3000 N. Rock Road
Newton, KS   67114*

Made in the USA
Middletown, DE
11 February 2020

84565476R20278